ZOE HARRIS

The Bookposal

Two Bookworms, One bookstore. One book unites two souls.

Copyright © 2022 by Zoe Harris

All rights reserved. No part of this publication may be reproduced, stored or transmitted in any form or by any means, electronic, mechanical, photocopying, recording, scanning, or otherwise without written permission from the publisher. It is illegal to copy this book, post it to a website, or distribute it by any other means without permission.

This novel is entirely a work of fiction. The names, characters and incidents portrayed in it are the work of the author's imagination. Any resemblance to actual persons, living or dead, events or localities is entirely coincidental.

Zoe Harris asserts the moral right to be identified as the author of this work.

Zoe Harris has no responsibility for the persistence or accuracy of URLs for external or third-party Internet Websites referred to in this publication and does not guarantee that any content on such Websites is, or will remain, accurate or appropriate.

Designations used by companies to distinguish their products are often claimed as trademarks. All brand names and product names used in this book and on its cover are trade names, service marks, trademarks and registered trademarks of their respective owners. The publishers and the book are not associated with any product or vendor mentioned in this book. None of the companies referenced within the book have endorsed the book.

Disclaimer: I do not support underage drinking nor smoking.

First edition

ISBN: 9798358169272

Cover art by Michela P.
Editing by Gerald Joyner

This book was professionally typeset on Reedsy.
Find out more at reedsy.com

*To my younger sister - Anything you
put your mind and dedication to,
you can
and will do it.*

She talked about books
with so much passion that you wanted to be
nothing but
the character she had fallen
so insanely in love with.

            UNKNOWN

Acknowledgement

First, I want to thank my previous teachers.

Crazy, I know. But they deserve light. To preserve privacy, I will not say names at all. But just know that I'm talking to you if you feel as I am. You've worked with my habits, and managed to deal with my incompetence throughout the years; especially in my writing.

To my 8th Grade Science teacher: What's Up? I promised you I would let you know when it's out. I'm giving you a shout-out because you knew. You felt it. You were one of the few teachers that just knew ahead of time I was going to get this out. That I was going to make it. Now, look at me. I wrote an entire novel, professionally edited, and self-published. I promise you, you have been in my mind this entire time. In every chapter, I remembered moments you'd just let me write. Let me embrace. And for that, Thank You.

Now for my friends. You guys have gone through absolute hell and back when it comes to my writing. Literally. I've made you guys read drafts, give me ideas, research with me, and give me advice even though you had no idea what to tell me. Just thank you to those friends who have supported me through it all. I know you guys want your names out, so here you go— Alexis, Jazmyn, Jamie, Mariyah, Neveah, Zahara, and Makaylah. I cannot thank you all enough.

For my very last bit, I want to definitely thank my family. Primarily my siblings. My younger sister is the one who gave me this fire. Who gave me the want to see my name out there. Make her and myself proud. Teach her that she can do anything she wants to do. Cheesy, yes, but especially if you put your mind to it. To my younger brother: I love you Lil dude! Can't wait to see you grow over the years, and the same message goes to you; Anything, absolutely anything you put your mind to, you can do.

    To my Dad: I know you've had to deal with my struggles, specifically my rushing, but we did it. We finally did it and I'm so happy.

    Lastly, to Mama. Just know Tiffany and her mom's connection reminded me of ours, which was why I did it.

I love you all and thank you for being there.

NOVEMBER 14, 2021

Senior Year of High School

One

CHAPTER ONE: FOOTNOTES

I walk through the door, the smell of Cinnamon Tea floating through the air, and the bell above the door rings. "Welcome to- Oh, hello, Tiffany!" Mrs. Deliare calls, struggling to place a large stack of books down on the counter. I rush over to help her. Standing up, she dusts off her hands.

"Oh, thank you, Tiff, but you didn't have to," She grunts.

"Hey, I'll help anytime," I smile. "What even is this stack?" I ask, checking out the spines. The first book I grab out of the stack is *The Hobbit by J.R.R Tolkien*. "New donations. You can go ahead and start searching through if you'd like!" She yells before disappearing into the backroom.

As I shuffle through the books, something catches my eye.

Anyone who's managed to find this, write back on the next page :)

It looks like a handwritten footnote, and not from that long ago. "Mrs. D!" I call. She walks from the back, a stack of papers and manila folders in hand. "Mhm?"

"How long have these books been in the bin?"

"Probably just overnight. You'll have to ask Jazlen," She replies, pointing toward the Adult Fiction.

Jazlen's a Senior in college, and she started working here 3 years ago, around the beginning of her freshman year.

With the book in my right hand, I tap Jaz's shoulder. "What's up?" She asks with a sigh, shoving the last few books from her hand into the shelf. "Did you unload the bin yesterday?" She stands there thinking for a bit. "Yea, why?"

"Someone wrote a footnote," I pause, scrambling to find the page. Finding it, I lean over to show her, pointing to the bottom. "This could be the beginning of your love story," She lightly teases. I nudge her shoulder.

"Shut up. That kind of bull is unimaginable," I groan, rolling my eyes. Walking back to the counter, I grab a pen from the container.

hi :)

I write a response back in hopes of not seeming silly. I put the book face down on the counter before heading back to the armchair where my bag rests. Sitting on the couch, I grab the book I'm reading out of my bag. It's *If We Were Us* by K.L. Walther, and it's pretty good so far. "What's that you're reading today, Tiffany?" Mrs. D says, leaning against the counter. I look up from my book and turn it roughly towards the cover. "If We Were Us," I read. She stands up straight before opening the register, a light *humph* exiting her mouth. "A contemporary Romance, all themed in a boarding school." I lightly laugh at a page, completely ignoring what she had noted. "Ah! A roommate romance!" Jazlen caws, jumping onto the beanbag beside me. She reaches her hand over the page to distract me from reading. Annoyed, I shove her hand out of my way before commenting. "Not necessarily. But if you refer to it like that," I break. "Then, sure."

I finish wiping down the counter top as Mrs. Deliare stops counting all the

CHAPTER ONE: FOOTNOTES

cash resting inside the register. "Here's your pay for the week, sweetheart," She states, handing me a wad of tattered tens and a few fifties. "Thank you, Mrs. D," I utter, swinging my bag over my shoulder, causing me to slightly crouch as it weighs me down.

"See you tomorrow!"

* * *

Walking into class, I see Avery and Emery sitting in the back at our clustered desks, waiting for me. "How much did you make for this week?" Emery excitedly bounces in her seat. "205," I reply, placing my bag on the floor. I quickly glance at Avery to find her typing on her phone underneath the table. "God, I need to get myself a job," She groans. "What happened this time?" I exhale. "Our momma refuses to buy me this jumpsuit," She pauses. Emery's phone dings beside me. "Just sent the link to y'all." My phone buzzes in my back pocket. As I grab it, the screen slowly loads from the terrible service. "Oh! That's what you guys were fussing about. You could wear it to Aaliyah's party Saturday," Emery cheers, scrolling through the reviews on her phone.

Avery turns her phone off before tucking it away into her bag. "Right!" The screen finally loads, and what's featured is a black jumpsuit with a triangular neckline. To prevent a boob slip, the top is held together by a gold-colored string. To be honest, if you put on some black heels, there's an automatic look. Quickly, we tuck our phones away as our teacher, Ms. Alliena, walks in. Shutting the door behind her, she grabs a stack of papers off the edge of her desk as the overhead bell rings. "Crap," Av whispers. "I completely forgot about the test today." Leaning back in her chair, Ms. A gives her on look as she places the paper on her desk.

Avery immediately sits back up and starts on the test. As she hands the paper to me, she whispers near my ear, "Adding 10 extra credit points for the essay you submitted yesterday." I smile at this and turn to nod a quick submission.

The bell rings, and anyone unable to complete the test quickly rushes to circle any opted answers, including Avery. "Dang, I only had 5 left."

"Better hope those randomized five are right," I laugh. Standing up, I walk over to Mrs. Ali's desk where I turn my paper face down and head back towards the back of the room, where my bag and desk are. Slinging my bag onto my shoulder, Ms. Alliena starts a conversation. "Have you girls gotten any news from the colleges?" We all stand in silence. Clutching onto the stack, she continues talking. "It's Senior year, better hope y'all got accepted."

"I'm applying at Berkeley next week," I declare as we walk towards the door. "Tiffany," She calls. I turn around. She looks me in the eye, pushing her curly hair back before giving me a smile. "Good Luck with the apps'. I know you'll get in."

* * *

I practically run through the door, slamming my bag onto the ground, excited to see the reply in the book.

Searching through the shelves for about an hour, I finally get to it.

I never thought anyone would reply, to be honest. It seems cheesy, but I thought it'd be worth a try.

I lightly chuckle at the response as I think of what to reply.

haha i thought the same lol

CHAPTER ONE: FOOTNOTES

As I begin to place the book back, my phone dings in my back pocket. The book falls out of my hand, and a few other things resting on the shelves crash to the ground.

AVERY| the guy write back??

I smile at the interest. It's Avery, I told her everything at lunch. I type back, also adding a picture of the page.

TIFFANY| yup

AVERY| aw . . . that's sweet!

Prancing back to the front desk, I turn my phone face-down on the table as Mrs. Deliare walks out of the back room, carrying a tray of apple cider. I grab a cup, soon sipping the warm liquid. The bell above the door rings, and a guy walks in. "Hello, and welcome to Yours Truly Bookstore," Mrs. Deliare says. He mumbles a quick *thank you* before pacing towards whichever section he's headed.

Eventually, he comes out of the aisle, a book in hand. *The City of Gold*. He walks up the counter where Jazlen's standing before placing it against the counter top. Grabbing the barcode reader, she scans the label.

"5.60." The guy starts patting the side of his pants as if searching for his wallet or money. After what seems like five minutes of him searching, he turns to me. He has dark brown hair and a cut that reminds me of my brother, Shiloh. A gold nose stud on the right nostril. "Any chance you could spare a brotha?" he jokes. I chuckle at the comment before grabbing my wallet out of my bag and handing him a few coins.

He cashes in, pausing in front of the door as he starts speaking. "Jayden, you?" I look up from my book, confused for a moment. "Tiffany," I smile. He looks at me in my eyes before saying anything else.

"Nice to meet you, Tiffany."

Two

CHAPTER TWO: FOLLOWING

I walk into the bookstore to see the same guy sitting in the beanbag, near my usual spot. I glance toward Jazlen as she does nothing but shrug. "Uhm, what're you doing?"

"Waiting for you."

"Why?" I ask, a dash of confusion in my voice. I give him an interrogative look of confusion before placing my bag down and sitting beside him. "So, *Tiffany*," He dramatically says, my name the most highlighted word that comes from his mouth. "I like the jacket," He points out. It's a pink, fluff-like jacket from Nike. "Thanks," I say with concern. He flashes a smile, playing with his hoodie drawstrings. "What do you want?" I groan, grabbing a binder from my bag. "Your phone number," He replies. I know he did not. Looking up at him, I watch as a smile slowly grows across his face. Laughing, he manages a response.

"Okay, I overdid it. I'm kidding. But I *do* want your number," He grins once again, but this time it's more sly. I roll my eyes. Opening the clips of the binder, I grab an empty sheet of notebook paper before ripping a piece off and writing my number down.

901-183-4723.

Quickly, I ball up the ripped sheet of paper before handing him the small slip. He smiles before grabbing his phone beside him. He types up the number and a ding comes from my bag. I look at it as he lightly nudges it with his foot, signaling for me to check it. I deeply sigh out of annoyance before just digging through my bag and grabbing my phone.

JAYDEN| Hey.
    ME| hi.

Looking up from his phone, he brightly smiles. "Locked in. Do you mind me getting a pic of you for your contact photo?" I shrug, sending him my latest selfie. "You're cute," He says as the message goes through, marking it as read. My heart begins racing at his compliment. "Thanks," I stutter, keeping my head down low while I shove my binder into my bag.
    "No problem."

Shelving the last few books, I push the book cart back behind the counter, waving at the customer Jazlen's handling. I look by the door and see Jayden still sitting on that beanbag, on his phone. "Finally. You've been in there forever," He sighs. I chuckle as I grab my phone from my pocket.

6:15 PM

"Jaz," I call as she hands the customer their change. "Mhm?"
    "Tell Mrs. Deliare I'm headed home," I reply, quickly gathering my things. Jayden looks at me as he asks, "You working a shift here tomorrow?"
    "Yup," I reply as I walk toward the door. "See ya then, Tiffany."
    "See you."

* * *

CHAPTER TWO: FOLLOWING

"So, how was you guys' day today?" Mom asks as she bites a mouthful of salad. "Got a promotion," My dad mumbles, not looking up from his phone. He seems to never get off it, no matter what's going on and mom hates it. Reaching over the table, she snatches the phone from Dad's hands. Mid-Scroll. Tough. He opens his mouth to argue, but one look causes him to quickly shut it.

A smirk aligns my mother's face as she points her fork at Shiloh. "Today was good, I guess," he grumbles. "We got a basketball game tomorrow," He adds. "You wanna go?" Dad asks as Shiloh quickly nods attentively. "So, Tiffany, how'd you do on that geometry test?" Dad adds in, alert now toward me.

"Good," I mutter, finishing the last bits of my Ziti. I stand up to place my plate into the sink when my parents both begin speaking. "Percentage?" They say in sync. "98," I smirk, laughter slowly climbing up my throat. A sigh of relief escapes from dad's mouth as he chuckles an unsure laugh. Walking towards the stairway, I tell mom and dad I'm working on an essay as mom tells me something. "Family's coming down soon. Keep that room straight."

✲ ✲ ✲

I sit on my bed, the blankets practically swallowing me. Grabbing my phone, I check Instagram and see a familiar face in my *quick-add*.

QUICK ADD:
JAYDEN MATTHEWS, ANAYA PORCHE, ALLEN GREY, LENA...

The account is private, and I press *follow*, and the **Requested** pops in place.

Three

CHAPTER THREE: MEET-CUTE

I wake up to heavy breathing in my face.

"Shiloh!" I yell as he laughs while backing away. "You didn't even brush your teeth!" I add on, falsely gagging. "Momma said get yo' nappy-headed butt downstairs for breakfast," He exaggerates, weening his arm towards my head. I beat him to his own before I smack him in the head. "Bro," he groans. I smile as he clicks his lips in attitude before walking downstairs, me following behind.

I shuffle downstairs after getting myself more presentable, at the least. "Morning, sleepyhead," Mom chuckles, placing the plates on the table.

"Go wake your father up, Shiloh. Tiffany, get the eggs and grits." I walk over to the counter, grabbing the food as told. Shiloh comes into the kitchen alongside dad. "Morning, baby," Mom smiles, kissing his cheek before placing the forks on each plate. He groggily replies with a quick, "Morning."

"So, what're your plans for today?" Mom announces, as no one says anything. Nothing but the sound of forks scraping the plate linger in

CHAPTER THREE: MEET-CUTE

the air. She clears her throat before repeating herself once again. "What're your plans for today?"

"I'm heading to the shop after school," I reply. "Shiloh and I are gonna head to that game," Dad points before taking a large gulp of orange juice. Mom checks her watch before briskly standing up and heading towards the sink, practically throwing her plate inside. Turning around, she glances in to be sure it hadn't cracked. "What's the rush?" Dad asks behind her as he heads toward the sink. Turning on the water, he rinses their plates. Mom rushes down the hall, not answering his question. Within minutes, she runs back in with her scrubs on.

"I got surgery at 10," She sighs, grabbing her jacket off the TV stand. Dad walks over toward her, pecking a quick kiss on her cheek. "Love you," She mumbles, swiping her keys off the counter before stepping into the garage, the door shutting behind her.

* * *

I unlock the door to find myself the first one in today.

Turning on the lights, I walk towards the cabinet where we store the book-box key. As I grab the key, I notice the book I'd written in wide open: With a new note.

Hey, what's your name? Mine's Jayden.

I smile.

Tiffany.

I walk out the front door, the bell ringing as it opens. I walk over to the donation bill, unlocking it to find the usual stack of books. Grabbing them,

I struggle to open the door again but manage.

Whenever we get new books, our method is that we add them into the system, alphabetically, before shelving them. As I do so, I hear a car pull up. Looking through the window, I recognize Mrs. Deliare sitting in the front seat. In the back, she has her granddaughter, Sasha. She bounces up the moment she parks, speeding towards the door as she notices me.

"Tiffany!" She bounces up and down, jumping to hug me. Sasha's 6, turning 7 later this month, and I've known her pretty much since the start. When I first started working here, she was 1 and I was 14. The door opens, and Mrs. D walks in behind her. "You just left me out there, huh?" She jokes, setting her purse down on the counter. "You and that guy still writing notes?" She adds on, motioning at the open book in front of me. "Yea," I chuckle.

Sitting down on the stool behind the register, I grab my phone from my pocket. Two notifications from Instagram are sitting on my home screen.

@JAY_MONEYX has accepted your request.
@JAY_MONEYX has requested to follow you.

I press them, as it leads to my in-app notifications. Before pressing accept, I check out the account.

Most of his photos are of him and his friends being ridiculous. A few are books. *The Hate U Give, Copper Sun, On The Come Up,* and *Monday's Not Coming* are just a few. Heading back to my notifications, I press accept. Within seconds he likes my photos, so of course, I gotta join in and like a few of his. A notification from my DMs pops up.

JAYDEN H| *Oh, so we playin' this game now, huh?* ▫

I press the notification to reply.

CHAPTER THREE: MEET-CUTE

TIFFANY M| *mhm.*

Liking each others' posts goes on for a bit, but eventually, he starts asking questions.

JAYDEN H| *You look familiar. Have I seen you somewhere??*
TIFFANY M| *it's me, dummy.*

I wait for a second and watch his profile picture going up and down.

JAYDEN H| *I know, just messing with you. Y'all open right now?*
TIFFANY M| *yupp*
JAYDEN H| *Lol, on my way right now.*

"Can you go shelf these books?" Jazlen asks seemingly out of nowhere, startling me.
"Sure."

"Guess your work release is in the afternoon, huh?" I hear a voice say from behind me. I turn around to spot Jayden standing at the end of the aisle. I give him a look, and he laughs. "Yea. What about you?"
"Oh, you know, just skipping class. The usual," He jokingly scoffs. Noticing a stack of books on the counter, I quickly shuffle over to get them. "Need help?" He asks, standing to my far left. I put the books on a book cart that's beside me before heading over to the Science Fiction section. "Nope. I got this. Been doing it for five years." Jayden continues to follow me around, watching me place each book on the shelf.

Looking around the shop, I see no one but me, Jayden, Jazlen, and Sasha. I figure Mrs. Deliare's in the backroom. "Mrs. D, I'm gonna go ahead and get to school. I'll be back at 4," I yell. "Alright, see you then, Tiffany. Thank you for shelving those books!" She responds, pointing a thumbs up out the door frame. Walking out the door, I realize Jayden's still inside. Turning around, I see him writing something down through the window. "You coming?" I call. My voice might be muffled, but Jayden hears as he raises a quick finger, signaling for me to wait. I open my car door and throw my bag on the seat beside me. Watching Jayden walk out, he heads towards the passenger's side. "I'm ridin' with you."

"I thought you were heading to school."
   "I go to the same school as you, I think."
   "How do you know?"
   He pulls out his student ID from his back pocket. *SouthWind High School*. "But still, go in your car," I reply, pointing out the window. Clicking his tongue, he opens the door, tossing my bag in the backseat before shifting his onto the ground. "You don't listen, do you?" I sarcastically ask, turning to the side and facing him. He looks me in the eye before speaking. "Nope."

He turns back forward, closes the door, then pulls his phone out of his pocket. I sigh before quickly putting the gear in reverse. "Bluetooth?"
   "Sure," I say, disconnecting my phone from the Bluetooth as he connects his. A song loads, and J. Cole's Album *KOD* plays through the speakers. "Dang, you don't seem the type to like him," I say, looking up at the mirror as I back up, sure to not ding any car. Once fully backed out, I face forward. I never take my eyes off the road. Momma and Daddy say I've been like that since I had those electronic cars.
   "Yea, I do. What kind of music do you like?" Jayden asks, with all his attention on me. His phone is face down in the cup holder and where I can visibly see, on silent. Stopping at a red light, I think for a moment.
   "J. Cole, Kanye West, Jay-Z, a bit of Megan," I begin, watching as the red light turns green. Turning the corner, I pull up into the school's teacher parking lot. I continue driving towards the back, where student parking is.
   Pulling into my spot, Emery and Avery are already parking and sitting in their car waiting for me. They notice me put my car into park and immediately get out. Emery's finger points to before her lips mouth, *Who the hell?* I chuckle before getting out and grabbing my bag from the backseat.

CHAPTER THREE: MEET-CUTE

Jayden gets out of his door. Noticing their looks, He nods. "Jayden." Avery shyly waves before she continues looking down at her phone, ignoring the conversation. Swinging his bag across his shoulder, Jayden mumbles quickly before fleeing.

"Be back after school, T."

Four

CHAPTER FOUR: BROKEN CLOCKS

J ayden opens the car door, throwing his bag before himself into the seat beside me. "Bad Day?" He nods silently. Connecting my phone to Bluetooth, I play *Love Yourz* by J. Cole.

He lightly grins at this, eventually looking up from his lap. "Not good news from my mom. No specifications, but it wasn't good," he mumbles, throwing on a phony smile. "I'm good, though." I put the gearshift to reverse but find myself not setting my hands on the wheel. Leaning onto his arm, Jayden looks at me, and I look at him the same way. The song instantly turns this into a connection moment, turning the energy from serious conversation to conscious romance. The eye contact is passionate, and there's something about his eyes.

Something about the way he's looking at me makes me want to melt into a puddle. We both lean in slowly, closer and closer, and- "Tiffany!" Someone yells, pounding on the window. Quickly distancing, Jayden leans against his window, and I unlock the car to look up and see Emery. I unlock the doors and open the backseat door before sliding in. "Avery drove off and left me. Just like that." She huffs. Struggling to get her bag to fit comfortably between her and the seat, she continuously shifts. I turn the music off, immediately disconnecting my phone.

CHAPTER FOUR: BROKEN CLOCKS

Eventually getting comfortable, she shuts the car door before her phone pairs. "Thanks," She replies, and I start driving in reverse. Saweetie starts playing, and Emery syncs with her. I sigh. Looking to my side, I catch a glimpse of Jayden falling asleep. "Whatchu smiling at?" Emery abruptly says.

I look back forward, pulling into her neighborhood. It's not that far from school, and I have no idea why they decide to literally drive. It would be only a 2 to 3-minute walk. Large architectural houses line the street, each one built precisely. "Nothing," I mumble, catching eye view of Em's house. "That was a lovely kind of smile. You like him?"

"Him?" I sarcastically point toward Jayden, looking in the overhead mirror at her. She looks right back at me as she nods. I pull into the driveway, shift the gear into Neutral, and eventually dial to park. My foot rests against the break. "Nah," I click my tongue. The doors automatically unlock as Emery opens the door quickly after. Flipping the bag across her shoulder, she gives me a look. "I'm serious!"

"Okay," She replies indecisively. Slowly walking backward, she adds, "But let me know when you do." She shuts the door behind her. I roll my eyes before flipping her off, and she reciprocated before unlocking and opening her front door.

* * *

The time reads 4:56 when I pull into the parking lot.

Reaching over the middle console, I attempt to wake Jayden up. "Jayden. Jay, wake up," I mumble, trying to shake him awake. He groans before sitting up. "We're here," I add before getting up and shutting the door behind me. He gets out on his side, rubbing his face to wake himself up. Opening the door for me, we both walk inside.

"Tiffany, I'm so glad you're here! I need you to grab that Christmas box from the supply closet."

"Why? It's still mid-November," I say, throwing my bag on the floor. "I'm entering the shop into the *Jingle Bells* walk for kids at St. Jude!" She yells from her office. I lightly *mph* before walking towards the register. Leaning on the counter, Jayden plays with a few things on display. Empty book racks, pen holders, receipt paper, and a few more random items. "Seriously, you seem out of it. You sure you're good?"

"Mhm." I stare at him, and he looks up at me.
"Isn't there a party somewhere this Saturday?" I nod.
"At Aaliyah's. Why?"
"You headed there?" He asks. "Yea. I'm going with my friends. Want me to send the location?" I ask with my phone in my hand, ready to type. "Yea. Well, I'm heading home. See you tomorrow," He waves before walking out the door.

* * *

ME| 2376 JASPER AVE. PARTY STARTS @ 10.
    JAYDEN| be there in 20

Five

CHAPTER FIVE: SLIGHT FESTIVITIES

I check the screen, a message Jayden sent an hour ago. "Tiffany, Avery's here!" I hear mom call. "Coming!" I yell back, racing down the hall towards the stairs. Reaching the end of the stairs, I notice Avery standing there, waiting for me. "Mhm! Lookachu!" She exclaims. I roll my eyes with a smile on my face. I'm wearing a light blue glitter dress, blue Air Jordan Maes', and a small silver clutch in hand. I jog down the stairs, giving Av a tight hug before I move my dress downward, getting rid of any wrinkles. We both walk toward the kitchen and into the connected living room. Dad's sitting right in the middle of the couch, so Avery and I have to sit close to each other.

The doorbell rings and I grab my phone out of my clutch, a text from Jayden pops up on my screen.

JAYDEN| I'm here.

Mom walks to the door when Av and I both perk up. "Yea, mom we got this, it's someone here to pick us up," I mumble, already knowing what she's gonna say. It's been a few weeks since my ex, CJ, and I broke up, and mom tries to get me to date any guy within my age range that she sees. If she saw

Jayden, she'd go ballistic. "Aw honey, I'd like to meet your friend, though," she says as she stops right in front of me. "It's good, really," I continue as Avery sneaks behind me to get to the door. "We'll be back by 11, ma," I say as I lean over her shoulder before giving her a quick kiss on the cheek. Hurriedly, I run to the door, which was left cracked by Avery. Jayden and she were right at the end of the pathway when I get to them. "Why'd you rush out here?" He asks, opening the back door. Avery automatically knew he meant her when he opened the door, so she crawled in the back. "No reason," I smile, walking to the passenger's side. "Okay," He pauses as he sits in the driver's seat. "Alright."

* * *

"There gon' be drinks there?" Avery stutters as we walk up the driveway. "This Aaliyah we're talking about. Of course, there will," I reply. A sigh of relief comes out of her mouth. "Good. I needa break!" she groans, jokingly pouting like a child. "Y'all must hang out like this often," Jayden asks, walking alongside me. "Yea, parties are me and Av's thing. Emery hangs out every so often, but-"

"She mostly stays at home," Avery interrupts, and she's right. Emery is an introvert, she hates being around parties. If she goes, it has to be a small crowd.

Reaching the door, I can smell the weed from here.

Track and Field by Enchanting plays when we get in. Smoke is in the air, couples are making out, and people yell along with the song. Yup, definitely a party Aaliyah's throwing. I look around to find myself standing in a crowd of people, along with Jay since Avery ditched me. "Want a drink?" he asks, pointing towards the kitchen. I nod yes, and he trods though the crowd and down the hall.

I wander around a bit, bumping into the dining room where people pass

CHAPTER FIVE: SLIGHT FESTIVITIES

a blunt back to back. Avery's one of them. Smoke rises from her mouth. I give her a look, and she gives me the same look back, but with attitude. Walking over, I sit in the empty chair beside her as she hands it to me. I try it, coughing hard as everyone around me laughs. Still coughing, I hand it to the girl beside me as she smiles she states, "It's alright, rookie. You'll get used to it."

Leaning back in my chair awkwardly, I hold in another cough to prevent any more embarrassment. Another round goes by, and thankfully right as I'm about to smoke it once again, I catch a glimpse of Jayden standing in the doorway, waving me toward him.

"Mhm, do it before you get up," Avery whispers as she nudges my shoulder.

Oftentimes, Avery somehow manages to convince me to do estranged things to "impress" a guy.

Hesitantly, I breathe outward before rolling my eyes and inhaling a puff. This time, I don't cough. Instead, a roll of vapor slips right out my mouth. "See?" Av smirks along with a wink. Hurriedly, I pass it to the girl beside me as I jump up and speed walk toward Jayden.

"Trying something new, huh?"

"Shut up. Avery was in there, and she's a lurer, and to be honest-"

"Hey, it's good," He interrupts, a chuckle in his voice. Shyly, I smile as I grab a cup from his hand. "So," I pause, realizing we're slowly walking back and forth down the hall, each time almost being separated by at least two people. "How's life?" He laughs, somewhat breaking the silence between the two of us. "Good," I reply. "So, you wanna talk about what happened earlier?" He asks, fumbling his words.

"What?" I ask, confused. Suddenly, the memory of what happened rushes through my mind. J. Cole playing in the back. The way he'd looked at me. "Uh," I pause, biting my lip right before taking a sip. The beer burns the small sore. And there it is. That same look.

The look he gave me in the car, but this time in a house with dim lighting. Our faces are close, and I can smell the beer on his breath. "Kiss me," I raspily say, an instant wave of regret washing over me. It feels as if people around us were eavesdropping with their eyes. He doesn't say anything, the air between us is empty and crisp. Backing away from him slowly, I glance between my cup and the ground, then back and forth. *Cup, Ground, Cup, Ground.* Anything to get out of this situation.

Why would I say that?

Six

CHAPTER SIX: BIBLIOKEPT

G limpses meeting, I notice Jayden's eyes no longer searching. They've rested. My heart starts to pound as his breath blows against the tip of my nose. His hand still clasped around my arm, Jayden slowly leans his face into mine, our lips grazing against each other as he kisses me roughly. My eyes drift closed, embracing every second. The grip loosens as his right hand slowly falls. His mouth tastes like alcohol, as expected. His right hand now completely free, he glides it up the side of my waist, giving me cool, yet comforting chills. The room feels empty. Like we're the only ones in the room. I break the kiss with a quick smile, Jayden's face distancing from mine as he smiles back.

The air between us afterward is haste, dry, and bitter. The rest of the party, instead of being unable to get enough of one another, we dodge each other.

Keeping away from the awkwardness that might be able to be avoided later on. Jayden might forget, but I never will. I'll never forget his silent admiration. Jayden told me he loved me right then and there. Through his eyes, through the kiss.

* * *

The hangover's possibly in effect now because my head is throbbing.

"Girl, that boy's fine as hell," Emery says, looking at a picture from his Instagram. I grab my laptop out of my bag and place it on my desk. "Yea. Well, we're just friends, believe it or not," I reply. Avery looks at the screen before liking the post for me. "Yea, you can say that all you want. I saw that kiss." I freeze at the comment, my phone vibrating in my hand before a notification appears on the screen.

JAYDEN| Wyd??

Emery peeks over my arm as she looks at the message. A look washes over her face before I shrug it off, sliding up and typing a response.

> ME| school, dummy, why??
> JAYDEN| You know that book that sits on the front desk? It's missing. Have you seen it?
> ME| no, why?
> JAYDEN| I'll explain later. Thanks for answering, though.
> ME| ok...

Turning my phone off, I put it back in my pocket. "What was that about?" Emery asks. "He's looking for this book. It's the one that sits on the counter," I reply, looking up at the board to write a few notes. Emery pauses before speaking. "You know what I'm thinking?" I hum as a reply. "That dude could be the guy writing the notes," She continues. "I mean, didn't you say that dude's name's Jayden?"

"Yea, but Jayden is a popular name, and you know that. There are like 5 Jaydens in this class right now," I reply, pointing towards each Jayden with my pencil.

"Think about it, though. Keep it in mind, at least?" I nod before opening

CHAPTER SIX: BIBLIOKEPT

a Word Doc to type notes as Mr. William begins the lecture.

* * *

I open the door to find Jayden sitting on one of the armchairs.

"Now that I'm not in class, where do you think it could be?"

"On the counter," he replies, not looking up from his phone. I sarcastically laugh as I swerve myself behind the counter.

"I mean, somebody coulda bought it, J. Afraid to say, but this *is* a bookshop. People *buy* used books," I say. He clicks his tongue, causing it to make that *'tick'* sound. "We have like six other copies. Chill out," I stand up to walk over to the computer.

Category Search: The Hobbit|

I press the enter key and five other copies are shown on the screen. "See?" I say, pointing to each one. He rolls his eyes. I sigh as I get up and walk over to the shelves. "No need to worry."

TOJ, TOK, TOL..

Grabbing the book, I toss it to Jayden. "Thanks," he grumbles, flipping to a page.

"Why'd you panic when you couldn't find the book? It's not like it's a big deal, right?" I say, walking back towards the counter. He glimpses at me, then back down at his page.

"No reason."

Seven

CHAPTER SEVEN: THE EXAMPLE (EX)

I pull into the driveway, noticing Avery walk down her porch stairs before opening my door. "Thanks," I mutter as she points a quick thumbs-up in reply.

I grab my bag out of the passenger's seat beside me as I close and lock the car doors behind me, walking alongside Av as we walk inside. Our footsteps echo on the marble flooring, and the room lit up brightly from the chandelier hanging above.

"Mom! Tiffany's here!" Avery yells as I take my jacket off before placing it on the coat rack. Mrs. Wilkens walks down the left stairway quickly. A bright smile is etched all over her face as she shakes my hand. "Hey, Tiffany. Nice to see you again! I'm pretty sure you're here to watch the twins open their admissions?"

"Yup!" I respond. Glancing behind her, I look at the massive display of trophies and papers within a casing. I've been to their house a million times, each time feeling like the first time I've ever stepped inside. Emery walks from the left room, her head down at her phone. "We'll be in my room," Avery glances, grabbing Emery and my hands before pulling us aside towards her room. I toss my bag onto her bed, sitting down on the ottoman placed right in front of her bed. I turn on the TV, and some random show

CHAPTER SEVEN: THE EXAMPLE (EX)

from *BET* automatically plays.

"Ignore that," she says, walking into her closet. Emery sits on her bed, her attention still reverted to her phone screen. I've seen the two so much, so I have no idea why it's so awkward this time. Avery walks out of her closet with a jumpsuit slugged across her arm and a pair of white cross heels hanging onto her fingers. "This good for tomorrow?" I glance away from the TV, and Emery finally looks up from her phone before we both reply with a quick 'Yes.' Avery sighs, tossing the outfit into a chair sitting in the corner closest to where she's standing. I finally stop clicking through channels, stopping on the show *Good Girls*, which plays on *NBC*.

"We should celebrate."

I suddenly say, obviously throwing them both off. "Celebrate for what, exactly?" Emery asks, her voice muffled from her mouth pressing against the bed. "Just us as Seniors. We lasted all through high school. And together, of anything." Lifting her head out of the mattress, Em's face seems as if she's about to agree with me. "Oh my god, You and I just came back from one literally not even a week ago."

"So?" Emery caustically mentions, her arms flailing all over. "Partying is your thing." Avery shrugs in confirmation. "Alright, party it is!" Avery's phone goes off, Jayla's voice swooning through the speaker not long after. "Hey, Trent's throwing a party tonight at his place."

"Isn't that the kid that just moved in next door?" I ask, pointing out the window. Emery shrugs and Avery nods. "Y'all down to go?" We look at each other before nodding quickly as J sends us the time and address.

* * *

"CJ's gonna be at the party."

"What?!" I yell, turning around. "Yea..." Avery mutters, showing me his

IG story.

"Hey, just ignore him. You got nothing to worry about," Avery states, fixing her lipstick in the mirror. "You got a new boo now." I glare at her. "What? You and Jayden be hanging out too often to just call y'all 'selves friends," she shrugs. I roll my eyes. "Plus, that kiss-" "Oh my god, will you guys give it up already?"

"Nope, you *kissed* him!" Avery yells. "A *drunken* kiss," Emery adds teasingly. I scoff, tying my hair back into two side buns. "Maybe it'll happen again tonight."

Walking outside, we watch as cars pull up and park, each one aligned up and down the street. The music pounding loud enough to hear from 5 blocks away. "Time to part-ay!" Avery yells, scrambling to the door. "Careful wit' them heels, Av!" Emery calls from behind her.

The whole house reeks with the smell of cheap booze. I grab a red Solo cup and fill the liquid to the brim. I smell the cup to see what's the drink when the whiff burns my nose. I cough. Hard. Falling backward lightly, I bump into someone. "Shoot, sorry," I stammer, not paying attention to who it is. "No problem-" the voice stops. Crap. Please don't let it be who I think it is.

I slowly turn around to see guess who? CJ. "Whaddup?" he says, laughing. CJ and I got together around the beginning of junior year. Obviously, we'd lasted a year before I'd found out he cheated on me with a girl named Clai a few weeks ago.

He stretches his hands out to do this handshake we'd made when we were together. His hand sits there.

Realizing I'm not touching his hand, he withdraws it back.

"So, how's life been going for ya?" I stand there, my arms crossed. I take a swig of the liquid, instantly regretting it. It stings the back of my throat pretty bad, but I withstand it.

He curls his right hand into a fist, hitting his left palm. "Alright, you don't wanna talk to me, huh? Guess I'll back off," He retreats. I exhale with relief

CHAPTER SEVEN: THE EXAMPLE (EX)

when I notice Em and Av coming for me. "You good? Need me to beat his behind?" Avery shouts over the blaring music. "Nah, I'm good. I didn't even speak to him," I answer. Em nods her head, but Av looks unsure. "You sure you good?" She continues. "Mhm," I murmur, walking toward the liquor bottles.

* * *

I check my phone out of reluctance.

**1:15 AM
15 Notifications
10 Missed Calls from *Mommy*
5 Messages from *Mommy***

Shoot. I look around for Emery and Avery. Emery's knocked out on the couch, and Avery's drunkenly arguing with some guy. Again. I shake Emery, trying to wake her up. She doesn't wake up. I forgot when she lays down, she's gone for the night. I waltz over towards Avery. "Avery, time to head out," I say, tapping her shoulder. "Okay. *Bye, Bye, Amuur*," She sings. He lightly waves, and I'm not sure if I saw him ask if she was gonna call him.

I walk outside, my legs wobbling with Avery holding on to my shoulder for dear life. I help her get into the front seat, handing her a brown bag. I store emergency bags in case of situations when I or they are blackout drunk. I close the door to turn around and find CJ standing there, carrying Emery bridal style. She's still knocked out. My throat closes. "Thanks," I strain, opening the car door. He places her in the back, laying her down. I close the door again, and we stand there for about a minute in silence. "Thanks," I murmur. We can still hear the music pounding from inside.

"No problem," He replies. Within moments he grabs both of my hands, pulling me closer. "I made a mistake." He hesitates.

I look downwards, and he uses his right hand to direct my face towards his. "Forgive me?" God, he looks so attractive right now. I nod yes, and he moves his hand onto my waist. For Pete's sake, he knows how I feel about him still. He cheated on me, and I stayed. But the last time was my last straw. I ended it all with him. Until now, obviously. He leans in to kiss me, and I kiss him back. The world melts away. Everything is back to normal. My (ex) boyfriend is kissing me, my friends are in the backseat wasted.

What could go wrong?

Eight

CHAPTER EIGHT: DISCOVERY

After the kiss, the rest of the night (or morning, whatever) goes by smoothly. I drop the twins back off at their house, not making a single sound. All I have to do is get to Starbucks, grab my mom's favorite latte, get dad's favorite donuts, and drive home. I'll tell them I came home at 12, slept a bit, went on a jog, and grabbed them Starbucks. Easy-Peasy.

I pull up in the driveway, the floodlight turning on. Grabbing the donuts box and the latte tray, I walk up the porch steps. I open the door, and the lights still off. Walking down the hall and into the kitchen, I check the oven's clock.

5:25 AM

I then look in the garage. Mom's car is here, and so is Dad's. I take my shoes off, place the food on the counter, and grab a pencil and paper.

hey, mommy! i know i came home a little late. i came home at 12, went to sleep till 6, and decided to get you guys breakfast. i'll be in my room if you want to check. i love you!

Plugging my phone in, my home screen glows with four messages from Jayden.

> JAYDEN| Who'se that?
> JAYDEN| Tiffany aare you single?
> JAYDEN| Hello?
> JAYDEN| Sorry about the previous messages, I drunk text often.

The last text was the most recent. I type up a reply.

> ME| no biggie. it's good. still wanna know who it is? lol

The moment I press send, I regret it. Why would I even say that? Gosh, that was so stupid.

> JAYDEN| Yea.

Dang. Outdone by him.

> ME| he's just an ex.
> JAYDEN| Didn't seem like it. You kissed him back, correct?
> ME| yea, but there were no feelings behind it
> JAYDEN| So, you're playing him?
> ME| what? no! why would i? what's up with you, jay?
> JAYDEN| Well you got to kiss him, didn't you?
> ME| what?
> DELIVERED

I have no idea whether or not that conversation was passive-aggressive or just him joking around. I walk towards my closet, looking for an outfit for the day. I'm just gonna go with a lazy outfit. A white tank, camouflage sweats, and green J's. I tie my braids up in a ponytail before heading across

CHAPTER EIGHT: DISCOVERY

the hall and into the bathroom. As I brush my teeth, I scroll through my Instagram. After brushing, I apply lotion and then walk downstairs. Mom sounds like she's awake. "Morning, Tiff!" I hear her say as I walk through the door frame. "Morning, mama."

"Thanks for the doughnuts, baby. I didn't feel like cooking," She smiles as she kisses me on my forehead. "No problem, ma. There may be a few missing from me snacking on the way back," I lie.

Opening the box, she spots two empty spaces. She chuckles before grabbing a chocolate sprinkle. "Where you headed?" She asks, sitting down at the table. "The bookstore," I reply as I grab my keys out of the drawer. Right as I open the door to the garage, I race to kiss her on the cheek. "Love you," I smile.

"I love you too, baby. Stay safe."

* * *

I walk into the shop to find Jayden writing in the book. "Jayden! What the hell!" I yell as I race towards him. I knock him to the side, and he falls to the ground laughing. "See, I knew it was you," He begins as he gets back up. Grabbing the book, he holds it up. "There is entirely no way that you thought it was a completely different Jayden, did you?" He asks, slightly unamused.

"No, I knew it was you, too," I lie. He laughs before nudging my shoulder. He whispers in my ear, "No, you didn't." Backing away with a smirk on his face, he shoves the book into his bag. For some reason, those single words were enough to send tingles down my spine. "Okay, so why do you need the book now that you know it's me and I know it's you?" I ask with confusion. Sitting himself down on the bean bag, he replies slyly, "Just for memories. Pure, amazing, memorable memories."

"Besides, I think what we did was cool. It lasted a good while before we figured it out."

"You mean a week."

"Yea, a good while," He responds, typing something on his phone.

I grab my brown paper bag out of the fridge, also collecting a Sprite can on the way out of the room. Placing the bag and soda can down on the counter, I sit down on the stool. "You and Jayden seem to be getting along fine, no?" Mrs. Deliare says, startling me. I place my hand on my chest to express my shock. "Yeah, I guess," I say, grabbing my sandwich out of the bag. She hums a little tune before replying.

"Yea, I find that sweet, the way you guys met."

"I find that sweet the way you guys met."

For some reason, that fumbles throughout my mind. What are these feelings? Why do I get all clammed up around him? Why do I get nervous when people ever so slightly mention us being together? What happened in the car? More importantly:

What happened at the party?

Nine

CHAPTER NINE: MIND OVER MATTER

JAYDEN| Morning. Coming to pick you up in a few, have 'yo butt ready

"Tiffany!" Mom yells. I fall out of bed from being alarmed. "Yes?!" I shout back, throwing on a pair of shorts as I drag myself closer to reaching the stairs. "Your friend is here!" She responds. What friend? Was someone supposed to be coming today? Nobody told me anything. I grab my phone from the end of my bed, seeing two missed calls from Jayden and two messages from him.

Two Missed calls from Jayden

JAYDEN| And you're probably still asleep cause you usually respond hella quickly.

Adrenaline being the cause, I race to my closet, grabbing the closest shirt I can find. Quickly after, I dig in my drawer, grabbing a pair of black leggings. Slipping my feet into Red Air Jordans, I then grab my phone, a ponytail holder, and purse.

I close the car door after sitting in the front seat. "Where are we headed?" I ask, putting my water bottle in the cupholder. He turns on the ignition. "Multiple places," He smirks before pulling back out of the driveway.

* * *

I shut the door as I look up at the tall building.

MEMPHIS NATIONAL RECORDS

The sign reads. "A record store?" I exclaim. "Mhm," he mutters, grabbing a tan-ish bag out of the backseat.

We walk out of the parking lot and onto the sidewalk near a crowded area. Someone's playing guitar in front of the building while people give them handouts. We get inside and the ambiance is comfortable. My feet are surrounded by a white, plush carpet, and the music is some kind of lofi. Shelves all around are stocked from top to bottom with records, a few cases contain record players. "Wow," I utter, still looking around. The ceiling has fairy lights, making the light dim, but still bright enough to read things along with the windows. Fake plant vines are scattered all across the walls, and a few vending machines line the sides. "I'll be right back. Look around," Jayden says as he slowly jogs toward what seems to be the check-out area. I roam around, eventually resting on the beanbags. This is the first time in a while that I've actually been comfortable in a communal area. Aside from the shop, of course.

CHAPTER NINE: MIND OVER MATTER

We left my house at around 10, and it's now around noon.

We've been sitting in this store for 2 hours when Jayden finally comes back.

He unlocks the car door as I climb in before he gets in on his side. Twisting the key into the ignition, the radio station 99.7 plays *Blinding Lights* by the Weeknd. Jayden turns the volume up a bit as he connects the AUX to his phone before almost immediately handing it to me. I smile at his thought as he continues to face forward to the road. People walk alongside the sidewalks, a few in jackets as the temperature had recently began dropping.

"15774." I type in the code, and it immediately lets me in. Going through music, I notice a playlist. A playlist made specifically for me. "What're you giggling at?" Jayden states, startling me. "Uh, nothing," I reply as I continue laughing lightly. We stop at a quick redlight, and he looks over my hand at the screen. "Oh, that," He pauses, the light turning green. I bite the corner of my lip, waiting for him to continue speaking. "I made that for you. Press play," He requests, and I do as he says. *Always n Forever* by Mariah The Scientist is the first one to play. "I had no idea you were into her."

"Mariah? She's not the best compared to SZA, but my sister got me into her," He chuckles. I roll my eyes jokingly before putting the phone face down into the cupholder.

Tucking my hands into my sleeves, Jayden lightly hums along with the song, tapping on the wheel. He pauses before looking at me, and I quickly revert my eyes back forward. "Were you watching me?"

"Me?"

"Yea."

"What? No," I pause, grazing on the sentence. I open up my phone to the messages notification signifying 6 messages from the group chat.

> EMERY| where'd you and dad go?
>> AVERY| we went to go pick up that dress i showed you and tiff.
>>> EMERY| ohh yea. well, can you stop at the beauty supply and pick me up some gel?
>>> i used the last bit this morning.

AVERY| alright. tiffany, you there?

I quickly reply at my cue.

ME| yea.
EMERY| wya? i thought we'd meet at vinyl countdown?
ME| about that...
AVERY| she's probably with jayden, lol
EMERY| it's no big deal. i'll just pick up my order.
ME| really? i mean, we always go together.

I look up from my phone, turning it off as I wait for a response. Moving the gearshift into park, Jayden takes the key out of the ignition as he unplugs his phone from the cord. Opening the middle console, he takes out a Bluetooth wireless speaker. "You ready?" He pauses, turning to face me. I nod and exit the car.

I watch as he grabs a bag out of the backseat again, and we walk over towards a picnic table, our feet crunching on the gravel with each step. I sit on one side as Jayden sits across for me. He then turns on the speaker and a loud, electronic *beep* comes from it, signifying that it'd been connected to his phone. Jayden looks up from his phone at me. "J. Cole?" he recommends, and I excitedly smile. He places it in front of me before I type in a specific album, *2014 Forest Hills Drive.* The intro begins playing, and I place the phone face up on the table. Unpacking the basket, he flips it over. My face must say it all. "Right now's about you," He states, handing a napkin to me. I grab a sandwich from the bag before taking a large bite. Glancing at me, he smiles a bit. "What?" I mumble as I cover my mouth, as it's full. "Nothing," He chuckles.

"Don't talk with your mouth full." I wipe my mouth with compliance. "You're not my dad," I playfully snark, looking at him in the eyes. He grabs a plastic container, opening it to strawberries as I take one from the top. Looking up, I notice him mumbling, singing along with the song.

CHAPTER NINE: MIND OVER MATTER

'03 Adolescence starts playing as we talk, and we get silent as if we were trying to keep one another from talking too much.

I wonder what's going on in his mind right now. "Like it?" he murmurs. "Mhm," I nod as my phone buzzes. Pulling my phone out of my pocket, I notice the notification from Emery.

EMERY| tiff, it's fine. i already have the record, i can hang out with jayla. have fun with jayden : -)

I guess Jayden peered at my phone because suddenly, he began apologizing. "I'm so sorry. I had no id-"

"Sh," I whisper, chuckling lightly as I place my fingers on his lips . It feels compassionate, in a way. "It's good. I didn't wanna go anyway," I continue. "Oh."

Eventually, we find another thing to talk about. And another. And another. And then it just pounds on top of each other as we'd found random things to talk about. Studying me for a moment, I give him a confused look as I swallow a spoonful of yogurt. I panic before quickly wiping my mouth. "What? Something on my face?" He shakes his head no before tossing a kernel into his mouth. "Why'd you bring me here?" I abruptly say. My phone buzzes again, causing the screen to glow.

5:45 PM

I quickly flip it face down. "No particular reason." I turn my head in confusion for a moment before I continue eating.

"Would you date me?" The sudden sentence leaves me in silence. I grab a blueberry from the plastic bag before taking a swig from my soda. The silence must worry him because shortly, his voice reads that he regrets the moment he opened his mouth. "Seriously, would you?"

"I-" I stutter.

He clicks his tongue. "I knew it," He murmurs.

"Ignore that question. It was stupid,"

"No. No, it wasn't," I manage to say. Heck it, I'm finna let my heart take over. "I would, indeed," I formally say. "Aight, Aight," He replies, a smile warming up his face. "So, you like me?" He adds. "Yea," I stutter again. I look downward, attempting to avoid what feels like awkward tension. I've never admitted to a crush before. All of em' say they like me, and I mostly ignore it because I never necessarily "like" anyone back. And when I do, they're always some kind of douche— CJ for example. But Jayden, he's different. He relates to me, book-wise and conversation-wise. I feel like I can just talk all day with him and never run out of ideas.

We don't even have to say anything to have a conversation. He's silent for a moment, so I look up to see what's going on. I look up to catch him glimpsing at me, his eyes gleaming. "What're you doing?" I laugh. "Deciding whether or not it's alright to kiss you right now." My bottom lip parts from the top in satisfaction. That was smooth, not gonna lie. "Well, it's alright with me," I smile as he reaches over to place his hand on my cheek, grazing the side of my face. His hands are smooth, giving me shivers right before he kisses me. I lean in closer, which causes me to bump my knee against the table as I stand up, but I don't care. I laugh, my body full of adrenaline. "Wow, I had no idea how much I'd enjoy that." He chuckles as well before sitting back down. "Yeah, guess we've been waitin' huh?" "Mhm," I reply before walking over to his side and sitting beside him.

"Jayden."
"Yea?"

                              "Can you kiss me, <u>again</u>?"

Ten

CHAPTER TEN: NOW THAT I'M YOUR GIRL

I pull back from the kiss, and he places one quick peck on the side of my cheek. I sigh.
    Now on his side of the table, I lay my head on his shoulder, my braids falling right with me. He moves a few before grabbing a hold of my hand. "Tiffany," he says. "Mhm?"
    "**Will you be my girlfriend?**" I look up, his eyes staring into mine. "Why not?" I beam, and he kisses my forehead once again.

The sun has set, and we watch as the streetlights turn on. Shuffling to the car, I sit in the front seat as he tosses the now empty bag into the back. Opening his door, he sits in the seat before plugging his phone in and turning the key into the ignition. I lay back, looking at the stars aligned throughout the sky. "Want the sky-roof open?" Jayden asks, noticing me looking out the window. I turn towards him, sheepishly nodding yes before laying my head back down. Within seconds, I hear the whoosh of the door opening and a cool breeze blowing densely against the back of my neck. I tense up, and he chuckles at that. "What?" I yell since the wind causes my voice to drown out. He smirks before giving me a reply. "You! You got real tense at that cold air." He presses the button, letting go as it sits at a gap. I laugh before grabbing his phone and typing in the password.

* * *

I wake up from the jolt of Jayden shaking me awake. "Wake up, Tiffany. We're here, and it's one in the morning, so you better get going." I shift around, turning towards his side of the car. "Tiffany," He murmurs, continuing to shake me even more. "Fine," I mumble, grabbing my purse off the floor and jumping out. The rocks engraved into the driveway remind me I'd taken my shoes off. Jayden grabs my shoes and hands them to me before closing my door and walking me to the porch. "Thank you," I whisper, rubbing my eyes. The Ring doorbell is broken, so just my luck. He smiles before giving me a quick peck on the forehead. "See you tomorrow."

"See you," I reply before turning around and focusing on getting the door unlocked. I grab the key out of my pocket and insert it, twisting the key way as the door creaks open. Pushing it broadly, I walk inside, the floorboards lightly creaking and moaning under my footsteps, so I have to be quick. I shut the door quietly behind me as I'm sure it hadn't shut too loudly. Tiptoeing towards the stairway, I walk up successfully.

Closing my door behind me, I walk towards my closet and put my shoes down, eventually changing into shorts and a tank top. Grabbing my phone out of my pocket, I sit on my bed, leaning against the headboard as I check missed messages before texting the group chat.

    EMERY| imma be honest, that restaurant you recommended, T, was hella cool.

        AVERY| what place did you even go to?

        EMERY| you idiot

        AVERY| what?

CHAPTER TEN: NOW THAT I'M YOUR GIRL

> **EMERY|** i'd typed it out on here earlier!
> **AVERY|** ohh i just went back, see it now.

It's crazy cause they literally live together, yet they prefer to text. I have no idea about those two.

The last sent message was from 3 hours ago, at around 10:47.

> **ME|** hey

Avery's the first to reply, which isn't surprising since she tends to stay up late.

> **AVERY|** HEY! finally, you're back. the hell were you?
> no, i remember where you went. with jayden. what took you guys so long?
> what did you do? where exactly did you go?

I laugh at her message, as I can easily imagine her voice saying each word in my mind.

> lol. we went to shelby farms, it was the sunflower field.
> we had a small picnic, talked a bit, and he asked me to be his girlfriend.

The message sits in the message bar, but I can't find myself sending it. Deleting the last sentence, I press the blue arrow.

> **ME|** lol. we went to shelby farms, it was the sunflower field. we had a small picnic, talked a bit, and earlier we'd stopped at that downtown record place.

My phone buzzes, Jayden's name popping at the top of the screen.

> **JAYDEN|** Thanks for the wonderful night.

I grin at the message, soon responding with one of my own.

TIFFANY| no, thank you <3 loved every bit of it

* * *

I wake up to realize I've fallen asleep with my phone in my hand. I unlock it and see a photo of me falling asleep from Jayden, along with a few messages.

ME| no, delete it, i hate it.
   JAYDEN| No, you look cute when you're tired.
   ME| better yet, burn the whole phone.
   JAYDEN| Lol.

We must've called to say goodnight, but I dozed off.

I get out of bed, walking towards my dresser to decide what to wear. I decide on a skeleton crop, white ripped jeans, and some Blue Air Max's. After grabbing the layout, I place it on my bed, head toward the bathroom, and get in the shower.

"Morning," Mom says, looking up from her laptop screen. "Morning'" I reply, grabbing a cup out of the cabinet. I notice a blender sitting in the middle of the counter. "Oh, yea! Your dad made you a smoothie. Strawberries, Blueberries, Almonds, and Milk," She explains. "Oh, ok," I nod, pouring the chunky concoction into my cup. This *better* be good. "Mhm, cause this is actually good, ma," I say, once again taking another sip. I probably have a surprised expression all over my face right now. "Hand me that," she replies, snatching the cup from my hands. After taking a sip, her face says it all. "Anyway, I gotta go,"

"Where to?"

"The mall wit' Avery and Emery."

CHAPTER TEN: NOW THAT I'M YOUR GIRL

Her face gives a look.

"And Jayden," I groan. She laughs. "This 'Jayden' better do you good. If he hurts you, you know how your dad is."

"I know," I complain. I walk towards the door, grabbing my keys off of the front table.

"I wanna meet this boy, too. When can we meet him?"

"Alright, love you, bye!" I yell, avoiding the conversation as I walk out the door, closing it quickly behind me. I get in the car and right before I close it, mom opens the garage door again, sticking her head out. "We'll talk about this when you get home, don't shut the door on me," She reprimands as I nod with a smile, closing my door and pulling out.

My phone buzzes in the cupholder, a notification interrupting the music in between.

JAYDEN| Hey, where are you?

ME| omw.

JAYDEN| Alright. See you when you get here!

ME| see you <3

* * *

I pull into the parking lot, noticing Emery and Avery's car next to an empty space before parking there. I open the door, hugging Em and Av like I hadn't seen them in years. Jayden walks over from his car, the keys jiggling in his pocket with each step. Standing beside me, he attempts to grab my hand. I pull back hesitantly, and he gives me the cockeye. "So, we down to start shoppin' 'till we drop?" Avery yells as we walk towards the entrance. Emery smacks her in the back, causing her to shuffle forward. "What was that for?" And the bickering began. We all continue walking, Avery and Emery still arguing as we go. "Seriously, I was just getting my lick back!"

"In the middle of the street?"

I laugh at the comment, turning to face Jayden to see if he laughed as well, but find his face stone cold. "Where to?" I yell over the two of them as I open the door. They walk first, then Jayden. We walk inside to be greeted as usual by the bungee jump. And as usual, Avery wants to do it. "Oh, you two can do it together!" She points as we walk up to the line. I look at Jayden as he silently nods. I nudge his shoulder, hoping my eyes say *Are you good?* "Yeah," He mumbles before continuing to speak. "So, we down or what?" He adds on, his smile lighting up his face. I bite my lip before I grab cash out of my wallet, handing the wadded-up ten to the vendor.

"Alright, no cartwheels unless you're a pro, okay? We don't need any accidents," She flatly says, opening the gate.

I snark a quick fake smile before handing my purse to Emery and stepping on the mat, the guide buckling me in. Jayden walks in right behind me and steps onto the mat beside me, quickly buckling himself in. "Jump when you're ready!" I take a large step before jumping, feeling like I'm flying through the air like a little bird. I hear familiar screaming behind me before I turn and see Avery jumping like a manic on another one. "What the hell!" I laugh. Avery continues jumping, and so does Jayden.

We get off as time quickly passes.

"I'm starving."

"Em, you're always hungry."

"I'm serious, y'all hungry?"

Emery says, pointing to the back where Jayden and I are walking. We both nod, walking altogether to the food court. "Imma go get me one of those big pretzels," Avery mumbles, quickly sprinting to the vendor. She steps into the line. We walk over to a table, Emery placing her bag and Jacket down. I sit on the left side, and Jayden sits right beside me, pulling out his phone. "I'm gonna get a giant cookie. You want one?" Em points at me.

CHAPTER TEN: NOW THAT I'M YOUR GIRL

"Yea, give me a second. Let me talk to Jayden real quick," I reply, and she quickly nods. I turn to him, shoving his shoulder playfully.

"The hell is up with you?"

"You were my girlfriend last time I checked," He grunts. I think for a moment, remembering what I'd done earlier. "I know, but I haven't told them yet." This single sentence is enough to make Jayden seem hurt. "Have you told anybody?" I shake my head no. He sighs. "Not even your parents?" Silence. "Look, Tiffany. I like you, so we're either together or not," He says. "And I know it's gonna take a while to get used to, and I really don't wanna force you into anything," He adds facing towards me, his eyes searching mine. He grabs my hand again, and I hesitate whether or not to keep my hand there. He looks at me, and my hand stays in his palm of his. "I'm just not used to this, that's all," I state. "It's good," He pauses before kissing me on the forehead.

"Now let's go get that giant cookie."

We hang around a little bit, Emery and Avery stopping at every hurricane simulator we pass. Stopping at Vans, we check out some shoes. Avery looking at some Uggs, and Emery checking out the newest Jordan's releases. Jayden and I look at some of the backpacks, giving each one a personal rating. "I have the matching shoes to that one. They're high tops," I say, pointing towards a bag with roses and vines scattered as the design. "I think I've seen them before," Jayden smirks. I panic in my mind, thinking of what to say. "Yea, I think I'm wearing them right now," I blurt, covering my mouth almost immediately. Jayden laughs as he places one hand over my shoulder. "I make you nervous, huh?" He mumbles, as I just lightly nod, trying my hardest to keep myself from saying anything else. "Your total is 29.56," I hear the cashier say before Avery follows behind me and Jayden, a bag hanging in her hand.

"What did you buy?" Emery says, popping up out of nowhere.

I silently thank god for saving me, because I don't know if I could keep my mouth shut any longer. "Some UGG slides, cause why not," she laughs, as we all guide out of the store. I grab Jayden's hand, and his fingers cross over with mine. "You guys dating?"

"Yup," I quickly respond. She smiles, patting my back roughly but also gently.

"One more stop," Jayden interrupts as we stop walking. We'd just passed a Barnes & Noble, so I already know where he was headed. "Well," I pause, grabbing my phone out of my pocket. "I should get going." Emery and Avery nod in agreement before they tuck their wallets back in their purses. "See you tomorrow, though?" I respond, quickly planting a kiss on his cheek. "Bye!" The twins call, walking away already. I walk backward, continuing to face Jay.

"I'll call you later."

Eleven

CHAPTER ELEVEN: SHE DRIVES ME CRAZY

~~~

I apply lip gloss as I look at myself in my mirror. Noticing a light slip crease at the bottom of my dress, I fix it before grabbing my purse. Grabbing my phone, I take a quick picture of the outfit before sending it to the group chat.

> EMERY| cute fittttt <3
> AVERY| betrayal. the fact you DITCHED US for a date

I chuckle at Avery's message before sending a reply.

> ME| shut up, you goofballs, it's a date. a date i've been looking forward to lately
> AVERY| WE DON'T CARE

A face-time request notification darts at the top of my screen as I immediately press it. *"Avery, we don't care about your abandonment issues, okay? Quit being the wet blanket."*

"Okay, for your information, it's generally not my fault that he dumped *me-"*

Emery interrupts Avery just as she's speaking. A line of her own words came out of her mouth.
"WE DO NOT CARE!"

She yells into the speaker. Avery's mouth hangs in shock. Within seconds, I hear a mini-debate coming right from my phone. A car horn begins honking in the distance outside of my house. I look out the window, spotting Jayden's silver face-time resting on the curb right in front of my yard. *"Love y'all like hell, but he's here."*

I say as I quickly revert to texting him.

> ME| omw out. on a call with these idiots, lol.
> JAYDEN| Lol. Alright. I'll be waiting.

"Bye, Tiff! Have fun!"

* * *

I walk downstairs to find Dad and Jayden talking in the kitchen. "Did you hear this boy? He runs track! I bet Emery's probably seen him around, huh?" He yells as he notices me peeking around the corner. Jayden clicks his tongue as he turns around and sees me, checking me out "casually". Dad knocks at his shoulder, knocking him out of the trance. "My bad," he mutters, rubbing the back of his neck. Mom comes from behind me, placing her hands on my shoulders. "You look amazing," She mumbles in my ear, growing a smile across my face.

"Leave the couple alone," Mom shushes before ushering Dad over to sit on the dining chair. Shiloh comes downstairs soon after, what my luck.

CHAPTER ELEVEN: SHE DRIVES ME CRAZY

"Who's he?"

"My boyfriend," I snap back, grabbing Jayden's hand. He sarcastically replies, his face smiling brightly the entire time he speaks, "Ew, you have a boyfriend? I had no idea people actually liked you." I knock Shiloh on the back of his head before he snickers. "I'm Jayden," Jayden requests, sticking his hand out. "You play C.O.D?"

"Yea."

"You good at it?"

"Yea," Jayden responds as Shiloh excitedly shakes his hand. "We finna have some fun, my dude."

"Have fun!" Mom calls behind us as we walk down the porch steps. I wave back, sitting in the car as Jayden opens it for me. He sits in his seat, putting the car in the ignition before we pull off. "Your family seems fun," He says, turning the volume down a bit, just enough for us to hold a conversation. "Yea, my bad about Shi, he's just-," I pause, thinking of the correct word. "Him," I finish, a chuckle releasing from his mouth. I laugh along when I realize he'd actually found my joke funny. Butter by BTS and Meghan the Stallion plays on the radio. I lightly turn it up to add some noise to pierce the silence. "Where's dinner?" I manage to say. He smiles, quickly looking at me as we stop at the red light. "A surprise," He smirks, and I give him a look. He shrugs, settling his hand back on the wheel. I smack my lips.

* * *

We pull up a few minutes later in front of a tall building. Multiple restaurants and shops are aligned across the street. I look to my right and realize we're at Beale Street. "Ever been here?"

"Only my favorite place to be," I reply.

Dad and I come here every other Saturday for Father-Daughter time.

I get out on my side, and Jayden comes out on his. He closes his car door, and he soon locks the car completely. "Ready?" He calls, holding his hand out for me to grab. "Ready," I smile, grabbing a hold of it. We walk up and down the block, stopping at a few stores along the way. The best thing about it all is we got here just as hit dark. All of the lights are on, and the sun is down.

While we're walking, Jayden spots a music shop right beside us. B.B. King's Blues Club. "I love this place," He chuckles, holding the door open for me. We walk inside, light jazz playing on the speaker. The walls are a dingy, yet comforting yellow. Multiple bean bags in every corner, and the walls are jacked with guitars and other instruments. I grab one of the guitars that seem to be set on a stand, imaginarily playing it. Jayden laughs at the sight of it. I begin pretend-playing the tune to the song playing overhead. Bright Size Life by Pat Metheny. "I never knew you were into jazz." He seems to be flirting. I lightly panic. "Uh, yea. I know a thing or two," I manage to lightly flirt back. I notice he lightly bites his lip before walking off.

JAYDEN

We walk around the street a bit, eventually agreeing on finding a spot to eat. Grabbing my phone, I recommend a place right across from us. "It's called BITE, and it's hella good. Went there for dinner with a few of my friends," I mumble, handing Tiffany my phone. She presses the menu, looking at the choices. "Alright," she smiles before giving my phone right back to me. I grab her hand, and we start walking toward the small restaurant.

We walk inside, automatically welcomed by a host, Doja Cat on the speakers, and other customers' conversations filling the room. "Welcome to BITE.

CHAPTER ELEVEN: SHE DRIVES ME CRAZY

Take-out or Dine-in?" "Takeout," Tiffany quickly replies. The host nods, walking us towards a bar. "Order here, and we'll have your order out within seconds." The host smiles before walking off. "What're you getting?" I ask, leaning on the counter. Tiffany's still looking through the menu. "So many choices. Oh, can we get a cocktail?" "Might have to give them our 'IDs'," I manage to stammer along, hoping she gets my voice "air quotes". She chuckles playfully, placing the menu upside down. "Hello, my name's Maria, and I'll be your waitress," a cheerful girl says behind us. "Yea, we're getting Takeout," I note. She nods her head, grabbing the notepad out of her pocket.

Maria takes our order before walking behind the bar and into the kitchen. "So," I say, tapping my fingers on the tabletop. This date is awkward for no reason. Tiffany smiles before laying on my shoulder. "Wanna head to my place when we get the food? We can watch a movie," she recommends. I nod before grabbing my phone.

> AIDEN| Hey, man. How's the night out?
> Y'all kissed yet? What did you guys order? What's the restaurant??

I smirk at Aiden's text.

> JAYDEN| Lol. No, dude. Quit being so nosy!

I type back before shoving my phone back into my pocket. Tiffany then sits up from my shoulder as the waitress hands us our drinks in Styrofoam cups. "Your order will be out in just a moment, anything else?"

"Nope," I respond, and she grabs our card before walking off.

TIFFANY

"Thank you!" Jayden thanks, grabbing the bag. My hands slide across the counter to grab our IDs before I shove them both into my pocket.

I watch as steam releases from the top before I grab his left hand as we walk out the door.

Walking towards the car, it begins sprinkling, then hammering down. Jay turns to look at me as he speaks. "Wanna make a run for it?" I think for a moment before giving him a response, "Bet." Holding hands, we jog to the car, both of us silently hoping he'd unlocked it while we were on the sidewalk and out of the rain. My hand wraps around the door handle, I pull, and it's locked. I laugh at myself before pulling the handle again, this time it opens. Getting in, the plush fabric in the car immediately gets soaked with water due to us leaning back onto the seats. Leaning back, Jayden places the bag of food in the backseat, moving the box that sits back there in front of it to be sure it not moving. He sits back up before buckling his seat belt and putting the car in the ignition, allowing me to immediately turn the heated seat on. It's under 60 degrees outside, and the rain doesn't make anything better. We pull out of the parking lot, leading out into the highway. Jayden turns up the radio as *Baby* by Ariana Grande faintly begins playing. I grab my phone out of my purse.

9:30 PM

2 Messages from Mommy

I press the notification, opening iMessage.

MOMMY| Baby, where are you?

MOMMY| Never mind. Don't forget your curfew at 10.

I sigh, placing my phone into the cupholder. He turns to me as we come

CHAPTER ELEVEN: SHE DRIVES ME CRAZY

to an abrupt stop at the red light. "You still cold?" he mumbles. I lightly nodded, and he reaches behind my seat, grabbing a black zip-up hoodie. He hands it to me, and I put my arms in it.

Within around 20 minutes we pull up in my driveway. "You sure your parents' good wit' me staying here?" Jayden asks. I sit up from leaning against the window. Hesitantly, I reply. "Yea, I'm positive." We then get out of the car and walk up the parkway towards the door. I hand Jayden my keys out of my purse as he passes the warm bag to me.

We open the door to find my mom and dad sitting on the couch, watching some show on *Black & Sexy*. Mom quickly pauses it, pacing over to me. Dad sits there on the couch, pouring himself a glass of wine. "Did you have fun? Did you get rained on? How was the night?" She pounds us with questions, left to right. "Mom, we're good. Tonight was awesome. Yes, literally it was pouring. And if you don't mind," I pause, taking my shoes off and placing them on the mat. "We're heading to my room to watch a movie," I finish saying, grabbing two plates out of the cabinet before rinsing them off. I turn around and see Jayden down the hall, standing right beside the stairway waiting for me. Walking into the kitchen, I grab two Sprite cans out of the box before heading down the hall back towards the stairs. "Leave that door open!" Dad calls behind us as we walk up. I hear laughter before Mom's voice immediately after, "And he speaks!"

* * *

"What movie?" I ask, sitting on the edge of my bed. Jayden starts opening the bag, taking out the takeout containers. Grabbing the chopsticks, I grab the remote to turn something on, continuously scrolling across the screen until I see Mean Girls. I look at him in question and he nods. I press play as the movie begins.

JAYDEN

The credits roll and I look to my side, noticing Tiffany knocked out. Grabbing my phone, a message from mom pops on my screen.

MOM| Where's Maddison? Have you seen her?

I already know. I stumble through the dark, searching for my shoes. After tripping over something, I finally locate them. "Babe?" Tiffany mumbles. She begins moving, feeling the area where I was. "I gotta go, Tiff," I whisper, tying my shoelaces. She groans as she stretches. Sitting up, she rubs her eyes. "Can't you stay till morning?" "Nope. My mom said it's getting late" I lie. I walk over to her, kiss her forehead, and she grabs my arm. "Wait," she says as she stands up. She leans in, kissing me. I kiss back, of course. She pushes back, as if remembering something. "You gotta go, 'member?" she smirks, sitting back down on her bed. I must look dumbfounded. "Uh, yea. Yea. See you tomorrow, babe," I stutter before quickly walking out.

* * *

Pulling into the parking lot, the moon reflects off the pond right beside me. Getting out of the car, I see a shadow sitting on a bench, automatically knowing who it is. "Maddie!" I call, jogging towards them. They shift, turning around. I see Maddison's black hair covering half her face, her

CHAPTER ELEVEN: SHE DRIVES ME CRAZY

black jacket hanging along her arms like too-big clothing. Sitting beside her, she immediately lays her head on my shoulder. "Mom's looking for you," I mumble as she rubs her head along my chin. "Why do you keep coming out here?" She sits there silently.

"Because," She pauses, taking a deep breath. "I can't just sit in front of mom knowing I'm hiding something from her."

"Tell her."

"I can't, Jayden," She stutters as she sits up, looking at me with tears in her eyes. "It would break her."

"Maddison, I can't hide this from her,-"

"Jayden," She interrupts, her voice breaking.

"Please, just promise me you won't." I look at her, feeling teary-eyed.

"I promise."

Twelve

CHAPTER TWELVE: UNBRANDED

TIFFANY

Last night was amazing. Takeout, walk down Beale Street, and a movie? Thank the LORD for my life. Walking towards my desk, my phone buzzes.

EMERY| how was y'alls night?? did you guys kiss? what did y'all eat? where'd he bring you?

I lightly chuckle at Emery's nosiness.

TIFFANY| good. yup. bite. beale street.

I reply, answering all four questions. Within seconds, she starts a call.

"What'd ya do?" I roll my eyes. *"Went to a few stores along the street. Found a record place you'd like,"* I reply, taking my bonnet off. My braids slowly fall from the light bun I put them in. *"Alright, how'd the kiss go?"*

CHAPTER TWELVE: UNBRANDED

I immediately freeze, remembering every moment of the night before. A muffled "ohmuhgurd" comes from her side of the screen. I look at the screen and find her brushing her teeth. She spits and places her toothbrush down. *"You guys did more than kiss?"* I lightly nod, not paying much attention. *"I thought-"*

"OH! NO!" I yell, finally realizing what she meant. *"Just a kiss,"* I mumble, a smile bordering my face. She starts laughing as if not believing me. I stand up and quickly shut my door, being sure not to slam it. I creep back to my chair before saying anything else. *"Fine. Just guess, k?"* I say. She nods before thinking. A look washes over her face. I already know exactly what she's about to say. Her mouth opens, and she doesn't even say anything. I automatically nod, and she shrieks with excitement. I shake my head. **"This might be just a high school relationship. I bet you it'll be over by January,"** I reply. She rolls her eyes, doubting me by the minute. *"Aight, whateva you say, T."*

* * *

Today I'm planning on doing absolutely nothing but sitting inside and watching *Martin* reruns. We're on Thanksgiving break, and until Thursday, which is Thanksgiving, I'm sitting inside all day.

I'm sitting on the couch when mom comes in. "Tiffany," She grumbles, picking up the empty chip bags off the floor. "What?" I groan, grasping the remote. "First, fix that tone. Second," She pauses, pushing my feet off the coffee table. "Family is coming over tomorrow. Well, at least a few of your cousins are. But you know how I am! This house has to be-" "Spotless," we say in sync. Her face turns stern, and I smile. "I know. I *promise* you I will *make sure* I clean up. Can I finish this episode first?" "No. Go clean your room now. Tell Shiloh he has to clean as well. You know how he is."

JAYDEN| Wanna hang out today? Picnic?

I grab my phone off the charger, seeing a message from Jayden. I groan.

ME| can't my ma's making me clean up from top to bottom.
JAYDEN| Whatta shame. I had plans...
ME| NO! what were they?? whatd you plan?
JAYDEN| Nothing. Clean up, and don't get yourself in trouble. <3

I fluff the couch pillow as I hear the Ring go off. "Tiffany! Open the door!" Mom yells over the vacuum, and Shiloh races down the stairs. I follow behind him, peering aside him. "Xavier, where you' at?" and he opens the door. "Boy, stop yelling in my house!" Mom calls from behind me, right as CiCi passes him. "Hey, Shi. Xavier's getting his stuff out of the back of the car. Where's your momma?" Shiloh points to the kitchen as he darts out the door. "Tiffany! Look at you!" She says, noticing me standing in the door frame which connects the living room to the kitchen. She quickly hugs me before noticing mom cleaning up in the kitchen, almost tripping over the power cord to the vacuum, which sits beside the table. "Lyana!"

Xavier and Shiloh both walk inside, hands full. I quickly hug Xavier as I pass him, causing blankets to fall out of his hands. "Why would you do that?" "My bad!" I call back, jogging towards the SUV. "Jayley?" I question, and she almost immediately raises her hand from behind the van. The cold wind blowing against my body makes me wonder why I care about this girl this much. Knocking on the car window, she turns around and grabs something. "Tiff-Tiff!" She says, a warm smile across her face. "Here," she says, handing me a make-up case. "Hold that for me." She grabs the last bag, a duffel, before closing the trunk door. Struggling to carry it, she manages as she speaks. "Now, let's get inside so we can talk. It's freezin' out here."

CHAPTER TWELVE: UNBRANDED

Jayley places the duffel bag on the ground next to the door as I put the make-up case next to it. She eventually walks down the small hallway towards the kitchen. I follow. "AH! Jayley!" Mom yells, racing over towards us to hug her. I clear my throat. "And I see Tiffany is finally speaking?" I scoff before shuffling towards the counter. Their freezer bag sits there full of food from their trip. I reach in to grab Chex Mix, but mom hits my hand. "I'm making dinner." Dad finally comes down, and then there's a whole 'nother wave of saying hello. "Tiffany, why don't you get Jayley settled in your room? Same for you, Shiloh. I left blankets for pallets sitting on both of your beds." I grab Jayley's bag, and we head upstairs.

Dad must've turned on my diffuser because the air smells like a Lemony scent. Jayley sits on my bed, peering around my walls. Posters are everywhere, and a few records are mounted on the wall over my bed. "You've changed, huh?" she sighs. I lay the blanket on the ground and reach into my closet for some pillow covers. "Yeah, I guess. Just got more interested in records and stuff," I reply. She chuckles. Standing up and walking around my room, she catches a glimpse of my record player sitting on my dresser. I hand the record *Colouring Book* by Chance the Rapper, and she places it onto the platter mat. *Blessings* plays on blast as she turns it down.

"Wow, I've literally always wanted these. Never found the time to get one."

The clock reads 10 PM when dad walks in, and dim lighting from the hallway lights up the room. "Might wanna wrap the night up, girls," He states, rotating his finger clockwise in the air. Jayley and I nod as he closes the door behind him. Jayley crawls over to a socket before plugging her charger in and heading back to her spot. My phone buzzes beside me, the glow of my screen lighting up my corner.

JAYDEN| Hey, you there? You haven't responded to me all day.

Crap, I completely forgot to tell him I had family coming down.

ME| **yea, sorry about that. my cousins came down today, I had to clean like a maniac. talk tomorrow?**

Thirteen

CHAPTER THIRTEEN: A FAMILY MEET-N-GREET

"Who you' textin'?"

I look up to find Jayley sitting on her knees in front of me, bouncing up and down in excitement. She looks like a child as she does so.

Turning my phone off, we're left in the dark as I quickly tuck it under my leg. I throw the topic aside with a quick, "No one. I like your shorts." A pouty look scours her face as she scoffs, shuffling back to her spot. "So," she pauses, reaching for something in her bag. "Anything I need to catch up on?" Rummaging through the blankets, I grasp the remote before I press a button, the screen of my TV illuminating the room. She looks me in the eye as she turns towards me.

"Well.." I begin. "Well?"

"I have a new boyfriend," I continue. "Oh," She replies. If her attention wasn't all on me at first, it definitely is now.

"What's his name?"

"Jayden,"

"Age?"

"17, just like me."

"Where did you meet?"

I pause, getting ready to see her reaction. I lightly laugh at the thought of this. She tucks her foot under her right leg out of anticipation. "Yours Truly bookshop." Her face looks disgusted, yet surprised at the same time. "That bookstore you work at?" I nod. "Uh," she sneers as she signals for the remote. I toss it in her direction, and she catches it with one hand. "Movie?" "Yea. You pick," I reply as I lie down. She scrolls through the options on the screen, eventually landing on a show called *You*. "I swear, this is the bomb. This ain't a movie, but an amazing show, wanna watch?" I give her a look, my eyes slightly squinting. "Guess that's a 'hell yea,'" she ignores, pressing play. I lightly chuckle, looking at the screen load up. I turn to my side, staring at one spot on my wall, slowly drifting asleep to the murmurs of the voices.

* * *

JAYDEN| Morning, babe, Hope you have a wonderful day. <3

I wake up in my room bright, full of daylight. Sitting up, I see Jayley still asleep, and the sound of voices muffled through the wall. I open the door, creaks moaning through the hinges as I head to the stairway. I walk down the stairs, and the scent of burnt bacon circulates through the air.

CiCi must be cooking. I walk into the kitchen, and I was right. "Mornin', baby," Aunt CiCi says as she places 12 pieces of burnt bacon on a plate. She smiles as Mom unsurely grabs a piece, the few pieces of bacon crumple in her mouth as she takes a bite. I snicker at her as she spits discreetly into

CHAPTER THIRTEEN: A FAMILY MEET-N-GREET

the trashcan. Grabbing a small bottle of Orange Juice from the fridge, I wander towards the bar stool, taking small sips. Shiloh and Xavier walk out of the hallway with the conversation of their game.

"No man I swear! LeBron is probably the BEST player you can have in that game!" They wander into the living room, continuing to argue. "Where's Jayley?" Mom asks, grabbing the carton of eggs as she takes only two out. "Still upstairs, she is *knocked out*," I enthusiastically reply. Aunt CiCi motions the plate of bacon towards me, sympathetically insisting I grab a piece. "Go wake her up. I need you guys to pick up some things from Whole Foods for me," Mom says, grabbing a sheet of paper as she hands it to me. A whole list of groceries is written on it. "Be back home by 2, and get out of the house to pick them up by 12."

I open the door to find the pallet laying empty. No one in my room. A pair of hands touch my shoulder, startling me. "Oh my god, Jay," I pant, placing my hand on my chest, expressing home much she'd scared me. "My bad. What'd you come into the room searching for me for?" "My mom said we need to head to Whole Foods," I say, handing her the list. She looks through it before wadding it into a ball and shoving it into her pocket. "Alright, give me ten."

Taking a selfie in the mirror, I send it to the group.

EMERY| it's cute. where you headed???

AVERY| is ur cousin in town?? seriously she is AMAZING.

Today I'm wearing a blue cropped top, along with black ripped jeans, white classic J's, and my braids in a ponytail. I grab a small sash-like purse and head downstairs. On the way down the hall, dad walks out of their room. He stops me midway. "Did your mom tell you what time to be here?" I nod. "Good, my momma's coming in town." "So is your brother!" Mom yells from downstairs. CiCi bursts with laughter as dad scoffs it off. He kisses my forehead before I continue walking down. "Love you too, daddy," I smile, and Jayley and I are off.

Jayley plugs her phone into the aux, playing *8 Days of Christmas* by Destiny's Child. "So, wanna finish talking about your boyfriend?" She asks, a joyful smile written across her face. I'd completely forgotten about the small conversation from the night before. "No, let's talk about you for once. How're you and-" "We broke up." Her face turns blank. "Oh. I'm sorry for bringing it-" "It's fine. He just started getting hostile, and I left. You didn't know." The car is silent, aside from the bells in the chorus of the song. "But otherwise, I'm doing hella good. My nursing exams are excellent, and I'm still best friends wit' Kylie," She gleams again, suddenly perking up.

Jayley seems so sad. People always expect her to be happy and upbeat. I've always hated that about her. She keeps those expectations flowing, making her hide all her emotions. "So, anything else I missed?" She continues. "I applied to Berkeley." She abruptly stops at the red light, causing us to bump backward in our seats. She looks at me, an eager expression on her face. "Oh wow! That's amazing, Tiff!" I smile. "I just have to write a personal essay on who I am and where I see myself in the future. But that should be easy." The light turns green, and she continues driving. We pull into the parking lot as she says something. "You got this. A small tip is: Know who you're writing about." I roll my eyes as we both open our doors to get out. Meeting at the back of the SUV, we start walking toward the doors. "Seriously. Ask yourself: Who Am I?" I grab a cart. She pushes it out of the way, almost hitting a kid. With no signification, she grabs my shoulders, making me face her. *"Who Are You?"*

* * *

CHAPTER THIRTEEN: A FAMILY MEET-N-GREET

We pull up in the driveway, and I get out to type the password to the garage out on the keypad, *42678*. The garage opens, and Jayley jogs in from behind me. Opening the door, she yells, "Ain't nobody gon' help us get these bags out or?"

"CiCi, go help your daughter!"

"Your daughter needs help too, 'yana."

Mom and Ci come in from the hallway, bickering along the way as they eventually jog into the garage where the car is. 4 bags in Mom's hands and 1 in CiCi's. Jayley and I laugh at this, grabbing the leftover bags. Placing them onto the counter top, we start unpacking each bag to put the items in the pantry and such. Ten minutes later, we're finished. Jayley grabs a glass out of the cabinet and pours a cup of lemonade. "It's 1 now. Go work on that essay for a bit. Trust me, you do NOT want to put that to the side," She chuckles to herself as she wanders into the living room, her phone perched up to her ear as she begins talking into the speaker.

* * *

I pull out my laptop, open my email, and reread the letter.

Tiffany J. Mohan,

 Congratulations! You have been admitted into the University of California-Berkeley. In order to complete your application, please write us a personal essay on who you are and where you see yourself in the future. This is mandatory. Once finished, please email it to headmaster. We will work hard to get your admission letter to you as quick as possible. Thank You, and hopefully we'll see you on campus!

And it's mandatory, dang it. My phone buzzes beside me, and a message from Jayden pops on the screen.

JAYDEN| Picnic?

I sigh at his message, soon typing up my reply.

ME| can't, babe. gotta get at least half of this essay done :(

Within seconds he replies.

JAYDEN| Alright. GL!
  ME| ty

I place my phone on the nightstand face down. No distractions. Pressing the 'pages' app on my laptop, I press the *Personal Letter* format. *You got this,* I praise myself. Before I'm even able to type my name, someone opens my door. Shiloh stands in the frame, staring at me. "What?" I say frustratingly. He keeps standing there, not saying a single thing. "Get out if you have nothing to say, idiot," I puff. He continues standing there. "Get. Out," I growl. "I'm. Not. In. Your. Room," he states, standing near the edge of my room and the hallway. "Oh my god, Shi! Just get out!" I yell, throwing a pillow at him. While he picks up the pillow to throw it back, I quickly race to my door and lock it. "MOM!" I hear him whine on the other side of the door. "Tiffany locked her door!"

I wake up at 2 PM to dad shaking me awake.
 "mhm?" I groan, wiping the drool off the side of my face. "Wake up, more family is here," He says, as he stands back up. "How'd you get in?"
 "Don't worry about that. Get your sleepy tail downstairs," he replies, as he walks out of my room and down the stairs. I get up and look in the mirror. My shirt is a little stained somehow, so I grab a t-shirt with the playboy logo on it. Nothing bad, I just like the logo as it's cute as heck. I walk downstairs and see my cousins Shannon, Alexis, and Marlon just sitting around the

CHAPTER THIRTEEN: A FAMILY MEET-N-GREET

dining table, the garage door open. They're all distracted by their phones. Shannon is 16, Alexis is 12, and Marlon is 20. Shannon notices me and places her phone on the table while she hugs me. "Tiffany! Hey, girl," she says, freeing herself from the hug. "Hey," I mumble. Eventually, Alexis sees me as well and hugs me, too. Aunt Delare walks in from the garage, shutting the door. After the door is shut, Dad walks in.

"Now, why would you do that? You knew dang well I was out there."

"Oops," she giggles, running from him. He chases her, running in circles through the hallway. He stops suddenly before moaning in pain. She pauses before squatting and absolutely dying of laughter. "Ha! I'm older than you and you got old man bones!" She laughs. God, I love her laugh. And how she aged. If you were to guess, you'd say 30, maybe even 26. NOPE, she's 45. "Hey, baby!" she cheers, hugging me from the side. "Hey," I reply, awkwardly pushing her away. "When does mom get here?" Dad asks, sitting on the chair beside Marlon. He moans in pain as he motions for Shi to get him an ice pack. Marlon perks up real quick, then back down. "Yea, she said around like, ten," Delare replies walking into the living room. Dad looks at me, and I already know. "Go-" "Get them an air mattress, I know, daddy," I reply, slightly groaning. Opening the closet under the staircase, I grab the air mattress box. We store at least five in the house in case some family drops by. Hopefully, other people will have enough common sense to go to a hotel. I walk down the hall into the spare room, setting up the air mattresses.

Shannon walks in from behind me, her rolling suitcase following her. "Thanks, Tiff. You know, we should really catch up," She says, placing the suitcase in the corner. She unzips it and begins ruffling through the clothes and such. She grabs a pair of shorts, a t-shirt, and her bonnet. "Yea," I reply as I put the sheets on the mattress. "Let's talk tonight, kk? I can sleep-" "Ah," I interrupt. "Actually, Jayley is sharin' rooms with me this year. Sorry, Shannon," I continue, throwing a pillow at her. She catches it as she stands up. "Yea, it's good. We all can just go somewhere tomorrow, I guess," She responds before walking out of the room.

Fourteen

CHAPTER FOURTEEN: A TURKEY DINNER

I should've known not to wake up. I should've known it was gonna be chaotic.
 I walk into the kitchen to find like, fifteen kids running around the whole house, and five more playing outside. The kitchen is full of cigarette smoke and the smell of food. Kanye West's song *Good Morning* blasts on the speaker, CiCi's phone sitting right beside it with Tidal pulled up. A playlist full of Kendrick Lamar, Summer Walker, Kanye, Tyler The Creator, and more sits displayed on the screen. CiCi, Mom, Delare, Marlon, and Dad help around in the kitchen. The counter is packed with ingredients, flour spread across the surface. "Mornin' Baby!" CiCi says, waving a puff cloud she'd just exhaled. I start to cough, and she just hits my back like I'm a child. "Ci, quit smoking around the food," Mom sighs as CiCi puts the bud out. She then walks over to her phone before changing the song to All We Got by Chance The Rapper. Looking around, Dad hands me his keys deliberately before rushing back to help mom ask she struggles to carry two tin pans. "Get the ice out of the backseat," He says, and I nod before walking into the garage. The headlights flicker as the horn beeps when I

CHAPTER FOURTEEN: A TURKEY DINNER

press the button.

Climbing in, I reach into the back to feel a wet seat. No, not just wet, but soaked. As I lift the bag, water pierces through small holes and I rush to take it out. Placing it beside the garage stairway, I rush inside, grabbing towels out of the laundry room. "Dad, it leaked." "It what?" He yells back, rushing into the garage before desperately groaning. "Alright, just, thank you," He pauses, grabbing two towels out of my hand as he unfolds them and places them flat onto the seat, patting as much as he can dry. He turns towards the door, walking inside as I hear his request. "We might have to go buy more ice, Lyana." I walk back inside, mom rushing past me as I shut the door behind me. "Go get changed, it's 11 in the morning and you're still in your pajamas." I groan walking upstairs as Shannon passes me with two pairs of pants hanging on her arm. "Which one?" She pauses, lifting both at separate times, "Tan-ish pink Sailors or dark blue wide leg?" I look at her, then at the pants, "What shirt?"

"The long-sleeved shirt with the cascade neckline." I think for a moment, "Dark blue wide."

"Then tuck your hair into a high afro," I comment, and she nods before shutting the door behind her.

I close my door behind me before walking towards my desk where my record player sits. Bending down, I look through the collection on my shelf. I'd been collecting records for a while, and it's gotten fun over the years. My hands grab a hold of Jodeci's Album, *Forever My Lady*. I take it out of the sleeve before placing it on the platter. I grab the Tone-Arm, place it onto the record, being careful not to make the needle bounce, and *Stay* plays smoothly through the speaker. I hum along with the chorus as I grab a Bronze-colored turtleneck before reaching for some black denim jeans. Placing a silk scarf over my head, I slide the turtleneck over my head and then skim on my jeans. I look on the shelf that rests above my clothes, holding my heels and boots. I mumble, singing along with the lyrics. Jayley walks in through the door, taking her ponytail down as she looks at my mirror. "Hey," I mutter, tossing the boots onto the surface of my dresser.

My phone buzzes on my nightstand, and Jayley hands it to me.

JAYDEN| Happy Thanksgiving!! I know we both won't be able to talk much today, but I just wanted to say hey.

I smile at this before typing back.

ME| happy turkey day to you too. hi :)

I take my braids down as I look into the mirror, deciding whether or not to put them in a bun or half-up, half-down. Jayley looks at me through the mirror, our eye contact locking as she automatically knows. "Half-Up, Half-Down. It'll go good with the kind of style you got today," She states, and I nod before pinning my hair up.

As I jog downstairs, the doorbell rings. "Whoever is near that door, go answer it!" "I got it, mama!" I yell back to reply, rushing to the door. Looking through the window, I see dad's mom, whom we call Nana, his father, whom we call Papa, and his younger brother, Jordan, struggling as he walks up the steps. "Nana!" I call, opening the door. "Tiffany! Hello!" She calls. "Excuse me, Ma," Jordan mumbles as he manages to slide through between the two of them. I direct him towards the living room, where they'll be sleeping. "Dad told me to tell you to put your bags here," I beam as I point to a corner. He walks over there and he lays the bags down. "Thank You," He voices before walking off. Nana and Papa walk down the hall behind Jordan, leading into the kitchen as I hear every greet them with warm welcomes. I follow behind them. "Tiffany," Mom calls, drying her hands on a towel. "Yea?" I respond, turning around. She grabs a glass dish out of the cabinet, placing it on the counter. "I need you to do something for me."

* * *

CHAPTER FOURTEEN: A TURKEY DINNER

The mac n' cheese is the best part of Thanksgiving. No argument. It's baked for up to an hour, causing it to be nice and crisp on the outside and hella cheesy on the inside. And as many amazing things I could say about it, I have no idea how to make it.

The pasta shells sit in a dish in front of me, cheese resting on top. Delare looks at me like I'm crazy before continuing the stuffing. Nana walks over to me. "Look, Tiffany. You mark the oven at 350 degrees, put the dish inside, and leave it there for an hour, then turn the oven off and let it sit for 30. You got that?" She says, handing mom a bowl. I nod yes as I turn the nob. "Where's Shiloh? I haven't seen him not once since I got here," Nana says, mixing the stuffing. Delare hands CiCi the Thyme, the glass container clinking against the counter. "Outside," I reply, placing the glass tray in the oven. She looks outside to find Xavier, Alexis, Shiloh, and a few other cousins outside playing. She laughs at the scene, and soon she and mom are talking about how much he talks about Star Wars.

I look around to try to find Jayley, but I can't find her.

Walking outside through the front door, I turn and guess who I find vaping? Jayley. She coughs, hitting her chest. She quickly shoves the pen into her back pocket. The vapor sits in the air, as she fans it away. "Hm, yea. Don't tell my momma," She says, chuckling to hide the fear in her voice. I stare at her, feeling a smirk slowly arise on my face. "Seriously, Tiff! Don't tell her, she'll kill me!" She whines. Not gonna lie, I've never in my life seen this girl whine. "Fine," I groan, stomping in place. She cheers in excitement before grabbing the pen back out of her pocket. She hits it again, the white vapor leaving her mouth. I chuckle before walking back toward the door. Mom opens it from the inside. "Come on, time to set up the table. Get that fold-up one out of the closet," She says, helping me inside. I open the closet under the stairway and grab the fold-up table. Jayley walks in from behind me. "I'll get the chairs."

I walk in from behind Jayley outside and find mom setting up the buffet supplies. She lights the little candle-like flames, placing them each under the trays. "Time to Eat!" She yells, tossing the lighter back into the drawer. A stampede of kids comes in from outside, and a crowd of adults come from all over.

Auntie Ciecle and Cousin Shannon lead the prayer.

"Thank the Lord for allowing us all to come into town like always, safely and smoothly. Please allow that for the ride back. Bless this food, God. Allow for each bite to bless our…" And the prayer continues, eventually ending with an *Amen*. Everyone grabs a plastic plate, and the feast begins.

Fifteen

CHAPTER FIFTEEN: JAYDEN ON MY MIND

The kitchen is left in disarray after everyone leaves.
We clean for up to an hour before we all decide to head to bed. It's around midnight when I lay down.

12:50 AM
106 Messages from The Real Housewives of Memphis

Dang, Avery and Emery blew up my phone with videos and photos from their dinner. They never put that phone down.

I check out every video and photo they sent, before sending my very own message into the chat.

ME| im tellin' y'alls mom to turn on y'alls screen time lol

The Bookposal

* * *

GMAIL: 1:56 AM

Tiffany Jessie Mohan,
The deadline for your personal essay is due within the next 24 hours. Please send your essay before November 27, 11:59 PM. Thank You.

I wake up hearing the *Gossip Girl* intro.

"XOXO, Gossip Girl," Jayley says along with it. I throw my pillow at her. "Ow! I had no idea you were awake," She says before tossing it back. It hits the lamp, but only the shade falls. I never had time to screw the top of the thing on there. Sitting up, I quickly fix the shade and grab the screw out of the drawer when I notice the email notification saying the sender is from Berkeley. Nearly dropping the shade in excitement, Jayley turns around with a concerned look as I shrug and place the shade on correctly, screwing the top on. I read it, panicking almost immediately. "Shoot, Crap, I completely forgot about that! Why would they assign it the few days of thanksgiving? No one pays attention-" Jayley stands up and hits my leg. "Calm down. Work on it. Now. It's not that hard anyway. Just tell them about you and your greatest achievements," She says, as it barely calms me down. I breathe in deeply, then breathe out. "I will not touch my phone."

"Right!"

"I will not be distracted."

"Right!"

"And I will- wait, there's a sale at H&M," I say as an H&M coupon pops up on my screen. She rolls her eyes, and I laugh. "I'm kidding. I will focus and get this done," I express, looking at her in the eyes. "By 11:59."

"By 11:59," I repeat. She nods before looking back at the screen. I grab my laptop from under my bed and open it. I press the file *Tiffany's Personal*

CHAPTER FIFTEEN: JAYDEN ON MY MIND

Essay from Monday, and I don't type. I can't type. I have no idea what to type. Finally, I think of something.

Hello, I am Tiffany Jessie Mohan. I am 17 years old, and I go to SouthWind High School. My boyfriends'|

I quickly delete the sentence, starting over.

I am Tiffany Jessie Mohan. I am 17 years old, and I go to SouthWind High School. I read, write, and talk to my boyfr|

And I press delete multiple times again. Why not 3rd person? That might be easier.

Tiffany Jessie Mohan is 17 years old and attends SouthWind High School. She graduates in the year 2022 and intends on becoming a student at the University of California-Berkeley. In her free time, she reads, writes, and talks to her boy|

"Nope, still the same," I groan, slamming my head down onto my bed. Jayley turns around. "Not going good?" I manage to shake my head no from under the covers. She pauses the show, walking over to me. I look up at her face, hoping for some kind of positive expression. She shakes her head no as she presses the delete key. She types something up.

My name is Tiffany Jessie Mohan. I grew up with one other sibling, a brother, and he is younger than me by five years. I am 17 years old and attend SouthWind High School. I've always been an A student, as my grades can express. I graduate next year, the year 2022, in May.|

She leaves the little bar there for me to continue typing. "I can't. I keep thinking about-" "Well then stop thinking about him!" she yells, walking back to her spot. She sits down as I roll my eyes before putting my fingers on the keyboard.

79

I would like to be an Investigative Journalist. My boyfri|

"I did it again," I sigh, and she presses delete.

I would like to be an Investigative Journalist. I see myself in the future with|

She leaves the rest for me to type.

I see myself in the future marrying my|

I give up, slamming my laptop shut before sliding it right back under my bed. "I promise I'll get it done before 11," I say, as Jayley looks at me with demise. "I promise."

* * *

EMERY| dana's having a party tonight @ 6. yall down?

My phone buzzes beside me, and I pick it up. Avery quickly replies.

AVERY| yea. knock on my door in 30.
EMERY| shut up, we live together.

I groan at this, still thinking about my essay. I feel someone's hands on my shoulders, and I turn around to find Jayley crouching over me. "Maybe you need a small break. The party doesn't sound like a bad idea," she says, as she pushes beside me. I turn my phone off before laying it back on the table. "Yea, but you said I-," "I know what I said," She pauses, scoffing as she realizes I'd used her words against her. "But maybe a break is just what you need." She grabs the remote, entering the app HBO max. I think for a

CHAPTER FIFTEEN: JAYDEN ON MY MIND

moment. Should I go to the party? I mean, I have many things on my mind, and a few drinks should get them out. "I'll go. I'm gonna go to the party," I say, as I look at her. "Okay, cool. No idea why you're telling me. I've spent six hours on the road with a rowdy 13-year-old. Yea, no thank you."

I hear the thunder from outside before it sounds like hailing. I look out the window to find absolute bucketfuls of rain falling from the sky. I look at myself in the mirror, unsure of whether or not to keep the outfit. As always, I revert to the group chat.

ME| y'all, should i wear this fit?? look outside before answering btw [Image]

EMERY| yea. it's cute, fashionable ig, and keeps you warm.

I shrug, shoving my phone into my back pocket. Walking out of the room, I bump into Shannon. "Whoa, where you headed?" She says as she blocks the doorway. Dang, could she just let me leave? "Jayden's. Bye," I quickly respond, trying to rush out of the room. She pushes me back once again. I roll my eyes. "Come on, Shay," I groan. She laughs. "Fine," She moves, also grabbing my arm. "But for real, where to?" I smack my lips before replying. "A party."

※ ※ ※

"Just tonight," I mumble under my breath before walking inside. "Just tonight."

I walk down the halls, searching for an available seat. Finally, after what feels like hours of searching, I can sit down in peace. I pull out my phone, and a notification sitting there on the home screen. *You have 10 more hours before your student application will be automatically declined.* There is entirely no way this decides to appear when I'm at a party. A party I didn't even want to come to. I press the notification, and as it opens it reads:

Hello Tiffany Jessie Mohan,

As you know, you have to fill out a student essay before 11:59 PM on November 27. If you have received this email, we have contacted you to let you know you have 10 hours left before we automatically decline your application. Thank You,

Derek Watkins
  Headmaster of California-Berkeley

I begin to pack up my purse, all of my things scattered onto the bench, as I was frantically searching for my phone before. Standing up, I notice Avery near the drink table, refilling her neon green cup. "Av!" I yell, doing a limp-like walk towards her; my bag wasn't organized, okay?! "Hey, I was looking for you. Where have you been?" She yells. "Look, I gotta go," I yell over the music. "You just got here, Tiff!" She groans, placing the cup down on the bar. "I know, but I only have 10 hours left before my application is declined." "Just chill out. Take a break for a bit. Jayden's lookin' for you," She yells, pointing over toward him in the corner. He's talking to some guys about something. He smiles as he notices me. Walking towards me, he stands beside me as he wraps his right arm around my hip. "So," he pauses. A slow-ish song plays. "Dance?" I nod, as he grabs my hand. He leads me toward the center of the room and we dance.

Flashbacks from the party ring through my mind. The kiss. His eyes. His voice. I lick my lips in anticipation, the tension between us rising. He clears his throat.

"I like hanging out with you, Tiff," He pauses, and I confidently smirk. He chuckles. "I'm serious. I'm extremely glad I met you, you have no idea." I lay my head down on his shoulder, and we continue dancing slowly as if we were at a formal. "I'm extremely glad you're my girlfriend," He says, causing a smile to grow across my face, and tears to lightly form in my eyes. "And I'm glad you're my boyfriend," I respond, the words flowing freely off my tongue as if they'd been sitting there, waiting for this very moment. I lift my head, our eye contact meeting. His eyes look the same way they'd looked at the party, but this time he's sober. He lowers his hands onto my waist, pulling me in once again. Within moments, our lips touch. His mouth is smooth, and he tastes like peaches just as before. He glides his hand from my waist up to my upper body towards my face, fondling my cheek as he pushes my braids away. I mute the world around me, only focusing on me and Jayden. Us. Unfortunately, my phone buzzes in my clutch. "Hold Up," I say, moving away from him, our lips departing. Grabbing my phone, I check my screen, and notifications from iMessage immediately load up.

10:56 PM
15 Missed Calls from Mommy
10 Messages from Mommy

I groan. Jayden looks at me with a certain look, and I nod. "Well, go ahead and head on home. See you tomorrow?" He states as he kisses me on my forehead. "Yea," I giggle, my view lingering on him. He smiles, pushing me towards the door. "Go," He pauses. "Talk later tonight instead?" I laugh, lightly nodding. "Okay, bye, for real this time."

I open my car door, quickly hopping in right as it begins to sprinkle again. The rain has been on and off since 5, and it's obnoxious. I put the key into the ignition, my headlights glowing brightly in the street. I take off my heels, placing them in the passenger's seat beside me. Tired of sound in general, I turn the volume on the radio down, leaving me in silence as I pull off the curb and drive down the street. Luckily, my house isn't that far from Dana's, so all I've gotta do is head around the corner and I'm at my place.

I open the door a crack, but this time it doesn't squeak. Aunt Delare must've oiled it. She fixes anything she can. Shutting the door behind me, I tiptoe towards the stairs in an attempt to sneak back to my room, as usual. This time is different. In the dark, I hear creaking coming from the guest room, before turning around and seeing a shadow standing in the doorway. I open my mouth to scream, but a hand swoops in just in time. "Shut up." My eyes adjust to the darkness, Jayley's face resting in view. "Jay?"

"Shhh," She shushes, her finger going up to her lips. "Dang. I guard for you and this how you treat me?" She sarcastically whispers. "Well, I'm gonna head to bed. As I would," I pause, one foot on the stairs. My heels rest in my right hand, and I feel a droplet of water fall onto my foot. "So, goodnight."

I walk out of the bathroom and see Jayley sitting in her usual spot. "Hey," she groans as she looks up from her phone. I lightly wave, quietly jumping into my bed. I plug my phone in as she tosses her phone to me, basically signaling for me to plug hers in, too. plugging in my phone. I plug hers in, and she lays down. Turning the TV off, I reach under my bed where my laptop usually is before grabbing a hold of it. I open it, type the password in, and head to the dashboard. Pressing Pages, I sit there and stare at the format Jayley had left me earlier, my fingers hovering over the keys, but not daring to press down. *God, why can't I just think?*

* * *

"Tiff." Jayley shakes me. "Huh?" I groan, wiping drool off the side of my face. I sit up from my keyboard. "Did you get that essay done?" She says,

CHAPTER FIFTEEN: JAYDEN ON MY MIND

looking at me in the eye. "Shoot," I mumble, typing quickly. "Maybe you could email the headmaster, Marlon had done the same thing-," She begins, but I mute her out since her babbling goes on forever. Quickly, I type the Gmail link in the browser, and an unopened email from Berkeley sits in my inbox, waiting to be opened. I click it as it reads:

Thank You for Submitting! You have now admitted your application to California-Berkeley University.

Attached to it is an email I sent. My essay. About me.

My name is Tiffany Jessie Mohan. I grew up with one other sibling, a brother, and he is younger than me by five years. I am 17 years old and attend SouthWind High School. I've always been an A student, as my grades can express. I graduate next year, the year 2022, in May. I would love to become a Journalist, as my grandmother has been one for 20 years. I can see myself in the future having 2 kids and marrying my current boyfriend, Jayden Hudsen. I would like to attend California-Berkeley because my parents Lyana and Derrick Mohan both attended and met there. The journalistic system has always been so interesting to me. For me to be applying to a University and becoming a student is such an accomplishment. I am prepared and excited about the skills that I will learn to become the best representative I am.

Sixteen

CHAPTER SIXTEEN: FROZEN IN TIME

Dad shuts the back of the trunk after Jayley crams the last of their bags. Auntie CiCi has a wad of blankets in her arms when she rushes outside. I jog to help her before a blanket falls. "Thank you, baby," she smiles as we put the stack in the backseat. Xavier grabs one from the top stack, his attention on his phone. "Wish you guys could stay," I say as I hug Jayley. "Yea," she mumbles. We let go of the hug & she heads to the passenger side. "We'll be back for Christmas," CiCi says as she hugs me. She rubs my back as adults do. Before they back out, Jayley rolls her window down. "Hope you get in, Tiff. You deserve it."

* * *

I feel cold air hit my legs, and I look up to see Mom frustratingly grabbing my comforter, as usual. "Get up." I groan and grab my phone off the charger. I pick out a blue turtleneck and black jeans. Heading to the bathroom, I take my braids out of my bonnet and fix my hair into a bun.

CHAPTER SIXTEEN: FROZEN IN TIME

"Good Morning. Tiffany, make sure your brother is ready. It's your turn to drop Shiloh off today," Mom says as I walk downstairs. I grumble a quick "Mhm" before opening the fridge and grabbing a canteen of yogurt. I hear dad jog down the stairs. "I'm heading to work," he says as I hear him kiss mom. "Bye, babe," She says, her keyboard keys clicking in the background. He wanders towards me, kissing me on the cheek. I can smell his strong cologne as it stings my nose. "Have a good day, Tiffany," He mumbles before heading out the garage door. "Shiloh!" Mom yells from the stairway. "Yes?!" he yells back. "Boy, if you don't get down here! It's time for you to go!" She yells back, walking back into the kitchen. He jogs down the stairs and runs into the kitchen, grabbing his bag off the chair.

Shiloh sits beside me in the passenger seat. "Can you turn on some music? It's too silent," Shiloh complains, still looking at that screen. "Yea," I reply as I type in my password. I back out of the driveway, and within seconds we're at the end of the street. *Christmas Calling* by Nora Jones is the first one that plays. "So, is school going well?" I ask. "Yup," he replies. I reassuringly nod. "That's good."

I pull up to his school, Highland Oaks Middle School. Grabbing his bag off the ground, he rushes out of the car. "Bye," he says. I wave and watch him walk into the building.

"As you know, we have roughly two more weeks before Christmas break, and then you'll be out of my class," Mr. Chester smiles. The class lightly cheers. "And we have already taken the exams required to announce class completion," He pauses. The classroom lightly murmurs. "I don't care what you do. You can play on your laptop, your phone, whatever. You can eat for all I care. I'll have a movie playing on the board until it's time for you to go." Not even seconds after he says this, the classroom erupts with sound. Avery scoots her chair closer to mine. "So," She yells, and I sigh. I roll my eyes as I look up from grabbing my book. "How are you and Jayden going?"

"Good," I mumble, flipping the page. "It'd be hella funny if you were wrong earlier." "About what?" I say, shifting positions in my seat.

"You said it's probably just a high school relationship and it'll end soon."

"Yea, it probably is. Now leave me alone," I reply, and she scoffs. I can feel her roll her eyes at me. "Whatever." She says. I hear her ruffle in her purse. She pulls her phone out, and I can see the glow on the screen. Mr. Chester turns on Home Alone, which the class isn't going to pay attention to. Avery digs in her pocket, eventually grabbing something. She hands it to me, the silver wrapper sitting there with the light's reflection aiming me right in the eyes. I grab it out of her hand and pop it in my mouth. Mint Wrigley's gum. I blow a bubble, in which Avery ridiculously pops. I roll my eyes and turn the page. A piece of paper falls out of place. I pick it up and unfold it.

Meet me after school at the ice skating rink. Trust me, it'll be fun - Jay

"What's that?" Avery says, snatching the paper out of my hands. You literally can't hide a single thing from her. Reading it, she awes. "Ooh Ice Skating date I see. Better not cut a finger off," She says teasingly, wiggling her finger in my face. I wince, my face scrunching up before pushing her finger out of my face. "He probably slipped it in a random page earlier today," I say, peeking a glance at the movie. "Well, whenever it was," Avery pauses. "You better go," she finishes, her voice near a whisper. She smiles lightly before reverting her attention back to her phone.

I sit in my car, the heat on. My phone buzzes in the seat beside me, a message from Jayden popping up on the screen.

JAYDEN| Alright, I'm here. Just where are you parked?
ME| i'm right beside the main area, parked between a silver Honda and a black GMC truck.

CHAPTER SIXTEEN: FROZEN IN TIME

Within seconds I see Jayden's car pull up behind me and park in the available space. I turn the key back off, the heat slowly fading away. I open my door and get out. Shuffling over towards Jayden, 3 beeps of my car going off, alerting me of its locking. Jayden wraps his arm across my shoulder. "Ready?" he says, kissing my forehead. "Mhm," I mumble, and we walk toward the entrance.

It's freezing, and I can see my breath in the air. I blow outwards, watching the fog float from my mouth. "Let me go get the tickets, get yourself some skates," Jayden exhales, handing me a wad of cash. I nod, and head over to the skate counter. "Size 8," I smile and hand the guy a 10. He walks towards the back, grabbing these white skates like the ones in the movies. "Lucky you, these just came in yesterday," he chuckles, handing me the pair. "Thank You!" I praise. I sit down on a bench beside the shoe counter and slip the skates on. Shoving my boots into the cubby under my bench, Jayden locates where I am before walking to me. "Hand me the rest of the cash so I can get myself some skates." I reach in my pocket and grab the leftover cash, just enough for him to pay for his. He nods thankfully before paying for his rental.

We finally get out on the rink. I grab onto the railing, lightly falling. "Careful!" Jayden says, helping me up. "I haven't ice skated in ages," I mutter, shuffling across the surface. "I can help you. Hold onto my hand." I grab his hand, which causes me to lose my balance. He stops me from falling. We're standing on the sidelines, my feet beside his. "Keep your other hand on the railing if you want." Which of course I do. We start moving. "You have to be extremely careful, be sure not to fall, okay?" Jay expresses. I nod, continuing to look down at my feet. "Look up, you can fall looking down the entire time," He says, lifting my chin. "Move your feet kind of like normal skating," He suggests. "Like this." He lets go of my hands, and I stand still like a water buoy. He wanders off, his feet moving back and forth between movements. He skates back towards me. "Your turn."

JAYDEN

Tiffany moves her feet as I showed her, and she begins moving. She's not even holding my hand or the railing, and she's moving. "Jayden, babe! Look!" She excitedly calls. I laugh and skate over toward her. I give her a high five and a kiss on the cheek. "Good job, baby," I exclaim, as I feel a smile crawl up my face. We skate one round together, holding hands. Noticing Tiffany's shivering, I offer for us to head inside and get hot chocolate.

***

Baby, It's Cold Outside by Esther Williams plays overhead. Tiffany takes a sip of her cocoa and places it down, fog from the heat forming against the table. My arm rests on her shoulder, and we're talking about random things. "What would you like for Christmas?" I ask. She looks upward as she thinks for a moment. "No idea," she replies, swirling the green stick around the cup. "No, seriously. What would you like? I'll get you anything."

"And I'm serious. I don't know. Heck, you don't even have to get me anything," She replies. I sigh, leaning backward. Guess I'll have to figure it out. Not bad, just I thought she'd know, which would make it simpler. We both finish our cups and within seconds, Tiffany's ready for another round around the rink. I groan. "Please? Last time, then we leave," She whines. I look outside, and it's getting a little dark. The overhead lights turn on. "Fine. But only because I've always wanted to skate in the dark,"

"Why?" she asks as we walk outside, and I pretend I don't hear.

We skate around again, holding hands like before. Both falling a couple of times, we laugh until our stomachs hurt. As a slow-ish song begins to play over the speaker, we realize we're a few of the last people out. "We should go. We've done more than one round," Tiffany laughs, unstably skating towards the entrance. Skating behind her, I grab her arm and pull her back.

TIFFANY

Jayden pulls me back to face him. We're standing face to face, looking at each other's eyes. I look at his lips, and he looks at mine. Within seconds, we kiss. His lips are warm, and the kiss is comforting. He glides his hand across my face, caressing my cheek. He pulls back. "Is this why you've always wanted to skate in the dark?" I say, my voice sounding as if I need to clear my throat. "Mhm," He mumbles. He closes his eyes and leans to kiss me again, this time longer. More passionate. We both part from this one together, as we notice one of the employees telling us it's time to get out for them to close.

We nod, giggling like little kids as we glide to the exit.

Seventeen

CHAPTER SEVENTEEN: MY TRUE LOVE GAVE TO ME

Jayden walks me to my car, and we talk the entire way there. I feel like I can never run out of things to talk about with him. We pause as we reach my car. "I loved the night," I say shyly. He smiles. "I did, too." I nibble on my bottom lip. "See you tomorrow," I say. He kisses me again on the forehead.

I get in the car, immediately turning on the heat. I toss my hat and gloves in the passenger seat and pull out my phone to check the time.

10:56 PM

We always seem to leave just in time. I turn up the radio, 104.5 playing distantly. Tonight was amazing. The skating, the drinks. The kiss. I smile as I re-imagine the kiss. It felt like the kind that goes on in those cheesy Hallmark movies. Fireworks, lights, cheering. Fuzzy, warm feelings. I've never felt like that in my life before, and I finally felt it. My phone vibrates beside me. I look at the screen, and a message from Jayden sits there on

CHAPTER SEVENTEEN: MY TRUE LOVE GAVE TO ME

the home screen.

JAYDEN| You have no idea how special you made this night for me.

I pull up into the driveway, racing to the door. I unlock it and kick off my boots immediately. I run up the stairs into my room. Closing the door behind me, I quickly respond to the text.

ME| i loved it, too.

Mom opens the door, and I quickly shove my face into the pillow. She always knows what you're feeling; And if you've kissed someone. "Hey," She laughs. Her laugh is heartwarming and makes you comfortable. Makes you feel like you can tell her anything. I muffle a reply. "Hi." She chuckles as she sits at the edge, near my feet. "I see you just got back," She pauses. "How was your night?" Those few words make me think back. "Magical," I reply, still muffled. "Well, your father sent me in here to check on you, you know how he is." She chuckles as she gets up. A laugh escapes from my mouth. She leans over and plants a kiss on the back of my head. "I love you." And she leaves, closing the door behind her.

* * *

I close my locker door and find both Avery and Emery sitting there, surprising me. I yell, startled. "You guys scared me," I whisper as I notice a few people turn to me. "Whatever. How did it go?" Avery says enthusiastically. Emery stands there, confused. "You don't have a single clue what you're here for, huh?" "We're supposed to do something? I thought we were just scaring her," She shrugs, walking alongside us on the way to our next class. We all have 3rd period together, and thankfully, Ms. Johnson, our Journalism teacher, put us all near the same desks. We walk into the class and begin heading towards the back of the room. "We went ice skating yesterday," I begin talking, explaining the whole night to them. "And it was so fun, I swear. We laughed and talked," I pause, grabbing the book *Red Queen* out my bag.

"He retaught me how to skate. Then after skating for a bit, we stopped for some hot chocolate. And as we drank, we talked about Christmas. What we'll get each other, the traditions," I smile, reminiscing the night before. "Then we skated a bit more," I chuckle. I pause, closing my eyes to visualize everything again. "Then we kissed." Emery shakes my arm with excitement, and Avery sits there waiting for me to continue. I look at her, and she looks at me. "What? You gonna say anything else?" I shrug, continuing to read the page. Avery scoots her seat closer to mine, looking at my book. "When's the next time you work at that book place?" "I don't know. I took a small break for Thanksgiving. She'll text me when I should come back," I reply, flipping the page once again. Mrs. Johnson walks into the room as the bell rings, a few more kids shuffling in to prevent being sent to the office. "Last and final exam of my class. If you finish it early before the bell, do not distract others," She says as she begins passing out the papers. Emery and Avery both scoot to their desks, Mrs. J's face already getting stone cold.

"You got this," I whisper to myself as she hands me my copy, and I start.

* * *

Jayden asked me last night what I'd like as a Christmas gift, and to be quite honest, I don't even know what to tell my parents what I'd like. I sit in the car, looking at Amazon. I check the time and see that it's 3:15, close to the time to pick up Shiloh. I put the car in the ignition before heading towards the school.

"Peace out, Jaycee!" Shiloh slides his bag in before getting in himself. "How was school?" I ask, probably sounding like my mom. "Good, we had our last state test today. I don't have to be at school for the next two weeks," He brags, poking my shoulder. I chuckle, turning the corner. "Alright, then. You're lucky."

We pull up in the driveway, and I look beside me to find Shi knocked out. Dang, that test must've dried him out. I shake him awake before heading inside, him walking right behind me. Dad's car isn't in the driveway, and mom doesn't get back from work until 10 tonight due to a surgery. Shiloh goes upstairs and I look in the fridge for a snack. Grabbing a Danimals and a bag of Lays' I head upstairs. Sitting on my bed, I turn on Home Alone and grab my laptop off the nightstand. I open a tab in Amazon and sit there, trying to think of the perfect gift for Jayden.

>   **ME|** ok so idk what to get jayden for christmas and i really wanna get him something
>   **EMERY|** idk.
>   **AVERY|** a watch? a journal? your love? a make out session??
>   **ME|** avery...
>   **AVERY|** what???

I chuckle at Avery's response when I finally think of a gift.

And it's perfect.

Eighteen

CHAPTER EIGHTEEN: HARD FALL

JAYDEN

I press *Place Order*, and the date for shipment tells me December 7, next Monday. Mom lightly knocks on my door before inviting herself in. I quickly exit out of the Amazon website, leading me to the tab mom had left open for me. "Have you decided on the colleges?" She asks as she sits on the edge of my bed. I sit there silently, staring at the screen. It has rows of colleges I could apply to. And it's not like I wouldn't make it, I definitely would. I just don't know what to do. Mom sighs frustratingly before reaching over as her fingers graze the mouse. She presses the first link on the screen, California-Berkeley, where Tiffany's going. "You said Tiffany applied here, so why don't you?" I look at her sideways. "What?" "I haven't even picked what I want to do in my life, plus they don't even have an undeclared major," I say, pointing to the list of majors. "Well then, you better think of one," She groans as she stands up. "Because you are way too smart to be acting like this." She kisses my forehead. "Dinner's ready."

CHAPTER EIGHTEEN: HARD FALL

I follow her down the hallway leading to the kitchen, Maddison already sitting at the table. "Hey," Byron, my stepfather, says as he gives me a side hug. I lightly shove him off my shoulder before sitting in my seat. My parents divorced about three years ago. She met Byron, fell in love, and married him a year later. Maddison begins to scoot food onto the side of her plate. The table is silent, aside from the Grizzles VS. Dallas Mavericks game playing on the TV. "Baby," Byron mumbles as he picks up his plate. Mom nods, already knowing what he's about to say. Walking over to the couch, he starts yelling at the screen. I peek at Maddison's plate and notice everything spread out, seeming like she was on her way to eating every single thing. I give her a look, and she peeks her head downward. "Dinner tastes good?" Mom says as she bites a forkful of mashed potatoes. I nod before getting up to get a cup. I walk toward the fridge and open it to grab the pitcher full of iced tea.

"Mhm," Maddie mumbles, dropping her fork. It makes an echoing clink sound, startling mom as she looks up at her. "Can I go now?" Maddison says, and Mom sighs. "No, finish those green beans," she points, and I watch as she sits back down. Maddison sighs heavily before groaning and scooting the green beans around, making conversation as she does so. "I made a 90 on my Chem test." Mom looks up at her in excitement before she takes another bite. "I'm so proud of you, honey. Really. Did you find any colleges? You know, you are a Junior, and you saw how fast time flew with Jayden." The room gets silent once again after her statement. "Hope you intend to join clubs before the school year's over," She pauses before she places her fork down suddenly as if she had thought of an idea. "Are you gonna join the dance team this year?" She adds, and Maddison lightly perks downward in negative emotion.

"Not this year," She pauses, moving the empty fork up to her lips. She fakes a bite, moving her fork back down on her plate before moving more things around. "But maybe next year." Looking at Mom, she plasters on a fake smile. Mom chuckles unsurely. "Done," Maddie compensates, practically tossing the plastic plate into the sink as she walks down the hall, not even waiting for mom's response. "What is up with that girl lately?"

She questions, taking the last bite of her food. I scoot the green beans into a pile with the mashed potatoes before taking a large bite, also finishing my plate off. "Probably nervous, she does graduate after I leave," I lie, following mom as she grabs the plate out of my hand. I open the fridge and pour myself another glass. "Yea, maybe that's it."

I walk down the hall towards my room. Passing the bathroom, I see Maddison hunched over the toilet, her fingers in the back of her throat, causing her to gag. "Stop it," I lightly yell as I move her away. I forcefully pick her up, and she wobbles over the toilet before placing her hands against the wall to balance herself. Wiping her mouth, she mumbles, "I had nothing to get rid of, anyway." Walking to the sink she washes her hands as I look at her, wondering what happened. Drying her hands off on the resting towel, she looks at me before stating something full of sass. "What?"

"Stop. I don't like seeing you like this. Quit it."

"No, not yet. It's not the right time." I inhale frustratingly before breaking the silence. "Look, I know I said I'd keep it a promise, but I'm telling you, I can't keep sitting here and watch you hurt yourself like this. " Walking towards the doorway, she kicks my foot in an attempt to stop me. Almost falling face-forward, I turn around and look at her face. She looks tired and weak, her glow not the same as it was a year ago. Her eyes water, tears soon spilling over.

Almost a year ago, Maddie stopped eating. I was the only one who'd noticed. About four or five months ago, I accidentally bumped into her while she was purging. She shut the door immediately, and since then, she hadn't been the same. A few minutes later, she'd come out and explain what was going on. The captain of the dance team told her to lose a few pounds. She did but found herself falling down a spiral. An unsafe spiral. She made me swear I wouldn't tell mom, and I promised her I wouldn't.

But I just can't sit here and watch it happen.

Nineteen

CHAPTER NINETEEN: SANTA TELL ME

TIFFANY

It's finally Friday, thank the Lord. I've been waiting for what feels like AGES for the weekend. Mom and I go Christmas shopping tonight, as it's a tradition. We've never missed a single weekend before Christmas. Never.

Mom knocks on my door before inviting herself in. She's wearing a blue-sleeved jumpsuit, brown boots, a black coat, and a small bag. Her hair is in a small afro puff that's bundled in the center of her head. "You ready?" She says, walking behind me. I nod. Heading into my closet, I pull out two purses, White and Brown. "This one?" I ask as I hold both. "Or this one?" Mom stands and thinks for a moment. "The brown one," She grins. I smile back before placing the black clutch on the doorknob. I grab my phone, wallet, and house keys (sometimes she forgets hers), before shoving them into the small clutch. Today I'm wearing a basic light tan sweater, gray jeans, and heeled brown boots. My hair's in a high braided bun. Dad walks out of their bedroom, Shiloh leaning against him. He goes up to dad's shoulder now. "Where are you guys headed?" Mom asks. Dad looks at Shi before he says anything. "Call of Duty marathon!" Dad cheers and Shi gives him that look. "Yea, don't do that."

"Why?"

"Because it's not as cool as it may sound to you."

"Yea, but it just-"

"Just listen to me: Don't do that."

* * *

We pull up in the mall parking lot, and the whole place is crowded. People have bags in their hands, scattering back and forth between the entrance and their cars. I get out along with mom, and we get to walking.

I spot a small book pop-up, so I tell mom I'm headed there. I walk in, light music playing overhead. "Welcome!" a cashier calls, and I wave. Walking down the isles, I notice the book I'm planning on getting Jayden.

It's called *Nothing Serious*, and it's by one of our favorite authors, Analease Seal. Originally, I was planning on buying it from Amazon, but apparently, it's a cheaper price here. I reach to pick it up off the stand when my hand collides with another.

"Shoot, my bad," The voice says. I turn and face a guy with curly hair. He's light-skinned and is wearing glasses. He clears his throat, and I realize I was staring. "Right, right. Um, so I need this," I stutter. He smirks. "Really?" God, not right now. "Yea," I say, reaching to grab it again. He smacks my hand. "Okay, Imma need you to go by the kindergarten rule: Keep your hands to yourself," I bark. He leans back, hands surrendering while making a sarcastic *psst* sound. I grab the book and clutch it tightly. "Okay, I'll just wait on the next restock, then," he chuckles. I stand there, confused on why we were both still standing there and staring. "Okay, let's start over. I'm Ryan," He pauses, reaching his hand out. I slowly shake it. "Tiffany."

CHAPTER NINETEEN: SANTA TELL ME

"Nice." He smiles. He slowly walks backward. "Well, hopefully, I'll see you again, Tiffany."

* * *

"Your total is 15.95." I shuffle through my purse and grab my wallet. Remembering I have a card here, I grab it and tell them to check how much is left on it. "20.75." She snorts before handing it back. "Mhm, keep it. I'd like to use it to buy the book." She smacks her lips with an attitude and begins typing in the card code, as the swipe is broken-down.

She hands me the bag over the counter, and I leave. Mom's car is parked right near the entrance. I open the door and get inside. "It's freezin' out there," I mumble, quickly turning on the heated seat. She continues driving and soon stops in the parking lot of a Dillard's. "I'll be back," she declares as she kisses my forehead. I smile and lock the door when she gets out.

JAYDEN| Hey, babe. Text me when you can. Christmas Party @ Maya's??

I begin thinking, deciding whether or not to go.

ME| eh, why not. out with my mom rn, tho. ill be home at... i'll say 6??

JAYDEN| Yea, 6 is good. I'll pick you up at 6:30. See you.

ME| see ya <3

* * *

I'm on a call with Avery and Emery when I hear the Ring trigger go off, letting us know the front door was opened. **"And he had the audacity to SMACK my hand!"** I exclaim. Avery snickers at the interaction. I give her a look. **"My bad. Did you hit his behind back? You better have."** I nod before looking out the window. I see Jayden's car park on the curb, and immediately I start rushing to get ready. From fixing my makeup to thinking about choosing another pair of shoes. **"No, keep those boots on. It goes."** Emery mumbles. **"Alright y'all, I gotta go. You know how personal my dad can get at times and I'm not quite ready for him to just start-"** "We get it. Go. Have. Fun." Avery smiles, clapping in between her words. Her bracelets bangle against one another. I smile back, grateful for how motherly she can be. Ever since the whole group was together, she always seemed to be the mom figure when it came to relationships and such. Gave advice, stuck there to the end, and would even put you first when it came to certain situations. **"Bye."** They both call before I hang up.

I walk down the stairs and towards the kitchen to hear Jayden and dad laughing about something. "Oh, hey, babe!" Jayden says as he notices me, getting up to kiss me. Dad gives him a look of warning, and he quickly removes his lips from my forehead. "So, Jayden just told me a story from when he was on the middle school basketball team," Dad proudly announces. Jayden chuckles at his gleaming. "Yeah, I sucked." "That was you?" I tease. He playfully nudges my shoulder with his. Taking his hands out of his pocket, he reaches his arm across my shoulders. "Well, we should get headed, Mr. Mohan," Jayden smiles. "Alright, then. Bring her home by 11:30. On. The. Dot." Dad's face turns stone-cold. Jayden nods. "Yes, Sir." "Have fun!" Mom yells over the couch. "Love you!" I yell back as Jayden and I walk toward the front door to leave.

Santa Baby blasts through the speakers, causing the sudden urge for me to sing along. As Jayden sings the next part, I look at him, but he doesn't notice. Am I <u>sure</u> this is just a high school relationship? Am I <u>sure</u> I don't

CHAPTER NINETEEN: SANTA TELL ME

feel anything more?

"What? Is there something on my face?" Jayden stops at the red light, noticing me staring. "Oh, nothing. I was just, zoning out," I chuckle. "Okay, then," He slowly nods. "Continue zoning out on my face then, 'cause it boosts my confidence," he jokes. I chuckle and lay back on the headrest. Jayden turns the volume down and continues to look straight as he drives. "Any response on your application?" I shake my head no, along with a frustrated sigh. He sighs roughly too. I sit up quickly before shifting into a comfortable position. "What if I don't get in? What if I wrote the essay wrong? What if I-" "Calm down," Jayden interrupts. "You're gonna get in." He pauses. "They'd be stupid to not let you in."

* * *

Jayden helps me out of the car, and we walk as slowly as possible to the door. Not that we don't want to be there. I just enjoy talking to him and he enjoys talking to me. Reaching the door, we don't even have to open it as a girl was holding the door open. "Thanks," I smile at her, and she reassuringly nods. Everyone's circled at the table, gifts sitting in the center. Probably dirty Santa. "What's up, Jay!" One of the guys says, standing up to do the bro-hug thing. "What's up, man? Hey, this is my girlfriend, Tiffany," He introduces. The guy waves. "Tiffany, this is one of my best friends, TJ." I look at him to wave. As he nods, I falsely nod back. "Well, the food's in the kitchen. Beer, Liquor, Hennessy, everything you need is hooked up in there thanks to Kia." TJ says, pointing towards a girl sitting on the arm of a gray couch. I nudge Jayden's shoulder. "Any drink? Virgin 'cause you're driving me home." I laugh.

"Uh, yea. Get me a Coke, please. Thanks, babe," He rushes as he heads over to sit with his friends. I blankly express before heading over towards the cooler. I grab him a can of Coke before pouring myself a splash of Vodka mixed with Sprite. Something I usually pour to fix my senses. I prance back over towards him and hand him his cup. "Thanks," he nods, paying attention to the TV playing overhead. The party isn't even turning out as expected. I know nobody, it's hella boring, and no one even seems to have even the *slightest* bit of Christmas Spirit. I notice an available spot next to Jayden, so obviously, that's where I sit. "Okay! Let's continue the round now, should we?"

Twenty

CHAPTER TWENTY: RECLAIM

Everyone turns their attention toward the girl. Jayden leans back towards me before taking a sip of the soda. "You enjoying the party so far?" he adds. I lie. "Yup. Everyone seems pretty cool." Kia begins handing out these separate slips of paper, each one with a number on it. "Alright, who's going first? Oh! How about Jayden's new girlfriend here, huh?" I must have a look of confusion on my face because they keep signaling for me to grab the number. "Right. Yeah, sure I guess," I awkwardly chuckle. *15. 15. 15. Find 15.* I find the box labeled 15 and open it.

Inside was a laced bodysuit. One that's WAY too revealing, and not my style. I pull it out of the box to show everyone. "Like it?" She asks. I lie, again. "Yea." I shove the suit into the box, tossing it aside. Jayden's friend nudges his shoulder. "No offense, man, but I think yo' girl would look fire in that." I glance to the side, hoping Jayden would be smart and stick up for me. Instead, he disappoints me.

Laughing, he replies, "Yea." He clicks his tongue, looking back up at the TV. That's it. I stand up when Jayden quickly grabs my arm, and I snatch my arm from his grasp. "Whoa, where you going?"

"In the car. I'll be waiting." As I grab my things, he sits there, dumbfounded. "What happened? You good?" He says, following me. Everyone looks around, and a few people whisper. My eyes water, causing my vision to blur as I blink them away.

"Yea, I'm perfectly fine," I jeer as I ragingly walk outside. I ignore the fact I never put my coat on. The door opens and Jayden comes walking through it. I walk down the sidewalk, reaching the car. He unlocks the doors.

"Okay, what just happened?" He yells as he's still trying to catch up with me. Turning around, I pull out an attitude. "What? Oh, nothing. Your friend just practically catcalled me, and you didn't do anything. No biggie," I sarcastically blow. "What? No, ignore Taylor. He's just a jerk. He flirts with everybody."

"Well, it ends with me. I can't believe you just let him talk about me like that!" I yell back. I shove the box into the backseat. Slamming the backdoor, I walk over to the passengers' side, but he gets there before me. "Okay, it was wrong of me, but I thought you said you were enjoying yourself."

"Surprise, surprise, Jay: I lied!" Jayden backs his head back like I just threw something at him. "What?"

"Your friends aren't my style. They joke too much, they didn't know a single thing about me, and worst of all," I pause.

"Your guy friends, god, they don't know how to treat women!"

"What do you mean?"

"I saw the way TJ kept groping his girlfriend. She seemed hecka uncomfortable with it. But she just dealt with it because 'he's her boyfriend.' Taylor harassed me and thought it was a compliment, and so do you." By now, he doesn't even know what to say.

"Take me home."

"Babe, I-"

"Take me home!" I yell, sitting in the passenger's seat before I slam the door behind me.

CHAPTER TWENTY: RECLAIM

***

We pull up in front of my house. "Don't even pull into the driveway, just stop here," I mumble, unbuckling my seat belt. "What?" He replies as he slows down. Jayden pulls to the side, eventually coming to a stop. I open the door and get ready to leave when he grabs my hand. "See you tomorrow." I sit there and stare. He sighs, letting go of my hand. "Bye."

Grabbing my keys, I unlock the door. A note's taped on the wall beside the door.

IF YOU GOT HERE EARLY, KNOW WE WENT TO BENIHANA'S AND WE'LL BE BACK AT 11. SHILOH IS AT JUSTIN'S HOUSE, BREANNE WILL DROP HIM BACK OFF HERE TOMORROW.

Kicking my shoes off, I open the coat closet under the stairway and shove the trench inside. I grab my phone out of my pocket and check the time.

9:15 PM

The fact that I'm home before 10 says something. I head upstairs and into my room. Opening my laptop, I call Avery. She answers, and I immediately notice Emery laying in her lap. I point toward her, and Avery waves me off. **"You're here early,"** Avery says impressively. Picking at a piece of skin around my nail, I look downward as I speak. **"Yea,"** I mumble. **"What's wrong?"** My eyes start to water, along with thoughts swirling around my head on how I was irrational for what I'd done. I take a deep breath, my voice shaking. **"I'd gotten this gift from the dirty Santa, and I swear it was lingerie,"** I mumble, laughing as I think back. Avery nods her head in agreement. **"One of Jayden's friends had commented, and Jayden didn't say a single thing."** Avery leans back and crosses her arms, and I look at Emery beside Avery and see her sleeping. **"Tell him how you feel. How the comment made you feel,"** She says, her hands moving everywhere.

Av's what I like to call a "Hand-Talker". She talks and expresses her comments with her hands. Emery uses her neck, but that's another conversation.

"But-"

"**No, I am not letting you guys break up over something you could easily solve. Did the comment make you uncomfortable? Tell him. Do you think he could've done better? Tell him. I'm sick of you being scared of commitment.**"

I stare at the corner of my computer screen. I *could* feel offended, but it's true. Every time something goes wrong in a relationship, I tend to end it.

But I like Jayden, and I don't want that to be us. I pick up my phone, but Avery stops me. Shoving her face into the screen, she begins to speak, "**In person.**" I place it back down. I look at the time and notice only ten minutes have passed. "**You know what, I'll talk to him tomorrow,**" I comment, throwing a smile onto my face. "**Sure,**" She adds. Looking down at Emery, she moves Emery's hair out of her face before reaching onto her nightstand, grabbing a bonnet, and putting it on her head. "**Goodnight, Av.**"

"**Night, Tiff. See you tomorrow.**" I hang up as the house sits silently. Closing my laptop, I hear an alert from Gmail. I grab my phone off the nightstand and look at the notification and see one thing I've been waiting for for a long time: <u>A reply from California-Berkeley sitting there on my screen.</u>

Twenty-One

CHAPTER TWENTY-ONE: ACCEPTANCE

D*o I press it?*
What if I was rejected?
But what if I was accepted?
What if they just emailed to tell me my essay was good, but my grades aren't good enough to let me in?

I take a deep breath in an attempt to push away all disapproving thoughts. I press the pop-up and move my face closer to the camera for the face ID. Alright, time to look at the opportunity of a lifetime. Closing my eyes, I feel my finger press the screen. *Should I open my eyes?*

What if it's just a reminder to others to turn in the essay? Heck, just do it already! Opening my eyes, I gasp in shock. As I read the email, my eyes begin to water.

Hello, Tiffany Jesse Mohan.
Thank You for applying to California-Berkeley University. We received over 150,000 applications this year guiding to administering into this University!

You have received this email either to be informed of Approval or Rejection.

Please continue reading under this bar to seek results.

*Congratulations, Tiffany Jesse Mohan!
You are accepted into California-Berkeley!*

If you would like to acquire a dorm for next semester, contact Mrs. Anderson immediately. The fee for housing: $15,150 for Single Dorms, $13,550 for Double Dorms, and $11,000 for a triple. Campus Tours are indeed available for any student or future student, so please email the headmaster with any questions and concerns. Visit the following link to check out the website, which provides more information.

Did I just get into my <u>dream</u> University? I continue reading the same sentence, over and over again, thinking I may have read it wrong. *You are accepted into California-Berkeley.* It finally hits me as I jump up and down in my room, probably looking like a 4-year-old throwing a temper tantrum. **I got into Berkeley!** Celebrating around the room, I trip and fall on something, causing me to hit the ground and the room to become black.

I wake up to mom shaking me awake and find myself on the floor. "Wake up. Jayley and them are here again." She smiles. I sit up as she sits beside me. "When did they get here?" I groan, realizing my phone wasn't plugged in. Grabbing my hand, she squeezes it. "Any update?" I immediately begin smiling. "I got the acceptance last night!" I shriek, throwing myself into her arms. "Really? Baby, that's incredible!" She cheers, hugging me back as she kisses my forehead. "Come downstairs and tell everyone the news." Mom smiles, walking over to the door.
   "Baby?"
   "Mhm?" I mumble, scratching my head, still half asleep.
   "I'm so proud of you."

CHAPTER TWENTY-ONE: ACCEPTANCE

* * *

I walk down the stairs and overhear everyone laughing and talking. "Hey, baby!" CiCi calls, walking over to hug me. I chuckle. "You're acting like you didn't just see me last month." Walking into the living room, I see Xavier and Shiloh playing Halo on the PlayStation. I lean over the couch and tickle Shi. "Stop! Quit it! I'm 'finna die 'cause of you!" He laughs, also trying to fight it. Jayley's laying on the ground facing up on her phone. I lightly kick her with my foot. "Hey," She mutters, typing. "Hey!" I excitedly reply. Mom walks behind the couch, putting her hands on my shoulders. I look up and see her, a certain face letting me know now is the time. I stand up and walk into the kitchen. "Guys!" I say, sitting on one of the chairs. I take a deep breath in as everyone's attention reverts to me. Turning to my right, I see mom smile, allowing me to feel looser.

"I got accepted into Berkeley."

Jayley stands up from the couch, throwing her phone onto the cushion. "Really? OH MY GOD! This is a big deal! I'm so proud of you! When do you do the tour?" She shrieks, racing over toward me, but CiCi beats her to me. She tightly hugs me, and I can get a huge whiff of the perfume she's wearing. Letting go, my dad chuckles at her reaction before hugging me as well. "I'm hella proud of you, T. You've worked so hard, and now look at you." He smiles. I smile back before heading towards the fridge. My hands grasp a Popsicle as Aunt CiCi starts talking. "Look at you! Berkeley has been your goal ever since, what, 6th grade?" I laugh at the comment. It's true, though. The moment I entered middle school, I knew I had to get my head in the game to get into a college: a good one. I found Berkeley, and now I'm going there! My phone buzzes in my hand as I put a spoonful of yogurt into my mouth. Looking at the screen, I see a notification from Jayden.

JAYDEN| Can we please talk?

Right. I completely forgot about what happened yesterday and that I planned to meet with him to explain. Putting the yogurt cup on the counter with the spoon still in my mouth, I type a reply.

ME| sure. the mall?

JAYDEN| No. Your place.

ME| why?

JAYDEN| Because I need to talk to you. In private.

The thought of the conversation dawns down on me, causing my happiness to slowly fade away. Jayley notices but doesn't say anything. "I'll be right back, let me call Avery and Emery to tell them the news." I throw a face smile on my face. Auntie CiCi claps her hands before she speaks, a large grin growing across her face as she glances at mom, and I can only imagine what she's about to say.

"Alright, baby. Just let me know what restaurant you wanna eat at tonight, irregardless of what your mother says." Mom coughs before correcting CiCi under her breath.

"Regardless."

CiCi gives her a look before I walk down the hallway and up the stairs, drowning out the argument I hear behind me.

"'Irregardless' ain't even a word, Cicilea."

"Yes, it is. I just said it, therefore it is."

"It's not."

"It is."

***

A few minutes later, I hear Jayley call me down right as I look out the window and notice Jayden's here.

CHAPTER TWENTY-ONE: ACCEPTANCE

I stand at the top of the stairs when Jayden notices me before coming up. "I'll just be upstairs, and I promise, the door will be open." He laughs. Jayley waves before walking back down the hall and into the kitchen. My phone buzzes in my pocket seconds later right before I grab it.

JAYLEY| don't worry about the door. i wont snitch. :)

Shifting towards my room, I sit on my bed and Jayden sits beside me.

"Can we talk about yesterday night?"

I look at him in his eyes as he waits for me to answer. Licking my lips, I answer. "Yea."

"Okay. Tiffany, I'm so sorry. I didn't mean to make you feel any kind of way, especially uncomfortable."

"It's alright. I guess I wasn't feeling right." I respond. Grabbing my hands, he pulls me closer before kissing my forehead. Glad we got this resolved. One less thing for me to stress about. Laying onto his shoulder, I stare out the window. "I got into Berkeley," I mumble, my voice high-pitched as I smile. He perks up, my head bouncing off his shoulder. "Oh my goodness, babe, that's awesome!" He exclaims, standing up. I kiss him, and he kisses me back. I move his hands onto my waist, pulling him between my legs as he stands, and he chuckles at my action. Moving back towards the bed, I sit down as he continues kissing me. Just then, Jayley walks in. Knocking on the doorway, she makes a clicking sound with her tongue.

Jayden hops up, staring at her awkwardly. "Yea, go ahead and quit that," she marks. We both laugh as she walks in and sits on the floor before grabbing my remote.

Jayden leans back, laying on my bed, and gets on his phone. I lay beside him, glancing at his screen every so often. "What movie?" Jayley mumbles, scrolling through my Netflix feed. "The Christmas Swap! Please!" I playfully groan. Jayden laughs at this, and Jayley darts a pitiful look before pressing play. She sits back onto a wad of blankets as the movie begins, then begins talking. "I just walked in on something, and I still don't know a single thing about you. Please, tell me who the hell you are, for Pete's sake!" She wails, with a slightly animated whine in her voice.

Jayden sits up and shuts his phone off before placing it face-down on my bed. "My name's Jayden. I'm 18, and my 19th Birthday's in May. I enjoy playing basketball, reading, and protesting. Kinda like Aaron from that show, I guess you could say. My grades are 'magnificent', as my mother calls it. And, my dream job is as a Neurologist. Don't even try to ask what my ideal college is because I'm sick of hearing it," He chuckles. Jayley slightly laughs along. "A guy who will watch the shows you watch, nice catch." I roll my eyes with a smile planted on my face. Jayley turns to me before saying anything. "Have you checked out Berkeley's dorms yet? I heard they got one hell of a campus!" She cheers, bouncing towards me. The voices of the characters in the movie speak over her throughout the sentence. She tosses the remote to me before I turn the volume down. "Nope. Planning it later today."

"You should do it like, now. If you don't get those dorms, I heard you'll have to get one of the last rooms. And those are supposedly not good."

I shrug, grabbing my laptop off the floor. I open it, type in my password, and head toward the email where the website is linked.

A new tab opens, immediately guiding me to the housing. Different options pop up, showing the types of housing including on-campus houses. Scrolling toward the eight different halls pop up before apartments seem to become an option. I sit up quickly, noticing that mom had just passed my bedroom door. "Ma!" I yell as she walks back. She stands in the doorway.

"Mhm?" She mumbles, looking up from her iPad. "Tour is on Thursday next week, so we can catch a flight on Sunday, hang out a bit till Wednesday, and get to the tour at 8 in the morning Thursday."

Twenty-Two

CHAPTER TWENTY-TWO: INTERNATIONAL

"Tiffany!" Mom yells, passing my doorway. "Yea?" I respond, shoving clothes into my duffel before walking back towards the closet. "Hurry up! I'm determined to get us out of here by 10. That way, we can get some breakfast, and get to the airport just in time, maybe a bit earlier." She knocks on the door frame before trodding off. My phone buzzes on my nightstand, and I quickly check the screen. Jayden's message sits on my screen.

JAYDEN| Dinner tonight at Owen Brennan's. On me?

I look at my packed bags by the dresser and then the duffel on my bed. *Almost packed, why not?* Grabbing my phone, I crouch down beside my bed, pulling up messages and texting Jay back.

ME| i can't today, tomorrow, or later this week...
JAYDEN| ?
ME| i'm heading out today to check out Berkeley :) we're spending time in Utah first tho, lol.

I look up at the time, and it reads 9:50. Standing up, I head towards my closet and grab something to wear. I'm not gonna wear anything too fancy, we're gonna be on a flight until 3, and I wanna be comfy. Looking through my drawer, I pick out a quick outfit. Taking my bonnet off, my braids fall aside me as I decide on a basic high ponytail. I check the time again. 9:56, and no response from Jayden. Mom knocks on my door frame again, signifying for me to bring my bags down.

I grasp for my rolling suitcase with my right hand, also trying to hold my gray duffel. I walk out my doorway, and Shiloh looks at me, a face of concern washing over him. For once, he has the decency to actually help me. "Thanks," I mumble, kicking over one of my bags. "You're only visiting for a few days, why do you need all of this?" "Just because," I respond, walking cautiously down the stairs. Reaching the bottom step, I dramatically drop the bags down as dad grabs them and tosses them over his shoulder. He walks towards the kitchen, where the garage door is. I rush upstairs, going to get the last few bags.

Shi waits in the doorway for me, and I toss the last bag to him. "If you decide on Berkeley," He pauses, walking beside me. We start to walk down the stairs. "Will this mean I won't see you again?" I pause mid-step, which obviously catches him off guard because he turns around to see where I went. "No, Shi, I can come home for the holidays." I stuttered, unsure of what to say. "You will always be my brother, no matter where I am." A glassy smile forms across his face. "When I head to Berkeley, we can call and we can text," My voice begins to crack, as my mind starts processing it all. "But that doesn't mean I won't see you again."

"That the last one?" Dad asks, shoving the bag into the trunk. I nod, putting a few small essentials into my carry-on. "Lyana!" Dad calls, and mom rushes out of the bathroom, things spilling over the floor. "Mom," I mutter, confused. "My shirt must've gotten under the stuff," She responds,

CHAPTER TWENTY-TWO: INTERNATIONAL

bending down as she picks up each thing, shoving them into a tiny pouch. "You ready?" I nod. "Alright," She hums, giving dad a kiss on the cheek. Shiloh hesitantly hugs me, and I hug him back. We both know this isn't the last time he'll see me, but he's just worried, and I can tell. Mom grabs the tickets from dad as we walk out the door, getting in on our sides as Destiny's Child blasts through the radio. "See You Thursday!" Dad calls, and Shiloh humorously chases after the car as we pull out. Mom peeks her head through the window right before we speed off. "Tell CiCi to call me when she wakes up!"

Dad puts a thumbs up before she presses her foot down, causing us to pull off.

"To a new beginning, huh?" Mom jokes. I smile, crossing my legs. "Yea, a new beginning."

***

Million Dollar Bill by Whitney Houston is mom's immediate song whenever I'm with her. We've always played it, ever since I was little.

Mom and I sing along with the song, knowing each and every lyric. She hands me the imaginary mic, and I sing the next line after the one she'd sang. The song ends, leading on to the very next one as we pull into the parking lot.

We get out, and I open the trunk, a few bags falling onto the ground. "I'll go get the trolley thing," Mom requests before walking towards the tall building. I nod lightly, hopping into the back and sitting on the platform. My phone buzzes in my pocket, and I excitedly reach for it. Shiloh's name pops up, and a smile gleams across my face at the thought of him thinking of me.

SHI| Jayden stopped by, and we played some 2K if you don't mind.

I look up and see mom rushing over, the metal cart bumping into each rock behind her. Quickly, I type a response.

ME| lol yea, I don't mind. hope y'all had fun. <3

"Alright," Mom pauses, dusting her hands off before lightly pushing me out the trunk. "Grab your bags and toss them on here." Within minutes, our bags rest on top of each other. I close the trunk behind us, and we walk into the building. "Get the tickets out of my bag, Tiff," Mom requests as we stop in line. "ID and pass, please," The security guard says, and mom scampers to grab her card out of her wallet. She hands it to them, and they hurriedly push us to the scan. We empty our pockets, and they place the suitcases onto the conveyor as they scan us. We get by, soon heading toward the front desk, checking in as Mom hands them the tickets and handles a few other things.

"Tiffany," Mom says, shoving me awake. "They're boarding us, you have to use the restroom or anything?" I groan slightly, stretching as I stand up. "Mom, I'm not a kid," I moan, grabbing the backpack that sits beside me. She gives me a look as she pauses in place. "No, I don't." She stops looking at me with that mother look she consistently gives before continuing to walk forward. "Alright, then. Here we come, Utah."

CHAPTER TWENTY-THREE: TURBULENCE

"Ladies and gentlemen, the Captain has turned on the Fasten Seat Belt sign. If you haven't already done so, please stow your carry-on luggage underneath the seat in front of you or in an overhead bin. Take your seat and fasten your seat belt. Also, make sure your seat back and folding trays are in their full upright position."

I walk down the aisle, finding my seat as I notice mom had stopped following me. Turning around, I see mom standing near her seat. "Excuse me," I smile, walking past a few people. "I swear, I thought I'd purchased seats right beside each other." Mom mumbles and I sigh, rubbing my face in frustration. "It's alright, mom. I'm 17, I can sit at a seat alone," I state, hugging her. "I'll text or come walk back here whenever I need you," I state, and she sits down. Walking back to my seat, I see a mother and her child, who looks about 5 or 6, sitting behind me. I smile, and the kid smiles back. I look at my seat, finding a blonde white girl sitting at the window seat, scrolling on her phone. She looks up, a smile drawn across her face as she looks at me.

"Hi!" She exclaims as I unlock the overhead bin, shoving my backpack in. I then close the bin before sitting down in my seat. "Hi!" She repeats. I suck my teeth before replying. "Hey," I grimace before grabbing my phone and Airpods out of my pocket. I connect my phone to them, but right when I put one in, the girl starts talking again. "My name's Cali! What's yours? You know what, don't even answer that if you don't want to. What're you heading to Utah for?" I roughly sigh before shoving them into my ears, ignoring her anyway. She shoves my shoulder, causing my Airpod to fall out of my ear. She catches it before it falls between the seat cracks. "What the hell?" "I'm Cali, and you are?" She hands the singular pod to me, and I place them both into the case, already knowing how this is gonna be. "Tiffany," I reply, shuffling through my bag.

"Tiffany." She pauses, laying back in her seat. "Pretty name." I shrug, grabbing a hold of a book. "What book is that?" God, she acts like a five-year-old. *"The Adoration of Jenna Fox,"* I mutter. I peek a glance out the window, although we hadn't gone anywhere. It feels like we've been sitting here for hours with this girl beside me. "Oh, I read that when I was a freshman. Nice Sci-Fi, huh?" She responds. I flip to my page where my bookmark is, beginning to read my spot. I nod due to my body being on autopilot. She leans back, finally being silent.

A voice emits through the speakers.

"Ladies and gentlemen, my name is Zachary Matthews, and I'm your chief flight attendant. On behalf of Captain Davis and the entire crew, welcome aboard American National Airlines flight 417, non-stop service from Memphis to Salt Lake City, Utah."

They continue speaking, but I dim out the voice as I turn the volume of my music up, also continuing to read my page. I hear footsteps walk down the aisle before hearing Mom's voice speaking to me. "You have some snacks?"

CHAPTER TWENTY-THREE: TURBULENCE

Quickly, I pause my music before speaking. "Yup," I reply, looking up at her. "Here's twenty bucks if you see anything on the cart you'd like." She starts digging in her wallet, handing me a crumpled twenty. I grab hold of it, shoving it in my pocket. "Just come walk back here if you need me." "Mom, I got this, I'm not 7," I reply, and she smiles. "I know, just," She pauses, thinking of what to say. "Stay Safe?" The girl beside me shakes my arm, pointing up at the speaker.

"Flight attendants, prepare for take-off, please. Cabin crew, please take your seats for take-off."

I silently celebrate before nodding and putting the earpod back into my ear. I feel us lift off before looking out the window and seeing us lightly incline. Finally, here the ride goes.

A few minutes in, the girl pokes at me, trying to get my attention, once again. "What?" I snark, and pull out the earpod. "How old are you?" I breathe in, trying to calm myself down. "17," I respond, focusing back on my page. "I'm 19. Well, my birthday's in May, so almost 20, I guess!" I falsely smile, this time not even bothering to try to listen to my music. This girl is going to speak to me the entire time.

"Ladies and gentlemen, the Captain has turned off the Fasten Seat Belt sign, and you may now move around the cabin. However, we always recommend keeping your seat belt fastened while you're seated."

They pause a moment before continuing to speak.

"In a few moments, the flight attendants will be passing around the cabin to offer you hot or cold drinks, as well as a light snack. Alcoholic drinks are also available at a nominal charge with our compliments. Also, we have movies playing on the display of each video nominate. Now, sit back, relax, and enjoy the flight. Thank you."

"Could you buy me something on the cart?" The girl mumbles, poking my shoulder. "Um," I stutter, flipping my page. "Sure?" I reply as she smiles before adjusting her position in her seat.

I read the last page as I look to my side and see Cali knocked out. Her head rests against the window, fog appearing from her breath as she inhales and then exhales. I look at the screen implanted in the headrest of the seat in front of me. The movie currently playing is Spider-Man: Homecoming. Stretching, I realize I can finally play music without interruptions, so I connect my Airpods with my phone, Mariah The Scientist playing on auto.

Laying my head back, I feel light bumps, but I ignore them thinking it was just light turbulence. I close my eyes and the bumping stops, but it just continues not even seconds later. Eventually, I realize it was coming from behind me, the memory of a mother and her child sitting behind me. I peek through the crack, the face of a little boy bursting with a smile and laughter as I mumble through the seats, "Hey, could you please stop?" I look through again, seeing that the boy nods before grabbing a cheese puff from a chip bag, and looking down at the iPad resting in his lap. I lay back, closing my eyes once again as I lay my head down on the neck pillow. Midway to deep sleep, the kicking begins again.

    I annoyedly sigh, an old woman sitting in the row beside me looks at me, concerned. I smile with a quick wave before leaning back and mumbling through the seat again, "Mrs, could you tell your son to stop, please?" But no voice replies. I look around the seat near the aisle to find the mother asleep, her seat leaning back as her son continues to kick my seat. "Could you stop?" I snap, elbowing the seat as a way to "Kick" back. But this time, the kid cries. I get out of my seat as attention turns toward me. I crouch beside his seat to comfort him, but it doesn't work. Suddenly, I remember the Airheads candy I'd packed earlier. Going back to my seat, I ruffle through my bag, grabbing a clutch of the plastic candy packaging. Reaching over the seat I offer it to the little boy. He snatches it, quickly becoming silent as his mom unhesitatingly opens it after he'd poked her

CHAPTER TWENTY-THREE: TURBULENCE

with it repeatedly. "Tank You," He says, smacking as he chews each bite. "No Problem," I mutter to myself.

There goes my early sweet.

Twenty-Four

CHAPTER TWENTY-FOUR: GROUND SPEED

The seat beside me shakes as I open my eyes and glance at Cali wiggling in her seat. "Stop it," I grumble, turning to face the aisle. She playfully hits my shoulder before the seat stops shaking. Sitting up, I press the flight attendant button. A brunette wearing a blue and white set walks over, water bottles in her hand. "I'm afraid I wasn't awake when you guys walked by with the cart?" "Oh, I'll be right back with it. Let me just give these to someone," She smiles, walking back toward the direction she'd come from. Cali's leg starts shaking. "Could you stop?" I moan, leaning against the headrest in front of me out of frustration. "I'm so sorry, I never really mean to do that. My leg just randomly starts shaking whenever I feel nervous," She replies, lightly rambling throughout the sentence. I sit up, looking at her. "What're you nervous about?" The flight attendant taps my shoulder as I turn around to find the cart wheeled up beside me.

I grab a bag of Salt & Vinegar chips and a Coke. "I'm on my way back from vacation. I came to Memphis to visit my parents this Thanksgiving,

CHAPTER TWENTY-FOUR: GROUND SPEED

and now I'm on my way back to my University. It's kinda nerve-wracking because I have to take a side test so I can get into my next semester's classes and I just-," I shove her side as I pop a chip into my mouth. "You're fine. You got this," I smile, grabbing another chip. She smiles before leaning back into her seat. Reaching in front of her, she turns on the headrest screen to the movie *Bring It On*. I check the time on my phone, and it read 4:50. The speakers overhead turn on as I tuck my phone back into my pocket. The voice of the attendant from earlier waves throughout the plane.

"Ladies and gentlemen, as we start our descent, please make sure your seat backs and tray tables are in their full upright position. Make sure your seat belt is securely fastened and all carry-on luggage is stowed underneath the seat in front of you or the overhead bins. Thank you."

Another announcement follows behind it.

"Flight attendants, prepare for landing, please. Cabin crew, please take your seats for landing."

Cali turns off the screen, shifting positions as she sits up and grabs the satchel that rests against her feet.

"Ladies and gentlemen, we have just been cleared to land at Salt Lake City International airport. Please make sure one last time your seat belt is securely fastened. The flight attendants are currently passing around the cabin to make a final compliance check and pick up any remaining cups and glasses. Thank you."

Attendants walk up and down the aisle, grabbing trash and cups from anyone who hands it to them. Cali doesn't seem that bad when she's silent. Plus, she's a freshman in college, so I could ask for advice. "Hey, you seem like a cool person to know, wanna be friends?" I ask, and her face glows right as I finish my sentence. "Yeah, sure! You need my phone number?" I nod, and I quickly pull out my phone to load it to contacts. She types up the number as we lean back in the seats, the plane declining as we reach the ground. She hands my phone back, the plane parking as it sits against the ground motionless.

"Ladies and gentlemen, welcome to Salt Lake City International Airport. Local time is 3:50 and the temperature is 60° Fahrenheit. For your safety and comfort, please remain seated with your seat belt fastened until the Captain turns off the Fasten Seat Belt sign. This will indicate that we have parked at the gate and that it is safe for you to move about."

The sign stops illuminating, and I unbuckle my seat as I rush over to mom. She sits up before stretching, signaling she'd been sleeping for the whole flight. "You ready?" She groans, and I nod before helping her up. We walk through the Jetway, our suitcases following behind us as the wheels make different-sized bumps throughout. We walk out, entering the arrival part of the airport. Cool air from the air conditioning hits my face, and the echoing voices of people talking surround us. We walk towards the baggage claim area, the small carousel circling as we spot our bags and walk over to grab them. "Let me go get the metal cart thing," I request as I spot a small family pushing one around. A security officer hands one to me, and I push it over to where mom and I had been standing. Mom places the suitcases on before taking over the steering and direction. I nod as I grab my phone out of my pocket, notifications from the group chat blowing it up.

 EMERY| you guys get there yet?
  EMERY| how was the flight?
  AVERY| don't forget to get us a souvenir!
  EMERY| OH, yea! get me a large piece of salt from the lake
  AVERY| i'm pretty sure she can't do that.
  EMERY| she can't? oh well, at least try to!
  AVERY| omg..

CHAPTER TWENTY-FOUR: GROUND SPEED

I laugh at the messages, which causes mom to turn around. "Whatchu laughing at?" "Em, she made a small comment," I reply, showing mom my screen. A notification from Jayden pops up as I quickly glide it upward, silencing it. "You should answer that," Mom teases, lightly punching my arm. I bite my bottom lip before opening it up, 3 messages from Jay popping up on my screen as it loads.

JAYDEN| Let me know when you land.
  JAYDEN| Quick Question, are you doing the lock-in later this month?
  JAYDEN| Hey, have you guys landed yet?

The first message was from a few hours ago, and the other two are the most recent ones, from only an hour ago. We go through the other things throughout the port, security, check-in, and a few others before we finally leave.

Walking to the rentals, mom checks in as they hand her the keys to the car. We walk down the sidewalk outside, soon heading to the parking garages as we walk up to a Silver Nissan. Mom presses a button on the keys before the headlights glow, signifying the doors are unlocking. Mom and I both unpack the bags from the cart, put them in the backseat, and hop in the car. "Okay, it is official," Mom pauses, gliding her hands along the steering wheel. "Our little vacation has begun."

* * *

The hotel wasn't that far from the airport, just about 7 or 8 minutes, depending on traffic. Erykah Badu lightly plays on the radio, and mom turns the volume up as we pull into the parking lot near the back of the building. "Let me go check in and get the little trolley. Start getting the bags out the trunk," Mom notes, putting the car into park as she grabs the keys out of the key starter. She kisses my forehead before hopping out, myself doing the same out my side. The car beeps before the trunk automatically opens before I pull the few bags out of the back, placing them on the rocky street. 4 Rolling suitcases and 2 duffels rest in the trunk. The others, such as our backpacks from carry-on, are in the backseat. Emptying the trunk out, I place them onto the trolley. Looking around, I don't see mom coming from anywhere, so I bounce onto the back before sitting in the trunk, the tailgate still open overhead.

Mom comes from around the corner seconds later, startling me. She lightly taps my leg before I hop down, closing the trunk shut behind me. I load the rolling suitcases onto the trolley and mom loads on the duffels. She shuts the driver's door from her side and locks the doors behind her. We walk towards the doors together, eventually walking down the first hall where our room is. She grabs the key from her back pocket, sliding it down the card reader and the small light over the handle glows a bright green before it unlocks. Mom opens the door, and we're immediately greeted by a bright room, the curtains wide open, the bed comforters white, and the lights on.

The room is large and spacey, with two beds aligned against the left wall from where we'd entered. There's a blue patterned rug near the beds, and one mid-century couch faced the opposite direction of the beds, making a small living room. A 65-inch TV rests on a TV stand aligned on the other wall, and then a small kitchen area on the left side of it. A wardrobe sits near a window, a small armchair sitting alongside it. Mom struggles to push the cart inside, eventually doing so.

Behind mom, I follow her inside, the door shutting behind us as I look around. I walk over towards the beds, sitting on the one I'd claimed. Mom chuckles as she unloads the trolley, moving it to the corner when it had nothing on it. She sits on the couch and turns the TV on, going through the channels just as if we were at home. "What do you want to do while

CHAPTER TWENTY-FOUR: GROUND SPEED

we're here?" Mom mumbles, pulling out her phone. The glow illuminates her face before she turns the brightness down. I walk over towards the suitcases, grabbing my backpack where my laptop and chargers were. "I found this website that can plan out your day for you, and I've been using it to think of places to go while we're here and in LA," I pause, plugging in my phone as it loads up into the website. "We could check out the Family History Library," I pause once again. Mom gets up before walking toward me, looking at the screen over my shoulder. "Alright, wanna head there now?" She points. "Yea, give me a second," I respond, walking towards the bathroom. A large window rests against the wall, lights aligned on the sides. Looking at myself in the mirror, I fix my braids, putting them up in a ponytail right in the middle of my head. Sharply inhaling, I grab my phone out of my pocket, opening up messages to see Jayden's previous messages, and replying with my own.

> ME| hey, we landed like, an hour ago.
>> my bad about not being able to reply, we've been looking for places to head to.
>> JAYDEN| Hey, it's good. Just glad you got there safely.

I smile, continuing to type.

> ME| yea, we're actually on our way to the family history library.
>> ill send pictures later, or you might see them on my instagram first, lol.

I shove my phone back into my pocket, and walk out the doorway, telling mom I'm ready to head out.

Twenty-Five

CHAPTER TWENTY-SIX: ADD-ONS

"Why exactly are we going to a library for in the first place?" Mom says, speaking over the music. I look up from my phone. "Because I'm trying to get as many library cards anywhere I can," I giggle, opening the Libby app. "I have a major book nerd, now, do I?" She laughs. I firmly grin before exiting the app. I check out Instagram, the latest posts loading slowly. Emery and Avery pose awkwardly in front of a gas station on their latest post, and I scroll to the next photo to see them looking perfect. I notice that's the profile pic now. Every post of theirs has at least three sucky attempts at anything before the last photo is of them succeeding with the pose. The car slows down as I look up to find us parked beside the curb near the library. "You go in by yourself, I thought they were gonna have something cool for us to do. Turns out, this is more of a *you* thing," Mom states, putting the car in park. I unbuckle my seat belt before opening the door and climbing out of my side. My heels click loudly against the brick pavement, abruptly stopping as I walk inside.

The floor is the basic, cushiony carpet that all libraries seem to have. I'm greeted by a glass sign, a projected screen that changes displays every few seconds. A mother and her kids pass me, and I open the door for her. She

CHAPTER TWENTY-SIX: ADD-ONS

mumbles a quick 'Thank You' before continuing to walk out. Walking up to the front desk, I'm introduced to three women typing briskly on the computers in front of them. Two white ones and one black one. The black one looks up at me, her curls bouncing in her face as she pushes them back. "Hey!" She greets, a joyful smile across her face. Her voice is calming and warm. I reply quickly, "Hi, I'd like to sign up for a library card?" She glides herself across to the other side of the desk, grabbing papers before rolling the chair back where she was. A brunette woman beside her hands her a clipboard before she passes it to me. "Just fill in this form, and provide me with your ID, Drivers' License, and other residency proofs." "I'm just visiting here from Memphis, and I was wondering if I could still get a card, by any chance?" I respond, grabbing the clipboard out of her grasp. I grab a pen out of the pen holder that sits in front of me. "Yes, you can, but you will have to pay a fee of $65 a year," She replies. "Alright, thank you," I thank, walking over to the couches near the window.

I finish filling in the document and hand it back to her. "The hotel I'm staying at is provided, along with my residency address," I state, and she nods. "Alright, you'll get your card within three to four business days!"

Walking out the door, the car is still where it'd been parked before, but I look through the window to find the car empty. I look behind me to notice the historical cabin, and mom standing in front of the plaque. Awkwardly, I shuffle over and tap her shoulder. "You ready to go?" "Yup. I found a cool restaurant to eat at," I reply, pulling up the website on my phone. The logo loads up, *R&R Barbecue*. Mom grasps the side of my screen, pulling it towards her. Scrolling through the menu, an option seems to grab her attention. "That Beef Brisket is looking pretty good," She laughs as we begin walking back toward the car. "Alright, then. I'll make an order real quick," I pause, standing in the middle of the sidewalk. Mom calls my name, and I quickly follow behind her, getting in the car.

We walk inside the music is absolutely on blast, allowing mom and me to realize we want to order To-Go. "It's too chilly to eat outside," I groan, falsely shivering. "Okay, we'll eat in the hotel, because I swear, I one-hundred percent agree with you," She smiles before continuing to speak with the waitress.

* * *

Whenever we stay at a hotel, mom always just opens the curtains knowing I'll wake up that way.

I can see the sunlight through my eyelids, and I turn my head in the other direction, groaning with refusal. "Get up, Tiff. I went downstairs and got some food from the morning buffet before they'd put it up. Blueberry waffles with powdered sugar and butter on top," She continues speaking, now pulling the blanket off me. I sit up, rubbing my eyes as I groan from the realization that my bonnet had come off in the middle of the night. Fortunately, I also sleep on a satin pillowcase that I'd brought with me. Standing up, I stretch my arms, soon walking to the kitchen. Opening the utensil drawer, I grab a fork and grab my plate before sitting on the couch. "What're the plans for today, T?" Mom smiles, her face still sucked into her iPad. "Well," I mumble, my mouth full of waffles. I grab the remote off the small table, changing the channel to Disney. Lemonade Mouth plays, and I turn the volume down a bit. I swear, I never seemed to enjoy that movie. I swallow before continuing to speak. "We could check out Red Butte Garden or City Library Plaza." "I'm not going to another library, Tiffany," Mom complains, looking up from the screen and dead in my eye. "Okay, fine. Red Butte Garden."

"I passed a place called Boondocks, it looks cool."

"Yeah, I checked that place out, too."

"Okay, so we can head there instead?"

CHAPTER TWENTY-SIX: ADD-ONS

"Nope, they're closed until tomorrow."

Mom groans, and suddenly our roles seem to have switched. Mom has my attitude, and I have Mom's. "Fine, Red Butte it is."

My dull reflection looks back at me. And it's not like my outfit is boring. Well, maybe it is. But I've come to a conclusion; Utah is always going to be colder than Memphis. Next time I decide to head down here, I'm definitely gonna pack more than just a layer jacket.

My sweater is striped with white and lavender, and my jeans are gray. I have a pair of stockings slipped under my pants and some basic tan UGGS. Grabbing my coat out of the closet, the mirror door bumps into the wall. I hear the kitchen sink turn off before I turn the corner and see mom putting the few dishes we'd used away. "Alright, so cold picnic?" I give mom a look before she starts laughing. Drying her hands off, she tosses the towel into the sink. "I'm kidding," She says, her cold hands grazing my face as she gives me a kiss on the forehead. "Let me get ready real quick, then we can head out."

Walking outside, I hold my sides as the cold breeze consistently blows against us. Trees toss and turn, and leaves circle around each other. "Hurry up so we can get in the car. It's freezing out here," Mom struggles to say. Her voice cracks with the last word.

We open the doors, and the car also freezing. The leather seats are cold to the touch, and the windows feel like ice. Mom turns the key into ignition as the radio turns on, 100.3 playing Santa Baby by Eartha Kitt. Mom sings along, and I hop in midway.

Stopping at a red light, we both look at each other as we realize the next line, already ready to say it in sync.

The Bookposal

    Giggling, we continue to sing along, more songs playing right after. A few minutes in, we pull into the Family Dollar parking lot. Mom digs in the cupholder, a wadded twenty-dollar bill sits in the palm of her hand. "Get some snacks. I want some Mike N' Ikes, Takis, Dr. Pepper, and Cheddar Popcorn. Spend the rest on you." I nod okay, opening the door and getting out on my side.

A bell rings over the door as I open it, and employees greet me when I walk inside. Rushing to the chips, I grab Takis and Hot Cheetos. Realizing I need a hand basket, I head to the front to grab it and walk immediately to the drinks. 2 bottles of water, one Sprite, and one Dr. Pepper. Going around the store, I collect the other things before going up to the register. I go up to a lane with a petite redhead, who couldn't be much younger than 15. Her face is dotted with freckles, and her hands move fast with each scan. Watching the screen, I watch the cost displayed go up with each beep. "That'll be 17.51," She yawns, holding her hand out as I place the crumpled bill in it. She grasps hold of it, unlocks the register, and grabs two 1's and a few dimes and pennies. Each item is placed in the bag as she rips them out and hands them to me, the receipt inside the bag, and hands the change to me. "Have a nice day," She blandly reacts, and I wave quickly as I jog out the door and towards the car. Opening the door, mom's voice rings through my ears as she sings Give Love on Christmas Day by New Editon.
    She sings, caressing my face as I put the bag in the back. Putting her hands back on the wheel, mom backs into the intersection, leading us down the highway. "Wanna stop at Subway to pick up the main course?" She suggests, and I nod.

We pass a few places that look interesting and every so often drives by a large mall of some sort. And I could've sworn I saw a limousine pull up to one of the hotels we'd passed. Mom parks right in front of the Subway, digging in her purse as she makes sure her wallet is with her. "Wow, you're actually going in with me?" I comment. "Yea, you don't know how to order my stuff," She snarls. "Wow, okay. That was one time! And I swear

CHAPTER TWENTY-SIX: ADD-ONS

you blurred all your words together on purpose." Mom unsurely ticks her tongue as the car beeps behind us. We open the door, a bell ringing as it shuts. What is up with Utah and the bells? Mom glances at the menu behind us as if she's choosing something new. A girl with Butterfly braids gives us a look as we walk up to the serving area. Mom shoves her entire finger against the glass as she points to each item she wants. "Olives, Lettuce, oh, and add some extra vinegar," Mom continues on as the worker rushingly adds each preferred topping.

"Your total is 25.11," The cashier says, handing me the two plastic bags as mom slides the card across the slider. "Thank you."
   "Have a nice day!"

* * *

We open the car doors, our breaths sitting still in the air as we sit down. "Maybe not a picnic," Mom chuckles as we sit in the car, waiting for it to warm up. I laugh along unsurely. "Indoor one?"
   "If in the hotel, then I'm down."
   We back out, heading back down the street in the direction we'd come from. I check my phone out of reluctance, 300 notifications from the group chat with Em and Av sit on my screen. I sigh aggressively, and mom seems to already know. "You just never know with those twins, huh?" I laugh. "They blew up my phone!" I reply, scrolling through the messages.

   EMERY| COME ONNN AV!!!
      AVERY| cant you just privately text me this? we literally are just a few steps apart.
      EMERY| im too lazy. TIFFANYYYYY

I continue scrolling, and messages more recent pop up.

EMERY| avery

    AVERY| what?

    EMERY| when is the lock in?

    AVERY| im not even going to respond to that. tiffany when will you freaking answer the chat?!

I open the message bar, quickly typing up a response.

ME| im here, my bad lol. ive been out all day with my mom

The car bumps as we drive over a speed bump, entering the hotel parking lot. Quickly, I shove my phone back in my pocket before getting out and grabbing my sandwich. Mom grabs the Family Dollar bag out of the backseat.

"I'm really sorry about us not being able to actually go anywhere," Mom randomly says. The elevator door opens, allowing us to walk inside. We step in, and mom presses button 7. "It's good, mom. I just now got the email, and I'm good with spending time indoors," I smile, leaning against the back.

The doors open, and we step out.

Walking down the hall, we get to our room and unlock the door before getting inside and placing the bags down on the table. "I'm just surprised it hasn't snowed yet." I wash my hands, eventually grabbing a plate out of the overhead cabinet. I place my plate on the table, my wet hands dripping water all over the table as I grab my sandwich out of the bag and place it on the plate.

It's 4 PM now, and generally, mom and I usually watch our show, Black-Ish by now. We sit down on the couch, display mom's phone on the TV (Yea, it actually is preferred), and just watch.

Twenty-Six

CHAPTER TWENTY-SIX: ARRIVAL

"Wake up," Mom calls, her mouth muffled from her brushing her teeth. I sit up for a moment, as I look through the window, surprised I hadn't woken up when she opened the curtains. Rubbing my eyes, I grab my phone off the nightstand, Jayden's messages resting upon my lock screen.

JAYDEN| Can we talk?

I sigh, rubbing my face to wake up. "Ma, Jayden wants to call, I'll talk in the hallway real quick," I say, pointing to my phone. She nods before taking a swish of mouthwash.

I press Jay's contact and put my phone up to my ear as it rings. He quickly picks up.

"Hey."

The air between us is silent.

"We can watch a movie when you get back?"

"Yea, I'd like that."

"Well, I gotta go. My mom wants me to go to this counselor to help me pick out a campus. Just wanted to clear the air between us."

I nibble on my thumb's nail, thinking of what to say.

"Okay, bye."

"Bye."

I could've sworn I heard him mumble a quick, 'I love you.'

The suitcase rolls behind me as mom carries her bags. She closes the door behind us, the key still resting in her hand. "To California, we go," She smiles, side-bumping me with her hip. "To Cali."

JAYDEN

"Have you decided yet?" mom says as she places the laundry basket on my bed. I push my chair backward before standing up. Sitting beside the basket, I start grabbing my clothes and folding them. "Jayden, you're a senior. You graduate soon, and you haven't even applied for colleges," She complains. I open my dresser's drawer, putting the folded Nike shirt inside. "Ma, I told you, I got this."

"Jayden, I don't think you 'got this.'" Mom puts air quotes around her sentence.

"Mom, I do. Just let me get some more time. I'll check with the counselors again tomorrow and see if I have any scholarships coming in."

Tossing the rest of my clothes onto my bed, mom groans lightly. "Jayden, you are too smart to be wasting your time. You have skills. 'Balling' skills and logical skills." She adds, putting air quotes around the word "Balling." The basket resting against her arm and hip, she walks out my bedroom door, leaving me in silence.

TIFFANY

Walking down the aisle, I check to be sure mom's still following behind me. She smiles as she sits down at the row I do. "I got the right seats this time," She cheers, placing her small bag in between her legs on the ground. I fidget with the light overhead, almost pressing the attendance button. I move my hands down to prevent myself from touching anything else. "Okay, this is the second flight, it can't be that bad," I mutter, grabbing a book out of my bag. *She Had it Coming*, by Mary Monroe. "We have your tour tomorrow," Mom says, shrugging at my shoulder. I nod okay before I continue to read. I flip to the next page, and mom leans back in her seat, the beads within the neck pillow pressing against each other and making a noise that's only loud due to the silence. "How long is the flight?" I say, looking up from the book. "Not long, about two hours," She replies, opening her hand out, signaling for me to get her eye mask. Shuffling through the bag, I eventually grab a hold of it and place it in her hand. She places it over her head and it lands on her eyes. "Wake me up when we land."

"We remind you that this is a non-smoking flight. Tampering with, disabling, or destroying the smoke detectors located in the lavatories is prohibited by law."

I close my eyes in the hope to drown out the noise. It works, but my mind soon drifts on into space as I slowly drift asleep.

I wake up to mom shrugging my shoulder. "You weren't supposed to fall asleep. But we're here." Her words sound jumbled together, but I'm able to piece the sentence around as I sit up and stretch, almost hitting my head on the overhead bin.

We walk out of the Jetway, moving in the direction of the parking garage port. Mom asks a few people as they point, and we find ourselves where we need to be, which is surprising.

The car is a Tesla, and mom is hella proud of herself for managing to reserve one. "Only 94 a day." "That's still a lot, ma," I respond, putting the last suitcase in the back. "Oh well," She responds, smiling as we sit down and she puts the gearshift forward. We drive down the street and head down to the hotel, the Omni LA Hotel near Cali Plaza. We pull down the streets, people walking up and down the sidewalks and streets. People talk, dance, and smile. LA seems fun. Passing the Hollywood sign, we pull into the parking lot it's packed.

People scramble from left to right, kids running around so you have to be cautious. All I can say is for it to be 5 PM, people sure seem to be up energetically. Streetlights illuminate the dark lot, and kids continue to play around. Finding an available spot, we park and get out. LA isn't that cold compared to SLC. Really, it isn't. Is it chilly? Yea, definitely. But I'm not shivering and rushing to get inside like Utah. Nope. The trunk swings open as mom presses the button on the key, and I grab as many suitcases as I think I can manage to hold. "There aren't any more trolleys," A woman says as she passes us. Mom nods and quickly says thanks to her before she grabs as many bags as she can grasp. "Well then, I guess we have to make due."

We walk through the doors, and it's packed inside, too. More people sit on couches, and a few families sit in the dining area, eating food out of takeout boxes. Mom walks over to the front desk to check in and gets the key before we head over to the elevators. One press of the button, and

CHAPTER TWENTY-SIX: ARRIVAL

people come pouring out of the Left ride. "Lord, if I had known it was this busy down here!" Mom exclaims, rolling the bags in front of her as we board. I chuckle lightly. "Well, this *is* LA." "It feels like New York! Am I sure this isn't Times Square?" I roll my eyes. Letting go of the suitcase handles, mom grabs the key out of her pocket to check the floor. Reaching over, she presses the number 4, and we start moving.

The doors open to our floor and we walk down the hall to our room. "Room 412," mom mumbles as we start looking on both sides. "Got it," She calls, seconds later. I follow behind her as she opens the door and we push the bags inside. "Oh my god," I mutter, feeling my mouth hit the floor. "It looks nice, doesn't it?" Mom states before going over to the window. She opens the curtains. "And it's a beautiful view." "You know what, you have the bed over there. I think I'm good right here," I reply, sitting on the edge of the closest bed. The door shuts slowly behind me. Looking out the window, we have a nice view of the Hollywood sign. I lay back on the bed, the sheets feeling nice and cold. "I like this." Mom laughs at me before taking her shoes off and sitting in the middle of the bed. "You taking a shower first?"

"Yea, give me a sec," I reply, typing on my phone.

    ME| [Image Attached]

        EMERY| OOOO that looks cool!

        AVERY| yall in LA? we got an auntie that lives down there.

        EMERY| omg, you talking about aunt brandy? she hella cool, t.

        ME| if you guys are recommending we stay there instead of here, i think we're cool.

        EMERY| your loss...

        AVERY| literally, lol.

"How are the twins going?" Mom asks, placing her suitcase on the luggage holder. "Good. Av got accepted into Clark," I respond, grabbing a T-shirt and shorts out of my bag.

"That's amazing! Isn't that in Atlanta?"

"Yea, Em's pretty frustrated about that."

I walk over to the bathroom, amazed by how it looks. This place is so modern and sleek, I love it. "Let me know what places Emery gets accepted into, alright?" "Okay." Before I close the door behind me, mom calls my name. "Hey, Tiffany?"
 "Yea?"
 "I'm proud of you."

Twenty-Seven

CHAPTER TWENTY-SEVEN: INTRODUCTORY

I untwist the last braid sighing loudly. Tossing it into the trash, I grab my phone and press pause on my song. As I was doing my hair, Jayden sent me a playlist, so I pressed it and started listening to it. It contains artists we both love, J. Cole, Ne-Yo, Kanye West, Jay-Z, Drake, and more rappers. Grabbing the detangling comb, I get a message from Emery.

EMERY| when's your tour?

Sighing, I place the comb onto the counter before unplugging my phone and replying.

ME| idk. i'm finna check with my mom.

"Ma!" I yell out the bathroom door. "Yea?" She replies quickly. I tune my voice down, remembering where we are. "When's the tour?" "Later today at 3." Quickly, I key in what she'd said.

ME| around 3. why?

EMERY| i was planning for us to look online for dresses for the dance.

I click my tongue in frustration. I forgot we even had a dance.

ME| awh, maybe tomorrow?

EMERY| yea

I slide my control center downwards on my screen before pressing play. *1 More Shot* by Ne-Yo sounds through on my Bluetooth speaker.

Turning on the shower, I put it on cold first as I step in. My clothes are still on, so I tilt my head forward as I wash my hair. The moment the water hits my hair, I immediately begin washing before grazing through my hair with the detangler.

I get out of the shower, my hair dripping all over the floor. Despite my attempt to keep my bottom half dry, it failed. Looking at myself in the mirror, memories from when I was younger pass my mind as I close my eyes. I graduate high school in 5 months. 5 **months**. How did time pass so quickly? Laughing, I remember something from 5th grade when Emery argued with some kid about whether or not Kettle Corn is better than cheddar. Opening my eyes, I grab a hair tie and start putting my hair into a large afro puff. Just as I clip in some butterfly pins, mom enters through the doorway. "Your hair's cute!" She exclaims, kissing me on the cheek. I smile. "It's almost time to head out, get some better clothes on."

JAYDEN

"Jayden, you have many different opportunities in your path. You just have to accept them."

CHAPTER TWENTY-SEVEN: INTRODUCTORY

Mom and I walk through the front door as she tosses her purse onto the couch. "Okay, what's up with you? Why have you been acting like this lately?" I don't say anything. "Did you even listen to anything Mrs. Mayun had to say? You have <u>eight</u> scholarships waiting on you." Sitting on the couch, I ignore her. "Jayden, listen to me." I look at her from the corner of my eye, and she smacks her lips. "Pick one before I pick it for you."

"Maddison."

I mumble.

"What?"
 "Maddison. I can't leave her, mom."

She stands there, confused. "What do you mean? What's wrong with her?" Her voice changes suddenly, in that caring tone that tends to soothe you every time.
 "She's anorexic."

TIFFANY

Closing the door behind me, I sit in the passenger's seat. Mom enters on her side of the door, soon inserting the key into the ignition. Mariah Carey's *All I Want for Christmas* tunes on, and mom sings along as we back out of the parking lot, going through the gate. I grab my phone out of my back pocket to text Jayden.

   ME| hey babe, you down for an online movie night?

Tapping my thigh impatiently, mom sparks conversation. "So, my little

Tiff-Tiff is turning 18 soon, huh?" I smile, rolling my eyes. Chuckling, she continues talking. "I'm serious! How does it feel?" she adds, stopping at the red light. For once, I *actually* have a response to that question. "Overwhelming. Tiring. Stressful." I reply, rubbing my face. My hand hits my leg when Jayden sends a response.

JAYDEN| Not tonight.

I roughly sigh, turning my phone off before putting it into the cup holder. "Boy Problems?" "Mama, stop, you make it sound so childish," I laugh. She laughs along, turning left around the corner. "I'm serious. I ain't see you and Jayden do your weekly dates in a while." "He's been busy lately. Probably with his applications," I say, reassuring her, or am I just saying this to reassure myself?

We pull up to a parking lot about an hour later, immediately turning our radio down. Destiny's Childs's Christmas album is our go-to when it comes to Christmas. It's on repeat in our house, every single year. Mom reaches towards the backseat, grabbing her purse before shoving the keys inside it. I get out on my side, and mom gets out on hers before locking the doors. We walk down the street, looking around at the large campus. Noticing a building that seems to be the office, we walk towards it, a group of smiling white women greeting us before they walk out behind us. Mom walks up to the desk, with me standing alongside awkwardly. "My daughter and I are here for a tour?" "What's your name?" "Lyana Mohan and my daughter's name is Tiffany Mohan." The woman smiles before immediately typing. "Alright, you're just in time! Your guide, Jesse, is standing right outside waiting for you two!" She exclaims, the smile still plastered onto her face. It's starting to scare me. "Thank You," Mom says, grabbing her keys off the counter.

"Hello! My name is Jesse, and I'll be your tour guide for today!"

CHAPTER TWENTY-SEVEN: INTRODUCTORY

* * *

We're at Blackwell Hall when I start to get bored. Looking out the window, I notice a group of people gathering around a bench. "This is our newest complex, with many people already nesting here. I recommend this place, especially for upcoming freshmen." I look at mom, and she can already read my eyes. Nodding her head toward the exit, I quietly thank her before jogging outside.

Approaching the crowd, I hear a guy singing *Best I Never Had* by Beyonce while playing the guitar. Unable to see above everybody, I shuffle through the small crowd finding myself in the front. The guy finishes playing, thanking everyone before the crowd disperses. There's something about him. Something about his face looks so familiar. He turns around as he notices me, his face glowing with joy. "Hey! Tiffany, right? I had no idea you went here." He says, folding the keyboard stand. I slowly walk towards him, my face possibly shifting towards concern. "Ryan. We met at that pop-up?" "Oh, yea! Ryan!" I laugh. He smiles. "So, you go here?" "Oh, I'm a Senior at SouthWind. Just here for my tour." He nods, turning back to gather his things. Tucking the keyboard and stand under his right arm, he grabs the bucket of change. "Let me help you," I say, rushing towards him, right as he was about to drop the bucket. Smiling, he points towards a building, where we both direct.

Walking down the hall, we reach a door, and he pulls his keys out of his pocket. Unlocking the door, he places the keyboard and stand against the wall by the door, then grabs the bucket out of my hands before tossing it into a corner beside the door. "So, you should probably go," He chuckles, rubbing the back of his neck. "Yea," I awkwardly replied. Stepping inside the dorm, he holds the door in front of him, ready to close it when I leave.

"See ya next year, freshman."

Twenty-Eight

CHAPTER TWENTY-EIGHT: LIFELONG PLANS

It's now around 6 PM, and it's almost dark outside. Jogging down the sidewalk, I head towards the parking lot where I see mom sitting in the car, waiting for me.

Walking up to the car, I knock on the window, and she looks up before instantly unlocking the doors. "You know dang well, I didn't mean you could wander off like that. I had no idea where you were, and you didn't even answer the phone!" She lectures, backing out. I buckle my seat belt, grabbing my phone out of my pocket before plugging it onto the charger. "It was dead," I mutter, leaning back into the seat. "Well, in that case, I shouldn't have let you go, now should I?" I roll my eyes before facing the window. She sighs, turning the radio on, Ariana Grande flowing through the speakers. Licking her lips, mom quickly adds to her lecture. "I have to trust you, Tiff. You're on your own soon." Picking at my nails, I reasonably ignore her. "Are you listening?" I nod.

CHAPTER TWENTY-EIGHT: LIFELONG PLANS

JAYDEN

If I had known telling mom was gonna get Maddie sent to a home, I would've never told her.

"Mom, please! I'm getting better. Give me more time. Don't send me there, please!" Maddie begs, but mom continues shaking her head no. Tucking a shirt into the corner of the suitcase, Mom zips the bag up, tossing it onto the ground. I look around the room and think of something. I tap Mom's shoulder, and she turns around impatiently. "Ma, look at how sending people to places doesn't do anything. It makes it worse unless they ask to be there," I say, just winging it. "Jayden, how long have you known? Why didn't you tell me?"

"Because I knew you would do something like this. I mean, look at you. You're sending my baby sister to a mental center."

"That isn't anything bad, Jay. They'll help her. They'll cure it."

Maddison freezes at mom's comment. *"Cure it?"*

She repeats herself once again.

"Cure it?"

Mom nods, packing the bag again, but this time frustratingly.

"You can't just *'cure'* anorexia. It's something that stays within your mind forever. Trust me, I've tried *'curing'* it myself, but the voice won't go away, mom. It never does." Maddison's voice breaks in between the sentence, but she continues.

"Give me time, mom. I'll try my best. Send me to therapy, get medication, *watch* me <u>eat</u>, I don't care. *Just don't send me away.*"

Chapter Twenty-Nine: Mindset

TIFFANY

"I thought you said we were staying for four days?"

"I did, but that was before I knew Macy and them were heading in town."

Mom quickly shoves her clothes into her suitcase, struggling to zip it up due to messy organization. I shuffle towards the bathroom and grab all of my things before tossing them into the small hand pouch. "I bought last-minute tickets and we leave in an hour. Hurry up, toss sweats and a hoodie on, I don't care. We just need to get out of here!" Mom yells before placing the last suitcase on the trolley. Yup, you read right, we finally managed to get the metal cart. My backpack sits on the desk chair, so I shove the pouch in. Tossing the bag over my shoulder, I check my look in the mirror, being sure my afro puff was in compliance appearance. "Hurry up!" Mom rushes, pushing the cart into the hall. Looking behind me, I see the bed sheets and comforter messed up. "Give me a second," I respond, rushing back to fix it. Mom clicks her tongue before pouting like me and pushing towards the elevator.

I sit in the passengers' seat as the trunk closes and mom sits beside me. The seat automatically adjusts to her height and such when she sits down. "Oh, you know Imma miss this," She sighs, pulling back. I chuckle as I plug in my phone and it dings in confirmation.

Ten minutes into the drive, and I swear she's going insane.
   Every thirty seconds, she looks at the middle console screen at the clock that sits in the top right corner.

* * *

We were back home 5 hours later, and to my surprise, we're back to Memphis before sunset. Our car sits in the parking garage as mom continues to rush to it. "Ma, we're here. It's Memphis, no need to run anymore," I groan, and she turns around to give me a quick look of despise. I surrender before hopping in the backseat. I'm not dealing with her chaotic phase right now. She puts the key into the ignition after putting the bags in.

We attempt to pull into the driveway, but we're blocked by two Nissans sitting in the way. "Head inside, and go tell Macy and CiCi to get their cars out of this small spot!" Mom yells as I walk out and close the door behind me. Walking up to the porch, I grab my keys out of the clutch and unlock the door. Smoke pours out. "Oh my god, Macy! You weren't supposed to leave it in that long!" I hear CiCi yell before rushing out of the dining room and into the kitchen. Closing the door behind me, I walk into the kitchen, waving my face clear of smoke. The smoke alarms go off, and Macy and CiCi start coughing as CiCi throws the cookie sheet onto the

CHAPTER TWENTY-NINE: MINDSET

counter. Fanning the smoke alarms, I laugh at the sight, and Macy turns to face me, her eyes glowing with excitement. "Tiffany! Look at you! You graduate in a bit, don't you? Send the graduation invites as soon as you can," She says, smiling big and wide. I chuckle. "Thanks, yup, I do. How's Andre?" I ask. Andre is Macy's son, and he just turned 2. CiCi ignores my question before asking hers. "I thought you guys were staying until Friday?" "He's good. Sadly, the little dude wasn't feeling well, so he had to stay in Chicago," Macy continues speaking, ignoring the grudging look Ci's giving her. I suddenly remember why I'd come in anyway. "Oh yea, mama said come get your car out the middle of the driveway," I say, Macy, laughing in the background. I raise my eyebrows in shock. "Both of you."

"Finally! I gotta head to the gas station tomorrow, and I don't wanna waste the amount I have!" Mom yells, noticing the three of us walking out the door. CiCi sits in the driver's seat of her car, and so does Macy. They both drive towards the side of the street, parking there. Just then, Jayley pulls in. Getting out, Mom gives her a look, and she automatically gets back in the car and parks on the curb. She gets out again, this time apologizing. "My bad," She snickers.

***

Putting my bonnet on, I sit on my bed and Jayley lies on the ground looking up at her phone. "How come you guys came back two days early?" She asks, sitting up. "Cause Macy came today. My mom said it caught her off guard, so we quite literally got here the exact day of my tour." I reply, grabbing the bottle of lotion that sits on my nightstand. "How was the tour?" She asks, facing me as she places her head resting in her hands. "Good, I guess. I wasn't there half the time," I laugh, slowly applying the lotion to my legs.

"Ha, same. Ditched my mom halfway through."

I laugh at this, tucking my legs under the cover. Annoyingly, the lotion causes the sheets to stick to my skin. "When's your dance?"

"Like, December 27, I think?" I reply, unsure.

ME| em, when's the dance??

EMERY| like right after christmas idk, ask avery lol

Plugging my phone in, I place it face down on my nightstand. "When do you go dress shopping?" She adds, finally laying down, but her face still looking at me. "Tomorrow. Heading out with Emery and Avery. I hope I can stop after and see Jay," I reply, laying down myself. I reach over to my nightstand, turning the lamp off.

* * *

Tomorrow's Christmas, and I'm generally surprised that half the family ain't here.

Jayley shakes me awake, repeating something over and over. "Jayden's here," She says. "Huh?" I mumble, and she quickly backs away. "Morning breath, but Jayden's here!" She repeats, but a little bit louder. I sit up, my head colliding with hers. Jayley laughs out of pain, and I start laughing as well. Jayden walks through the doorway. "Hey," he mutters, putting his hands in his pockets. "Hey," I reply, still laughing. Jayley points towards my head, indicating to take off my bonnet. I shrug it off, and Jayden walks closer before sitting on the edge of my bed. Jayley continues standing there, and I give her a look as she gets the hint before wandering out of the room. "Call me if you need me," She mouths, and I nod. Keeping my legs under the

CHAPTER TWENTY-NINE: MINDSET

cover, I sit in criss-cross applesauce, facing Jayden. "So, I realized I haven't been spending time with you lately," He pauses, grabbing my hand. No. He can't.

"And I've just had a lot on my mind that I want to tell you."

Thirty

CHAPTER THIRTY: CONNECTION

"Jayden, please don't say what I think you're about to say," I interrupt, my eyes already watering. He looks at me, confused for a moment. Suddenly, his face changes as he realizes. "What? No! I would never," he replies, looking hurt at my comment.

"**I love you.**"

My heart begins pounding **hard** at this singular sentence.

Worriedly, he begins stuttering. "My bad if you weren't ready. I just-."
He pauses due to me kissing him immediately.

I find myself sitting on my knees, and he places his hands on my waist as he pulls me closer. He kisses me harder, and I can't help but feel butterflies. He pushes me backward, my head now hitting the pillow as he leans on top of me. We pull away, breathing heavily and giggling like little kids.

Jayden falls beside me, laying upward on my bed, his arm resting on top of my shoulders. He moves me in, and I lay my head on his chest.

"**I love you too, Jayden. *I mean it.***"

CHAPTER THIRTY: CONNECTION

* * *

We sit there for about an hour, just talking and mumbling on and on about unlimited things. "Okay, I also came here to tell you something," Jayden says, his voice becoming stern as he sits up. I sit up along with him. Tucking my hands into my lap, I look at him, noticing his eyes turn a light red.

"Maddison has anorexia. I've been busy due to looking for ways to help her. I told my mom, and she wants to send her to one of those rehab centers. Tiffany, I don't know what I would do without Maddie. She's my baby sister. I was supposed to protect her," He rambles and by now, tears are pouring in streams down his face. Laying his head onto my shoulder, I lightly caress the back of his neck. "Baby," I whisper, his ear up close to my mouth. He lightly mumbles a quick 'yes.'

"I'm here for you, no matter what. You're there for me. Whenever I'm down, *you* manage to make me smile. Whenever I need someone to talk to, *you're* my therapist. *I'm* here *for you*, just like you're here for me."

I wake up to find myself snuggled underneath Jayden's arm. My phone's on the nightstand, so I reach over and grab it to check the time.

5:50 PM

Sneakily, I manage to get away from his grasp and out the doorway. Walking downstairs, I hear mom and another person laughing and talking. Realizing my bonnet is still on, I quickly snatch it off, and the plaits I'd braided my air into fall down.

"There she is! Tiffany, say hi to my friend Ashley!" Mom says, pointing her finger at a young woman sitting cross-legged in the armchair across from her. Shyly, I wave a quick *hi* before walking into the kitchen and seeing ten

Styrofoam containers wide open across the counter, containing shrimp and chicken fried rice and different variations of sushi. Jayley walks in from the guest room, a plate with chopsticks in her hand. "My bad," She pauses, serving herself more rice. "I meant to wake you up." I scoff, grabbing two plates out of the cupboard, one for me and the other for Jayden. "What was that about?" Jayley asks, pointing up at the ceiling. "Family stuff," I pause, grabbing two spoons out of the drawer. Sneering, she grabs a plastic cup from the stack and grabs a bottle of Sprite out of the fridge.

"You're a good girlfriend. I would've spilled within seconds," She laughs, pouring the soda into her cup. After she places the bottle down, I grab it from her reach before pouring the last amount into the two cups. Tossing the empty bottle into the trash, I take a bite of rice off my fork before turning around and searching in the cabinets for a tray. "It's under the stove top," Jayley mumbles, leaning against the fridge. Opening the cabinet door, I look there and find it, placing the plates and cups onto it.

Heading up the stairs carefully, I see Jayden on his phone while leaning against my headboard. Putting the tray onto my nightstand, I sit beside him before grabbing the two plates and handing him one. "Thanks," he mumbles, taking a bite. I numbly smile, having no idea how to boost the mood. Wiping his mouth, Jayden decides to speak. "Thanks for being there for me," he sniffles. "No Problem, babe," I mumble, chewing the mouthful of rice. A piece falls out, and I quickly wipe it off my bed, positive he didn't see. "I saw that," He chuckles, nudging my shoulder.

"Whatever, it fell out of my mouth! I'm not 'finna put that back in my mouth, ew!" I yell, nudging him back. Playfully, he false punches my stomach, and I false punch his shoulder. Within seconds, we're play fighting. "Ah! Okay, I ain't see nothin'!" He jokingly shrieks, causing Shiloh to run through my doorway. "Jayden's here? When did he get here? Wanna play GTA? I added a new mod," He motors, going on and on. I stand on my mattress as I grab a pillow. "Boy, get your big-headed forehead outta here!" I yell with a laugh between my sentences, throwing it at his head.

"Mhm, no, you are not hitting my little dude," Jay says, joy filling his

CHAPTER THIRTY: CONNECTION

voice. Jayden grabs my fur pillow and throws it at me. "Wow, I thought you were on my team, babe!" I sarcastically say, falling onto my bed.

"Hey, if you can't beat 'em, join 'em," He shrugs as he and Shi throw piles of pillows and blankets at me. I take a moment before grabbing a pillow, examining how Jayden looks at Shiloh. He treats him like his own brother, and they bond perfectly. Shiloh and CJ never got along like that. Matter a fact, CJ *hated* kids. I snap out of it when a pillow hits my forehead. "Ha!" Shiloh laughs. "Oh, get over here," I blow, a smile plastered on my face as I move closer to him. I plan on picking him up on my shoulder and tossing him onto my bed, but instead, Jayden tosses *me* over his shoulder. "Put me down!" I laugh, and Shiloh pushes Jayden toward his room. "Throw her on my bed!" He calls as Jayden tosses me onto Shi's bed. "Okay, y'all win!"

I check the time on my phone as it reads 2:56 AM. Looking up, I find Jayden and Shi finally exiting their 2K game as Jayden crawls onto the bed and heads toward me before laying down. Shiloh changes the input to Apple TV, and I watch the white bar circle around the Netflix app as he presses it. He gets into his profile, and immediately presses a show he'd been watching before. Sneakerheads, it reads. I'm pretty sure it features King Bach. Shiloh sighs deeply before shoving his entire body between Jayden and me, separating the two of us as we laugh lightly. Putting my phone down on Shiloh's nightstand, I lay my head down on the pillow, slowly finding myself drifting asleep as the characters on the show argue.

* * *

I wake up from the middle of the bed consistently pulsating in a way. Opening my eyes, I see Shiloh's face engulfing my eyesight. "God, Shiloh, get out of my face!" I shriek, accidentally slapping Jayden's back as I push

Shiloh off of me. Jayden turns around, his face groggy. I chuckle awkwardly. "My bad."

"Shut up, Tiffany, no one cares about your apologies. It's Christmas, get up," He adds, jumping off the side of the bed. I sit up as Jayden stands up, walking behind Shi as he follows him down the hallway. I hear three knocks on a door before someone opens it, probably my dad. I walk to the doorway seeing dad's confused face as he grabs his robe off the doorknob. He puts it on, calls mom's name, and they both walk out the room following Shiloh downstairs. Jayley comes out of my room with her bonnet on crookedly, and I point towards the stairway as she immediately tosses it off. I knock on the Guest room door before CiCi answers and I let her know of the "news". "I know it's Christmas. Give me five," She mutters, shutting the door behind her as I hear bumps in there. Her clumsy behind could've knocked over the night table.

I walk downstairs to Mom and Dad handing out the gifts, Jayden sitting on the couch near a pile that must be mine. Shi's ruffling through paper, putting the gift he'd just opened behind him. Mom smiles before leaning back on the neck of the armchair. Marlon rests on the ground with a pallet surrounding him, and pillows on top. He sleeps weirdly for a 20-year-old man. The floorboard in the hallway creaks before CiCi walks in an Opaque robe as she hands mom a camera. "Jayden, it's 8 right now, I think you should be headed home," Mom mumbles, her attention revoked towards the camera as she adjusts the lens and viewfinder. "Yea, you're right," he replies, standing up. His shirt is still on, so all he has to do is grab his coat from under the stairway, his shoes, and keys, and he'll be out. Walking towards me, he mumbles something in my ear. "I have your gift at home, stop by a bit later. I'll send the address." I nod lightly as he pecks a kiss on my cheek before heading towards the coat closet and grabbing his out. "Bye, babe."

"Bye, Jayden! Merry Christmas!" Jayley calls, sitting down beside Auntie Ci.

CHAPTER THIRTY: CONNECTION

Jayley was the last one to get her gifts. CiCi walked to the stairway and grabbed multiple bags from there. Gucci, H&M, Louie Vuitton, SHEIN, and some others. She places them on the table as Jay rushes toward them and digs through the bags, tissue paper flying everywhere. "I think the girls and I are gonna go dress shopping today," I sigh, standing up with my gifts in a pile cradled in my arms. "We have one more gift for you," Mom says. Dad grabs the camera off the table as mom walks over to the couch. She turns the laptop toward me, and I find myself face-to-face with an apartment listing.

An apartment I'd begged for since 2019.

Thirty-One

CHAPTER THIRTY-ONE: CHRISTMAS GLOW

"You guys?" Mom and dad nod. "We will pay the rent until we know for sure you're on your feet," Dad says, his voice slightly breaking. "Oh, and you have a roommate!" Mom adds on. I look up from the listing, looking at Dad's face.

"Our little Tiffany's almost an adult, and it's scary to see."

JAYDEN

"Good morning, Jay!" Mom says, noticing me walking through the door. "Morning," I groan, placing my car keys on the console table. Through the air, I can smell sweet spices. Following the trail, I head into the kitchen to find Maddie flipping pancakes along with mom beside her, her face gleaming with happiness. <u>Real</u> happiness.

"Jayden, I need you to get along with Bryant today," Mom says, placing the

CHAPTER THIRTY-ONE: CHRISTMAS GLOW

plate of pancakes in the center of the table. I scoff, grabbing forks from the drawer. Bryant comes from down the hallway wearing a white short-sleeved T-shirt and Nike shorts. "Good morning," He mumbles, kissing mom on the cheek. "Morning, babe," She smiles, giving me a corner look as I exhaustively nod. Maddison sits in the chair beside me while mom and Bryant sit facing us. Silently, we begin eating. "So, have you gotten any reply from applications?" Bryant asks, cutting a piece off the pancake.

"Yea," I grumble. "Wow, Jayden, that's amazing! What places?" "Clark Atlanta, Allen, Alabama," I pause, plastering a forced smile onto my face. Taking a bite of the egg, Maddie nudges my arm. Mom's eyes largen. "Oh wow, Jayden!" She exclaims, dropping the utensils onto her plate. "I'm so proud of you," She says, walking around the table to hug me. Maddison looks me in the eye, already knowing about Berkeley. We both have logins to each other's email, just in case of a situation like this. She kicks my foot underneath the table, letting me know to say it. Forced, I strainly say it, "And Berkeley." Mom pauses in her tracks, the fork in her hand falling out. "Berkeley?"

"Consider it a Christmas gift to you," I mumble, leaning over to hug her tightly. She pats my shoulder and I look up to see tears trailing down her face. I missed this. Missed her hugs, her love, and her warmth. I've spent so long being mad at her for marrying someone else that I never even realized what I was missing.

TIFFANY

EMERY| dresses??

   AVERY| yup. tiff, you down?

I pick up my phone as I felt the vibration, two texts from the group chat sitting on the home screen.

ME| yea, give me like an hour?

Standing up, Jayley pauses the show, causing everyone to groan. "Where you going?" "Oh, come on, forget her, Jay. Continue on the show!" Shiloh whines, throwing a pillow at her. She ignores him as the screen is still on pause. "Emery and Avery want to go dress shopping for the dance tomorrow," I reply, walking behind the couch. I feel mom's glare against my back. I turn around before adding a sentence. "That good with you?" "Yup," Mom mumbles, taking a sip from her wine glass. "As long as you're using your money, have fun."

I put my hair in two low afro puffs. Looking into the mirror, I place four different colored butterfly clips on both puffs.

Heading downstairs, I hear Dre from *Black-Ish* whining as I pass the living room door before I head toward the garage. I grab my keys off the rack and grab my phone out of my back pocket, seeing a missed call from Jayden. Quickly opening the door, I connect my phone to the car's Bluetooth, and he quickly picks up.

The new message tone rings through the speaker, a notification from Emery.

EMERY| zoey and jayla are here too. where are you?

ME| omw rn

"**How's Maddie going?**" I ask. "**Good. She's been eating, and mom is being sure she doesn't relapse,**" He replies as I can feel his excitement. "**Good.**"

I turn the corner to *Arabella's Boutique*, a place I've passed by before but never bothered to check out. "**Hey, babe,**" I say, spotting a parking space and parking within it. "**Hm?**" He mumbles. "**I just pulled into the lot.**

CHAPTER THIRTY-ONE: CHRISTMAS GLOW

Wanna call later?"

"Yea. I Love you, have fun."

* * *

Shutting the car door behind me, and spot Emery, Avery, Jayla, and Zoey all getting out of Jayla's silver Honda. "What's up, girl? Ready to get our shop on?" Avery expresses as Emery and Jayla both give her a look of *'Don't ever say that again.'* I chuckle, walking onto the sidewalk. "What's our budget?" "None, I guess. Our mom just handed us the card and told me to 'Have Fun,'" Avery responds, putting air quotes around her sentence. The group shrugs as we walk through the doorway into the shop.

Ed Sheeran lightly plays throughout the store, and the theme seems to be a formal black, aligned through and through with clothing racks. "Alright, so who are we gonna search for a dress first?" Zoey sighs, looking at a turquoise-shaded dress aligned with gold-colored rhinestones and a silver belt. "Mine," Avery and Jayla both say in sync, soon giving each other the eye after realizing what they both had said. What was at first the stink eye, soon determined who would go first, dueling into a staring contest. Jayla wins as Av blinks before rubbing her eyes.

Laughing with victory, Jayla guides us through an aisle full of medium-puffed dresses as a clerk comes over. "Hello, my name is Rae. May I assist you in any kind of way?" She requests. She has caramel-toned skin, and her hair is in tribal braids as she has a thick layer of lip gloss applied on her lips. "No, but we will ask for you if we need any help," I smile, and she politely walks back behind the counter. Shifting throughout the rack, Zoey's hands grasp onto a hanger that holds a long, black dress with a slit that stops at the inner high thigh. Holding it up, Jayla looks up as her eyes glow. "Hand that to me," She demands as Zoey surrenders the dress to her. I walk to the other side of the rack as Avery follows behind me.

"How's Jayden feeling?" She mutters, looking at a blue dress. "Good."

"Has he told you any of his application acceptances?"

"No," I reply, humming along with the Song *Till it Happens to You* by Corinne Bailey Rae, that's now playing. Looking over the rack, I see stacks of dresses resting upon the ottoman that sits beside J. "Jayla," Emery says, her face saying it all. "I'm gonna try these on!" Jayla defensively exclaims, struggling to pick each hanger up. "I'll be back," She strains, and we all laugh at this as she shuffles towards the dressing rooms.

I grab a blue dress with gold embellishment within the chest area that glides along the sides. I hover it over my torso as I look in the mirror alongside me. Zoey and Emery both walk over toward me. "That's cute. Try it on," Zoey announces, shoving me toward the dressing room. "Okay, okay!" I laugh.

Entering the dressing rooms, I notice each room closed off by black curtains and the walls full of pictures of other girls in dresses. Quotes from people like Nicki Manaj, Beyonce, Megan Thee Stallion, Kilumaunti, and others hang in gold frames. Jayla walks out of her stall wearing a plain white dress with silver lining across the side and front. "Isn't it cute?" She says, looking at herself in the mirror. I nod before walking into the stall beside the one she'd just walked out of.

Slipping out of my clothes and into the dress, I hear someone walk in before the sound of Emery's voice echoes throughout the dressing room. "You done?"

"Yea, almost," I reply, looking at myself in the mirror in front of me. I move the curtains out of the way, and Emery looks at me with a shocked expression before signaling for the others to come in. "Wow," Zoey says, freezing in her tracks. Jayla gives me a look before walking over to me and fixing a slight ruffle issue.

"That's the one you getting?"

"What?"

CHAPTER THIRTY-ONE: CHRISTMAS GLOW

"Nothing, it's just the first one you've tried, and look at the whole store," Jayla pauses, waving her arms around the room. I shrug, as she is right. "I'll keep this in mind."

* * *

We end up spending 3 hours in the store, dancing and laughing and playing at every moment. "Your total is 1,745," The cashier smiles as Avery shrugs and hands her the card. Swiping it, they quickly zip the dresses into dust bags before handing them to us. Jayla ended up picking a light purple dress with rhinestones lined on the sides, the lower part with a small train, and white lacework along the front and back. Emery picked a light blue dress, somewhat basic with no train and just an average glittery dress design. Avery went with a matching dress along with Emery but got it with adjustments. The straps are silver chains, and the waist has little silver-glittered roses. Zoey found a black dress also *somewhat* basic but has a diamond Swarovski crystal rose on the top right, along the chest. I ended up with the dress I'd first tried on.

Walking through the door, we check the clock as it read 6:50 PM. "Y'all wanna get Subway?" I offer, and everyone gladly accepts.

We all took the same car this time, the one the twins had arrived in, as it's the largest of us all.

My finger hits the cold glass as I point to what I want on my sandwich. "Toast the bread, and make sure to melt the cheese," I direct, and the worker nods. The group sits along the side of the place on the far left side, and I could hear them from where I was, across the room. As I hand them the cash, the stove's alarm goes off. Quickly, they grab it out before steadily placing the turkey, lettuce, olives, tomato, and my other requested toppings on it. Reaching over to hand the sandwich to me, I give them the amount in cash before prancing back to the table, catching a heart of the conversation.

"We should stay the night at Em and Av's place tomorrow night!" "Yea, but we just got the guest house renovated. Plus, the theater got add-ons!" Jayla adds her own two cents. "My mom got this cute spa set I think we could use. I mean, it *is* the night before the dance."

Everyone argues. "Hold up!" Zoey interrupts, causing the table to get silent and everyone within the building to look at us. "Flip a coin," She adds as the group groans. "Do you always have that stupid coin wit' you?" Avery snaps, leaning her head back. Stubbornly, Zoey nods before slapping it in the palm of her hand "Heads," Jayla says, and Emery groans as she already knows she has to get tails. Flipping the coin in the air, Zoey grabs the coin before slapping it onto the surface of her hand. "And Tails wins!" Zoey cheers as Emery pulls out her phone before typing. "Alright!" She states, putting it face down on the table. "I just sent y'all the address in the group chat."

JAYDEN

ME| Hey babe, wanna call later?
Delivered

Shifting back and forth between my PC and phone is hella difficult. Every thirty seconds, I find myself leaning over my phone screen to see if Tiffany replied. "Jayden! Come eat!" Mom calls as I blankly reply.

Walking down the stairs, I pass Maddie with a smile on her face. "You eat today?" "Yup. Breakfast, Lunch, and a few snacks," She proudly announces as I hug her closely. We walk into the kitchen to see the TV display the Home Alone DVD screen and the table packed with food mom had spent all day cooking. Turkey, Stuffing, Mac N' Cheese, Chicken, Greens, Casserole,

CHAPTER THIRTY-ONE: CHRISTMAS GLOW

Tamales, and just random foods she enjoys making. "We can make a gingerbread house later tonight right after the movie," Mom smiles. I smile back before sitting down in my usual spot. Bryant comes out of the living room, looking slightly more presentable. I give him a look before I see mom give me the same look. Quickly, I look down at my plate as we say grace.

Thirty-Two

CHAPTER THIRTY-TWO: NEW TROUBLES

TIFFANY

"Give me like five minutes!" I call from the stairway. Emery rolls the car window up before playing Doja Cat on blast. I knock on the door, standing on the wood floor awkwardly, clutching onto my sides from the cold. I hear a door chain unlock from the inside, a young woman with her hair in a tight ponytail soon answers the door. "Hello? May I help you?" She says, a smile glistering across her face. I think for a moment before coming to a realization: I've never met his mom, and she's never met me.

CHAPTER THIRTY-TWO: NEW TROUBLES

JAYDEN

"Who's that?" Maddison and I ask in unison as mom quickly turns around with a stern look. I stand up, signaling for Maddie to stay put as I walk towards the door. "I'm here for Jayden?" A voice says, and I can immediately put a face to it. Mom opens the door wider, allowing Tiffany to look at me. "Hey," She says, her face growing into a smile. Mom mumbles that she's headed back to the kitchen before walking behind me, leaving Tiffany and me staring at each other. "Hey." "I don't have much time, but here," Tiffany mutters before handing me a wrapped gift. Grabbing it, I invite her in, realizing she's been standing in the cold for a bit. Walking inside, she sits down on a small couch mom had moved beside the door a few weeks ago. "Open it," She points as I close the door. Sitting beside her, I begin unwrapping the paper, revealing *Nothing Serious*, a book we've both been looking forward to reading.

"Oh my goodness," I laugh. "What?" Tiffany says, a wave of worry flowing through her voice. "I got you the same book," I reply, leaning in for a hug. She sneaks in a kiss on my cheek as I let go. A tiny giggle escapes from her mouth, possibly from relief. "Let me go get it," I stammer right before racing upstairs.

TIFFANY

Jayden rushes upstairs to get my gift, leaving me in the dim entrance. All over the wall are family photos. Vacation pictures, Toddler photos, birth photos. I stand up and walk closer to the wall of a picture of a little boy wearing a party hat gathers my attention. Cake's smeared all over his mouth. The photo right under it has a picture of a young girl, not much older than 1 or 2, holding a block in her hand while a line of slob leaves her mouth. "You must be the infamous Tiffany," A sarcastic voice blows from behind me. I turn around to be face to face with what looks like the girl I was looking at in the photo. She's skinny, with her hair in a lowish ponytail, and she's wearing baggy clothing. "Yea. Maddison?"

"Mhm," She mutters. Her skin doesn't look much different than Jay's, with a warm undertone. Slowly walking towards me, she pauses, not even inches from where I'm standing. "I know I'm younger than him, but don't freaking hurt Jay, okay?" She says. Jayden comes down quickly right then. "Okay, here you go," He states, out of breath. The book sits in his hand as I grab it. "You had no idea where it was, did you?" "Nope. Not a clue." Before walking to the door with him, I turn back around towards Maddie, quickly coming to a realization the girl on the photo was her.

"I can assure you, I wouldn't dare."

Jayden and I walk outside, laughing and talking. I look at the car and see Avery knocked out in the backseat, Zoey singing along with New Edition, Jayla on her phone, and Emery giving me an annoyed look. "I should get going," I chuckle, leaning into his chest. Resting his chin on my forehead, he plants a kiss on my scalp before lightly moving me toward the stairway. "I love you," he says, his lips cruising into a grin. "I love you, too."

Words linger in my mouth.

And I mean it.

I sit in the passengers' seat, closing the door behind me as Emery sits up before placing her hands on the wheel. "It's about time," she sighs, backing out of the parking space. "Whatever," I scoff with a smile as I buckle my seat belt. It's dark outside, and the time reads 8:41. The book Jayden gifted me sits in my lap. As we pass a streetlight, the cover glistens. "What'd you get him?"

"A book,"

"Ugh," Em blows, making a weird face. She may have to look forward, but she will express her normal emotions facing forward. "What do you mean, 'ugh'?" I laugh. "He and I are bookworms." "And I find it adorable." Zoey interrupts as she pats my shoulder. Jayla laughs at that. "Of course

CHAPTER THIRTY-TWO: NEW TROUBLES

you do, you love reading *just as much* as her," She adds on as we slow down at the yellow light. "But you gotta get him things other than books, T." I roll my eyes. "You do realize," I continue, "A book is what got me and him together in the first place."

My head bobs against the window as Emery pulls into my driveway as we come to an abrupt stop. I look in the back to see everyone but Jayla asleep. "See you tomorrow, T," She says, leaning to the front seat to change the music. Grabbing the book from between my legs, I open the car door and hop out. I rub my back pocket to be sure my phone hadn't fallen out. "Thanks, Em. See you tomorrow."

"See ya then, Merry Christmas!" Emery yells out the window before I back away from the car. Slowly but surely, Em backs out the driveway and into the street. Walking up the porch and ringing the doorbell, I look through the window and see Jayley rushing downstairs to open it, with a distant yell from my mother. "It's Tiffany! Finally," She yells back, lightly muttering as she opens the door. "I heard that," I snicker as I toss my shoes off. J laughs lightly as well before closing the door behind me, grabbing my coat, and resting it inside the closet under the stairs. Placing the book down on the table beside the door, I walk into the kitchen and glance into the living room, everyone is in the same spot as earlier when I left.

I walk in, the floorboard creaking under my footsteps. "Shut up," Shiloh mumbles as I hear mom smack his thigh. "What?" I hear him yelp. I smile before sitting between mom and dad. Dad sighs as mom grabs a hold of my hand. The movie on the TV is *Best Man Holiday*. Mom's had it on repeat ever since it came out. The scene playing is the dinner scene, her favorite. Harper shoves Lance's shoulder at a remark, and mom laughs hard. "Oh my god, Lyana. It's not that funny," Aunt CiCi groans as she slugs back into the armchair she's sitting in. Mom stops laughing immediately before giving her a look. The TV continues to play in the background. "What? We've seen this a million times, and you laugh at the same scene *a million times*," She adds on. Jayley stifles a laugh. "I mean, come on! It's not funny anymore!"

"Okay, then how about you pick the next movie? It's not like you're gonna pick something we've never watched."

"What do you mean?" Oh boy.

"You pick *This Christmas* every dang year and laugh at the <u>same</u> scene every dang year!" Mom says, her tone increasing. CiCi stands up, and so does mom.

"Well, maybe that shower beatin' is what <u>you</u> need!"

"Oh, come on! The same 'diss' too! You're from Memphis, for god's sake. Pick somethin' different!"

Dad stands up as CiCi and Mom close in on each other, now arguing chest to chest. "Alright, how about the kids pick the movie?" he says, pointing towards Jayley, Shiloh, and me. "Uh," Jay stammers, laughter held like water in a dam behind those lying eyes. "I don't pick good movies." "Yea, and I just don't wanna pick," Shiloh adds. "Fine," I groan, snatching the remote off the coffee table as everyone sits back down. I look beside me and see mom's arms crossed like a two-year-old who hadn't gotten their way. Scrolling through for what feels like hours, I finally find a movie. It's called *The Perfect Holiday*, and we watch the trailer. "Be careful, your mom may make this movie tiring' too," CiCi mumbles as mom defensively sits up before giving up.

I wake up to look around the room with everyone knocked out. Jayley's arms are all wild over my body, Mom's leaning on CiCi as her hands are in her hair, seeing as she'd been massaging her head. I rub my eyes before looking at the TV where CoryxKenshin's playing Sonic. Shiloh was probably up all night and turned this on once he realized everyone else was asleep. Sitting up, I slowly walk out of the living room into the kitchen before opening the curtains by the kitchen table to find the sky a purple/blue shade. It looks like cotton candy, like the day Jayden asked me

CHAPTER THIRTY-TWO: NEW TROUBLES

to be his girlfriend. I'm still wearing my clothes from yesterday, an orange and yellow striped sweater with black jeans. Reaching towards my back pocket for my phone, I touch nothing before realizing I must've dropped it between the couch cushions.

Sneaking back towards the couch, I lift Js' left foot where I was sitting and reach between the cushions. Nothing. I move in Shilohs' direction, fiddling under his body, this time actually grabbing my phone. I pull it out from under him, his body shifting a bit before getting more comfortable.

6:15 AM
12 Messages from Emery
2 Missed Calls from Jayden

I slide across on a call from Jayden, my phone immediately dialing him. I watch the screen as we're on face-time. "Hey," He says, his voice groggy, causing my internal self to freak out. "Hey, babe," I reply before closing my door. Sitting on my bed, I put the call on speaker and then reach for my laptop from underneath the bed. Opening it, I load up Google, type in the Berkeley link, and press enter, automatically loading me into the website. "So, what was your institution choice?" I say, pressing the housing option on the website banner. Berkeley housing pops up, and I click that once again before all dormitory options show on display, Residence housing is the first option. Sadly, freshmen have to live on campus first year, so I have to wait a bit before moving into the apartment mom and dad rented out. "I got accepted into Berkeley," Jayden smiles, waiting on my reaction. "Oh my god, we'll be going to Berkeley together! Yes! I can't wait, literally, I wonder if we can request to be roommates, but then again I feel like that's a bad idea," I ramble, seeing Jayden laughing on the screen.

"Hey, we can try," He responds, the screen going on pause.

I nod as I continue to scroll through the website. "I can't believe it. Just like that, all 4 years in high school are up," I sigh, snapping my fingers. He chuckles behind the phone. "You should've gone to the tour when my mom and I did, god it was amazing!" Jayden continues to 'mhm' as I continue speaking. It doesn't bother me, I tend to ramble on about anything. Especially when I'm excited. "Well, then," he pauses, his face popping back on my screen. "I guess we'll find out who our roommates are in June," He says, gliding his hand across his head. "I gotta get ready to go meet my friends," I say, checking the time. "Hey, have fun. Get your little makeover for the formal," He twinkles. "Let me pick your polish color when you get there. Send a picture of the options." He smiles before laying down onto his bed. I giggle lightly, my finger hovering over the hang-up button. "Okay, I will. Love you." I respond. "Love you, too."

Thirty-Three

CHAPTER THIRTY-THREE: MANY MANI'S

I watch the silver car pull into the driveway as I tug on the ribbon tied around my hair.

My curls bounce as it slowly crawls up my head and into the center of my scalp. Slipping my feet into my shoes, I bend down to tie the laces as I stand in the doorway. I hear knocks on the door before the sound of the door unlocking and the hinges creaking. Mom's voice floods the hallway, the echo bouncing upstairs. "Tiffany!" "I know, I'm coming!" I call, grabbing the backpack that rests in the center of my bed. Since I'm staying the night over at the twins' place, my bag is full of clothes, my hygiene needed things, and my bonnet. My dress for tonight is at their house. Pulling the straps across my shoulder, I walk downstairs. "Have fun at the dance, Tiffany. Emery, don't forget to tell your mom I said to take a picture of you girls and send it to me." "I will, bye Mrs. M," Emery replies before waving as she jogs down the walkway and back towards her car. I follow behind her, getting excited as I look through the window and see Jayla and Zoey in the backseat.

I open the door as I climb in, sitting between J and Z. Avery sits in the passengers' seat in the front, and Emery climbs into the driver's seat, putting the gearshift in 'drive'. I toss my bag into the trunk. Pulling back, we drive down the street near the intersection. "Let me pick the music this time, you chose it last time, Av," Emery requests as we merge into the right lane. If an argument doesn't start right now, I'm genuinely going to be surprised. I see Av close her eyes as if calming herself down, before reluctantly disconnecting her phone from the Bluetooth. We stop at a red light, allowing Emery to quickly connect her phone to the car, turning on the album *good kid, m.A.A.d city* by Kendrick Lamar. She turns the volume up to 54 as she bops her head along, rapping the lyrics with Kendrick. "Where to first? Nail salon?" Avery says over the music.

"Yea, I need a new set, anyway. Is this a cute design?" Jayla says, leaning forward as she hands Av her phone. Avery nods her head with a quick 'yea' and 'this is cute!'. She hands the phone back to her. Jayla turns the screen to me and Zoey as we look at it as well, agreeing with Avery. Emery sings along with the song, "handing" an imaginary microphone to Avery. She gives her a grimacing eye look. Pushing Em's fist away from her face, she continues to speak. "Okay, so there's a nail bar right off Cordova that N'yla recommended we go to." The GPS beeps as Emery almost makes a wrong turn. "Don't miss our turn because of your stupid music," Av mutters, pointing at her face. "Get that thing out of my face, trust me for once, A," Emery snarks. I look beside me to find Zoey sucked into an ebook. "Mrs. D said she misses you," I say, striking conversation. Zoey used to work at Yours Truly for a while, but when she moved she'd said it was about 2 hours away from her new place. She looks up. "I do, too. But I live too far from that place now. I'm not finna drive one hour to work at 8 in the morning, drive back to school at 12, and drive there again at 4. Yea, no."

We pull into the parking lot, the engine turning off but the music still on. "Turn it off." Emery ignores Avery's comment and continues to rap along.

CHAPTER THIRTY-THREE: MANY MANIS

Emery's hands wave everywhere as she continues to sing. We all get out of the car, leaving Emery to sing the song by herself. I hold onto my shoulders as I shiver lightly. Zoey's still sucked into her phone, and Jayla mumbles a song by NBA Youngboy under her breath. Avery bangs onto the car window, knocking Emery out of her song trance. "Okay," She says, closing the door behind her. The headlights flash as the beeps signify its locking. "I'm ready."

We walk into the tall building, opening the metal doors as we step inside. Immediately, we're met with a draft of cold air. "Are you serious? Cold air inside of a building during winter?" Avery groans. "Chill out, I'm pretty sure each shop has its heating system," Emery says, pushing her shoulder. We walk down the corridor, looking at each door for the significance of the business taking place there. Finally, a tan-colored door with a pink dot and the Name 'Spoil Me Nail Bar' rings a bell in Av's mind. "This is it. N'yla said she gives this woman top 10," She says, knocking on the door before a young woman opens it. "Hello, My name is Takydra, and welcome to Spoil Me Nail Bar! I'm sure we're going to spoil you!" She cheers, welcoming us in. We step in, slipping out of the cold and into warmth. "I am so sorry about that chill in the hallway. We've told the landlords about it, and they refuse to turn the heat on," She adds. "It's alright. We got a recommendation from a recent customer?" Takydra leans in as if she could remember a person from the name. "N'yla Peters." "Yes! She's normal here. Every two weeks, a new set." She smiles as we all sit down. "Now, what are you all here for?"

"Acrylic."
   "Manicure."

We all give Zoey a look as the owner lightly chuckles before continuing to go down the line.

"Acrylic."

"Same here, Acryl."

"Acrylic."

We all reply on our terms, her finger pointing at each of us as a sense to speak. "Alright, so Acrylics will be $55, and your basic manicure is 25. Daisy, get these girls rung up at a station!" The owner says to a girl wandering behind her. "Hope you guys feel like princesses here!" She adds on before opening the door for someone else. We separate to our stations as the woman sits down in front of me. "Okay, my name is Daisy, and I'm going to be your nail tech for today. Is there any specific style you're going for?" She asks, placing my hands into a tray of warm water. I think for a moment. "Yes. I'd like this design," I pause, pushing my phone towards her with my elbow.

I had made the set my wallpaper, that way she didn't have to dry my hands off the moment I'd walked in. The nails on my screen are a basic peach-tan mix, with different totals of diamonds on each nail. Jayden loved it and said it matched my dress. "Okay, I'll have this done in about 45 minutes."

Thirty-Four

CHAPTER THIRTY-FOUR: PLANS

My hand is cramped by the time the tech is done with my nails. They're about a quarter to an inch long, so to pop my fingers, I have to point them outward. "Oh my god, I love it!" I cheer, holding my hands up to the light as if I'm inspecting it. They look just like the photo. "Thank you, glad you love it," Daisy laughs, rinsing off the bead brush in a bucket of freshwater. I stand up, stretching from had looking downward at my phone uncomfortably. I look at the other tables where Em, Av, J, and Z sit. They're not done yet, but seem to almost be. I walk over and sit beside Emery. "That's a cute shade," I point. They're white near the base cuticle and silver glitter aligns the tip of the nails. Every other nail has a diamond pattern placed precisely. The nail tech tucks Em's nail under the UV light as she mutters that she was done, but Emery needed to sit under the light for 15. I grab my phone and take a picture of my nails before sending it to Jayden.

ME| [Image Attachment]

JAYDEN| **Ha! Look at that! Does it match your dress as I'd thought?**

ME| **yup!**

JAYDEN| **Can't wait to see you tonight, babe. I bet you'll look amazing.**

ME| awww, shucks, your so sweet. can't wait to see YOU in your tux tonight.

Aiden told me you guys had spent less than us?

JAYDEN| Hey, you guys didn't have a budget due to Avery and Emerys' splurging.

ME| your right

JAYDEN| Anyway, we can text a bit later? What time do you want me to pick you up?

ME| Maybe around 8?

JAYDEN| Okay. I love you.

ME| i love you too.

I shove my phone back into my back pocket. "Jayden like the outcome?" Avery says, waving her hands in the air. "I like it, it's cute and it suits you!"

"Yea, he did. I said it matched my dress perfectly."

"That's because tan goes with anything," Jayla interrupts, her nails also done. Avery's design was a dark blue with gold embellishments, and Jayla's was white as well, kind of similar to Emerys'. They must've both picked from the portfolio.

"Okay," Takydra says, holding the card scanner in her hand as she walks over to us. "Who's paying?" Avery raises her hand, her hard within her palm. She swipes the card, the total popping up with $246 and some change, including tax. Zoey then walks over, her nails painted a basic black. "Black is what you decided to go with?" Emery groans. "Whatever. I'll choose something more sufficient towards Prom season, but until then, I'm sticking with this." Avery tucks the card back into her wallet, and we all wave as we walk out the doorway. "You just earned new customers," The twins says in sync. "Thank you! So glad I did! When will I see you two again?"

"Probably next week, our cousin, Kiesha's getting married, so," Avery notes. "Alright, see you two then. Bye, girls!"

CHAPTER THIRTY-FOUR: PLANS

JAYDEN

Aiden places the suit down onto my bed as he sits beside it, gently brushing the collar as if something were there. "Imma be fresh up in there."

"Yea, with no girl," Jeremiah says as his face is still glued to the TV screen, Call of Duty Modern Warfare displayed. The controller clicks as the thumbsticks click along the rims. He yells at the screen as a person on the opposite team shoots him consistently, causing him to die. "Shut up, Jere," Aiden defenses, and Jeremiah turns around, a defiant look on his face as he places his hands in the air, signaling 'Surrender'.

"So, the girls are out doing some makeover thing before the dance," Aiden declares, finally getting his hands off of his tux. "What are we gonna do?" Jere and I both look at each other before we shrug. "I already got my hair cut just yesterday," I respond, grabbing my suit out of the closet.

The dust-bag crinkles as I move around to place it on the bed, slowly unzipping it as I carefully pull it out. I think before I finally get a thought. "You guys get corsages?" Aiden looks at me with a *'Are you serious?'* look, and I turn at Jeremiah, finding him trying his hardest not to laugh. "Why would you even ask me that?" Aiden stutters. "I don't know, I guess I'd forgotten?" I reply. It's not necessarily a lie, either. I did forget. For like thirty seconds, and then the moment that sentence left my mouth, I remembered. "Oh well, yea, I did," Jeremiah replies, changing the input on my TV to the Fire Stick. I toss him the remote before heading toward my desk and opening the top drawer. A red velvet box lies in the middle. I open it, a red rose pin and corsage sit right in the middle. I grab it out, checking to be sure it wasn't damaged. Aiden breathes over my shoulder.

"Dang," He mumbles, reaching to touch a petal, but I move his hand away before he can. "Don't even bother. I've seen how you handle things, and I'm not letting this become one of your relationships." Jeremiah stifles a laugh as Aiden gives me that look from not long ago. "Wow," Jere mumbles, a laugh hiding the rest of his sentence. "That was-"

"Harsh." Aiden finishes his sentence, sitting on the edge of my bed. "It was funny, though," Aiden continues, and I'm surprised he even continued to speak to me. "Okay, since you like to bring up the fact you're single so much," Jere pauses, pressing play on my Netflix 'Play Something for Me'. "You sure you're gonna be good tonight?"

"Yea, why wouldn't I?"

Jeremiah and I both glance at each other.

"Okay, I can see why. But I'm good, I swear."

"Okay, Aiden. Don't come to us during the last dance just because you have no one to dance with."

"He will, he'll be with Mrs. Morgan again." Jeremiah begins slow dancing with the air as we burst out laughing, Aiden staring at us with a content look, and it slowly turns into a grimacing grin. "I won't."

CHAPTER THIRTY-FIVE: I WANNA BE LOVED BY YOU

TIFFANY

I look in the mirror as I feel Emery zip the back of my dress. She backs away as if we were in a Barbie movie. If so, this would be the part I'd start shining, and my dress would magically get a glow-up. My hair is in a bun, similar to that one picture of Yara Shahidi. Right in the center, Avery places a glittery rose crown. Glitter falls from the crown, landing on my forehead and close to my hair. Hell, that'll take some time to get out. I turn around, everyone wearing their dresses. Jayla's wearing the light purple dress, her leg peeking out of the slit as she helps Zoey zip-up hers. Finally, they both turn around, clambering with "oohs" and "ahhs" as we all compliment each other on our looks.

We talk for a bit, thinking about how the night may go when the twins' mother calls us all down. The best part about this is that this isn't even prom. God, what will that be like? Will my dress be puffier? Will it feel even more magical? We all take turns gracefully walking down the marble stairway as Mrs. Wilkens claps for each of us. Right as I reach the middle stair, Jayden walks in, his face glowing with joy. "Oh my god," He mutters, grabbing my hand as I step off the last step. He twirls me around. "You look amazing." Butterflies form in my stomach, causing me to feel flustered and weak. "You look handsome," I reply, grasping his hand.

"Thank you," he responds as Aiden walks in and grabs Emery's hand, regardless of the lack of romance between the two, they seem to have fun with each other. Avery looks at her with a compensating look. "It's alright, I'm pretty sure I can find a guy tonight." Emery smiles as the rest of the group follows behind us. Our heels click on the ground as it echoes against the walls. "I love you, Emery and Avery. You girls have fun tonight," Their mom says, and Mr. Wilkens walks from the kitchen, standing behind their mom.

"Get some pictures for us," he smiles. Mrs. Wilkens does an expression before scrambling into her room and power walking back. A camera is in her hand. Stand in front of the door and smile," She says, and we pose. The light flashes as the picture is taken, and we disperse from the small group. "Now for real, go have fun tonight."

We walk down the porch stairs, talking as we then go down the walkway, stopping at a white stretched limousine. I feel my eyes widen, and Jayden nods. "My God," I gasp. Jayden opens the door on our side, allowing Zoey, Jayla, Avery, and me to get in before him. On the inside, there's a minibar alongside the walls, and the place is padded with seats. We slide across, sitting side by side and in front of each other, depending on where you sat. Jayden sits beside me before closing the door and holding my hand. He tucks it underneath my thigh. "The driver already knows where we're headed," Aiden says, getting comfortable in his seat. I look in front of me where Jayla sits and see her on her phone, giggling at the screen as she puts the tip of her nail in her mouth. Emery nudges her lightly, alerting her attention. "My bad," She mumbles, a large smile continuing to take place

CHAPTER THIRTY-FIVE: I WANNA BE LOVED BY YOU

on her face.

Avery reaches over and presses the overhead sunroof button, and it slowly opens as the wind blows through. We take pictures, and Zoey's being her usual crazy self as she stands upon the seats and stands in the sunroof, yelling random things.

"WINTER FORMAL 2021!"

* * *

We pull into the school's parking lot, everyone in the lot is either walking toward the building, taking pictures, or getting drunk in their car. Getting out, I fix my dress before grabbing Jaydens' hand. My clutch is in my grasp as I open it to grab my ticket. "Make sure you have it, Emery," I snark jokingly. She reaches into her jacket pocket before waving the small purple slip in the air. Emery tends to lose things. A lot. So when it came to the ticket, I made sure the girl had it stored in her case, easy for her to grab a hold of when we got here.

Getting inside, we walk through the corridor, where food is served. We're welcomed by the inside blanketed with curtains and string lights. There are selfie stations, food, bars with non-alcoholic drinks, a charging station, and a few other sections. Continuing to walk down the hall, we can hear the music from the gym where teachers are standing and talking, letting people in only have they have a ticket.

    Ms. Alici looks at are tickets as we're let in, greeted by groups of people dancing and laughing. "Oh my goodness, Avery! That dress is *literally* glowing!" A girl says as we pass her. Avery quickly thanks her before wandering off along her side. My hand stays within reach of Jaydens' as we walk towards the center of the floor, letting go as we separately dance together. *White Christmas* by Bing Crosby plays on the speaker, and snowflake holograms display across the wood floor as everyone slows down. "Seems like it's the first dance," Jayden mumbles, grabbing my hand. Pulling me close, we begin doing a slow dance, his hand placed on my waist and my hands tucked around him.

I lay my head on his shoulder, not saying anything. I feel like I could sit like this for hours. Not be tired, hold him for hours.

Within moments, the music speeds back up, *Winter Wonderland* echoing in the gym as Avery's movements get within my vision. I see her talking to a guy, waving her arms around as they argue in what seems like a playful way. "Can you get me some punch?" I request Jayden, and he gives me a thumbs-up before wandering off into the crowd.

"Hey," I smile. Avery and the guy both pause as they look at me, confused. The guy has an Almond tone, and a light fade cut, similar to Aidens. "Right, hey. Tiffany, this is Justice. Justice, this is Tiffany," Avery greets as he reaches over to give me a handshake. His hands are warm as the clutch mine. He smiles as he lets go of my hand, shoving it back into his pocket. "I literally just met him, and he seems pretty chill," Av continues to speak, placing her hands on her hips as she gives him a look.

A look I know too well.

Thirty-Six

CHAPTER THIRTY-SIX: WE ARE INFINITE

Jayden comes up from behind me, poking my collarbone as I turn around and grab my cup out of his hand. "Hey, who's this, Avery?"

"Justice," She smirks, breaking her eye trance off of him. I poke her shoulder before grabbing her forearm and dragging her with me.

I pull her aside, almost knocking over a girl who wobbles in her heels. "My bad," I chuckle, and she gives me a hating look before she wanders off with her friends. "I saw the way you looked at him."

"What? Who? Me?" I look at her with the "Duh" kind of look. "I swear, I don't like him! I just freaking met dude, how could I like him within literally two hours?" I look at her the same way again and she groans. "Okay, whatever. 'Don't listen to Avery, she sluts off with anyone and everyone', I see how it is, Tiff," She air-quotes as she lifts the lower part of the dress as she begins to walk off, laughing the conversation off.

"Av!"

"Don't like him, oh my god!"

I shuffle back over to Jayden as I see Avery still talking with Justice.

"What was that about?"

"I think Avery finally has a crush."

"On who?"

I nudge my head in their direction, and he nods in confirmation before a smirk aligns his face. "We'll see. I'll be right back, let me go find Aiden and Emery." I nod as I watch him leave in the distance.

The microphone screeches, leaving everyone's ears in piercing pain. Within seconds, the calming voice of our Principal, Ms. Davis, waves over the speaker. The sound of chatter dulls down. "Hello, Jaguars. Welcome to the 2021 Winter Formal!" Everyone claps loudly, the group coming towards me along the way. "I'm really glad to see all of these faces. Really. Look around." I glance around, seeing Justice and Avery flirting with each other, Aiden and Emery arguing, Jayla taking a picture with Zoey, and Jayden continuing to look up at the stage. "These are your friends. Your classmates. Quite literally! Think about it. This whole room is filled with Seniors. Class of 2022." The room gets silent, light stifles of laughter here and there. Looking around a second time, I see everyone's attention actually on the stage. "This isn't your last dance. Prom will. And then graduation. Half of this speech will be saved for your big day. Your cap throw day." Everyone claps once again before she signals for it to get silent. "Have fun. Just know, I'm proud of you. All of you."

She walks off the stage, and everyone continues to do what they were doing before, the room roaring with sound. I check my phone, the time read 10:56. "Hey," I say, getting the group's attention. "It's almost time to head out, let's get a picture, huh?" I suggest as they all 'humph' in agreement. A blonde girl offers to hold the phone and take the photo, and we all gather together in our poses. "Say Christmas Formal!"

"Christmas Formal!"

CHAPTER THIRTY-SIX: WE ARE INFINITE

The corridor is full of kids scrambling to their cars. People are smiling, laughing, playing, joking. "Okay, so we have 2 more hours with the limo," Jeremiah mumbles, shoving his wallet into his pocket. "Are we down to ride around town until we have just 10 minutes?"

"Yes!"

"God, yea!"

"Mhm!"

We all agree before getting into the limo and telling the driver we had no exact location for that time. Just riding around. "Oh! I remember I read *The Perks of Being a Wallflower*! Charlie and his friends stuck their bodies out of the sunroof when they went through the tunnel!" Zoey exclaims. Not gonna lie, pretty cool idea, and a nice way to end the night. The driver agrees, and we're on our way to the closest tunnel. Lights are illuminated, allowing us to see. The sunroof is large enough to hold at least 5 of us as we stand, so that's what we do.

Just Me, Avery, Emery, Jayla, and Zoey.

* * *

Sadly, the night comes to an end as the limo stops in front of the twins' house. Aiden and Jeremiah had already been dropped off at their apartments, and we were the last to be dropped off. I'm the last one to get out when someone grabs my elbow, keeping me from walking away. I turn my head to see Jayden, my body relaxing. "I loved the night," he pauses, and I see his eyes glance toward my lips. "I did, too. Can't wait for the Lock-In next week, huh?" He nods lightly. Closing my eyes, I lean in as I feel his warm lips touching mine. His clutch is released from my arm, and his left-hand pulls me close around my waist. It feels like a dream.

I fall back from the kiss, giving him a look before I quickly walk towards the porch, Emery standing at the door for me. "Bye, Tiffany," He requests, sitting back inside the limo. "Bye," I respond, and he closes the door behind him before him and the driver head off.

I sit on the edge of Avery's bed to sigh out of relief when I take my heels off. "My feet have never felt so good!" Avery says, her feet inside of a foot-bath. I chuckle at the sight as I toss the heels separately towards my bag, they bang against the wall before they fall.

Laying back, I feel the tight fabric of the dress against my legs, preventing me from being able to rest my legs on the mattress. Emery and Zoey are in her room, and Jayla is in Avery's room with me. "You wanna get in your pajamas first?" I ask, sitting up propped onto my elbows. "No, you go first," She responds, tossing a braid over her shoulder. The TV remote in her hands, she switches through apps, I guess trying to see which one is best. "Alright," I sigh, standing up as I go towards my bag and shuffle through until I find my shorts and Tank top. I get a hold of it and walk through the doors and into the connected bathroom.

My feet become cold as I step onto the cool marble. The bathroom seems to stretch on forever, the corner tub on one side and the shower having its room. The counter top is a wood-marble combination, the actual counter top is marble, and the base of the counter is wood. The mirror is one large square vanity mirror, and the sink's a silver-gold tone mix.

I place the pile of clothes onto the counter top as I realize I want to take a shower. Leading back out the door, I signal I'm just grabbing some other things out of my bag, and Zoey stays put. "If Avery comes back and I'm not out yet, just tell her I'm in the shower." Zoey nods, her face glued onto the screen as she watches Never Have I Ever. I reach into my bag and grab a new bra and underwear before rushing back into the bathroom, closing and locking the door behind me.

I reach my hand into the shower to see if the water was warm enough for me before I get in. I grab a shower cap out of a glass jar on the counter top and put my hair in an afro puff before I slip on a bonnet and place the

CHAPTER THIRTY-SIX: WE ARE INFINITE

clear plastic cap onto my head. The water hits my head, making the sound of rain falling on an umbrella.

Turning the water off, I grab a towel off the rack and wrap it around my body before walking out, the glass door slowly shutting behind me.

I apply lotion before slipping my shorts on, and pull my tank over my head as I open the door. Jayla immediately stands up, her clothes already in her hands as she walks behind me and into the bathroom. The door lock clicks behind her.

I look in the bed to see Avery clicking away on her screen. I toss myself beside her, startling her lightly. "Geez, Tiff! You enjoy giving me a heart attack, don't ya?" She jokes, rolling her eyes. I look on the screen in front of her, her email quickly dinging before the notification from Clark Atlanta University slides across the screen before fading away. She freezes, and I can immediately feel her tense up. "Press it for me."

"No, you do it. It's your admission."

"Yea, but what if they say no?"

She doubts, sitting up. I sit up as well before grabbing her hand and intertwining it with mine. I clutch tightly as I tuck it between our feet. "You got in, I promise you did. I know you did." She breathes in roughly before leaning onto her elbows and pressing the email app. Pressing the email, she gasps as I read the first sentence.

Hello, Avery Lilliana Wilkens,

You have been accepted into Clark-Atlanta University.

Thirty-Seven

CHAPTER THIRTY-SEVEN: A PERFECT WORLD

"Oh my god, oh my god, oh my god!" Avery exclaims, quickly sitting up before she gets up out of her bed and walks out of her room. I hear knocking on a door from the hallway before the hinges creak, and I hear her voice. "I got into Clark."

"You what?!"

"I just got the acceptance email, and I swear, I freaking got in."

"Have you told mom and dad yet?"

"No, you and Tiffany are the first to know."

"Go tell them!"

I hear Emery and Avery rush down the stairs and I follow behind them, ecstatic to hear their parents' response. Excited, they both walk into the kitchen where both of their parents are, sipping wine. "I got in." Avery pauses, her foot bouncing up and down out of nervousness. Their dad places his glass onto the table before grabbing the remote and pausing the show. "What?"

CHAPTER THIRTY-SEVEN: A PERFECT WORLD

"I got into Clark. I just got the email and-"

Avery's voice stops as her mom quickly stands up to pull her in for a hug. "Oh my god, my baby. Go get your laptop and let me see it!" Avery rushes past me before I hear her feet harshly thump on the stairs.

Zoey slowly walks down from the other stairway, confused. "What just happened? I saw Av rush into her room and she's on her way down now." She walks over towards the fridge, freely grabbing a Capri Sun before closing the door shut. Avery then slides on the flooring, being sure not to drop her laptop as she places it down onto the counter, speedily typing in the password. Her parents lean into the screen, taking a few moments to intake the information. Within moments, her mom breaks down in sobs, shoving her face into Mr. Wilkens' chest. He rubs her back before they congratulate Av and we head upstairs, now awkward after witnessing their mother have a full on breakdown. I don't blame her, we leave so soon and the years went by so fast, it's just that it's very awkward, sitting there and watching your friends' parents cry.

The time on the large clock in the hallway says 2:15 AM. I step into Avery's room, the lights automatically dimmed down to a dark pink as the clock reaches 2. Avery follows behind me, plugging in the computer before she puts it onto her desk. I lay down on the air mattress that sits on the floor, staring blankly at the ceiling. I hear her laying down on the bed, excitedly making erratic movements. "Oh my god, I freaking got into Clark Atlanta, Tiff," She mumbles. "Has Em gotten her email yet?" I ask, and she eerily becomes silent. I already know the answer. The bedroom door creaks and a ray of light shines across the floor as I see Jayla sneak in.

"Hey, my bad about being out for so long. Em needed to update me on a few things," She mumbles, creeping towards the mattress and laying beside me.

"Anyway, I think we should get some shut-eye."

"Avery? Are you okay? Are you sick?" Zoey says, sarcastically gasping as she sits up and quickly rushes towards her. I continue to look at the ceiling, feeling myself drift away.

"What?"

"Avery, you just said we should get some *sleep*!"

Giggling follows. "What? I think we should. It was a long night, plus, I think the lock-in is later this week, and I *so* wanna help with the decorations tomorrow!"

***

Waking up in the twins' house is a bit different. The lights are automated, and their rooms are huge. Avery's extra, so she has this little chime speaking asking her to wake up.

I wake up to the lights turned on fully and sit up to see no one else in the room but me. Listening in a bit more, I realize I hear the sound of the shower running, and I quickly get up and reach for my phone to check the time. 9:57 AM. I rub my eyes before patting my head, checking to see if I had put my bonnet on. My hands grasp the silk fabric before I sigh out of relief and type the password into my phone. Multiple messages from Shiloh load on my screen, with a few from Jayden, Mom, and Mrs. Deliare mixed.

SHILOH| Jayden's coming over to play the game with me.

JAYDEN| Let me know when you wanna hang out a bit, okay?

MOMMY| What do you want for dinner tonight?

MRS.DELIARE| Hey, Tiffany! Is it alright if you came over and worked a few hours today?

CHAPTER THIRTY-SEVEN: A PERFECT WORLD

I'll add a bonus to your check. Thank you!

Quickly, I type up replies to all of them before I hear the shower turn off. I stand up shakily, leaning forward to reach out for Av's dresser. I dig in my bag, grabbing the outfit I'd packed for today. I look up at her closet door to see my dress hung neatly packed in the dust bag on the knob. For today, I'd packed a gray and white sweater with a white skirt, some black leggings, and asked Emery if I could borrow her UGGs until I get home since we wear the same shoe size. The bathroom door swings open, and Jayla exits wearing a black butterfly sweater and black jeans. She walks over to her duffel bag, where she pulls out a pair of Grey Air Jordans. "Where's everyone?" "Right, you're always the one to wake up after everyone else. Mrs. W made some breakfast about 15 minutes ago, it should be warm still if you decide to take a shower after." I shrug, clicking my phone off as I toss it aside. "I'll go ahead and get in. The food can be reheated." Tossing the bag over her shoulder, she walks out into the hallway.

I lock the door behind me, tossing the pile of clothes onto Av's counter as I wait for the water to heat up. Looking in the mirror, the mirror slowly fogs up, and I draw a smiley face against my reflection. A memory from when I was younger flashes back in my mind. We were in 7th Grade, and it was our first sleepover together. I was nervous, terrified I would embarrass myself in front of my best friends. I was, and still am, an easy person to entertain, so Emery thought of a stupid, yet calming idea to help me ease my anxiety. She'd turned on the shower and we spend literally an hour just drawing on the mirror. I remember her parents' reaction to the fingerprints all over her mirror. She'd earned herself a grounding that night.

Walking downstairs, I head into the kitchen to everyone still sitting at the table. Zoey gets up and walks toward the counter to get seconds. Grabbing the tongs as she places the last 2 waffles onto her plate. I click my tongue, and she looks up at me almost immediately. "My bad," She chuckles, putting one of them back. "I got a little excited there." "A little?" I respond, hearing Avery's giggle. I grab a plate out of the cupboard before putting it down on the counter top, get the waffle and place it on, and then get a separate serving of the eggs resting inside of the pan. I walk over to the table and sit in the available chair by Av. She laughs once again at the screen. Cutting a piece of the waffle off with my fork, I dip it into the maple syrup tray that sits in a bowl beside me. Moving it towards my mouth, I chew lightly whilst intensely staring at Avery. She finally looks up to take a sip of orange juice from her glass. "What?"

"Who are you talking to?"
"No one."
"What're you laughing at?"

She takes a moment to respond, and I see her fingers flying across the screen.

"Justice, I gave him my number last night."

I lick my lips, the sweet taste of the syrup overcoming my mouth as I walk to the sink and place my plate inside. "Oh?" Walking back over to the table, I look over her shoulder and at the screen.

> JUSTICE| wyd?
> AVERY| just finished breakfast, wyd??
> JUSTICE| omw to uofm. my mom wants me to apply there, so im down to check it out.
> AVERY| cool! well, I have news...

"Jeez! Nosy much?" Avery shrieks, holding the phone up to her chest. I hold my hands up in a surrender pose as I see Jayla stand up from the couch. She shoves her phone into her pocket. "Well, I'm out. Kaia is outside waiting for me, so I'll see you guys later," She says, waltzing over to the front door. It opens, then closes, leaving a loud echo that bounces throughout the hall.

CHAPTER THIRTY-SEVEN: A PERFECT WORLD

"I gotta head out soon, Jayden and I are working extra hours at the shop today," I add, grabbing my phone out of the front pocket of the bag. I walk to the couch and toss myself over, landing on the cushions. "Okay," Emery mumbles before I hear the clinking of the plates. "I'm gonna go check if I got a response," Em mumbles as I see her rush upstairs. "I think your application affected her."

"Yea, I could see why. University of Memphis is all she's talked about the last month since she'd applied."

"Mhm," I mumble in response. An email from Berkeley sits on my screen, letting me know information about my dorm. I'll know who my roommate is in June around the 15th, and the actual information-information will be emailed to me on January 8th. Avery sits beside me, leaning against my shoulder with a wide grin plastered onto her face. "You're smiling mighty hard, Av." "I am? I mean, I don't know why I would, but I am?" I nod in response and she covers her mouth instantly. "God am I glad I'm not white." I chuckle at her thoughts as I open up messages.

ME| hey, what time do you think you might get here?

Jayden responds almost immediately.

JAYDEN| Right around the corner. :)

Standing up, I swing my bag onto my shoulder as Avery stands beside me and walks to the door with me. Looking out the window, I see Jayden's car pull up. "Let me know what response Em gets, okay?" I say, hugging her. She nods, face still down at her phone. "And let me know if you get a date with him," I add on, teasing her as she punches my shoulder. "I will."

Thirty-Eight

CHAPTER THIRTY-EIGHT: TRUTH IS...

EMERY

I rush to my computer, opening my email for the thousandth time. Nothing. Not one response, only from Sims patreons. Clicking the 'X' to close the tab, I push away from my desk and head to the hallway, and walk down the stairs. Avery leans against the door, a grin still on her face. "You told him?" I ask, standing beside her. "Yup, he said he got his yesterday." I bite the inside of my cheek. *How did everyone get theirs before me? I'm the one that reminded them.*

I'm the one that sent it first.

Why did Avery get hers before me?

She couldn't even decide between taking the scholarship from Emory or applying Clark-Atlanta, so why'd she get hers first?

CHAPTER THIRTY-EIGHT: TRUTH IS...

TIFFANY

We pull into the parking lot and see Mrs. D's car in her usual spot before we get out. The doors click behind us as we grab each other's hands. Jay opens the door for me, and I walk inside, Christmas music still playing overhead, and the book Christmas tree still sitting in the corner. "Hey!" Mrs. Deliare says, walking from behind the counter towards us. Books rest in her hands, and Jayden and I's hands separate as she hands them to us. "Shelve these and then I want you two to work on getting the lights off the book tree," She says, walking towards the backroom. "When you guys finish that, let me know."

I walk to my aisle, and Jayden walks to his. Moving books aside to make room, I manage to shove the one in my hand onto the shelf. Feeling something in the way of one book, I reach my hand back there to feel someone else. "Jayden?"

"Tiffany?" We laugh, and I put the last book onto the shelf. Turning the corner, I'm face to face with Jay, a smile on his face as he reaches out the grab my hand. I grasp onto him, standing there as I try to give him light hints. My eyes revert from his eyes to his lips, back and forth, back and forth. He licks his lips, snapping me out of my trance. "You want to kiss me, huh?" He snickers. I nibble on my lip, lightly laughing at the playful sentence. "Yea."

EMERY

My phone dings and I leap to grab it, nothing but an H&M notification sits on my screen. I sigh roughly, Mom's attention worriedly on me. "You alright?"

"Yea," I mumble, looking back at the TV. She looks back to it as well, a light 'humph' mumbled under her breath. Another ding, and another notification from a useless app. Another one, and another one. God's testing me today. One more ding and I break down. "Okay! I get it, I'm not getting in!" I yell, my voice breaking. Mom's arms collide with my body, instantly comforting me. "You alright? What's going on?"

I don't respond. I can't respond. I can't breathe, I just *can't*. She rubs my shoulder in consolation, my face still embedded in my hands.

"Is it about Avery?" I nod.

"And her application?" I nod once again, and I feel her head fall onto my shoulder. "Hey, it's okay. Do you know how many applications UofM gets?" I shake my head no. "Up to 10,000. They said it's <u>double</u> that amount this year, Em." Sitting up, I wipe my face.

"You got in, I can feel it. Matter a fact," Mom pauses, grabbing her phone. I watch as she pulls up a website, every so often a light tantrum from it not cooperating. The University of Memphis website sits on her screen, a yellow banner displayed across the top.

<u>**NOTICE: We will be sending out letters this year. All families should receive letters from December 24-January 18. Thank You!**</u>

TIFFANY

Our lips collide as my hand falls out of his grip and crawl their way to his neck. He chuckles lightly ending the kiss. Someone clears their throat. "Ahem." I look up to see Jazlen standing there, her face attempting to look unamused. "Mrs. D wants you to get the lights off the tree?" Her face gives it away as she tries hard to look serious about her sentence. "Right," I stutter, awkwardly smiling as I look back and forth between her and Jay. He follows behind me before Jaz stops him. "Mhm, no. She said you need to get the new years stuff." She grabs the keys out of her pocket before placing them into his hand. "It's in the basement, right beside Valentine's

CHAPTER THIRTY-EIGHT: TRUTH IS...

day box," She smiles, Jayden turning around and heading towards the door. "Bye."

Stepping onto the stool, I unwind the light from the star at the top of the tree. "You guys are dating now?" I nod. "You never told me! I mean, I saw some chemistry, but I didn't know you guys were like, dating!" I get down, the ball of lights tangled in my hand. "You still write in that book?" I shake my head no. "So he was the guy?" I shake my head yes this time. "God, this is so cheesy. Something right out of a romance novel, ya' know?" She laughs, continuing to speedily speak. "Yup," I impatiently reply. "You should write in that book again, though. That would be one hell of a way to remember that day." I nod, actually picking up on the idea. "Yea, that's a good idea, actually," I say, going behind the counter, putting the lights in an empty box. Jayden comes from the basement, a huge container in his hand. Placing it onto the counter, he opens it, multiple random things popping out. I place the lights in the box behind the counter, quickly kicking it back in place with my foot.

"So, Jazlen had an idea," I state, grabbing a New Years' foldable. Jayden shuffles through more things before stopping to revert his attention to me. "What is it?"

"Well, she said that it'd be a good idea if we started writing in the book again."

"Write in the book again?"

I nod in confirmation. He shifts positions, his left hand now leaning against the counter. "Well, it's not a bad idea. I liked that." I chuckle lightly, feeling like Avery and her comment from earlier. *"I'm glad I'm not white."*

"You down?" I say, placing my finger on the top of his hand. His hand grabs it.

"Yea, I'm down."

Thirty-Nine

CHAPTER THIRTY-NINE: LOCK-IN

My bag's packed for the lock-in, and the fact that I'd just had a sleepover at Em and Av's house last week is beyond me.

I hear a truck beep and I look out the window before jogging downstairs. Mom's sitting on the couch, Shiloh's playing the game also on the couch, and Dad's on some call arguing with one of his friends. "Come on, man. I told you to get a suite. Ain't nobody finna stand out there!" I laugh at the sight of that as I quickly open the fridge and grab any snacks I can, shoving them into my bag. "Hey, don't get all that stuff! I just went grocery shopping, and I'm not feeding your little friends. Grab a bag of chips, candy, soda, and leave," Mom calls over the couch. I sigh before putting everything back inside. I grab a Coke from the bin before closing the fridge, eventually leading to the pantry and grabbing Skittles and a medium-sized bag of Takis. The Ring doorbell goes off, and I speed to the door, dragging my bag behind me.

I open the door to be greeted by Emery dragging me down the porch steps. "Calm down, we'll get there before they lock the doors. Give me a second," I say, getting her grip off me. I walk back up the steps, going to the door and locking it behind me. I grab my phone out of my pocket, quickly sending a text to mom.

CHAPTER THIRTY-NINE: LOCK-IN

ME| just left. check the ring, i said ily guys!!

Jogging to the car, I climb in the backseat and sit next to Avery. She types away at the screen, and I see Justices' name in the contact bar. It's been a week since she'd met Justice, and they've been <u>hitting</u> it off. Avery gasps dramatically, her knees bouncing up and down as she puts her phone face down in her lap and turns to me. "He just asked me out. Well, on a date. But it's this Saturday!" She exclaims, holding onto my upper arm. I smile, giving her the same amount of excitement she'd given me. "God, what am I gonna wear? I mean, something warm, but something attractive at the same time, you know?" I roll my eyes, facing back forward as I get a hold of my phone. Zoey sits beside me, her head drowned in a book. "You're a bigger bookworm than me!"

"Nah, I just got my phone taken," She replies, laughing. "Tough," I sigh, opening up my messages.

ME| hi. you guys there yet?

JAYDEN| Yup, Aiden and I just pulled up. The lot is packed.

JAYDEN| New announcement, they lock up the place in about 15 minutes, where you guys at?

I read the last message, rushing Emery to drive quicker, but also within the speed limit. "I'm trying, dang-it!" She shrieks, pulling the corner roughly.

I grab my bag off the ground and feel my phone buzz in my hand. Two messages one from Mom, and one from Jayden.

MOM| Lol, tell the girls I said hi!

JAYDEN| Want us to stand in the front? Yk, that way it'd be easier to get a hold of you :)

I reply to Mom's message but ignore Jayden's since I see him standing right beside Aiden's car. "Jay!" I yell, closing the door behind me. He turns around, tapping on the car door to signal for Aiden to get out. "Hey, babe!"

He replies, leaning in to kiss me on the forehead. He drops his hand beside mine, requesting we hold hands, and I accept it. Avery, Emery, Jayla, and Zoey get out, their bags in hand as we walk to the school building.

"Five minutes left."

A voice announces through the speakers, causing everyone in the lot to walk inside along with us. Fortunately, there is no ticket into the Lock-In, but you do have to have your ID to be sure of being a student. I show the office woman mine, quickly tucking it away after she looked at it and gave a thumbs-up. "Please walk towards the gym, where all students are. You will receive a centerpiece chalkboard stand where you write your name and put it near the area you will be. Thank you!"

Walking towards the corner, we find ourselves claiming a spot where we're by the concessions, but a decent distance. "Okay, who has better handwriting?" Zoey says, holding the chalkboard in the air, along with a piece of chalk in her other hand. Jayla and Avery speak in unison, annoyed once the two of them realize one another were requesting.

"Are you serious? You always get to write the things, let me do it for once!" Avery yells as people turn towards us now.

"Yea, no. Your handwriting is literally so difficult to read!"

Arguing for about five minutes, it goes back and forth before I decide on a deal-breaker. "I'm thinking of a number 1 through 17."

They both sigh harshly as I point to Av, her guess going first.

"9."

"7."

"Avery's closer," I state in response, grabbing the chalk from Jayla's hand.

CHAPTER THIRTY-NINE: LOCK-IN

Avery teases, sticking her tongue out before writing.

<u>Jayla Parkson</u>
   <u>Avery Wilkens</u>
   <u>Emery Wilkens</u>
   <u>Tiffany Mohan</u>
   <u>Jayden Hudsen</u>
   <u>Aiden Turner</u>

* * *

A few hours in, and it's boring as hell. It just got dark out, and a few people had already gone to sleep.

"See, I only came because I thought it would be fun since it is senior lock-in. I heard so many good things about it since freshman year," Aiden mumbles as he leans back and lays his head on Emery's lap. She begins to rub his scalp, his eyes opening and closing in an attempt to stay awake.

"Maybe there's a party afterward?" Em unsurely states. Jayden shrugs. "Maybe, but we'd be invited if so," Zoey grumbles lightly as I reach into my bag, thinking about whether or not to change into my pajamas. The thought process leads to yes, and I get up, telling everybody where I'm headed to walk to a teacher, also letting them know.

After changing, I sit back down onto the pile of blankets, tossing my clothes into my bag. Half the group headed to sleep within the few minutes I'd changed, leaving Jayla, Avery, and Me the only ones awake. I grab my phone, checking the battery before I open the app Netflix. 35%, enough to till I get tired. I reach in my bag for my Airpods, quickly connecting them as I press play, the show *All American* slowly loading onto my screen. Feeling someone tap my shoulder, I pause and turn around to face Avery.

"They're finna shut the lights off, and Jayla decided to go ahead and head to sleep," she says, yawning as she ties the ribbons of her bonnet. "Alright," I respond, turning back towards my phone.

She lays down beside me, her face turned towards me. "We graduate next year, T," She mumbles. "Yea," I respond, turning my phone off as it becomes pitch dark. I hear a few mumbles here and there. I can't see her, but I remember where she laid down. Suddenly, emotion rushes all over my mind, leaving me feeling scrambled.

I'm a freshman all over again in 9 months.

9 months.

Forty

CHAPTER FORTY: NEW YEAR, NEW ME

"The lock-in was hella boring," I say to mom, my mouth muffled as it's full of fruit. I take a quick sip of water before popping another strawberry in my mouth. "Ours had games, the ones you see at field day," Dad comments, walking towards the sink. I walk behind him and place my dishes inside, too. "Anyway, low key excited for Graduation!" I shriek, walking in the direction of the stairs. "They sent in a letter about your gown. I'm picking it up Tuesday," Mom calls behind me, and I hum in response before rushing upstairs.

EMERY

Mom shakes me awake as I feel a paper ruffle against my arm. "Emery," She says, repeating my name once again. "Emery." I toss her hand off my side in an attempt to get her to leave me alone. Realizing what she was doing wasn't working, she pulls the blankets off of me along with the layered sheet. "Okay," I groan, turning to my side as I look at her. Sticking the paper in my face, I see <u>her</u> face glowing with a smile when realization kicks in: UofM. Ripping the paper from her hands, I ravage through the seal, finding myself face-to-face with my acceptance letter; and a scholarship.

TIFFANY

Kanye West's *All of The Lights* blasts through my room as I bob my head along with the beat. Clicking away at my screen, I get a notification from the group chat, but with Jayla and Zoey as well.

EMERY| GUYS!!

The group blows up with responses.

ZOEY| WHATTTT
   JAYLA| what is it?
   AVERY| You could've come downstairs and told me instead of blowing in the gc yk

Emery sends the shrugging emoji before an immediate message is sent after.

EMERY| [Image Attachment]

An image shows her acceptance letter to UofM, along with another piece of paper sitting beside it. Reading it, I get excited with each word.

ME| OMG! you AND got a SCHOLARSHIP?!!
   EMERY| :)

Shiloh knocks on my door as I turn around, looking at him stare at me. Walking over to me, he sits on the edge of the bed before laying down alongside me. "What's going on?" He mumbles, reading the message. A

CHAPTER FORTY: NEW YEAR, NEW ME

smile slowly glows across his face. For what feels like the first time, Shi's genuinely showing interest in my life. "She got a scholarship?"

"Yup," I nod, turning my phone off. I tuck it under my pillow as I lay back. "I leave in a few months," I mumble, placing my hands on my chest. Shiloh sighs roughly. "You gonna be alright when I leave?" His lip tuts to the right as he turns his head, looking at me. "Yea, I'm getting your room," He responds, nudging my arm. I sit up, throwing a pillow at his stomach. Still lying down, he tosses it back, missing by an inch as it dashes by my head. "In all seriousness, though," He pauses. Getting off my bead, I grab the pillow off the ground, swinging it around in my grasp. He also gets up, walking back towards my doorway.

"I'm gonna miss you, T." And I watch as he opens the door and leaves, the lock clicking shut behind him.

* * *

Walking downstairs, I hear pots and pans clanging together before the cabinet door slams shut. I step into the kitchen, greeted by the scent of mom's cinnamon bun cake. Slowly walking toward mom, I look on the stove to see a pot full of oil, and a plate with fried fish placed beside it. "New year's dinner is finna be bomb, Tiff. Your grandma sent me her classic recipe for the fish you guys be tearin' up," Mom shrugs, the oil popping as she places a new piece of the fish inside. She puts the tongs onto a towel on the counter, walking to the fridge as she grabs bottles of champagne. Dad walks out of the living room as he opens the cabinet over the fridge, pulling 2 glasses and placing them on the counter. I give him a pleading look, hoping he'll be down to let me get a glass this year. "Tiffany," He pauses. "What?" I say, my voice whining on. "You know what I'm about to say." I cross my arms before leaning against the counter top. "21st Birthday."

"How about 19th?"

"20th," He points, walking to mom as he kisses her on the forehead from behind. "And that's it."

"Can you turn on the countdown, T?" Mom calls from the kitchen, the sound of clattering plates almost overcoming her voice. Grabbing the remote, I click off of Hulu and switch the input to live TV, finding the channel containing the countdown within just a few scrolls. A news reporter's face surrounds the screen, talking about the crowd and the excitement for the countdown.

"As you can see, the time says 11:56, leaving many people out excited and energetic for the countdown."

Mom hands me a plate over the couch before calling Dad and Shiloh down. Shi stumbles on a strawn shoe as he grabs a plate off the counter and sits on the ground, putting the dish onto the table. Dad's still in the kitchen, pouring the champagne into the glasses. "Babe! 1 Minute before countdown!" Mom calls, rushing dad. "I'm coming, hold up," He replies, frustratingly grabbing the glasses as he rushes into the living room.

"10, 9, 8, 7, 6, 5, 4!"

Memories of the year before pass through my mind, similar to how people say others feel before dying.

"3!"

Friends.

"2!"

Family.

"1!"

Home.

CHAPTER FORTY: NEW YEAR, NEW ME

"Happy New Year!"

We all call, cheering as the sounds from the TV blast throughout the room, making us feel as if we were there. Mom and Dad clink their glasses before taking a sip, and Shiloh dances to the music playing on the TV while blowing the sound maker in his mouth, different events and headlines from throughout the year are displayed on the screen. My eyes water, thinking about everything. It sounds cheesy, but it's true: *This is one of my very last months here. At home.*

* * *

JANUARY 2022; NEW YEAR

Tuesday, and we're back in school. Today's January 5, 2022, the official new year. This not only means it's a new year, but it means just 13 excruciating days until I get my dorm information.

I sign my name at the top of the page as I hand the slip to Mrs. Anderson. "How'd you think you did?" Emery murmurs as she turns around, facing me. She hands me a stick of gum, and I unwrap it before popping it into my mouth. "I'm a straight-A student, I'm positive I got an A," I pause, grabbing *Concrete Rose* by Angie Thomas out of my bag. "As per usual," I add, sitting up. Em clicks her tongue, turning back forward as I open the book to my page. The class intercom turns on as Mrs. A quickly responds.

"May you send Tiffany Mohan to the office, please?"

Emery kicks my desk from behind her, signaling her version of the all mighty classic "Oohing" sound. Packing my stuff, I swing my bag over my shoulder as I push Em's head forwards. "Study for the Exam tomorrow, T," Mrs. Anderson says as I walk out of the room and down the hall.

Now near the front of the school, I open the office door as cool air immediately blows through, leaving me freezing as I step up to the desk. "Oh, yes. Mr. Bates needs you in his office." *Mr. Bates? The principal? Why would he need me? I haven't done anything. Has someone sent a video of me doing something? Drinking? Smoking? That was one time!*
    I consciously smile before walking to the hall where his office is separated, heavily knocking on the door. "It's open," I hear a muffled voice say, and I open the door. "Tiffany?" I nod, putting my bag down on the ground. It leans before falling onto the floor as I sit down. "Yes, okay, great!" I bite the inside of my cheek. "I've called you down here to let you know of something very important towards your graduation day." He stands up, fixing the bottom of his suit.
    "You've been selected as Valedictorian of your class."

Forty-One

CHAPTER FORTY-ONE: ELECTORAL

※

"Me? Valedictorian?"

He nods his head yes as he walks over to a tall file cabinet sitting against the wall behind me. "It was a tough decision between you and Liela Brown, but we picked you." I look downward, sitting down as my mind tries to process what he told me. "Oh my god," I pause. "I'm valedictorian!" Mr. Bates hands me a file, holding all of my grades for previous years and the current year. My GPA stands at an exact 4.6. I rifle through the papers, watching my average go up and down much like a roller coaster, but eventually landing on 4.6. "And hopefully, you'll be able to keep that honor up to May," He adds, now sitting in his chair. I hear the keyboard typing away. "Liela is salutatorian, so she'll also have a speech, but just know you have valedictorian." His typing stops as I stand up, the bell ringing above to signal the class switch.

"I'm proud of you, Tiffany. I kept my eye on you throughout your whole journey here, and I'm so glad I did." He holds his hand out for a shake. I grasp his hand proudly.

"Keep it up, Mohan."

I walk out of the office, waving out to the front desk women and a few others who pass me on their way to class. Heading to the hall with my locker, I see Emery, Avery, and Jayla notice me. "Tiff!" Em calls, leaving the others as she rushes towards me. "What was that about? Did you get in trouble? You never get in trouble!"

"I know, and that's what I thought," I respond, putting in my locker combination. "But, no. I didn't get in trouble. I have news, but I can't just tell you alone." The locker door gets jammed for a moment before eventually opening with a rough pull. "Why not! I swear, I'm really good at pretending. You could tell me, and I'll act like I ain't know!" Emery pouts. I swap my bag and books for my previous class to my Spanish II journal. Shutting the door behind me, I quickly respond, "No, it needs to be genuine."

***

Avery and Jayla catch up to us through the crowded hallway as we walk. "Emery told us you got called to the office. What happened? Did someone snitch on you?" Jayla says, ready for any response. I chuckle lightly as I get to my class. "I'll tell you guys at lunch, that way Zoey's there, too."

"Forget her! We wanna know, T!" Avery whines, punching my shoulder. I rub over it to signify pain. "You can wait. See you guys in an hour," I smile, ending the conversation as I walk into the class. The desks that are usually there are replaced by four seated tables. Jayden sits in a spot, already writing the needed information to the bell work. "Hey," He mumbles, continuing to write. "Hey," I respond, sitting next to him. He pecks a kiss onto my cheek while I open my journal. I click my mechanical pencil, the lead slowly but surely coming out. Reading the board, I quickly write alongside him.

Write out your morning routine in Spanish. Please use complete sentences.

I write my list, listening as the classroom gradually gets louder as more

CHAPTER FORTY-ONE: ELECTORAL

students walk in. The seat in front of me becomes taken by Aiden, who kicks my shin slyly, and I kick him back. "Oops," I mutter, Jayden chuckling under his breath. "Whatever, Tiffany. What's up, Jay? Hey, do we still have practice today?" "No, coach said as much as we need to work hard, we need just one day for a break." I look at Jayden's notebook, each sentence neatly written out.

- *Hacer la cama.*
- *Cepillar los dientes.*
- *Elige ropa para el dia.*
- *Despierta a mi hermana.*
- *Ayudala con cualquier tarea sobrante.*
- *Haz el desayuno para mi y mi hermana.*
- *Paquete de bolsa.*
- *Subetee al auto llevanos a mi hermana y a mi hasta aqui.*

Jayden catches me looking and glides the sheet over to me, allowing me to read it more fully. "Aiden, you should get started on the work, man. Seriously, you are failing the class right now." "Okay, and no one had to know," Aiden responds, muttering under his breath as he slides low in his seat, typing away on his phone.

The rest of the room fills up, a girl with bright red-dyed hair and a gold nose ring sits beside Aiden. He flirts with her a bit, and she does the same, every so often clutching onto his shoulder, grasping ahold of it like those cringy Disney movies.

Everyone becomes silent as we hear the door close against the frame, Mrs. Hill sitting on the surface of her desk. "Welcome back! Today we're not doing much due to everyone coming back from break. Write the bell work down and when I see that everyone is done, I will pass out worksheets. The class should be done before you leave today."

***

Sitting my head up, I noticed I'd fallen asleep as I look around the room and see people talking. I check my watch, three minutes before the bell rings. Jayden chuckles as he looks at me from his phone, sneakily pecking a kiss onto my cheek. "You awake?" I roll my eyes as I stretch, packing the things that'd sit on my desk into my bag. Aiden and the girl continue to flirt, and I nudge Jayden's shoulder as he shrugs in response. "Lord knows how long they'd been flirting." I chuckle before getting another glance at my watch once again. One minute. Standing up, I toss my bag across my shoulder as Jayden tucks his phone into his pocket and slowly pulls his bag onto his back. The bell rings overhead, and everyone rushes to the door as I peek behind me, the girl covering her mouth with shock as she looks at her friends, Aiden standing up along with her.

She giggles as they shuffle out the door, standing in the hall waiting for her as she stands and says something.

"I'm gay."

Aiden's face turns to stone as she stifles a laugh behind her red face.

"So, my bad. I just like messing with straight guys." She prances through the door, her voice booming as she laughs with her friends walking down the hall. Jayden and I walk to him, tapping his shoulder as we falsely console him.

"I swear you had Emery."

"Yea, but she said she isn't looking for anyone right now."

I see Em walking towards us with Avery and Zoey beside her. "Hold up," I mumble, separating from them as I walk towards Em.

"I thought you said you liked Aiden?" I lean against the lockers as she enters her combination. "I do," She unsurely replies.

CHAPTER FORTY-ONE: ELECTORAL

"Okay? He said you rejected him."

"Yea, I did."

"Okay? Why did you?"

She shrugs before grabbing her Chemistry textbook. "He just got rejected by a girl he didn't even know was gay. He thought she was straight." Emery laughs hard, shocked at my comment. "Who? Ainslee? Bright red?" I nod.

"Yea, she came out last year. That's hilarious." She shuts the locker door as she stands up. She continues to walk down the hall with me. "Yea, my bad. I kinda didn't accept because I had no idea if it was a crush or not. You and Avery have been shipping us for as long as I can remember, and I never liked him until now."

We stop in front of her class. "Well, you know you like him now, so you better go and accept that offer," I respond, watching her walk into the class. She gives me a look of confusion as to why I wasn't walking behind her.

"Free period today," I say.

"Oh, alright. See you at lunch, then."

✶ ✶ ✶

I sit down and place my tray against the table, watching as Avery's face glows in anticipation as she speaks, "It's lunch, now."

"I know," I respond, taking a bite of the burger that was served. "So, what were you sent to the office for?"

"Av, everyone isn't even here, yet!" She groans impatiently before taking a sip from her white thermos. Zoey comes from the line, with Emery waltzing behind her before they take a seat. Avery pauses before she speaks, giving herself a moment to take a bite from her salad. "Okay, they're here now. So?" I laugh before I give her an answer. I wish I could wait for Jayden, but he has third lunch instead of first, with us. I cover my mouth as I chew, swallowing before I speak. "Okay, so the reason I was called up front was," I continue.

"I'm our class valedictorian."

Forty-Two

CHAPTER FORTY-TWO: BUBBLY

Walking through the door, I lock it behind me as I toss my keys into the bowl that sits on the table. The lights are off, no sound except what sounds like the TV in the living room. Slipping my shoes off, I walk into the living room and lean against the couch, the pillows toppling over and hitting mom in the head. "Tiffany quit it. You do too much sometimes," She mumbles, tossing them onto the ground. I jump over before responding. "My bad." I grab the remote and pause the show, the name of it hovering downward as it reads Insecure. She's on episode three, season two. "I have news, but I don't know if you want to hear it now or if you'd rather hear it at dinner," I shrug. She clicks her tongue before snatching the remote from my hands. "At dinner, that way it'll spare you and your daddy some time." She presses play on the remote, and stutter lightly before speaking in a full sentence. She sighs roughly before pressing pause once again. "Did you get my gown?"

"Yes! I forgot to text you, it's on your bed. I got it around 1 earlier today." I nod as I slowly walk out, her face expressing relief as she continues to watch her show, leaning back onto the cushions.

The box sits on my bed, and my cap sits right on the top. A note sits beside it.

They said you guys can paint the caps this year. I'll give you 250, I found a cool artist I know you're gonna like. Love, Mom.

Taking the cap off, I smile at the note as I toss it aside, removing the top to the box as a clean, black gown rests inside. My eyes water once again as I lift it, shaking it to allow the sleeves to part from the fold. I hear a knock on my door frame as I fold it back into the box, tossing it beside my nightstand. Shiloh walks toward me, handing me batteries.

"I took those out your remote."

"Oh. I had no idea, you just snitched on yourself."

"Oh well."

"Stay out of my room, Shi."

He turns around as he slowly walks backward. "You got 5 months left with me, I better make it the time of my life."

JAYDEN

Maddison hesitates as she smashes all her food together in one corner of her plate, quickly scooping it up with her fork. I give her a look as she takes a bite, slowly chewing it with despise before swallowing. Mom points towards her cup with her fork as it dings against the glass. "Why do I have to take a sip after <u>every</u> bite?"

"To be sure it washes down."

Maddie rolls her eyes as she takes a sip, standing up to put her plate in the sink. I stand up and walk behind her and do the same thing, leaving mom the only one at the table as she shuffles through her magazine. "Jay, I pick up your graduation gown tomorrow after work, watch Maddie, will you?"

CHAPTER FORTY-TWO: BUBBLY

She asks as I walk towards the hall. "Yea, I don't mind," I respond walking into my room. Shuffling through my drawer, I grab a pair of sweatpants and put those on before sliding on a hoodie. Walking into the hallway, I grab my keys off the counter and head towards the door, sliding my feet into my slides that sit on the shoe stand. "Where you headed?"

"Tiffany's."

"Alright, tell her I said hey," Mom pauses. I unlock the door and before I walk out, mom mumbles something. "She's a catch, Jay. Don't let her go, you'd be a fool if you did."

TIFFANY

The doorbell rings as I rush downstairs, already knowing it's Jayden since he'd texted me saying he was on his way. Opening the door, Jayden stands there with two bags, steam and the delicious scent of fried rice rising from them. "May I come in?" He mutters, and I let him in. "Ma, Daddy, Shiloh! Jayden's here with the food!" I call, grabbing a bag from his hand. We both put them onto the table, quickly getting the takeout containers out of the bag and putting them onto the counter. "Hey, Jayden!" Mom calls, leaning in for a hug. Dad pats his back politely as he walks towards the cabinet and grabs five plates. He puts the stack into the center of the counter island, grabbing his as he gets a spoon and begins serving himself.

"So what was it you had to tell me, Tiffany?" Mom says, putting soy sauce in her rice. Jayden grabs my hand under the table, clutching it tightly. "I'm Valedictorian," I smile, Mom and Dad's faces both becoming blank. Shi continues to take bites of his food. "Oh my god, praise him!" Mom cheers, getting up as she walks over to me and plants a kiss on the middle of my forehead. "Babe, that's awesome!" Jayden praises. "What's your GPA?" Dad mutters, taking a sip of his water.

"4.8. On. The. Dot," I exclaim, planting my fist onto the table in between words. "Congratulations, T! I'm proud of you," He exclaims, walking to the sink as he puts his dishes inside. Mom serves herself another spoonful of rice before placing a serving of noodles onto her plate.

"Jayden, how about you? Have your admissions been accepted?"

"Mom," I mumble, lightly kicking her foot as she gives me a look before she glances back at Jayden.

"It's alright, T. Yea, actually. I've been accepted into Berkeley along with Tiffany." Mom smiles to display happiness, and it's actually fairly genuine. "Jayden, that's awesome. You two won't be separated the next few years, now, huh?" Jayden chuckles under his breath.

"Unless they break up," Shiloh adds, causing us all to become silent. Mom gives him a look, and he rolls his eyes before heading to the counter. He comes back with an egg roll in hand. "So, do you know your roommates yet?" Mom continues to add on to the conversation from before.

"Not yet. We get the email in June," I respond. Mom quickly finishes her plate before walking back towards the sink and dropping it inside. "Thank you for dinner, Jayden. I really appreciate it." Jayden nods before helping himself one more serving of rice.

"No problem."

I finish my food not long after Mom had. "Shi, you got the dishes tonight," I remind Shiloh before he groans and heads over to the sink, slowly opening the dishwasher and unloading the few dishes inside. "I should head home," Jayden states, checking his phone. "Okay, well, stay safe! Don't forget to tell your mama I said hi," Mom yells over the couch, waving goodbye as he walks towards the door. He says a quick okay and his goodbyes when I follow behind him before speaking, "I'll walk you out."

The chill wind hits my body and goes through my pajama pants. Jayden and I both walk down the walkway and towards his car. Standing in front of the driver's door, he pauses for a moment, looking at my lips. He continues the conversation, continuously looking back and forth once again, trying his

CHAPTER FORTY-TWO: BUBBLY

hardest not to interrupt me. It gets silent between the two of us, nothing but the sound of passing cars. "Can I kiss you?" He groggily says. "Yea," I respond, licking my lips before he does so, causing him to smile before leaning in.

His hands trail along my sides, allowing me to move closer than we already were, our bodies colliding as he leans against me and I lean against his car. His lips still against mine, I chuckle and he chuckles too, allowing the kiss to end as quickly as it'd started. "I love you so much, Tiffany, you have no idea," Jayden mumbles. I don't say anything, my mind going blank of anything but one.

Maybe I do.

Forty-Three

CHAPTER FORTY-THREE: MY WORDS TO YOU

MAY 16, 2022

A few hours before graduation, and I never thought I'd be rushing as much as I am now.

"Shiloh! Hurry up!" Mom calls as she puts connects the clutches of her necklace. I shuffle around my desk, looking for my diamond earring before it catches within my glance. Looking in my mirror, I see Mom standing in the doorway stiffly. She's wearing a medium-length evening dress in a dark red shade, it tightly tucked against her body. She pairs the look with silver stilettos and a pearl bib necklace. "Hey, you go ahead and get there. Use your daddy's' car," she mumbles, patting her hand against the door. I nod before quickly grabbing my cap and watch as Mom walks down the hall and into their bedroom. Heading downstairs, I nearly fumble as the ends of the gown lightly tuck underneath my feet. Dad sits at the

CHAPTER FORTY-THREE: MY WORDS TO YOU

kitchen table, already dressed and ready. "Mama said I need to use your car to get there before y'all," I mutter, tapping his shoulder. He looks up from his phone unamused before digging in his back pocket and handing me his keys. A dry smile grows on his face, "I love you, drive safe, baby." He plants a kiss on my forehead before I walk off into the garage.

The student parking lot is on its way to being full, with a few students pulling up on their own. People walk alongside the sidewalks, taking pictures ahead of time and just talking with their friends. The email the principal had sent out said they wanted us in our gowns before we got there, that way people won't spend all their time in the restroom. Attempting to find a spot near the SUV that I believe is Emery and Avery's, I just decide to park next to a red Honda Civic. I grab my clutch out of the passengers' seat, placing the keys in the wall pocket as I step out, seeing Em and Av wander over towards me. "Dang, you're the first one!" Avery shrieks, pulling in for a hug. I hug her back before going to hug Em. "Yea. Jayden texted me on my way here, he's about five, ten minutes away," I respond. We step onto the sidewalk as we walk toward the building. "Alright, yea I'm good with that. Zoey and Jayla both said they should get here within the next thirty, and Justice-," Avery pauses, catching herself talking about him. She covers her face as she comes to an abrupt stop, embarrassed she'd even brought up his name.

"Come on, it's no big deal, we already know you like him anyway."
"Do not."
"Do so, it's so freaking obvious, Av."
"It is?!"

She panics for a moment, Emery shrugging her off as we continue walking.
"But he did say he should be pulling up pretty soon. Look out for an Orange Mustang with a back license plate that says BETTER, but two 3s as the Es."

Emery looks at her as a guy holds the door open for us, and I politely wave a quick *Thank You*. "I find it adorable. I'm just frustrated we hadn't gotten a custom plate. Do you know how cool that could've been?" We walk down the hallway, greeted with multiple decorations, the gym decorated for the Prom next week, and a banner that says *CO' 22!* Mr. Bates stands in the corridor, where a crowd of kids stand as he collects our attention.

"Students! All students, please head to the backroom of the auditorium. Any parents that are currently here, please move towards the Auditorium itself, and be sure your tickets are in hand!"

The hallway echoed with the voices of people chattering on and on in the conversation, soon coming to a stop as we near the backroom door. A teacher squeezes through the doorway packed with kids before announcing another thing. "We will line everyone up in the front once the audit gets more of a crowd. Please be sure you look nice and have the image quality that you want. Congratulations, students. You've made it." I stick my head through the curtain like a little child, watching the dim room fill up with more people. I look in the fourth to last row and catch a glimpse of Mom, Dad, Shi, and Nana sitting there. Shiloh sees my head and waves as I pull it back. "I think we're 'finna get out there, EA," I say, grabbing the twins' attention. The line we're in thins out, slowly pouring out the curtain and into the auditorium, a crowd of people clapping as we walk and stand into place.

The speakers screech as Mr. Bates taps it lightly, grabbing everyone's attention as the room becomes silent and a bit more lit.

"*This thing working? Okay, yea, it is.*"

The crowd chuckles, enlightening the mood.

"*Here we are. Class of 2022, standing right in front of us. Wow, time flew, you know? For your parents, you're looking at the child that you made. For mothers, you've birthed. A child you raised and is now entering what we like to call 'The*

CHAPTER FORTY-THREE: MY WORDS TO YOU

Big Kid World'."

Silence throughout the room.

"But for me as a principal and teachers around us, it's crazy because we also watched your kid grow. We watched them become who they are. Especially those teachers from the middle and elementary school, I see you! Over here checking out the kids you taught. I can hear it in your minds already, 'I taught that boy!'"

More laughter immerses, also earning a chuckle from me myself.

"But seriously, it's crazy how fast time flies."

Mr. Bates turns towards us, giving us a hand motion.

"I mean, I bet it feels like just yesterday you guys were just starting to walk down the halls, huh?"

We all nod in confirmation, a few people whimpering in an attempt to hide their tears. He laughs in the mic, soon taking it out of the stand.

"Yea. I remember my graduation. Boy, that time flew! I swear, as a kid, you wished so hard to grow up but once you did, you wish you could be a kid again."

I think about that deeply, and it's true. When I was around 14, on the first day of High School, I had already wished I could graduate then and there. But now that I am now, I would do anything to go back and slow down. Relive everything.

"Alright, let's get this show on the road, now. I know a few of you want to get the hell out of here, and I respect that. But first I'd like for our Salutatorian and Valedictorian to speak."

The crowd goes wild, definitely mom and dad as they stand up while I walk up the steps, smiling as I grab the microphone from Mr. B's hands.

"Thanks, no really," I begin as the large room becomes silent. A few people mumble throughout the crowd, but then stop.

"Hey, I'm Tiffany Mohan," I pause, thinking of what to say.

"I'm 17, turning 18 in June. And I guess I'm Valedictorian." My words slowly build up.

"I ended with an exact 4.0 GPA. Crazy, I know. I've spent literally my entire high school years partying and having fun, obviously with study time. But I had no idea I'd be here, on a stage, and Valedictorian. It's the opportunity of a lifetime if you ask me."

The room gets a light wave of laughter.

"And if I could say one thing for this entire class, it would definitely, be I'm outta here!"

Everyone laughs at this comment.

"I'm serious but I'm also kidding," I chuckle.

"I can also be sure that on everyone's behalf, it all went by hecka fast. Like I remember the exact day my best friends and I had walked into this building, already having a feeling we were finna have the time of our lives. And we did! We really did. I made my friend group, with Zoey and Jayla," I point, and they both wave.

"I met a magnificent man whom I adore."

CHAPTER FORTY-THREE: MY WORDS TO YOU

I look at Jayden as he looks at me back, his eyes full of love.

"And myself. Like, really I did. I figured out a ton of stuff. That Algebra is pretty easy depending on what you do. That the baby project was actually more nerve wracking than imagined." Again, I cause the crowd to laugh.

"But to any younger siblings, hint hint, Shi," I add, Shiloh, waving his arm in the arm as people laugh. *"Don't say you want time to fly by fast. Because trust me, it'll go a lot faster when you do."*

I step off the stage, applause following as Mr. Bates grabs the microphone from me.

"Alright, here's Salutatorian, Leila Brown, with her speech."

Forty-Four

CHAPTER FORTY-FOUR: TURN YOUR TASSELS!

The band plays, and the line begins moving as a few people begin to get called up, one by one. "Avery Wilkens." Everyone claps, especially in the front row, where I notice their entire family is. Mrs. Wilkens cheers loudly, causing Av to fluster up and laugh roughly. Mr. Bates hands the diploma to Avery and shakes her available hand. "Avery is on our dance team, one of the top dancers that allowed us to win championships."

"Congratulations, Mrs. Wilkens," Mr. Bates mumbles as she walks down the stage and the next girl, Anaya Perks, walks after her.

"Aiden Spears." Aiden walks up, the entire line cheering as he grabs the paper from Mr. Bates' hand and walks down the staircase, doing stupid things along the way down. He pounds on his chest jokingly before walking into the area.

About an hour in, Emery's name is finally called, everyone in line clapping and cheering. "She's also on our Track team, winning our latest champi-

CHAPTER FORTY-FOUR: TURN YOUR TASSELS!

onship and earning a scholarship to the University of Memphis!"

The auditorium cheers loudly as she smiles and does a peace sign. Walking down the stairs, she also gets into the small area.

More time goes by, and more claps ring throughout the room. "Jayden Hudsen." I clap loudly, causing Jayden to burst out in a smile at the sight of my appraisal. He takes off his cap, pointing towards the bottom section as he maneuvers it towards his mom. She gasps as he smiles brightly before disappearing throughout the crowd. The design was different sections or areas of memorable moments or people to him. The one he'd pointed towards reads *Momma, I Made it!*

Jayla's after him, and she smiles brightly whilst pausing on stage for her mom to take a picture, Jeremiah shoving her since he was right after. They both walk down the staircase together, a specific look plastered all over her face as she looks at him, unamused. I bounce my foot up in down out of nervousness, and more people clap once again as a girl named Nila walks the stage.

Finally, I'm called as my heels click against the wood flooring, and I smile brightly, grabbing a hold of the diploma as Mr. Bates hands it to me. He mumbles something under his breath.

"You have a shine, Tiffany, a very bright shine, and I cannot wait to see what you ignite with it."

Once the whole class has received their diplomas, Mr. Bates says another speech, this time a bit shorter.

"Again, I am extremely proud of this class. I've seen some extraordinary people, and I cannot wait to see what they do."

He pauses as he grabs the mic out of the microphone stand, walking towards our group slowly.

"Congratulations, Class of 2022. Turn Your Tassels!"

I smile joyfully as I turn my tassel on the left, laughing as Emery realizes she'd accidentally had it on that side the entire ceremony. "Freak!"

"It's okay, you can just put it on the right." Avery tries to calm her down, but she continuous to ramble on. "I could, but then it wouldn't be right. You know what, I'm just gonna keep it on the left."

Mr. Bates throws his hand into the air, signaling we toss our caps in the air. We all do so, and they immediately crash back down seconds later. "Oh my god, Tiffany. We did it! We did it! We graduated high school!" Avery bounces up and down, her hands grasped onto my arm. My eyes water, this time I feel a tear drop down as I see the group come and surround me. "I had an amazing time with y'all," Jayla mumbles, putting her fist in the center of us. Zoey puts hers in, as everyone else also does, along with a small note. We all cheer, doing the SouthWind chant as they play music overhead and allow parents to spill over and take pictures. "Tiffany!" I hear Shiloh call before I turn around and see him walking towards me with mom, dad, and Nana behind him. "Congrats, T!" Nana says, hugging me tightly. "Thanks, Nana." She hands me a card as she lets go. "I know I've said it a lot lately, Tiff, but I'm really proud of you." Mom then reaches over and hugs me, signaling for dad to take a picture of us. "Hold up." He turns around, talking to someone before handing them his phone.

"1, 2, 3!"

We all smile, the flash brightening in our faces as I think to myself:

I'm on my own now.

CHAPTER FORTY-FIVE: MAGGIE L

Mom and I pull into the parking lot of a strip mall near downtown. I get out, looking around to see if I could identify anything. It has a formal vibe that kind of reminds me of carriage crossing but isn't exactly carriage crossing. Closing the door behind me, I watch mom walk over to the front of the car and meet me there as we walk across the street. Mom looks at every storefront window, checking each name until we get to one particular one; *Maggie Louise.*

Classical music plays overhead as we walk in, greeted by a cool breeze. "Hello! Welcome to Maggie L!" A worker greets as she hangs up a dress. "Hi, my daughter and I are here for your prom dress category?"

"Yes! Alright, just follow me, we have a number of different dresses in different colors," She says as we follow her into the back of the store, met with a formal room with color-coordinated dresses hung up and mannequins wearing separate ones. "These are our choices! My name is Mary-Ann, and just let me, or any other employees, know if you need any assistance!" And she wanders off into the front.

The first dress I see is one a mannequin is wearing, an all-red mermaid dress, similar to the one I'd worn to the winter formal. It still in my hand, I walk over towards a mirror and hold it in front of me, seeing how it would look. "Ma," I say, catching moms attention as she turns around from looking at the blue dresses. "No, didn't you say the theme was a celebrity-like look? Why don't you pick something white or gray?" I shrug as I put it back. "Yea, but some things that don't seem to go with the theme sometimes do, you never know." I shuffle through the rack, my eyes catching hold of a champagne-colored sequin dress. It glides across the floor as I pick it up and head toward mom. "Try it on, let's see how it looks."

Walking into the dressing room, I pass a girl who looks around 14 or 15. She struggles to pick between two dresses, obviously having tried them on already. "Struggling?" I ask. She puts the dress onto the hook on the outside of the door. "Yes! I put this other one on and both of them are cute on me." "What's the theme?" "Hollywood." I glance at the dress she's wearing right now before pointing toward her phone, and she lightly nods. Opening her camera roll, the gold dress that sits on the hook is on her, and I admit it does look cute on her. I glance at the one she's wearing right now, a silver tan that reminds me of a dress Kim Kardashian has worn to one of the METs. "That one," I say, pointing at her. "Kim Kardashian wore something like that at 2019's gala." She smiles brightly before grabbing the dress that'd been hanging on the door. "Thank you," She says before walking out. "No problem."

I zip up the dress before turning around and looking at myself in the mirror. It looks tacky. Especially since I'm planning to get a lace front, it just won't look right with the one I'm getting. Quickly, I take a selfie before sending it to mom.

ME| [Image Attachment]
  MOM| Yea, that's a no. I found a gray rose design dress.

* * *

CHAPTER FORTY-FIVE: MAGGIE L

We're on the 15th dress, Yes, I counted. The past 14 just didn't look right on me, but this one did. It's all white and is a long mermaid dress. My upper waist is shown but is also covered by a gray fabric similar to pantyhose. Diamond embroidery aligns all around the fabric area.

I walk out, mom awes at my sight and I can already sense the familiar thought swirling around her head.
   "This is <u>the</u> one."

Forty-Six

CHAPTER FORTY-SIX: SECOND IMPRESSION

"Alright, did you want some curl in it? Maybe just some bounce? Or some shine?" Mom mumbles words together as she wipes her hands off with a damp towel.

"Uh," I mutter, popping a kernel of popcorn in my mouth. I chew lightly as I flip to the next page in my magazine. "I mean, I don't wanna ruin my hair with a straightener," I pause, popping another into my mouth. "So just something basic, I guess," I respond as I look in the mirror. It's back like when I was little; I sit on a stool whilst mom does my hair in some fancy style. Except for this time, it's for an actual fancy event.

My hair tightens as I look and see mom had put my hair in a top bun. "Just enough room for that crown." "Mom," I laugh, standing up. Glancing in the mirror, I politely pull down two strands of my hair near my hairline, smiling as I stand up straightly. I look in mom's room, my dress sitting neatly on her dress form. It's a shimmery white, and extends down to a mermaid end much like my Winter Formal, but not exact. A chunk of the left torso is cut out and replaced by mesh and diamond embellishments that reach up to my left shoulder.

CHAPTER FORTY-SIX: SECOND IMPRESSION

"You ready to put it on?" I hear mom say as she sneaks behind me, her hand resting on my shoulder. I nod lightly as I walk towards the stand, gawking adoringly. "I'll be in your room getting your shoes, just walk out and knock on the door," She mumbles as she walks into the hall, closing the door behind her. Slowly, I unzip the silver zipper along the back before pulling it upward and slipping it off. It sits upon my forearm, waiting to be worn. I look in my reflection, feeling emotional for the thousandth time. "Dang," I mutter to myself before slipping my current wear off and putting the dress on.

JAYDEN

I pull into her driveway, escatic to see what she looks like. Tiffany hadn't sent any clues or any thought of what the dress would look like, she just told me to wear white, which I did. Looking at the overhead mirror, checking for the millionth time to be sure nothing was on my face. Quickly, I grab the corsage that sits in the plastic container and rush out, slamming the door behind me.

As I walk up the pathway, I continuously smooth my tux over and over, nervously breathing hard. It's not my first time meeting her parents, but it's certainly the best impression. I ring the doorbell before knocking lightly behind it. A shadow walks towards the door as I stand there, waiting to be greeted.

"Hello! Jayden! So nice to see you, and don't you look nice!" Mrs. Mohan greets, a smile brightly painted on her face. "Don't mind me," She mutters as she closes her robe and slips her feet into the pair of slippers that sit beside the door. "Wanna come in?"

"Right, yea," I respond, walking inside. For the first time, I'm actually looking around. Picture frames sit on the walls, not as many as mine, but enough. Walking into the kitchen, there are certificates and letters and tests sticking to the fridge. I sit at the table as Mrs. Mohan walks towards the pantry.

"You know, we need to have another dinner with you sometime, Jay. Really, I'd like know who you are."

"Tiffany doesn't talk about me?"

"Oh, she does."

She pours herself a glass of wine before putting the bottle back in the fridge. "It might be enough, but I'm sure I'd like to know more. Who are you? What are your intentions with my daughter?" She sips as I awkwardly chuckle. "Kidding, Kidding. That's Mason's job. But really, I want to know if you intend to bring y'alls relationship any farther." She gives me a look before sitting up, realizing she'd been leaning against the counter. I look at the ground, really thinking about what she'd said.

Forty-Seven

CHAPTER FORTY-SEVEN: LOVE YOURZ

"I'm ready!" The hallway echoes as I hear Tiffany's heels click downstairs, more footsteps trailing behind her. She walks into the kitchen, and I stand as I awe insight, absolutely adoring her.

Feeling the container almost fall out of my hands, I stutter before walking over and handing it to her, leaving me more in awe. She smiles, her eyes glowing. "Thanks," She beams, slowly opening it as she looks at it, really giving the sight a look. I'd picked a white rose with just a few adjustments. Aiden and I had spent all night gluing small diamonds onto every other petal. "Oh my god," She says, fumbling to pull it out. "Here, let me help." Reaching over, I grab the ribbon and tightly tie it around her wrist. Before moving away, I pull the other one off of my suit and clip it onto her dress. She bites her bottom lip lightly as I move away. "She looks amazing, Mrs. M," I sparkle. Mrs. Mohan smiles brightly as she walks toward the counter and grabs her phone. "Mason, get behind them and smile." Mr. Mohan follows her order as stands behind us, both of his hands on top of Tiffany's shoulders.

The flash quickly shines brightly as she takes the photo. Tiffany rushes to see it, laughing lightly, the way she always does.

"Jayden, come see!" She calls, waving me over.

The look she'd just given me. It confirms it all.

I do.

TIFFANY

Dozens of photos later, I finally interrupt the photo-shoot and remind mom and dad of the dance. "Ma, Dad. Prom?"

"Oh shoot, right!" Mom mutters, shoving her phone into her pocket. "I love you," She says, kissing me on the cheek. Daddy walks over before giving me a tight hug and walks Jayden and me to the door. "I love you, baby girl." He mutters, opening the door for us. I walk out first as I turn around to see Jayden not following behind me. Looking in the doorway inside, I notice them both talking, mostly dad, though.

JAYDEN

"Your dad's hella protective," I mutter as I get in the car. I buckle my seat belt as the ignition turns on. "Ignore him." I chuckle before backing out.

"It's his job, I don't blame him." Shyly, she grabs her phone from her clutch before staring at the screen.

J. Cole begins to play, and I check the radio screen to see what song is playing. *No Role Modelz*. The volume's not high, but not too low. Just enough for the right mood. I mutter along with a lyric.

Stopping at a red light, I see Tiffany typing on her phone. "Nervous?"

CHAPTER FORTY-SEVEN: LOVE YOURZ

She looks up at me before turning the screen off and nodding. I put my available hand on the middle of the console, waiting for her hand to grasp a hold, then it does. I gasp silently, looking at her as she smiles.

"I see you getting excited."

"What? Me?" She says as we begin moving again.

"Mhm. I can see in the corner of my eye." She laughs as if it was at her sentence. "Why are you nervous?" I respond, chewing off a piece of the previous topic. "No reason."

"No, there's a reason," I respond as we pull into the parking lot, the music seeming to pound through the walls as people scramble out of the space I lead to park in.

Putting the car's gear in park, I grab the keys out of the knob and sit there.

"Seriously, I want to know."

"Baby," She laughs tiredly. I laugh too. Licking her lips, she starts talking.

"It's prom. You're my boyfriend. Anything else to add?"

"You're nervous because I'm your boyfriend?"

"No. Yes! No, but yes!"

She stutters, meaning to say one thing and then another.

"Yea."

"Oh?"

She nods once again, this time leaning into my face as my elbows sit on the console. "Mhm," She mutters, our foreheads touching. *Love Yourz* begins to play, and I turn the volume up. Moving closer, she purposefully grazes her lips across mine before I move my hand and place it onto her face, moving her closer as we lean into a kiss. She giggles, causing me to laugh as well. I pull back, looking as her eyes are still closed. Opening her eyes, she sits there for a moment. Realizing Love Yourz had been playing, she smiles brightly. "I love you."

"I love you, too."

Forty-Eight

CHAPTER FORTY-EIGHT: FORMALLY YOURS

TIFFANY

Biting my bottom lip, I hold in a wide smile before grabbing my clutch off the ground. "Let's go." Jayden turns off the car before getting out on his side, eventually leading himself towards mine and opening the door for me. "Thank you." The train of my dress follows behind me, slowly hitting the ground as I step down.

Walking down the corridor, I see many groups of people in more formal wear than before. Emery's wearing a gold-colored evening gown, a mesh-like fabric coating it. "Oh my goodness, you look gorgeous!" She shrieks as she notices me. "Thank you. How are you and Aiden?" She smacks her tongue in false frustration. "Real good. We're not dating, yet," She pauses. I notice her quickly peek a glance at him as he does with her. "But hopefully soon." Avery then waddles towards us, her dark red trumpet dress tucking underneath the bottom of her heel. "You and Jayden both look amazing. Matching, I see. Told Em to try to go that route but she hadn't listened," Avery says, shrugging Emery's arm. Em flakingly smiles before actually smiling, possibly spotting Aiden in the busy crowd. Hearing his voice behind me confirms my guess. "Hey," He says before taking a sip of what's in his cup. "Did they spike it this year? I hear last year's Senior Prank was spiking the punch with student consent but not teachers'." He says, sounding as if he were hoping it had been. "Did they tell you to be careful?" Avery responds, speaking to him as if he were a baby. "Mhm," he mumbles, drinking the rest of the red liquid. "Well then, it is."

"Really? Thank god, I had prayed for this. What's a party without liquor or some crap like that?" I make a face at him, causing him to quickly shut up.

Not long after arriving, slow music begins to play overhead.
"First dance of the night. Find the love of your life and head towards them."

I see Justice walk over, a smile growing across his face after spotting Avery. "You two still talking?" I say, pointing at him. Avery quickly nods. "You two dating?" I add on, feeling Jayden tug on my hand. She shakes her head no before waltzing to him as they begin dancing. I turn towards Jayden, and he slowly walks me to a blank spot where no one is.

He places his right hand onto my hip as I find myself putting my hand into his left hand, Jay holding it onto the side. Gently, we begin swaying side to side, my head laying on his upper chest.

The music plays lightly, the ambiance perfect. I feel Jayden's chin rest on my head, causing butterflies to fly around in my stomach. Looking up I smile at him before he twirls me around as if I were a princess. "You look amazing." Shyly, I smile as I lean back in and lay down against him again. "Thank you," I mumble, the music speeding back up as the lights get brighter.

"First dance of the night, check! The second dance is in one hour. Don't go

anywhere, we'll be right back!"

Jayden holds my hand as he guides me towards our table, where everyone's already sitting. Avery giggles hard at a comment Justice had made, and Emery pretends as if she doesn't like Aiden, but it's obvious. Jayden pulls out a chair for me, and I quaintly sit down before taking a sip of the punch he got me, cautious of the alcohol spiked throughout.

JAYDEN

Tiffany places her cup down before wiping her top lip. Her hand falls into her lap, soon fidgeting with the silver ring that sits on her finger. "You alright?" I ask, already knowing. She tends to do that when she's insecure and doesn't know what to do. Her words fumble as she comes up with a response. "Yea. Just a bit nervous."

"And insecure?" She freezes at my words. "No," She hesitates, continuing to play with the ring. I give her a condescending look. "Maybe a little, but how would you know?" I point to her hand, guiding her towards her answer. "I always do this?" "Only when you're nervous," I say, scooting the chair closer to her. We sit face to face now, her hands in my lap as I slide the ring back onto her finger securely. "Don't be. You are <u>the</u> *most beautiful woman in this room.*"

"You want dinner after?" I ask, waiting a moment after saying the previous sentence. She nods before yawning. "Alright." Pulling my phone out of my pocket, I text mom letting her know T wants somewhere to eat.

> ME| Hey, mama.
> Tiffany wants to get something to eat around the time we leave, so we'll be out longer.
> Any ideal places?

The three dots on the screen pop up and down, eventually disappearing as her response shows into place.

MOM| **Alright, baby. Curfew is at 2.**
   A good spot your father used to take me was that St. Orleans spot downtown.
   Tell her I said hi! Hopefully, we can have dinner with her and her family soon.

An idea pops into my mind with that sentence.
   What if we had dinner with her family *now*?

CHAPTER FORTY-NINE: WINE N' DINE

TIFFANY

Jayden pokes at my arm as the slow music begins again, everyone at the table, including us, standing up. "Last dance?"

"I thought there were three dances?"

I place my hand on him, realizing he's leading us into the box step. "There are, I just have a surprise I want to show you before the night's over with."

My heart beats fast, yet slowly as the lights dim, giving the ambiance a flirtatious perspective. I lift my head off Jay's shoulder as we move gracefully, our bodies suddenly knowing what direction and tone we should be dancing in. He glances down at me with a certain look in his eyes. Suddenly, a thought from earlier in the year rings throughout my mind once again.

Am I sure this is just a high school relationship? Or is it something more?

JAYDEN

"I'll be back, let me go tell the twins we're heading out," Tiffany says, pointing her thumb in their direction. I nod lightly before grabbing a cupcake off the nearby snack table. My phone rings in my pocket, an iMessage notification from the restaurant I'd reserved, letting me know our table was ready. I follow behind Tiffany, noticing she hadn't walked away far.

Tiffany leans against the table, rambling on and on about random things with Avery. "You just got over here," I pause, sitting in the empty chair. "How are you already in a different conversation?" She shrugs before turning towards me, a light smile gleaming across her face before sitting upward. "Anyway, we're finna head out, Jayden wants to bring me somewhere."

Emery and Avery both glance at each other before prancing over and tightly hugging T. "Have a nice summer, call me as soon as you guys head to your campus, okay? Avery, call me as soon as you get into Atlanta," She mutters against their shoulders.

Avery said she's headed out next week to go ahead and get settled. Is it a pretty early settlement? Yea, at least I thought so. But she'd explained she wanted to get a few things packed down, which I can 100% agree with.

Then Tiffany said her parents recommend we head out to LA in two weeks, giving us enough time to get a few student things out of the way, so it's pretty much the group's last time being all together like this. And I gotta admit, it's pretty emotional.

Aiden looks at me with a grin before walking over silently and doing our handshake we'd made years ago. "See you at break?" I reach my hand out, his quickly meeting mine as we hug one another.

"Hell, yea. You bet I'm coming back for it, I wouldn't miss my ma's thanksgiving dinner for anything!" He laughs, and Jeremiah follows behind him. "See y'all later."

CHAPTER FORTY-NINE: WINE N' DINE

"Yo, you want us to come over next week to help with packing?" Aiden offers. I think for a moment before replying. "Yea, Yea. Thursday."

* * *

Opening the door, Tiffany walks through first as I walk to the host. "Hello, my name is Aanya, and I'm the host. Now, do you have reservations, or?"

"Reservation," I interrupt abruptly as she quickly types on the glimmering screen implanted in the podium. "Alright, name?"

"Hudsen. Jayden Hudsen." Her nails clack on the screen. Turning around, I see Tiffany paying attention to a Grizzles game playing on the TV overhead, everyone at the bar cheering as they make a shot. "Alright. Table 32, follow me!" Anaya smiles before leading us to a two-on-two table, sitting not too far from the bar. "Your waiter, Darcy, will be on her way." I grab Tiffany's chair back, allowing her to sit down before placing her clutch onto the table. I take my suit jacket off and neatly place it on the back of my chair before sitting down. The legs make a sound as they glide against the ground. "Alright," I pause, opening my menu.

"Anything in particular?"

Fifty

CHAPTER FIFTY: ROYL

TIFFANY

I look at my menu, my eyes immediately glancing across something that catches my eye. The place has a New Orleans look, which I like, so I'm pretty familiar with the menu. He clicks his tongue, seeming to have been afraid of my silence.

"Anything?" I bite my lip, deciding whether or not to pick the simple thing, or if I should just pick something new.

"Alright! My name is Darcy, and I'll be your waiter for today. First, may I start with your drinks?" The girl pulls out a notepad from her pocket. "Uh, yea. Actually, we have a few more people coming, so is it alright if you come back a little later? " Jayden says, and she gets nods.

"I'll give you fifteen minutes."

"Babe, who's coming?" I ask, confused. He hadn't told me anything, and if Em and Av were coming, I wish he'd told me. He responds once the waitress walks away, "It's a surprise." I playfully pout as he grabs my hand and kisses it. "Trust me, you'll love it."

CHAPTER FIFTY: ROYL

I hear the door close from across us, a familiar voice popping up once it shut.

"I'm part of a party?"

Jayden raises his hand once he hears, and I turn around to be greeted face-to-face with my family.

"Mama?" I say, confused. They grab a seat from the long table, Shiloh sitting right beside me. Turning towards Jayden I ask, "I see them everyday, what's so surprising about this?" Jayden nods at Shi before replying. "Oh, wait a second. Trust me, your parents don't know it, either."

"So," Mom continues, placing her purse into her lap. "How was Prom? Jayden told me you guys cut it short due to this dinner." I nod. "Yea. It was really good. Emery and Avery had beautiful dresses, and Jayla and Zoey said they were both Prom Runner Ups."

"I'm pretty sure Avery is, too, actually," Jayden interrupts. "Yea, I wouldn't be surprised if she is."

"Well, it's nice to hear the night is going well. You guys planning on my recommendation and moving out soon?"

"Yea, Yea. I think it's a good idea. That way we can get our schedule set up, and our dorms fixed," Jayden responds, his hands intertwined with each other as they sit on the table. After sitting silently for the entire time, dad begins speaking as he opens up, "That's what I did when I graduated. My brother and I moved out three weeks after Prom."

"What was Prom like for you guys?" Shiloh asks, looking up from his phone. I have no idea what he expects out of them, because he suddenly got excited once the topic of Prom popped up. "Your father and I weren't together then," Mom says. "But, mines was magical. Might be your description of it, too, Tiffany." I smile at her sentence. Suddenly, Jayden jumps up as three people pop in, and I quickly recognize two people out of the three; Jayden's Mom and sister, Maddie.

The Bookposal

"Jayden!" His mother says, hugging him. Maddie looks at me, trying her hardest to search through my eyes and know me. She grabs a chair and sits beside Shiloh. Maddie and him begin talking.

"Mom, this is Mrs. and Mr. Mohan, Tiffany's parents," Jayden greets, as my parents get up to shake her hand. "Nice to meet you, and please, call me Lyana," Mom says as Mrs. Hudsen sits down. "This is Mason, my husband," She adds on, and Dad waves. The waitress comes back after seeing everyone sit down, filling all 8 of the seats. "Alright, is this everyone?"
 "Yup!" Jayden responds. "Okay, so, let's get started?"
 "For a starter, I'll order us all Fried Calamari?" Jayden asks, and everyone nods in compliance. "And for drinks," He pauses, allowing each of us to order our own. "Sprite," Shiloh says, and the waiter begins writing. Maddie then says her drink, "Sparkling Water with a zest of lemon."
 "Virgin Bloody Mary," I say, adding my order. The adults then order their drinks, my mom being the most pointed out. "Ruffino Pinot Grigio, with Martini salt along the rim, but not quite a Martini."

We order our food not long after we got our drinks, allowing us plenty of time to eat and talk about one another. My mom got to know his mom, My dad got to know his Dad, and Shi got to know Maddie.
 The plates soon arrive, and I dig in quickly after a prayer. I look at Jay before I speak. "About the packing, we can get the boxes and such starting tomorrow or later this week, then get them shipped to LA by Sunday. Monday, we leave. My parents said they'll handle the tickets, blah blah blah," I pause, taking a bite of my food.
 "Then our journey begins."

Fifty-One

CHAPTER FIFTY-ONE: GOODBYES

Folding the ends of a box, I seal it with the last bit of tape before dad walks in and grabs it from in front of me.

I look around the room, all of my posters and small break-down furniture to bring into the dorm are gone, causing the room to feel dull. "That's it?"

"Yea. Mom got started on my clothes while I was asleep," I laugh, glancing at the half-emptied closet. "Okay, well," He pauses, standing in the doorway as the box in his hand is barely weighing him down. "Your mother is in the kitchen putting some of the older pots and pans in a box for you." Before walking away from the doorway, he adds one more thing. "She's been saving them for you. Even if she had to wait 18 years." We both laugh as he heads off, and I sling my backpack over my shoulder, along with grabbing the handle of my suitcase. Slowly, I walk around the room to gather one good look at an empty room I'll be seeing on Thanksgiving day. Memories of sleepovers, incidents such as Emery's first period, sad moments such as Avery's first boyfriend dumping her, and many others. I close my eyes as I stand in the doorway, just a footstep away from the steps.

To a new beginning.

Walking down the stairway, I watch Shi as he rushes towards me and grabs my duffel out of my hands, sprinting down the hall before yelling. "Ma said I get your room!" I chuckle as I turn the corner into the kitchen, Mom packing plates and silverware just as Dad had said. Struggling to get to her, I plant a kiss on her cheek as I put the backpack down on the ground and help her with the last few things. "Look at my baby!" She shrieks, pulling me in for a hug. I hug her back. "Okay, so you got the tickets? The seats are right beside each other? Do you know where your dorm room is? How about your hotel?" "Mom, Mom," I interrupt. "Relax. I'm almost 18, I got this. Trust me." She beams with happiness, yet a small glimmer of fear shines through her eyes. "I'll be alright. You guys coming down for my birthday?"

"Heck yea! You'll get to show me your dorm, and your roommate! Gah! I can't wait!" Dad walks through the garage door right then, opening the pantry as he grabs the can of Pringles and pops a chip into his mouth. "You ready?" I glance at Shi before clamoring towards him and practically suffocating him with a hug. "See you in a month, okay, Shi-Shi?" He gives me a look. "What'd I say about that nickname?" My eyes water as I cock my head to the side, giving him a bit of a sarcastic attitude. "Imma call you Shi-Shi from now on." Standing up, I push his head with my hand before walking to the door. Mom rushes over as she realizes I'm going to hug dad.

"See you guys soon."

"Bye, baby."

"Don't forget to see everything at the freshman settle-down. They added a small course with everything to do with taxes, bill paying,-" I stop dad mid sentence with a look. "Dad, I got this." Opening the car door, I step inside, close it behind me, and pull back. "Love you! Stay safe! Text me the moment you land!"

* * *

CHAPTER FIFTY-ONE: GOODBYES

Pulling into the parking lot, I text Jayden to let him know I'd just pulled in. I see him and his mom on the balcony before she calls down. "Hey, Tiffany!" Stepping out, I wave as I walk down the sidewalk and towards the stairway. "We got all his bags in the corridor right inside," Mrs. Hudsen adds on as I reach his floor. "Thank you! How's Maddison going?" I say, leaning against the railing. She quickly responds. "She's doing amazing. Getting better, feeling better. Let me go get her, perfect timing for a photo, huh?" Waltzing inside, the door clicks behind her as it leaves Jayden and I staring at each other outside.

I sit on the now empty chair beside him. "High school flew by pretty fast, huh?"

"Hell yea. Feels like I just started yesterday." I laugh lightly. "Well, my parents literally hoarded my every attention. I had to practically pry myself away from her eyes' view." Jayden laughs at my comment. "I had to try my hardest to keep my mom from crying at everything she'd put in a box," He adds on, reaching his hand over the patio table to hold mine. I clutch his hand as Mrs. H walks through the front door, Maddison and Bryant behind her. "Bryant, stand in the back. Jayden and Tiffany, I want you two to hold hands in the front. Maddie, you either get in the back with Bryant," She points everywhere for us to stand.

The flash leaves a bright light in my eye as we all gather around Jay's mom to look at the camera display. "I literally love how the sun is treating my skin," Maddison glows, pointing at her face. "Yea, you look cute! I see you, too. Lookachu with butterfly braids," I tease as she playfully thanks in an exaggerated way. "Well, you guys should get headed out," Bryant clears his throat, initiating Mrs. J's tears. Maddie tightly hugs me before moving on to Jayden, but this time seemingly to have a struggle letting go. "Call us if you two have any issues, and definitely let us know the moment you land." Jayden and I nod, our hands intertwined as we stand at the stairway, ready to walk off. "I love you, mama," He calls, and we both step down, talking about our excitement for when we get to Cali.

Fifty-Two

CHAPTER FIFTY-TWO: ARRIVAL

"Nadia. Nadia. Nadia. Hello, my name is- Nope," I quietly mumble.

"What're you saying?" Jay asks, laughter ringing throughout his voice. An announcement over the intercom somewhat blows off part of his sentence. "My roommate's name is Nadia, and since we go ahead and move into the rooms, I wanna be able to know what to say just in case I bump into her. First impressions last, you know." Coming to a pause in front of the baggage area, I stand on my toes as I struggle to look over the slow conveyor belt. "Yea, well my roommate's name is Denver. You don't see me rehearsing what to say, do you?" He responds. Squinting, I catch sight of our suitcases. "By the couple with red lace printed shirts," I point out, the couple turning around and glancing at us as we rush towards them.

My suitcase meets the ground with a thud as we maneuver our way through the crowd, sitting on a nearby bench. Jayden pulls out his phone from his pocket, soon pulling up the car rental website. "Just for right now, but when we get settled," he pauses, typing his name into the box. He looks up at me as the screen confirms our rental, a 2020 Honda Civic. "We'll have an official, right?" I smile, nodding to his sentence as I lay my head down against his shoulder. We sit there silently, the airport booming with

CHAPTER FIFTY-TWO: ARRIVAL

sound. Jayden shrugs, causing my head to bounce as I look up at him.

"You excited?" I make a sound signifying my expression before I sit up, accidentally knocking my bag off as I scoot closer against the bench. "Yea. I mean, I'm also terrified, you know? We've survived on our parents for as long as we can remember, and now we're about to be on our own." He sighs heavily before he releases his arms off my shoulders. "Sure, but," He pauses as he stands up and grabs his bags, letting me know to do the same. I stand up as well, struggling to keep all of my bags in hand.

"We're alone together."

***

"Jayden Hudsen?" The woman behind the desk swivels her chair towards her desktop, her nails clicking away at the keyboard. Jay looks up from his phone before nodding. "Honda Civic, Model 2020, Hatchback, correct?" "Yup." Digging under the surface, she hands him keys with a blue tag wrapped around the key chain. "$50 a day. Return to any rental lot, but for prevention of fees, we recommend you come back to this specific airport," She gleams a smile as we exit the line, the person behind us stepping forward.

Going on about two escalators and riding around on one Zip-car, we finally reach the garage. I follow behind Jayden as we walk into the garage, each footstep echoing into the distance. "We're here, in California!" I exclaim, nudging his shoulder with excitement as I hear my echo repeat after me. Glancing at me, he peeks a smile before planting a kiss on my forehead. He looks down at the keys, reading the number 35 that's plastered onto the blue tag. It confuses us for a moment, but after paying attention it eventually becomes understanding. Each parking space has a number which to where your car is parked. We walk down each aisle, continuing to look for our number.

Pretty quickly, I find our number.

Lifting the trunk door, it slowly opens as I let go. Sliding the handle back in place, Jayden lifts his suitcase before I do the same. We do this back and forth for a while before nothing is left sitting on the gravel.

I close the door behind me as I sit in my seat, the leather cushion squeaking as I move around. Jayden opens before sitting in the driver's seat as he puts the car in the ignition. Kanye West plays on the radio at a loud volume, causing us to get startled as it blasts through the speakers. Out of reflex, I turn the volume down as he backs out of the space, the dim lighting soon illuminating with a glow as we exit the garage and into the busy city. LA. Los Angeles. Not only here for good, but with someone I love. I peek a glance at Jayden for a moment before grabbing my phone out of my pocket. "So, any specific place you wanna check out before we head towards the dorms?"

"Not anything specific. Just wanna unpack and wind down," I chuckle. He nods in agreement, quickly reverting his attention back to the road ahead.

A message notification falls down the top of my screen from Emery. Pressing it, an image of her dormitory was decorated from top to bottom. Luxury items are thrown in here and there.

> EMERY| literally blingeddd this place out. lmao. anyway, how was the flight?
> ME| lol, it was good! this time, no horrible incidents happened.
> gratefully i got to keep my candy
> EMERY| good, you still know you hella crazy for giving that little boy that candy!
> ME| ill send a picture of the dorm once we get there.

Jayden pokes at my arm, catching my attention. "Why'd you wanna get down here so quick? We got at least a month or two."

"Cause. The tickets were on sale," I reply, stifling a laugh behind my stray face. "Okay," He replies, a chuckle hidden throughout the response. I

CHAPTER FIFTY-TWO: ARRIVAL

open Gmail as I look at my home screen, a notification from U-Haul sits underneath the email from GoodReads. Pressing it, it displays across my screen.

<u>U-HAUL DELIVERY: #26785028710</u>
  <u>HELLO, TIFFANY JESSIE MOHAN.</u>

<u>*This is an automated message to let you know your packages have been delivered! We hope you enjoyed this service, and use us next time you intend to move.*</u>

There are more words listed underneath the spacer, but ignore them as I exit the app and turn off my phone. "My stuff arrived," I say, leaning against the headrest. Jayden turns the volume down as he averts his attention to me. "I think mine gets there Saturday?" He responds unsurely, gesturing towards his phone as I grab it. I type in the password and open his email. Nothing. "Who'd you use? U-Haul?"

"Nope. My Town movers. My mom wanted me to use them since we'd had a discount," He chuckles. "So, here I am, using a crappy moving company no one has heard of." I bite my lip as I press the 'Junk Mail' tab. Just as expected, a ton of update emails rests inside.

<u>MY TOWN MOVERS - ORDER #4726591038</u>
  <u>THIS IS AN AUTOMATIC MESSAGE TO LET YOU KNOW YOUR DELIVERY WILL ARRIVE BY 6:30 PM THIS FRIDAY. REPLY UNDER THE LINE WITH ANY QUESTIONS AND CONCERNS.</u>

<u>SINCERELY,</u>
  <u>MY TOWN MOVERS - BEN THE AUTO-MAIL</u>

* * *

Quickly, I unbuckle my seat belt the moment we pull into UC Berkeley's parking lot. Parking in a spot, I practically jump out as I rush to gather everything out of the backseat; My laptop bag and stuff stacking against each other on my back. "Yo!" I hear a familiar voice call from behind me. I attempt to turn around, but the bags prevent me. Footsteps gather closer to me as the voice gets closer as well. "You need help?" "Ryan!" I say, dropping the bags in my hands immediately and hugging him. "God, yes." He smiles before crouching down to grab my small clutch. Jayden comes around from his side as he opens the trunk. Looking down as he shuffles things around, he starts talking. "Thanks, man. Hey, could you get us a cart-" He pauses before looking up. "Ryan?"

"Jayden?"

"**You two <u>know</u> each other?**"

Fifty-Three

CHAPTER FIFTY-THREE: NEW DORM, NEW ME

They both begin laughing before hugging and giving one another a pat on the back. "Yea, I've known this little dude for ages," Ryan teases, smacking the back of Jayden's head. Placing a bag down, Jayden asks him, "We'll catch up once we get settled, but could you get us a baggage cart?"

Ryan looks at me, a strong smile plastered across his face. Stuttering, he replies, "Yeah, Yeah, sure."

The cart squeaks and bumps as we push it along the sidewalk. "You know what you guys' dorms are? Tiffany, didn't you say you had Blackwell while you were here in December?" "Oh, yeah, I do. Babe, how about you?" I point my thumb towards Jayden as I wait for his response. Stopping in front of the door, Ryan scans his Student ID before he unlocks it, us following behind into the crowded lobby. "Right, I think I got the same as you." I smile before I struggle to pull my phone out of my pocket. "Okay, my dorm number is 316." Ryan nods before pushing the cart in the direction of the elevator. I press the arrow going up, and the light confirmation of the chute coming down to us flashes. The doors open, and Jayden lets go as Ryan pushes the cart inside. I walk after him, Jayden following behind me as he attempts to fit in. "That's tough, man. Only enough for me and T."

"Nah, babe, you can come in. You two have been best friends for some time, I just met him." I offer as my foot sits outside the doors. Jayden lightly nudges me back inside.

"Tiffany, you're good. I'll head up by stairs, alright?" I nod lightly before he pecks a quick kiss on my cheek. "Leave your door open."

The doors close as he steps off and wanders towards the stairway. I press the third floor, and we quickly begin moving upward. "So, you know who your roommate is yet?" Ryan mutters, striking conversation. "Yea," I reply, stepping out as the doors open again as the bright corridor causes my eyes to strain. "Nadia Alexander, I think," I say unsurely. He clicks his tongue. "Rooming with a Sophomore."

"That's bad?"

"No, that's one hell of an advantage. Plus, Nadia's cool. She'll show you the ropes." I bite the inside of my cheek as we find the room, the door already propped open. Peeking inside, I see a girl with darkish green dyed hair shuffling around her suitcase, her phone shoved between her shoulder and ear. "I swear, I don't even know why she tried it with me." Ryan knocks on the door before walking inside, leaving the cart in the hallway before he grabs a few bags.

"What's up, Ry?"

"What'd I tell you about calling me that, Nadia?"

"My bad," She giggles, planting a quick kiss on his cheek. Ryan checks his apple watch with a sigh before speaking. Her phone beeps as she tosses it onto the unmade bed behind her. "Tiffany?" I nod as I drop my bag on the ground, expecting her hand to shake mine. She laughs before bumping into my shoulder and walking into the hallway. "Alright, then," I mutter, bending over to grab my bags once again. The empty bed is the closest to

CHAPTER FIFTY-THREE: NEW DORM, NEW ME

the window, the mattress perfectly white aside from one stain, which looks light pink. A knock comes from the door before I hear Jayden's voice flood the room. "Hey, babe," He mumbles, awing at the light sight of Nadia's side of the room. I let go of the sheet corner I'd been holding as I stand up. "Hey." I loop my arms around his neck as he kisses my forehead. Just then, Nadia walks through the door, clearly giving the look of *'Who is this?'*. "Jayden," I pause, introducing the both of them to one another. "Nadia Alexander, my roommate." She smiles, tagged along with a wave before she lays on her bed and grabs her phone out of her left pocket. Reaching under her pillow, she pulls a light blue stick out of her pillowcase. Placing it close to her mouth, I watch as Nadia inhales a puff before slowly breathing out, vapor coming from both her nose and mouth. "Nadia," Ryan shrugs, lightly punching the side of her head. "What?" He maneuvers his eyes towards me before she shrugs. "Okay? She can deal with it." Annoyed, I breathe in roughly. I walk back towards my bags, unpacking the sheets I'd packed as I begin placing them onto the mattress.

    And if there's one thing I dislike about making my bed, I would say it's putting the fitted sheet on. Every time you get one corner on, another corner pops right off. And to make matters worse, my bed is a twin bed, that's scooted all close against the wall. You move to different positions and throw your body against the bed just to mess up a different corner that you worked OH so hard on.

Everyone in the room stops talking as they turn to me while I struggle to put the sheet on. Nadia chuckles behind a stray face, Ryan bites the bottom of his lip to prevent a smile from popping up, and Jayden laughs as well before offering to help me. "Babe."

    "Wait," I say, aspirating for a breath. "Let me help you," He continues to laugh, reaching for the left corner that'd lifted. Working together, we manage to keep the sheets in place."Thank you," I sigh, pushing my hair back as it grazes my shoulder.

    Ryan sits on the edge, about shoulders' length apart from me as he begins speaking. "Additional class sign-ups are going on in the student union around 6:30 later today," he pauses, turning to me as I toss him a smile. He nibbles at the corner of his mouth as he continues speaking. "Nadia and I aren't gonna be there, since we've already picked our classes and no longer want any additionals. I recommend not getting any classes that no students have signed up for. There's a reason why."

"He's saying this cause he made the mistake last year," Nadia interrupts, laughing between words. Ryan takes off his slide and throws it at her head as she laughs even harder. It hits the wall before sliding along the side, slipping under the bed. She reaches under the bed and begins explaining as she tosses it back to him. "He picked a midnight oral discussion class. Got stuck in there till like, 2 in the morning." She continues giggling as Ryan stands up quickly and struggles to jokingly suffocate her with a pillow. "Alright, thanks for the advice," Jay shrugs.

"Finna head to my room, I'll text you my number," Jayden says. I nod, now working on the comforter. And I'll be honest, it's coming together! I mean, aside from if someone had already seen, you'd never know a big, pink stain was under my sheets. Fluffing up my pillow, Ryan taps my shoulder. "Heading out. Party tonight, you down?" I don't respond, thinking whether or not I should. I mean, Jay and I just got here, I'm practically jet lagged, and it's not seeming to go "as expected". But again, it's _college_!

No parents, no rules, just freedom. As I continue to decide, my mouth opens before I can make an official decision. "Sure! Where at?" He smiles at me once again at my response. He nods his head before reaching into his pocket. "I'll text it to you. What's your number?" I chuckle as he hands me his phone, the contacts app wide open. *901-463-3625*. The bar blinks as I tap the 'name' bar. Quickly, I type my name out.

tiff

Handing the phone back to him, he sends a message to me to be sure of the right number. My phone vibrates against the nightstand, and I grab it off just as it nears the edge. Face ID causes it to automatically unlock, and

CHAPTER FIFTY-THREE: NEW DORM, NEW ME

Ryan's message rests upon the screen. "See you tonight."

Fifty-Four

CHAPTER FIFTY-FOUR: PARTY GIRL

I knock on the door, quickly greeted by Ryan.
"Hey!" He exclaims, opening it wide enough for me to walk through. Walking inside, I look at both sides of the room. It has two colliding personalities, the left side with a plant-lover style look, and the right side has a fraternity style. Ryan sits on the bed on the right side as he ties his laces. "Your side?" "Hell yea." He responds, his voice wavering with initiation. A Tupac poster is plastered behind him, along with a stoplight neon sign beside it. Six hat hooks stuck against the wall, one cap hanging on each. Standing up, he grabs his wave brush before looking in the mirror that hangs on the back of the dorm door and brushes his hair. "So, whose party is it?" I state, continuing to glance around the room. "One of my friends, Kiya. Off-campus place, so we gon' be driving a bit," He responds before he tosses the sponge onto his bed. "You ready?"

"You mean, are *you* ready? You shoulda done that before I got here." He smirks before a chuckle submerses from his voice. "Oh well. Couldn't help but pamper when you got here." His voice gets a tad bit deeper in this sentence, catching me off guard.

God, is he flirting? Awkwardly, I laugh it off as I walk through the door before he closes it behind him. Walking down the echoing hallway, I can't

CHAPTER FIFTY-FOUR: PARTY GIRL

help but notice how unearthly silent it is. I mean, it is a college campus, I would expect at least a tad bit of bustle. He presses the call button, and the light ding fades as I hear the lift escalate down to us. "So, what're your classes? You get to the student union and check those out?" The doors open as I begin speaking, both stepping inside as I press the 1st floor. "Yea. Signed up for noon Marketing and 8 PM Creative Writing." He hums, as if he were holding something back. "What?" I laugh, shrugging his shoulder. His hands are tucked into his pockets, lightly swaying. "Nothing, just listening to you."

* * *

Pulling onto the street, I can't help but notice a crowd surrounding the front porch of the house to the left of us. Getting out, I hear the music pounding from inside. The door slams behind me before a beep sounds. I stand along the sidewalk, waiting for Ryan. He walks aside from the car and towards me. Pumping his arms in the air, he chants random words for a moment before speaking to me. "Hyped?" I look at him from the corner of my eye. He laughs before lightly flicking the back of my neck. "Never, ever say that again. I swear it's the most cringe crap I've heard," I reply, a chuckle buried in the back of my throat. We cross the street, finding ourselves walking directly through that crowd I'd mentioned earlier.

Looking around the crowded living room, it looks like people are actually having the time of their life. And it's not like the parties I had gone to back in Memphis weren't it and all, but it's just the one I'm in right now just has a different feel. Everyone has their own crew. Their own presence allows you to not help but wanna speak to them. Ryan taps my shoulder as I manage to compile what he might've said through the loud music. "Finna be in the corner. Text me if you need me." Nodding, I watch him dissolve into the crowd.

I make my way around the place, unable to help myself from feeling left out. After being shoulder to shoulder with tons of people, I manage to get through to the kitchen. My hands clutch a red cup while my eyes scan the counter top for drinks. Vodka, Tequila, Hennessy, Beer. Any variations I can think of just aren't anything of my tasting. The spiked fruit punch isn't what I'm looking for, and neither is the Teaquila, which is Sweet Tea predominately made with Tequila. I know it sounds gross, but it's actually pretty good.

Without notice, a girl with light brown braids comes onto my side, picking up a variety of bottles before pouring the concoction into my empty cup. She's a warm chestnut shade, clear gloss aligning her lips as she lightly nibbles on her top lip. Not long after, another girl pops up, tapping her shoulder before speaking. "You don't mix lights with dark, 'Veah." I glance inside as she points toward the cup. A faded brown is mixed in with the light, an even darker shade popping up as droplets fall from the Hennessy bottle. "Okay? She's just gonna have the best hangover ever," Chestnut responds. The other girl shuffles her weight onto her other leg before clicking her tongue. "More like the worst. You remember what kind of hell you were going through that one night?" Frustrated, the girl who I'm guessing is 'Veah, slams the bottle against the counter, causing the leaning cans of beer beside it to fall and spill. "Mariyah, don't bring that up again!"

"Oh, yes, I'm bringing it up again. You had the most torturous night ever! Don't even think about putting this poor girl through that crap, too."

She crosses her arms.

'Veah scoffs before grabbing a spoon out of the plastic cup and begins swirling the mixture around, snatching it out of my hand before taking a swig. Her face scrunches up as if it were sour. "Good?" I ask. She inhales an exasperated breath before taking another sip. Her friend beside me taps my shoulder, waving me away from the counter where she is. "My bad about 'Veah. I swear that girl just does anything." I laugh at this, hoping to now catch her name. "Tiffany," I say, hoping it hadn't been too sudden

CHAPTER FIFTY-FOUR: PARTY GIRL

for me to say that. "Mariyah. And as said, that," She continues, pointing to Neveah, who's now slouched over the bottles and adding more to the cup that was once mine. "Is Neveah."

"Party Animal, huh?" I add, continuing to look at the girl as she grabs a plastic shot cup and pours the drink into it. She scoffs before a response releases from her mouth. "You wish. The girl's only doing this cause she's having a moment."

"A moment?"

"Sometimes, she tends to just do stupid stuff. This included." Her left-hand swishes against her shorts. Reaching into her back pocket, she checks the time before looking up and noticing Neveah had wandered off. She mumbles underneath her breath before actually speaking to me. "Crap. It was nice meeting you, but I gotta go. She literally went somewhere else, and that's not quite the best idea." I raise my eyebrow in concern. "She tends to," She pauses, looking up at the ceiling. "Catcall guys?" She says, a bit of laughter in her voice. "Anyway, I really gotta go. Berkeley, right?" Slowly, she walks backward toward the doorway where a large group of people are. I nod. "Yea, hope I see you around campus."

Fifty-Five

CHAPTER FIFTY-FIVE: 808S AND HEARTBREAK

I wake up in my dorm, my head pounding as if I'd spent the whole night drinking, and the open window directly beside my bed doesn't make it any better.

"Whatever you smoked last night was strong as hell. You threw up like three times last night," Nadia says. I look towards the small closet on her side and notice her putting her braids in a tight bun. Opening my mouth, I manage to refrain from laughing, as I know it would make it worse. Turning on my back, I reach for my phone on the desk next to me. My hand feels nothing but the smoothness of the wood. "By your leg," Nadia adds before crouching down and grabbing her tote bag off the ground. I grip my leg, my phone within grasp as she requested.

My face ID opens it, despite the fact I have a disgusting trail of vomit by the crease of my mouth. I look at the camera, wiping it off in disgust. "Yea, you should probably wipe that off." Nadia tosses a pack of baby wipes to me, hitting me in the head before she bursts with laughter. "My bad." She continues to lightly snicker as I roll my eyes, the throbbing of the headache

CHAPTER FIFTY-FIVE: 808S AND HEARTBREAK

no longer as strong as before. Opening the pack, I reluctantly grab a wipe and place it at my fingertips. Wiping my face, I feel the cool of the wipe as it gives me instant chills. I crumple it up, placing it on the desk. Sitting up, more pain from the headache comes back again, and I curse myself out within thoughts for the stupid decision.

"Where 'you headed?" I mumble. "Lunch. Believe it or not, I do not spend my entire life at parties."

"I spend entire nights."

My feet hit the ground, the dizziness from the night before instantly coming back. My stomach grumbles from hunger. Getting up, I head towards the mini fridge, greeted by the empty shelves.

"We need food," I mutter, shutting it behind me. She nods, shutting the mascara wand that was once in her hand.

"We can head out when I get back. Make a list, we're gonna stop at Walmart first."

* * *

If I could say one word to define adulting as of right now, it would definitely be frustrating.

First of all, we have to go grocery shopping. Living back home, mom obviously bought all the groceries herself, and the same system would go by, too. I would unpack for her, look at the receipt, and say "That's a lot of money."

Not that big of a deal, right. But the prices were usually around 350. 350! That's how much it cost to get food, and for it to be gone in just a few days!

Pulling into the parking lot, the radio abruptly shuts off as I open the door. My phone buzzes, alerting me of a reminder I had typed for myself once I arrived to the lot.

Nadia's car trails behind me, as she refused to use my rental. "Other peoples' hands have been all over your stuff," Was her excuse. I agree, but we touch everything everyone else has already touched. She pulls beside me, her car still in motor as she waits for me to get out. I turn the car off, get out, and she does the same. Her car beeps as she locks the doors behind her, walking alongside me. "You got a list?" I nod, grabbing a cart from the cart corral. "Don't forget the ramen, that's an essential." I chuckle as we walk inside, the bustle from everyone around us igniting almost immediately. "Alright, I eat Nutella bread for breakfast," Nadia continues, grabbing a banana from the produce aisle beside us. "So we need Bananas and Nutella."

"And Bread." I interrupt. She rolls her eyes before snatching the list out of my hands. "How about we split this up, huh?" I give her a look. We stand in front of the tomatoes. She reaches in my bag, and I pop her hand real quick as she pulls out a pen. Marking the paper, she grabs her phone out her pocket and takes a picture. "I do this half, and you do this half. We'll head to Kroger after." I look at my half, containing almost all of the snacks. Nadia continues to stand there, staring at the photo as I turn the cart and head towards the bakery. "T!" She calls out, everyone near the cashiers turning around and looking at us. She prances over to me, noticing the attention she had gathered. "Get things for your hygiene basket. We have enough to buy all of this, and personal supplies," She shuffles through the wad of cash within the wallet. We both put our share of grocery money in not too long ago. "60 for the both of us?" I grab the 50 and the ten in her hand. "Yea, sure."

"You have my number, right?"
"Yea."

She types my name in the message bar, and it automatically fills in.
"Okay, text me when you have everything you need, got it?"
"Got it."

And we both separate.

CHAPTER FIFTY-FIVE: 808S AND HEARTBREAK

JAYDEN

ME| Down for dinner tonight?

I shove my phone in my pocket as I walk towards my door, my hand grazing on the handle. My roommate, Devan walks by from his small closet. "Where you headed?"

"Lord knows where. My girlfriend's been out all day." He laughs at my sentence. Confused, I give him a look as my hand falls from the handle. "Nothing, man," He sarcastically replies. He sits on the beanbag by the mirror before leaning over to tie his laces. Looking at his shoes, I immediately can name the pair. Jordan XX2, I've been trying to get my hands on them forever.

"You've just been on the phone with her pretty much every night you've been here. You haven't even talked to anyone but her. Hang out with other people." His voice sounds agitated as I sigh roughly. "Well what else am I supposed to do?" He clicks his tongue as he continues to be aggravated. "I don't know, Join clubs? Go to parties? Meet other people?"

"There's hardly anyone around the halls."

"Cause they're all out doing stuff! Your girlfriend is doing this stuff, why can't you?"

I pause, leaning against the wall as I'm now further away from the door. He stands up and heads toward me, his face expressing invitation. "Follow me, I'm heading out with my friends. Try to talk to other people, maybe?" I smile before following behind him.

"Bet."

Fifty-Six

CHAPTER FIFTY-SIX: ESCAPE TIME

JAYDEN

I follow him towards the cafe, where a group of guys laugh loudly, gathering pretty much all of the attention in the room. One of them (who has dreads) stands up and walks towards us as Devan does the chest bump with him. "What's up, Tony?" He laughs. "Nothing much. Hey, who's this?"

"Freshman. No friends, at all whatsoever." He glances at me before turning back to him.

"Only person he's hung out with is his girlfriend."

"Join a club. What's been in mind?"

"Okay y'all. I'm pretty sure he's confused, give yourselves some names."

The guy with dreads raises his left hand before giving himself a name. "Tony." The dude that had just stood up says his next, then everyone else as a group. "Allen."

"Liam."

CHAPTER FIFTY-SIX: ESCAPE TIME

"Xavier."

I wave lightly before introducing myself. "Jayden."

"Nice to meet you, Jay." We all sit at the table, trash resting in a pile. Liam asks me the same question he'd asked earlier. "What's a club that's been in mind?" I shrug. "You haven't even seen any of the clubs?" He asks again, this time sounding astonished. Xavier pulls a laptop out of his bag before typing away. He suddenly turns the screen towards me, a list of each and every student formed organization. My fingers graze the mouse, scrolling up and down until I reach a group that catches my attention. *American Red Cross at Cal.* "What's this?" I ask, clicking the link. Devan, beside me, glances at the screen before speaking, "One of the main medical revolving clubs. The other ones suck." I scroll on the page, looking at the things they do.

"Where do I sign up?"

TIFFANY

The cart bumps as the wheels roll across the parking lot, the plastic bags making an annoying sound as they rub against each other.

I turn around to notice Nadia continuing to trail behind me, but her head sucked into her phone screen. Reaching our cars, she bumps into me from behind as I come to a stop. "What the hell?"

"You bumped into me, Nadia." She sighs heavily before grabbing her car keys out of her back pocket. I grab mine out of my purse. Both beep at the same time. Opening her trunk, she begins loading the bags in, "You got things for your hygiene basket?"

"Yea. We stay within the budget?"

She pauses in her tracks, acting as if we hadn't. "Gotcha! We did. Only one dollar away from literally being directly AT the amount."

Relieved, I let out a long breath before putting the last few bags in my backseat. "You sure you set your mini fridge up the right way?"

"Yea, I'm sure, Tiffany. Ryan set it up for me, anyway. So if it doesn't work, we can just blame it on him." She laughs before closing her trunk door and grabbing her vape pen from her pocket. Breathing in, she blows out a puff of vapor, as usual. "Soft Tacos tonight, you know." "I know." I respond. We both push the carts back to the small corral. "Alright, then," She pauses. "See you at the dorm."

JAYDEN

I press send to confirm the email towards the group organizer. Devan claps his hands in sarcasm at a comment one of the guys had made.

"Hey, babe!" A familiar voice calls behind me, and I turn around to meet Tiffany. "Hey," I respond as she sits beside me. "Nadia 'n I just came back from Kroger, but I just got your message. Dinner tonight, still?"

"Yea."

"Where?"

I think for a moment, quickly glancing at Tony in front of me, who's mouthing a random restaurant nearby. "Uh, let's just do dinner here? Movie in my dorm?" The moment the sentence leaves my mouth, I hear Devan roughly sigh in frustration. "Alright. What time?" Flipping over my phone, I check the time. "8. Devan will be at a frat party, so we'll have the dorm all to ourselves." I watch as a fond smile creeps across her face at the thought. "Okay, I'm down. You pick the movie, alright?" I nod. Standing up, she leans over before she plants a kiss onto my forehead. "Love you, baby. See you tonight."

"God, Jayden, you're stuck."

Liam gives him a look before Xavier laughs at the two. "Tony, what the hell do you mean by that?"

I watch as Tiffany jogs back over to Nadia. She gets to her before they

CHAPTER FIFTY-SIX: ESCAPE TIME

both walk inside Blackwell hall. "That! I mean that!" Tony yells, his hands waving at me. Turning back towards the table, I give him a look of concern. "Jayden, the way you look at her," He continues, a light chuckle stuck in his throat. "It's literally as if she's your only focus."

"And what's so bad about that?" Xavier interrupts, trying his hardest to defend me, although I don't need it. "I'm just taking note of it, letting a dude know. He can't go wandering around campus with that gazing look, now can he?" I fade into my thoughts as I hear the group arguing.

Tony's words repeat in my head over and over again, unable to erase that sentence.

"...literally as if she's your only focus."

Fifty-Seven

CHAPTER FIFTY-SEVEN: NEW BEGINNINGS

TIFFANY

I hear the door shut behind us as we walk back in the room, the only sound we hear involves the buzz of people walking by the building outside. A knock echoes across the room just as Nadia sits down. She groans before standing up, causing me to lightly chuckle as I unpack the bags. Neveah's voice floods through the room as I hear the door open. "Hey, the student advisor said Tiffany rooms here?" I watch as Nadia's posture changes, her body now leaning against the wood door. "It depends. There are multiple different Tiffany's throughout campus." I don't hear Neveah's voice after the remark. "Her hair's down in an afro. Curly hair, but I think it's better to be described as probably 4a?" Nadia doesn't respond, but instead moves out the way. "Bingo," I salute before standing up. "Hey, glad I found you. Mariyah found a party at some sorority, you down tonight?" "Nah, sorry. I'm hanging out with Jayden tonight. Nachos and Horror," I

CHAPTER FIFTY-SEVEN: NEW BEGINNINGS

respond, crouching back down as I attempt to fit the last few things into the mini fridge.

"You're good." Turning around, she looks at Nadia. "Not tonight," She says, which throws me off. I stand up, looking at her with sarcastic shock. "I know, T. But I got something to do tonight." Her body maneuvers back to 'Veah. "But I'll come at the next one." Neveah nods, walking out the doorway and into the hall. "Alright, see you later, T."

NADIA

I close the door shut behind the girl before slowly walking back towards my bed. Rolling onto my back, I pull my phone from underneath the pillow. Unlocking it, I immediately head towards Instagram. Ryan's latest post loads up a video from the party him and Tiffany had gone to a few days ago, him downing shots. I continue scrolling to a photo of him and T, a red solo cup in each others hands, along with another photo of them laughing at something and the photo blurry. I Double tap to like, then scroll.

"Anyone on campus you interested in?"

I sit up and notice Tiffany standing at the edge of my bed.

I scoff, turning my phone off before walking towards the bagged food and unpacking it.

"Nah. Focusing on my studies for now."

"What about Ryan?"

The sentence freezes me in my tracks, obviously catching me off guard.

A smile slowly creeps up her face. "I saw the way you looked at him yesterday."

I roll my eyes, ignoring the comment as I continue to load the fridge.

"I mean, you should tell him."

"Tiffany, I don't like him. Simple as that."

"What about the kiss?"

"We've known each other for years, it was more like an accompanying kiss."

"Oh, really?" She replies.

"T," I uncomfortably laugh right after my reply, standing up before kicking the bags around my feet and walk towards the door. Putting on my slides, I hear the weight against the mattress lift up before Tiffany's voice, "Where you headed?" My right hand glides off the table as I feel the smooth card in the palm of my hand. "Ryan's," I pause, before opening the door. "Unpack the groceries, and god, please separate our snacks."

* * *

I knock on the door, almost immediately stopped by it opening. A white dude with curls stands there, staring at me unamused. "What?" He finally says, catching me off guard as I lightly flinch. "Ryan?" Moving out the way, I walk through the doorway, welcomed by a the strong scent of weed. Ryan sits on the ground, a blunt laced in between his two fingers. "I hope y'all know how to get this smell out."

"We do," the guy mumbles, closing the door behind me.

"Okay, whatever. Ry, I got somethin' to tell you." He blows out a puff of smoke before standing up, stretching and putting the stick onto the nightstand. Quickly, his grasp wraps around a can of Lysol. He tosses it towards the guy, and he does this quick thing that seems to almost immediately clear the air. "How did you-"

"What'd you need to tell me?" Ryan interrupts, throwing off my train of thought. "Right, um," I pause, looking at his roommate. Ryan turns before giving him the same look. "Dylan."

"Alright, Alright," he mumbles, opening the door before closing it behind him. "Ryan," I begin, trying my hardest to figure out what I'm about to

CHAPTER FIFTY-SEVEN: NEW BEGINNINGS

say. He hums before moving closer to me, my crossed arms the only thing keeping us apart.

"I like you."

Unfolding my arms off my chest, he places them to my side. Our noses touch. "I got that," He chuckles lightly, a smile growing across his face. "So," I look at him. "Feel the same way?" His hands graze my right arm, slowly rising onto my neck and soon my face. He nods slowly, and

before I'm even able to react, his lips part with mine, leaving me with nothing but silence.

TIFFANY

My phone buzzes rhythmically before I lift it and find a link to a website from Jayden. Pressing it, it automatically opens to the campus site, but a headline that reads *The Daily Californian*. I scroll a bit, enough for me to realize it's the campus paper. I press the information tab, quickly sent to a link providing the location to sign up. I screenshot it, slide a hoodie and some shoes on, then head out.

Walking down the hall, I notice Neveah walking down, Mariyah laughing alongside her. "Where you headed?" I quickly jog to get to their pace. Mariyah calms down before listening to my reply. "Uh, the student office. Found out there's a student paper?" She stops walking to clap her hands as if she'd just remembered something. "Right! Crap, I meant to send a picture of the poster I saw." We continue walking, now near the elevators. I smile, flattered at her thought. "Thanks. Where are you guys going?"

"We just finna ride around. Never been to LA, so why not check a few things out?" I nod before pressing the down arrow for the elevator. "You guys joining anything?" Mariyah opens her mouth to speak, but Neveah stops her. "Nah. Nothing that catches my eye."

"Freak you, 'Veah. I was just finna say that, but you just had to stop me."

The doors open, and we step inside. Mariyah presses the first floor. "I mean, unless they have a true crime kinda group I haven't seen, I'm pretty much not joining anything," 'Riyah continues, the attitude from her snap faded away. I nod, reaching for my phone out my back pocket. Jayden's name sits on my screen with a message I missed.

JAYDEN| You check it out? I just saw their sign-up poster and immediately thought of you.

Smiling at the screen, I type a reply.

ME| yea, thanks, baby. headed to the student office now.

The doors open once again, this time we're greeted by the cold air that sits in throughout student floor. We step out and I glance around, looking for the office before I catch view of it. Turning around, I realize they had already wandered towards the doors. "See y'all later!" I call before heading towards the office. Without looking, 'Veah throws a thumbs up before they walk outside.

* * *

Walking through the doors, I'm greeted by a black woman manning the front desk.

"Hey! If you're here for any sign-ups," She continues, her hand now raised and pointing towards a cork board on my far right. "Head over there." I smile as a 'Thanks' before quickly walking over. A girl with wavy curls stands near the board, signing a piece of paper before noticing me. "Oh, my bad."

"No, you're good. It might not even be for me," I respond before looking at the top of the page. I do so, almost immediately embarrassed when she

CHAPTER FIFTY-SEVEN: NEW BEGINNINGS

hands the pen to me. Laughter ascends from her lips. I sign my name before looking at the other side of the sheet, noticing it asking for your office assigning email. I write it down before placing the pen into the cupholder that sits on a table beside the cork board.

The girl and I walk alongside one another as we walk out the office. "I couldn't help but notice you'd signed the same slip of paper?" I bite my lip, remembering the embarrassing moment. "Yea," I chortle. "What's your name?" Quickly, she adds something on. "Not to seem creepy, but we may end up working together."

"No, I get it, not creepy at all," I laugh. We both walk near the outside doors. "I gotta head out, but I'm Tiffany." She nods as a smile grows across her face before she responds. "Alright, I'm Ever." I turn around and walk away, but not fully before I realize the conversation hadn't been ended properly. "Nice to meet you, Ever."

II

SEPTEMBER 6, 2022

Freshman Year of College

Fifty-Eight

CHAPTER FIFTY-EIGHT: WELCOME TO HELL

My phone buzzes beside me, the most aggravating sound one could hear exiting from it; an alarm. Tired, I stretch my arm over and feel nothing but pain.

My hand collides with the wood, making a loud thump. "Crap," I mumble to myself, writhing in pain. Now awake, I feel around at my bed before finally feeling my phone. Right when I grab it, the sound stops. Flipping it face-up the screen is pitch black, with no sound at all coming from it. "Shoot," I mumble once again, frustrated that I hadn't plugged it in the night before. "Nadia?" I groan, looking over at her side of the room.

Nothing but silence. She might've gone out with Ryan. Getting up, I look out the window and watch as everyone walks around campus. I walk towards the outlet where my cord sits and plug it in before watching as the screen quickly illuminates with the Apple Logo. Slowly, it loads to my home screen where the time is displayed. Reading it, it takes me a moment before realizing: **It's the first day of classes and I'm late.**

9:20 AM

Rushing, I quickly snatch my bonnet off and waltz towards my dresser, ruffling around to see if I can find anything. A black TLC T-shirt finds its way into my grasp before I grab a pair of white leggings. "Crap, Crap, Crap," I say to myself, thinking I'm mumbling it. Looking in the mirror, I notice my curls matted against my head and shake it before watching it immediately take its shape once again. I glance down at my phone, the time blazed on the screen.

9:27 AM

How'd it take me 7 minutes to literally grab a random shirt?! Rushing, I grab my bag I had sitting by the bed and slip into my slides, ignoring the fact my toe rings (they're cute on me, don't worry) aren't even on. Before exiting all the way, I look at my reflection in the mirror one more time. "That's good," I mutter, quickly sprinting out seconds later.

I dash across campus as I probably look crazy. *Now, I know what you're thinking: Why are you rushing? It's college, it's alright.* No. It's not. I'm determined to set a perfect impression for my teachers and give myself a head start into the college life, that way I'm practically set for the entire year. But No, my alarm had to go off literally two hours late! Finally, I reach the main building, glancing at the clock over the doors.

9:31 AM

Shoot, the class ends at 9:45. Now speed walking, I look around the walls as I notice each door has a name plate, much like high school. I remember my schedule did read that News Media is on the first floor, so all I gotta do is walk down one of these halls. I have terrible luck, so I quickly pray before racing down the left hall. I look at the plate that reads Prof. Smith, thanking god for my not-so glorious recovery. I open the door, greeted by an silent classroom. My eyes dart around as I look for a spot for me to sit. I find a seat and sit in it. Silent chatter waves throughout the room. God, you would think the murmurs stop by now. "Name?" I look up from my

CHAPTER FIFTY-EIGHT: WELCOME TO HELL

bag as I notice she's speaking to me. "Uh, Mohan. Tiffany Mohan." She nods before walking behind the podium and writing on a slip of paper. "Right." She pauses. I open my journal, quickly realizing people had theirs open. I look at the board behind her, seeing the notes written across. "We won't do this again, Mohan, will we?" Really? I'm being called out my a professor already? People don't snicker, but instead look at me as they wait for a reply. "Yea, no."

If I could think of one positive outcome that comes out on my side, is hey, at least the class was short? "Alright, to end the day, I want you to pick a partner in which you will work on one video segment." Everyone in the classrooms sighs. She shuffles around her desk in attempt to look for something. Everyone begins to stand up to leave as she raises the sheet up into the air. "Each segment must be at least 3 to 5 minutes long. More information will be sent to each of y'alls emails. Keep your eyes out!" The class murmurs a reply before we pour out.

Walking out the doorway, I feel a tap on my shoulder. I turn around, and meet myself face to face with someone familiar. "Hey, I had no idea you had news media." Ever. "Hey, yea, I thought it's something nice to add into the schedule. Planning to become a journalist," I reply, moving onto the side and out of everyone's way. She looks at me awkwardly, and I do the same. "Well, just wanted to say hey, I guess," She adds. "Nice. See you."

"See ya."

I check my phone.

9:47 AM

My next course isn't until 12, so I can wander around, I guess. Walking down the echoing corridor, I pass a large room and look inside, catching glance of a familiar shirt. Looking through the window a bit more, I notice it's Jayden. The name plate outside the door reads that it's Biochemistry. An elective I remember Jayden picking right before we'd moved in. Accidentally bumping into the glass, I gather the attention of

The Bookposal

pretty much everyone in the class. Awkwardly, I sprint away before feeling a light vibration against my back from what I'm guessing is my phone. Now outside the building, I'm surrounded by a chilly breeze and a crap load of people walking around outside and talking. Walking towards a nearby bench, I take my bag off and grab my phone, quickly greeted by a message from Jayden.

JAYDEN| Hey, lol. You alright? Sounded like it hurt..

I awkwardly chortle at the message, still embarrassed.

ME| yea, im good. it didn't i swear. hows ur class?

He doesn't respond, probably paying attention to the lecture. Standing up, I toss my phone briskly into my bag. I look around the campus around me, thinking of where to head to next. My eye lingers around a tall building, looking much like a Greek museum. Wandering towards it, I look at the signs around it and very quickly realize that it's the campus library. It's huge, and I can only imagine what the inside looks like.

I walk in, instantly regretting the fact I hadn't brought a jacket.

It's chilly outside, but it's freezing in here. You would think the heat would be turned on since, you know, fall started. "Hello!" A woman greets before prancing towards me. "Hey," I reply, my hands rubbing along my arms. "Sorry about the chill, the headmaster refuses to turn the heat on until later this month. But may I help you?" I look around, quickly gathering the hint of something very important. Stacks of textbooks rest upon almost all the tables, half of them open. "Excuse me, but we have textbooks?" I ask, and she turns around towards those tables. "Yes! We just bought a new batch of every textbook on campus," She pauses in her sentence before asking me a question. Her voice lingers a bit, uneasily asking, "You didn't order any textbooks, did you?" I shake my head no. "Oh, dear. Follow me, alright, hon? You're gonna need these every day for every class. Each one

CHAPTER FIFTY-EIGHT: WELCOME TO HELL

is $100, but since you seem to have to get the older ones," She continues, now walking behind the front desk as I stand in front of it. "I'll only charge you $50 per book. Sound like a deal?" Rapidly, I nod my head yes before bending down the grab my phone from my bag.

> ME| i may or may not have ordered textbooks..
>
> MOMMY| Tiffany! How could you forget that? Are you serious? You're in college now. You have to start being more responsible.
>
> This is the last time your father and I are saving your behind! How much do you need?

I sigh roughly. Should've known a lecture was gonna come from this.

> ME| Mb, mama. she said $50 per book. ill find out what classes ill need it for and get the price to you.
>
> MOMMY| Alright. We'll just send $900 to your savings account.
>
> Do not spend on anything other than CLASS-REQUIRED things, okay?
>
> ME| okay. love you guys.
>
> MOMMY| Love you too.

Standing back up, I look at the librarian. "Okay, my mom said they just sent some money into my account."

"Got it. I see your schedule for the first few weeks, seems like you have about 5 classes that require textbooks." "What's the total?" I ask. She types onto her computer before replying, "$250." She continues typing before she stands up. Walking back to my side, she grabs 5 different books and stamps something inside before she hands them to me. "Have a nice day, Tiffany. And don't forget to get this done ahead of time for the next round, alright?" I nod. "See you soon, I hope."

Turning around, I reply, "Oh, you definitely will."

Walking into Blackwell hall, I head into the elevator, bumping into Jayden. "Hey, babe," He says before planting a kiss on my forehead. "Hey," I strain.

The books are heavy as heck, and I have to carry all of these on my own. Quickly, he grabs the top two books from the stack, then a third one, leaving me with only two books. "Jayden, you don't have to." "Yeah, but I want to," He responds before holding the stack with his left hand and pressing my floor with his right. "How's the first day so far?" He asks. I instantly think back to the class, awkwardly walking in at 9:32, being called out, having to get the old books instead of the new ones.

"Sucky," I respond. The doors open and he lightly chuckles at my response. We walk down the hall and turn left onto the side where my dorm is. Reaching the door, he offers to hold the two books I still have while I unlock the door. I unlock it, open it, and he places the stack onto my mattress. "Thanks," I say, giving him a quick kiss on the cheek. "No problem." He looks around before sitting on my bed beside the stack, and I grab a few of the books and put them under the bed. "What time is your next class?" "12," I respond. The books now under the bed, I sit beside him. I lay my head onto his shoulder, and he leans back further onto my mattress before inviting me to lay onto his chest. Back onto the previous topic, I ask him the same question, "What time is yours?" "1." I look up as I give him a look of confusion. "I had a 7 AM." I lightly laugh before glancing back at the headboard of the bed.

"Wanna grab lunch before class?"

"Hm." I mumble, moving higher towards his neck.

His chin collides with my head, but its comforting. Remembering his question, I respond quickly, "Yea." Sitting up, I pat his stomach and before he props onto his elbows. "Where to?" "We could stay on campus and just make something with the food me and Nadia bought," I say, a dash of squeakiness in my voice as I recommend the decision. "Yea, I'm down. What'd you guys buy?" I stand up and head towards the mini fridge that's packed full. Opening it, a few things spill out, but I just read them before putting them back in. "We can make soft tacos?" I suggest. He stands up as I toss the bag of soft tortilla shells and catches it. He stretches before replying, "Sure." I grab the small container of Parsley before the ground beef, cheese, and iceberg lettuce. Standing up, I shut the door with my foot

CHAPTER FIFTY-EIGHT: WELCOME TO HELL

as my arms are full.

"We'll borrow spices from Neveah, I'm sure she's got some," I say, walking through the door he holds open. "Alright." We walk down the hall and towards the other side, where Neveah and Mariyah's dormitory is. I knock on it, causing the Parsley and lettuce to fall out of my grasp. "Crap," I mutter, and Jayden crouches down as he grabs them. The door opens, Mariyah seeming as if she'd just rolled out of bed.

Reading my mind, she immediately says, "I got a 2 AM class, my next is at 1, then I'm thrashed with my others." Unsurely, I nod before continuing with my original intention. "You got any spices?"

"Yea, why?"

"Well, can we use some for these soft tacos?" Moving out the way, we walk through before the door shuts behind us. Her pink bonnet flops with each step she takes, and her slippers making a satisfying swoosh sound as she walks. Reaching into a bookshelf, she digs through a brown wicker basket before handing me the basics. Onion Powder, Chill Powder, Garlic Powder, and a small container of Ms. Dash.

"Here, return them as soon as you're done," She says before exasperatingly laying onto her bed. I looked around while we were waiting, her side has these string lights with photos and small memorabilia pinned on. Her wall was a brick wall contact paper, with posters of Chadwick Boseman, The Simpsons, Megan Thee Stallion, and of course, Tupac. "Thanks, 'Riyah," I thank, stepping into the hallway as Jayden follows. Sometimes he just reminds me of a little chickadee, following your every move. "Shut the door behind you!"

**

I take a bite of the taco, embracing the juices and simple spices.

I've been living off of ramen and take-out for the past 4 weeks, and I don't think my body could handle any more of that torture. I grab the napkin sitting on the table beside me and wipe my mouth. Jayden gazes at me with a look of satisfaction washed across his face. "Did you just poison me or something?" I mutter before taking another bite. He lets out a bit of laughter before a hear a reply. "No, I swear." I laugh, too before I take a sip from the cup of water. "How's college life going?" he asks.

"You sound like my mom," I mutter, grabbing a chip from the bag between us. "I'm sure I do. How's it going?" He nibbles on the taco as I mumble a reply. "Difficult."

"How?" He freezes, his mind probably off tracking onto something else.

"It's frustrating, stressful."

"It's only the first day."

"Well, I'm going through hell right now," I add before squeezing a bit of lime into the taco. I laugh, remembering what happened earlier this morning. It's funny now that I look back on it. A chuckling sound in my voice, I respond.

"Hey, we all are."

CHAPTER FIFTY-NINE: BACK TO REALITY

JAYDEN

Suddenly all the stress from before fades away as we talk more.

"Right! Who knew Nadia would soften up around Ryan like that?" Tiffany laughs as we talk about the two. She smiles before eating the last few bites of the taco, lettuce and meat spilling out from the other end. Trying her best not to laugh, she holds her hand in front of her mouth. "Napkin," She says, her mouth muffled and full of food. I chuckle before grabbing a napkin, noticing the one she had earlier was used. Reaching over, I wipe her mouth. "Here," I mumble, retreating quickly before I hand her another one for her hands. She grabs it out of my grasp before wiping the oil off. "Thanks, baby."

Folding the used napkin, I grab my plastic cup along with Tiffany's trash as well. She stands up and pushes the chair in, walking towards me as I head to the trash. "So, didn't you say your parents bought you a place?"

"Yea," She responds, typing on her phone. We walk out the doors, leaving the chilly cafeteria. "Why aren't you staying there?"

"Cause," She pauses, putting her phone into the her side pocket. "I wanna move in on campus first. It would suck to not really get the full 'feel' of college, you know?" We both stop walking as I give her a look of confusion. "I hope you get where I'm coming from," Her voice lightly dulls down as she speaks. "I do," I continue. "I think." She laughs playfully as we walk back into her dorm building, chilly air hitting our heads from above.

"Anyway," I pause before grabbing my phone out my back pocket. Tiffany stands along my side as she waits for me.

"I should probably get going, my class starts pretty soon." The time reads 1:50. Glancing at the screen, her body stiffens as she backs away slowly. "Crap, Crap, Crap!" "What? What happened?"

"I'm literally an hour late to my next class! I had the time memorized, and," Her voice begins breaking. Looking at me, her face seems to hold back tears.

"I was supposed to be in there at twelve, and it's literally one freaking fifty." I rush to her side, moving her onto the nearby couches in the main area. People glance at us as I move in front of her.

"T, it's okay. You have tomorrow. You don't have to be on time to all of your classes at once." Tiff responds, the sound of her voice wavering in and out as she attempts to fight back more tears, "Yes, I do. It's the appearance I'd set in high school, it has to be here, too." I place my hand onto her chin, moving it up to allow her eyes to meet mine. "Tiffany, you've set all of these expectations for yourself here that you're panicking. Look at me," I pause, noticing her eyes dashing around us as others pass by. "College is the time we learn more about ourselves. Let ourselves loose and find out more on who we are. You're a hardworking partier, T." She chuckles as she wipes her tears. "Stay that way. Don't try to impress people just for the sake of it. We're here for four years. They'll forget about us once we leave."

Leaning in, she hugs me tightly as we stay there for a few minutes. Hugging, embracing and enjoying the moment.

CHAPTER FIFTY-NINE: BACK TO REALITY

The moment I realize she may be the one.

TIFFANY

I wipe my nose before we let go, words immediately leaving my mouth before I can process.

"You should head out."

"You good?" I nod my head in confirmation, not sure if I even believe myself. He plants a kiss on my forehead before slowly heading towards the automated doors, quickly jogging out onto the crowded campus. Heading towards the elevator, the doors open as I'm face to face with Ever. I move out the way as she exits. She stops in front of me, the doors shutting from lack of movement.

"You got the email yet?"

"Email?"

She grabs her phone as it unlocks, opening the app Outlook. She presses something in her inbox, an email confirming her initiation within *The Californian*. Quickly, my shove my hand into my pocket before opening my app myself. I sit in silence as I stare at my inbox, the latest message from the owner of the newspaper.

"Want me to sit here and open it for you or something?" Ever says, her voice between a mix of sarcasm and genunity. My left thumb grazes along the silver ring that rests on my pointer finger, slowly fidgeting with it as I stare. Ever clears her throat, startling me out of my zone out. "Right, right, yea." I stutter before quickly pressing the email. My eyes dash across the screen, quickly trying to process what was sent.

Tiffany Jesse Mohan,

Hey! This is Analease Jordan, the primary student owner for <u>The Californian</u>. I've sent this email to contact you about your signature on our latest sign ups. Now, don't be scared. Well, actually, be scared. Because this email is to either let you you if you've been chosen as one of the few; literally few, as it's 13 of us; students behind the paper. Your verification will be placed under the following line:

———————

YOU HAVE BEEN ACCEPTED INTO <u>THE CALIFORNIAN</u>.

Very soon, we will be gathering within the main student union; in the office building, the seating area; to discuss one another and get to know each other Friday afternoon at 7:45 (PM). Please bring a black ink pen, you will fill out some forms providing us some information about you. Thank You, and I can't wait to write with you! <3

XOXO,

Analease J. :)

"Seems like we'll be working together, eh?" Ever says as I look up at her, a smile planted across my face. "Hell, yea." I press the button for the elevator that directs the chute upward. "Can't wait," She sarcastically blows. The doors open before I prance in. "See you tonight."

JAYDEN

Walking alongside Devan, I tell him a bit of my realization towards Tiffany.

"So, you actually <u>love her</u> love her?" I nod as we walk up the stairway, passing a nearby couple. "Alright," He roughly inhales as we reach our dorm. It's the first one to your right if you come by stairs. He takes out his card before sliding it in front of the card reader. It unlocks, letting us inside. Sitting on my bed, I kick off my shoes, being sure I'm not creasing the front. Laying back, I grab my phone out of my pocket, sliding up on a message Maddie's recently sent me. Devan clears his throat, gathering my

CHAPTER FIFTY-NINE: BACK TO REALITY

attention, before continuing to speak. "Do something about it." I chuckle uncomfortably and unsurely as my eyes scan the text.

MADDIE| i relapsed.

CHAPTER SIXTY: BITTERSWEET

TIFFANY

"You know what you need?" Nadia says, tossing the clothes she'd thrown on the ground this morning back into her dresser. "What, N?" I reply, unamused. My face sucked within the textbook between my legs, a notebook on my upper right thigh as I take notes. "A break."

"I can't take a break right now, it's the beginning of the year, I can get backed up." She scoffs before sitting beside me. "T, you just told me you had a near panic attack in the union today," She pauses. I continue to look down and take notes. "You need at least an hour worth a break. What'd you say Jayden said?"

"That I put all of these expectations of myself into my head."

"Right. You did, at least that's what it seems."

I roll my eyes. "Seriously, come to the party with me tonight. Join one of the sororities or something. You said you liked Track?"

"I said I liked watching track."

CHAPTER SIXTY: BITTERSWEET

"Well, go to one of the meets when the season comes!"

I take a deep breath before I close the textbook shut. "Alright, I'm down." She tosses on a smile before grabbing the blue pen off the nightstand. "It's at 10 tonight, Delta Sigma Theta. I'll text the address to you later." I give her a thumbs up. She stands up and walks towards the door where her shoes sit. She slides her feet in before bending over and crouching to tie them. Standing back up, she places her hand onto the door handle before opening it a crack. "See you later, T. Give yourself a break, alright?" I toss a thumbs up before she leaves, keeping the door a crack as Mariyah pops in right after. "Hi," She says. I place the book from earlier onto the ground and slide it under the bed, just enough for me to find later on. "Hey," I respond before sitting back onto my bed. She leans against the wall across from me, giving me a look. "What?"

"Nothing." I give her the same look before she walks over and sits along the edge of my mattress. "You heading to the Sorority party tonight?" I nod. Grabbing my phone out my pocket, I head to messages before typing a quick thing to Jayden.

ME| there's a sorority party tonight. you down?

"Yea, Nadia managed to get me interested." She chuckles before standing up.

"Alright, well see you tonight. Try your best not to not have fun, okay?"

"Since when would I not have fun?"

"Since you got here. You've had this determined attitude since 'Veah and I've met you. Loosen up."

This is the third time someone's told me to "loosen up". Am I really losing my pizzazz? My party animal? "Mariyah, you have no idea how much of a true party lover I am. I gotcha tonight, you'll see the true Tiffany at that party, alright?" She holds her arms up as she quickly surrenders sarcastically. "Alright, Alright," She pauses as she backs up towards the door. "See you tonight, then."

I look back at my phone before quickly texting Avery a quick message.

ME| i think im losing my shine..

The three dots quickly load up before I watch as her reply loads onto the screen.

AVERY| um.. no one LOSES their shine. it just gets tangled up with other things. what's going on?

ME| it's just stressful yk?

AVERY| i admit, i'm not going to parties much, either, but that's when it was high school. we're adults now, we can't really do what we did the past few years, you know?

ME| yea

Avery calls me instead of replying. I answer as she smiles brightly, standing up as she shows off her room decor that sits behind her. **"When I tell you Clark is exactly as I thought!"** She pauses excitedly as I playfully laugh at her action. **"The track team is bomb, I'm doing hella good so far. Beat my 400 meter personal best from high school, 46 seconds, with 41 seconds! Woo!"** She cheers, her arms flailing everywhere. "Proud of you, Av. Guessing you're not also continuing the cheer team?"

"Yea, no. **Em somewhat convinced me to step out, cause what if I get some kind of offer for the Olympics or something? I'd be distracted with both dance and track too much to really pay attention to any of my classes, too.**"

I shrug in agreement.

"**Well, enough about me,**" She pauses, her face moving closer to the camera. "**Time to talk about you.**" I smile brightly as I think of what to update her on. "Okay, um, I joined the campus paper. First meeting is at 7."

CHAPTER SIXTY: BITTERSWEET

Unconsciously, I check the time. 6:36. **"First day sucked. Like really. I got into my German course and found out they expected for me to already know the basics."** I watch as Avery holds back a laugh at this. "Whatever. Oh, and I made some new friends."

"Aw, Tiffany got over me and Em's lack of presence," She coos as I flip her off. "Then to sum it up, I'm gonna head to the Californian's meeting."

"Californian?" She repeats, her voice questioning what I'd just said. "Yea. It's like the schools' newspaper. People actually read it, surprisingly."

"That's literally awesome. My little journalist!" I chuckle lightly at her reaction. **"How's Jayden?"**

"Good. He joined the schools' Red Cross group or something. He's enjoying it so far from what I can tell," I reply, glancing out the window.

"Oh, and how's Em doing? She talk to you?" I chime in.

"Yea, she's doing good. She call you yet?"

"No. Texted her a few times. She's been busy."

"Yea. She joined the schools' varsity dance team, said her schedule's been jacked up since. Practices every other night for like, 3 hours. Then she's deciding to maybe join Cross Country, so she practices for 2 hours on her own everyday."

"Wow."

"I know. But hey, she's on Memphis' top dance team, you know?"

"Yea," I nod. I watch as she checks her watch before reverting her attention back to me. **"I gotta head out for my next class, but it was nice hearing your voice, T. Talk tonight?"**

"Yeah, tonight. Miss you, Av," I reply before hanging up, hearing the small sound come from the speaker.

* * *

I check the time once again, this time it reads 6:50. Time to head out.

I put my phone in my back pocket and slide on some slides that sit beside my bed as I stand up. I'm wearing skinny jeans, a tank top with one of

Jaydens' hoodies over it, and my hair is in one overhead afro puff. Over time, I've very quickly realized that I do not feel like dressing all classy for everyday occasions here.

I walk towards the door as it automatically opens, Nadia coming in from the other side. "My bad. Where you headed?" She asks walking past me as I move out of her way. "My meeting. It's in ten," I respond, now standing in the doorway. "Okay, well there's gonna be food at the party, so don't stock up on snacks to eat in there for now." I close the door behind me as I exit, but she opens in once again as I turn around and meet her face. "Stock up on things to bring up here, though," She says with a smile as she swiftly pulls her head out the crack and closes the door after speaking.

In the elevator, I meet Ever, who's already pressing the button for the main floor. "Hey," I say, and she replies back. "You know this meeting confirms if we're really getting in or not, right?" "Yea," I respond, picking at my uneven nail. I've gotten my acrylics removed, so since then I've been trying to grow my nails out. It's going good so far, except for the fact that sometimes I'll chip one and then it'll just make me have to file it lower than the others. The doors open into the cool lobby, and we both exit as four other people enter after us.

We head towards the doors and jog to the main office building. We stand in front of it, the tall building towering over us as we quickly head up the steps. Walking inside, it's crowded as hell. Other club owners also decided to host their meetings within the building, so it causes it to be nothing but loud and packed. I turn around when someone taps my shoulder and notice it was Ever. "Down there, the group is down there," She speaks, her finger pointing towards a group where people are seated. We walk over, sit down, and are immediately greeted by the head owner. "Hey! I'm Analease, as you know, and I'm the head writer of The Californian! So glad to see you guys here. Now, for us to begin checking out everyone's listed credentials, let's get to know one another, huh?"

No one responds, nothing but the sound of the crowd around us. "Okay, then. Not getting to know each other, then," She says before tucking a strand of her hair behind her ear. She sits down on the beanbag beside

CHAPTER SIXTY: BITTERSWEET

Ever, grabbing a clipboard that sat on the ground before speaking.

"Okay, when I call your name, say here, come to me, and I'll hand you a form. Fill out the form, including any previous experience towards writing or Journalism at all. You'll hand it in to me as soon as you're done, and everyone should get an email with the confirmation or decline later tonight." Clicking her pen, she continues, "There will be 20 people out of the 30 of you here that get a confirmation email. The ones declined, you can try again next year. Those who get confirmation, I will also include a meeting date to allow me to interview you. You'll get your news later that night. Any questions?"

No one raises their hand nor speaks, probably stunned by how she'd said that. "Alright! Justin? Audrey? Veronica? Maya?" Each name separated by a quick response by the person she called and them standing up to get the form. Finally, she gets to my name. "Tiffany?"

"Here," I reply, standing up and walking over towards her. She hands me the sheet and gives me a look before I sit back down. Glancing at Ever, I notice that she'd noticed. Her eyes read as if she's asking me what happened, and I just shrug. Reverting my attention back towards the form, I begin filling it out.

It feels like I'm writing my personal essay to have gotten here all over again. I mean, everything on the first two pages were just asking for some background, including information towards previous writing opportunities.

But then I flipped to the third page, and it just felt like I was at home and struggling to write my personal essay all over again.

Where do you see yourself in five years?

I rub my thigh in frustration, trying to think but I can't.

"Five minutes left!" She calls, and I watch as multiple stand up and hand her their forms. Glancing back down at my paper, I click my pen over and over as I realize I might just have to write a random thing and turn it in.

Where do you see yourself in five years?
I see myself raising a family and becoming a world-traveling journalist.

Quickly, I stand up and hand her the paper before I speed walk towards the doors to leave. "T!" I hear Ever call. I thought she might've left by now. Turning around, I wait for her as she jogs towards me. Now caught up to me, we begin walking back to the dorm building. "You good?"
"Yea."
"I saw you panicking, you sure?"

I bite my lip to prevent myself from spilling over again. "Yea, I'm good, I swear," I reply, lightly stuttering between words. "Alright," She mutters, and I watch as she slowly lets the topic go. "You seen Jayden?" I ask. Her face scrunches up as she replies,"Who?" Right, not everyone you know knows Jay, Tiffany. "Never mind," I respond. I pat my sides for my phone, but very quickly realize that I have leggings, so I had to leave it in the dorm. "Shoot," I mumble, quickly speeding up my pace. "T!"
"I'll catch you later, okay? See you at the party tonight!"

Sixty-One

CHAPTER SIXTY-ONE: URGENCY

I walk inside the house beside Nadia, probably looking hella lost.

"Loosen up. Smoke something. Drink something. Do something," she says, music muffling her voice. I nod before we walk into the kitchen, greeted by a pack of girls standing around the island, drinking and playing flip-cup. "God, yes!" I hear one of them yell before ascending into laughter as the guy across from her downs a bottle of beer. I head towards them, grabbing a red cup from the stack beside them. Reaching into the cooler, I grab a beer before pouring half of it in it.

Nadia walks over to me as she mixes Tequila and Vodka before adding a spritz of lime inside. Taking my cup, she pours it into the sink before replacing the mixture with one of her own. I watch as she grabs a can of White Claw and pours it in, along with one shot of Tequila before handing it back to me. I take a sip, my face scrunching up at the taste. I hate it, but enjoy it at the same time. "I'll be back. Stay here, or not," she says before wandering off into the other room.

The parties here are definitely dialed down significantly more than high school parties. I'm used to people blasting music on the highest volume, along with the room packed to the brim, but that could just be the parties

I've grown up with. Looking around the kitchen, I glance at the few people talking. Laugh, joking, making out, even. Jeez, this is embarrassing. I have no one to talk to, and to make matters worse, I look crazy looking around, trying my hardest to identify someone.

Looking to my right, I notice Ever talking to a guy. His hair seems to be a duke-style cut, along with his beard as a short stubble, as if he'd just shaved a few days before. Diamond studs are pierced in his ears. "Hey!" I say, lightly startling Ever. "Hey," She mutters. She holds her hand out at the guy, signaling something as he pulls out a cigarette box and puts one in her hand. She grabs a lighter out of her back pocket before placing the stick between her lips and lighting the bud. Her fingers grasp along the sides before lifting it from her mouth, a puff of smoke quickly exiting as she breathes out.

"This is Liam, my brother. Liam, this is Tiffany, someone in the school paper with me." He shyly waves before taking a sip from the water bottle in his hand. Ev laughs before harshly coughing from inhaling the smoke unexpectedly. "Crap," She strains, her hands grabbing a hold of Liam's water. She snatches it out of his hands before moving the cigarette to her left hand and taking a sip, causing him to angrily sigh. Removing the bottle from her mouth, she laughs, this time without interruption. "What?"

"Dang it, Eve. You know what," He groans before snatching the bottle from her. She rolls her eyes before moving the cigarette back to her right hand and into her mouth. "Anyway, I was asking how Kara was?" Ever says, giving me a side eye as I slightly feel ignored. "Yea, yea, she's good. Law school's doing her well," He mumbles, reaching for his phone in his back pocket. Ever clears her throat before speaking to me.

"So, you gotten an email yet?" I shrug, quickly pulling my phone from my pocket. Nothing in my notifications, and I unlock it and open Gmail to be sure. "Nope," I respond, my phone vibrating in my hand from a message from Jay popping up on my screen.

JAYDEN| I'm in Memphis.

CHAPTER SIXTY-ONE: URGENCY

I scoff, quickly typing away at my screen as I watch his bubbles pop up right after my message had been sent.

ME| ?? why

JAYDEN| Maddison relapsed. I might stay a week or two to support her.
Send any assignments I miss. I'll send my schedule. Told my professors I'd be out.

Staring at my screen, I continue watching as the bubbles load.

JAYDEN| Talk to you tomorrow, okay? I'll let you know how she's doing when I get there.

JAYDEN

I pull into the dimly lit parking lot before rushingly heading towards and up the stairway, stopping at the correct floor, and walking to the door. I knock on it, but no answer. Digging in my pockets, I grasp my keys and turn the knob before entering.

"She's not going," I hear mom yell. Shutting the door behind me, I head towards the kitchen where the two are.

"Rayn, I'm not arguing with you on this. She's going to the center and that's final."

I watch as he walks towards me, his shoulder bumping into mine as he turns towards the stairway and heads up. Mom's elbows rest against the counter as she rests her head in her hands, pulling her hair in frustration. "Hey, Jayden," She mumbles, not bothering to react to me. "You're just gonna let him decide Maddie's future?"

"Jayden, I would rather not speak about this right now with you."

"She's not even his child," I continue, ignoring her request. I listen as my voice increases in volume. She sighs roughly. "She is."

"No, she's not."

"Dang it, Jayden, can I get some demand in my own house?"

"Go ask Bryant that! You've let him decide half the things around here since y'all got married!"

I yell, my frustration now taking over.

"Jayden," She pauses, lifting her head. Her eyes are red, and her hair is messed up. I hear her whimpering, her voice shaking as she attempts to speak. "I can't do this right now."

I hear footsteps come down the stairs before turning around, face to face with Bryant. "Don't even try," He mumbles, walking towards us and then to the fridge. "I'll drop her off tomorrow. I'm sure they won't mind the last-minute decision." His hand grasps a beer before he shuts the fridge door and twists the cap. He takes a sip, his dreads falling onto his shoulder as he walks towards the couch and turns on the TV. "Bry-," Mom mumbles, her voice breaking as she manages to form her words. He doesn't hear, but I do.

"Bryant." Her tone becomes sterner. He turns the volume down, watching as mom stands up quickly and paces towards him.

"She's not going."

"God, we're still on that?"

"She's not your daughter!"

"And?"

I watch her fists clench together before releasing them promptly. "Bryant, she's staying, and that's final."

"Well, if she stays, I leave." Glancing at Mom, I watch as she bites her lip before saying something else.

"Then leave."

CHAPTER SIXTY-TWO: ASSOCIATION

TIFFANY

I wake up with my head mashed into my pillow.

Sitting up, I notice Nadia across the room typing away on her phone, giggling at it every so often. The sun beams through the curtains, giving me a pounded headache. Quickly, I shove my face back into the pillow, but it's too late. The damage has already been done. "Good Morning!" "Hey, Nadia," I mumble, wiping my mouth. I sit up once again, glancing back at Nadia's bed when I notice she'd gotten up. I hear her voice from behind me before the mini-fridge door closes. "You should get up, you have your AM."

"Imma be honest," I pause, regretting my life decisions.

"I thought I would've missed those already."

I hear her chuckling before the creaking of the bed frame beside me. "It's 7:25 right now. I get up early all the time, believe it or not." Standing up, I rub my eyes. Slowly, I walk back to my bed, my eyes squinting as I face the window. A notification from Jayden sits on my screen.

JAYDEN| Might stay here a bit longer.

I sigh quickly before grabbing it and turning the brightness down and typing.

ME| yea, yea, you're good. love you

I toss my phone onto the bed before I take a large swig of my water, half the bottle gone as I put it back down. "I should get ready, too, to be honest," Nadia says before putting her phone and vape onto the nightstand. "I have an AM." Uninterested, I nod lightly as the bottle meets my lips once again. As she slips out of her bed, I get more of what she's wearing. A tank top, Nike shorts, white ankle socks, and an anime-patterned bonnet. She takes that off as her braids stay in fall to her shoulders. A satin scarf is wrapped around her scalp. Heading towards our plastic dressers, I watch as she grabs a pair of Grey sweatpants, another tank top, and a bra and underwear. Nadia tosses them onto a chair before she slides her feet into her flip-flops and grabs her shower basket off the shelf.

"You should come down, too. Around this time, the showers are clear. If you wait any longer, it's gonna be packed, and you may have to go to class reeking of sweat." I sigh before laying back on my mattress. "Okay, I got it. I'll be down in five," I respond. "Alright," She replies before exiting. I hear the door shut behind her as I'm left in silence.

Standing up, I head to the dressers and grab a bra and underwear as well before walking towards the closet and grabbing a pair of light Grey jeans and candy-corn colored sweater. I grab my shower caddy from the shelf and hold it. My phone buzzes against my mattress as I walk to the door, giving me the impulse of wanting to check it. Placing the basket back down, I walk over and grab it, quickly reading the notification, with nothing but a reminder from my period tracker reminding me to drink water. I toss it back down, walking towards the door to grab my basket once again and

CHAPTER SIXTY-TWO: ASSOCIATION

exit.

Walking down the hall, I notice people slowly leave their rooms and come down the hall towards the showers, causing me to speed up a bit. I reach the showers pretty quickly after that, grab a towel, and slide my feet out of my slides and into these free flip-flops before placing them onto my shelf and hopping in the shower.

* * *

I can say that one thing I'm gonna have to get used to is public showering.

I mean, over the summer there was barely anyone here, so it was practically like home. Not many people showered in here, and when they did, they would wait until the person inside would come out. But now that the semester has started, god it's awkward. And it's not like there aren't stalls, it is. It's just that it's so many people in the room.

People walk in and out, the door opening and closing every thirty seconds. You hear people talk the entire time, leaving you to wonder if they even actually lather themselves with soap. And I know, we all talk. But the amount of copious chatter that I can hear throughout the room makes me think I'm the only one actually getting myself clean.

Reaching over, I feel the knob before shutting the shower off, quickly wrapping myself with the towel I'd brought with me before grabbing my basket and walking out. Someone walks in right after me, practically slamming the door behind them. And the amount of people that can fit in a shower room is crazy. I mean, there has to be at least like, 10 girls just standing and talking by the mirrors. And probably 10 more by those small cubbies!

It's not like they're embarrassed to be in here, either. I mean, some are so comfortable that they shave while talking, rinsing the razor off in a nearby sink after every stroke. My flip-flops soaked, I grab my things out of my little cubby and walk out. The ground feels weird after every step, each time my I step down, my foot lightly submerges within the wet foam sandal.

Arriving at the dorm, I notice a scarf hanging on the handle, symbolizing Nadia possibly changing. While I admire the idea, I'm left awkwardly in the hall.

Imagine it: A girl in your hall wrapped in a towel, clear plastic shower cap, soaked sandals, leaning against the wall and waiting outside a door. You'd never know; but probably infer; that it was hers.

The door handle turns, the scarf quickly falling off as Nadia grabs it and tosses it inside before exiting. "There you go. I'll be back, I gotta go brush my teeth," She adds, her toothbrush and stuff in her hands. "Alright," I reply before walking into the room. I shut the door behind me, turn around, and notice the curtains were closed, which gratefully had been done already by Nadia.

After putting my clothes on, I realize I hadn't put the scarf back on the handle outside. Fortunately, Nadia brushes her teeth long enough for me to get my clothes on, preventing any embarrassing accidents from happening. "I like your outfit," She mumbles before putting her little bag back onto the shelf. I thank her quickly before grabbing mine from beside hers. "I gotta head out, now. My class starts in five minutes, and I swear I can't be late for the first time today," She says, rushing to grab her bag from the chair that held her clothes. "Peace out," She adds before rushing out of the door past me.

The bathrooms are surprisingly empty right now, possibly because half of this hall supposedly has an 8 AM class. I place my bag onto the small bookshelf beside the sink as I pull out my toothbrush, putting the toothpaste onto the bristles. I put the toothpaste back into the bag for a moment before turning the sink on. Right as I do, I hear a sniffle come from a stall behind me, then it's quickly muffled. I turn the water off and stop myself from

CHAPTER SIXTY-TWO: ASSOCIATION

brushing as I ask who it is.

"Who's in here?" No reply.

Shrugging it off, I turn the water back on and brush my teeth, spitting every so often when I need to. Hearing the sniffle again, this time it's followed by light weeping.

"Hey, whoever is in there, I hope you're alright. If you don't mind, let me know who you are. I'm Tiffany."

"T?" A familiar, but unrecognizable voice asks. It sounds dismal and much out of place. My mouth begins moving before I can even stop it.

"Ever?"

The words exit my mouth, quickly greeted by something sliding under the door. I walk over but leave it on the ground as I crouch over and look at it.

"You're pregnant?"

JAYDEN

I wake up sprawled on the couch, my leg resting on the ground. Sitting up, I look around in the dim room, no one in the kitchen or living room. I stand up and walk into the kitchen to find a note sitting on the counter.

I headed to work and Bryant left this morning. I'll be back at 8.

Watch Maddison, and make sure she eats the sandwich I made for her in the fridge.
Mom

I rub my face to wake up before heading towards the fridge, quickly grabbing the Saran-wrapped sandwich and a Gatorade bottle. Placing the two onto the counter, I grab a plate from the cabinet and grab the sandwich to place onto it. Unwrapping it, I put it onto the surface before going to the pantry and grabbing the bag of chips to put on the side for her.

The stairs creak as I walk up, each floorboard louder and louder after each step. Now in the hallway, I walk towards Maddie's door when I notice it is open a crack. "Mads?" I say quietly, just in case she'd be asleep. "Hm?" I hear before watching her sit up. I walk in, opening the door wider before sitting on the edge of her bed. "Hey," I mumble. "Hey," She responds, picking at her nails. "You alright? Did you sleep well?"

"Not well, but I got sleep," She says before standing up. Maddison did well while I was gone, her body frame becoming more full than when I had been here last.

It was silent between us as if there was some kind of hidden tension I didn't know about. And as much as I would love to bring up what happened, I don't wanna force her to say anything she doesn't want to say. "You know you can speak around me, Jay. It's not a secret what happened," She mutters before putting pajama pants on. "Right," I mumble.

I watch as she takes her bonnet off, her flattened hair falling onto her shoulders. "I was doing so good, you know?" I nod.

"And I don't know what happened. I don't. Like I remember just looking in the mirror and speaking to myself; God, you're getting bigger."

I don't say anything, nor nod. No response at all. She walks towards her closet, shuffling through everything in sight.

"I walked to the bathroom, bent over the toilet, and shoved my fingers in my throat. Everything we had gone through left, along with the food from that day."

She turns to me, two pairs of pants hanging on her arms. One light Grey with rips and one light blue with rips as well. "Which one?" I point to the right one, the Grey before she nods and tosses it to me, putting the blue ones back. She doesn't say anything else at that moment, just the sound of the hangers scraping against the metal rod. Maddie pulls out a tan knitted turtleneck sweater.

"Maddison, you know why I'm down here, right?" She hums in her reply. "I'm here to be sure you're okay."

"I know."

CHAPTER SIXTY-TWO: ASSOCIATION

"So, what's going on?"

She takes a deep breath before slipping her top off, a tank top resting on her torso before she puts on the sweater. "I don't know. I just got the urge to, and I did. I did and it felt good, so I did it again yesterday morning."

I blink roughly before replying.

"Maddison, what happened?"
"I told you."
"I know when you lie."

Her jaw tightens.

"Bryant commented, okay? He commented and it made me feel bad. I vomited, and as I said, it felt good, so I did it again," Her voice whimpers. Frustrated, she slips on some socks before grabbing a pair of shoes from her closet. "Maddison, as much as I want you to take this journey at your own pace, it seems it's not working."

I stand up, my hands in my pockets.

"Jayden, what the hell do you mean? You've been out for the past 4 months, you wouldn't know what's going on."
"I have *you*."
"And what if I stopped telling you what I did?"

I inhale roughly, licking my lips in frustration.

"You have food downstairs."

She takes a bite of the sandwich, and I watch as she chews slowly. She swallows, giving me attitude as she notices. "What're you looking at?"
"You."
"Why is that?"
"So I can be sure you eat."

She angrily chuckles before rolling her eyes and taking another bite.
"How's Berkeley?"

I keep my eyes on the plate, remembering what she used to do the first few weeks.

"Good."

"That's cool. How's Tiffany? She knows you down here?"

"Yea," I respond, watching as she grabs a chip and washes it down with a swig of the Gatorade. "You guys have been dating a good bit, you notice that?"

I laugh at her sentence.

"The hell you mean by that?"

"What it sounds like. Do you remember when you were with Jazmine? Y'all didn't last not even a month,"

She giggles at her comment, causing me to throw a towel that sat on the table at her.

"No, but I'm like dead serious, you notice you guys have been dating a while? Like do you see it going any longer?"

"God, I can't believe I'm talking about my relationship with you."

"Jayden, do you?"

Her voice gathers more tension, making me listen. I tap my heel against the ground, thinking.

"It's not that hard to freaking answer," She muffledly replies, her mouth full of bread.

"Yea."

I respond, nibbling on my bottom lip as I try to hold back a smile from thinking about her.

"Hm," Maddie mumbles, grabbing her plate as she stands up and places it inside the sink. "How so?"

"Maddie," I groan annoyedly.

"I'm serious! It's good to think about how you see yourself with her."

"Oh, thank you, since you're such an oh-so relationship expert," I sarcastically blow. Leaning against the counter, Maddie looks me in the eye.

CHAPTER SIXTY-TWO: ASSOCIATION

"I'm serious. *I've never seen you so happy with anyone else as much as you are with her.*"

Sixty-Three

CHAPTER SIXTY-THREE: LIFESTYLE

TIFFANY

"Ever, what're you gonna tell Liam?"

Now in my dorm, Ever bites her nails as we both sit in front of the test, it resting on a paper towel placed on top of my nightstand. I nudge her shoulder, causing the tip of her fingers to slide out of her mouth quickly. "I have no idea." Her feet cross each other, and I watch as she nervously continues to nibble her nails. "We just got here. How in the world did this happen?" Her voice shakes. "Freak what Liam says, what will my parents say?" I inhale deeply, keeping a bubble in my mouth as I try to comprehend what I'm seeing.

"You should go ahead and tell him, Ever."

"No way. I should wait a bit. Maybe take another test. This one could be inaccurate."

She stands up before grabbing it and frustratingly tossing it into my trash bin. "Hell, I'll head to the clinic." I nibble at my bottom lip as I try to think of what to say.

CHAPTER SIXTY-THREE: LIFESTYLE

"Pregnancy tests are usually what tells people in the first place, you know."
"It's possible this is an impairment."

Still sitting, I turn around and watch as she rubs her hands on her face, groaning in frustration. "What am I supposed to do if I am pregnant? Abortion? Deal with it? Adoption?" I shrug. "T, I can't drop out. But I also know I can't deal with a kid right now," She chuckles uncomfortably. Her phone buzzes in her pocket before she grabs it. "Shoot, I gotta go. My meeting's right now," Ever rushes to grab her jacket off my chair and slides her shoes back on. I stand up as I walk towards her, leaning in for a hug.

My chin tucked comfortably between her shoulder and her head, I mumble, "Hope you can figure this out, Eve." We let go of the hug, and she smiles reassuringly as a tear lightly falls down her left cheek. "Thanks, T. Don't tell Liam anything, Okay?" I nod. "I'll let him know when I'm ready." I open the door for her as she slides the jacket on, quickly exiting before I shut it behind her. It opens almost immediately after, with me not even that from it. Nadia quickly pushes me out of the way, tossing her bag onto the ground before rushing towards her dresser and pulling things out. "Whoa, Nadia, what the heck are you doing?" I exclaim, picking up each thing that'd fallen on the floor.

I toss them onto her bed before she turns around with an orange body con in her hands. "I need you to get out. Like, right now. Ryan just freaking asked me on a date, and we're leaving in twenty," She says before pushing me towards the door.

"Dang, okay!" I reply, moving back as she whines in frustration before I grab my phone. She pushes me out once again, this time I'm out and she closes the door behind her.

* * *

Never went to 'Riyah's room. I just went downstairs to the halls' student union and sat on the couch.

My phone buzzes in my hand before a notification slides on my screen, the sender from Analease.

Hey, Girl!

Currently emailing to let you know you made it to the next round. Anyway, you're my next appointment, actually, at 5:60 PM. Can't wait to see and get to meet you. And this time, not from the boring sheet of paper you filled in before this. Thanks, and don't be late.

XOXO,
  Analease <3

I catch myself smiling at the screen as I finish reading the email. God, I'm so nervous. I made it to the very last "round" towards the application, and I'm so close! All it takes is for this meeting to go well, and I should be in. A message from Jayden slides down my screen as it buzzes in my hand.

JAYDEN| Hey.

Sitting up more comfortably, I type a response.

ME| hey, babe. how's maddie?
　JAYDEN| Doing good. Something someone said triggered her.
　Wanted to check in, how's school going? Did you get to your interview yet?
　ME| not yet. scheduled for 5, so it's soon! <33

Suddenly, it feels as if we have nothing to say. Literally, nothing that we usually talk about seems to be the right time to talk about.

JAYDEN| Well, I wanna hear your voice later. Face time tonight?
　ME| yea, i love you.

CHAPTER SIXTY-THREE: LIFESTYLE

JAYDEN

I scroll through Tiffany's following before I bump into Emery's account, quickly pressing it and checking through her posts.

Her profile picture is of the three of them, Her, Tiffany, and Avery. The most persistent photos throughout her page seem to be ones that include shopping, cheer and dance, and track. I press the messages button, my fingers tapping on the screen as I type out a message to her.

> JAY_MONEYX: Hey, I'm down in Memphis and I got something to tell you.
> Meet in thirty?

I stare at the screen, waiting for her response. It's not like she's gonna take forever, at least she shouldn't, as she's online. The bubble moves in the corner before it disappears and is replaced by her text.

> JAZEMX: yeaaaa i don't mind. where at?
> JAY_MONEYX: Carriage Crossing?
> JAZEMX: bet, i was finna hit up that macys later today, anyway. ttyl

And just as quick as she replied, she left.

Sixty-Four

CHAPTER SIXTY-FOUR: INVITATION

TIFFANY

I pull up to Hearst Hall, greeted by the multitude of people walking by. And it's not like it's too many people, it's just the amount of groups that seem to gather here.

I open the door, surprised by the lack of sound throughout the lobby. There's no one talking, and when they do, it's a low whisper. The building map is planted onto a nearby wall, so I walk towards it as I search for Ana's office. Hall B24, it reads. I walk to the hall labeled B as I glance at each door, waiting for the number to pop up as I feel like a freshman again. After what feels like ages, I find it, soon knocking on the door and standing there.

The handle twists, and it opens as I find myself face to face with Analease, her inviting me in almost immediately before guiding me towards a corner.

"Please, sit," She pauses, her speech sounding as if she was speaking formally. I sit down, hesitantly placing my bag onto the ground as she offers to hold it on the shelf beside her. "Thanks," I respond, having no

CHAPTER SIXTY-FOUR: INVITATION

idea what else to do.

She pulls a file from her desk, opening it as she pulls out a piece of paper. Looking closer at it, I notice it's my application from earlier. "Alright. So, I looked at your application and your background is hella efficient! I mean, you did your high *and* middle schools newspaper, back to back?" She exclaims, her face beaming of excitement. "Yea. I've always been assigned to do interviews around the schools, you know? Along with looking up some things going around." Analease turns around before putting the file on a shelf behind her, the papers still beside her. Her hands hoover over the keyboard as she decides what to type. "I was looking around the internet when I'd found a few of your articles. You did one last year on the dress code?"

"Yup. I actually free wrote that one. We had the choice to do our own prompts, and I chose something that made pretty much everyone around the building frustrated. I contacted the board about it, to be honest." Her body perks up, giving me a hint I'm doing a good job. *BINGO, T!*

"That's awesome. We need more writers that are comfortable going out there to get the information. Oddly enough, some people in the paper are a bit afraid to get their toes wet," She says, her hands off the keyboard.

She moves back towards my application, flipping the page to the very back one; the one I'd struggled with. "Now, I noticed your many attempts on this page?" She slides it over to me, the many erase marks and previous written paragraphs in the background. I nibble inside my cheek, thinking of what to say. "I actually struggle with that question quite often, believe it or not." She leans back as she listens.

"I struggled, and especially on the college essay. And it's not like I don't know what I'm gonna do in life, because I know exactly what I wanna do. It's just that I get nervous, I guess. I get clammed up whenever I see that question."

I watch as Analease grabs a pen and writes something down onto the paper, but she goes too fast for me to read.

"Okay, now time for me to ask some questions, huh? You should probably know how this goes. I ask you questions, you respond with the appropriate answer. And me being a Senior here, I'll also go off topic every thirty seconds," She says, laughter lightly spilling out with her last sentence. I laugh too, but only for the impression. "Ready?"

"Ready."

"Tell me about yourself."

"Well, for my hobbies, you'll commonly find me writing or reading. I'm trying my hardest to begin knitting, but that's not within my field, I guess."

She writes what I'd said down in a notebook.

"For my job and school life, I tend to get everything ahead of time. Before the deadline. My mom had always said 'On time is late, and Early is on time' throughout my entire childhood, so I've lived by that with pretty much everything. If you am recruited into the paper, I'm offering myself to write towards the news around not only the campus, but California in general."

Ana nods, writing in the notebook once again.

"Your strengths?"

"On time, Consistent, Diverse Vocabulary, Creativity, the list could go on."

"Weaknesses?"

"Sometimes I'll get off topic, but eventually get back on. I'll also often get stressed, as you can tell from my application. I've noticed over time that I tend to not listen to needed critique, so you could count that as stubborn."

My right leg begins bouncing up and down out of nervousness, the silence slowly overwhelming me.

"Last question, alright? Half of them were answered on the application already," Analease chuckles before turning her body directly to mine.

"Where do you see yourself in five years?"

CHAPTER SIXTY-FOUR: INVITATION

JAYDEN

I sit, bored, in the drivers' seat of the car, parked in a space in front of Great American Cookies.

A Silver Range Rover pulls up beside me and parks, Emery hopping out the drivers' seat. She knocks on the window, unknowing I'd already seen her. I shove my phone into my pocket and get out, quickly locking the doors behind me. "Hey, long time, no see!" Emery says, leaning into a hug. "Hey," I respond before awkwardly standing there after she releases. "We should probably get out of the street."

"You're right," She laughs as we walk onto the sidewalk.

"You mind if we talk about this while in Macy's? I have this return, and they have a new Kate Spade I've been waiting on forever."

"Mind if we get a cookie first?"

"Sure," She responds, and we walk towards the building.

* * *

I open the door for her as she walks in, her boots clicking against the linoleum with each step. No one is in line, so we can immediately choose our desired cookies. Emery goes first.

"Two Macadamia Nut, One Domino, One Birthday Cake, and," She pauses before looking at me. "Uh, Two Chocolate Chip." The guy nods, adding my two cookies into the box. "Anything else?" Emery looks at the menu before adding something else.

"Fudge Brownie."

We walk out after she paid, one cookie in each of our hands. "You really didn't have to, it was literally nine dollars."

"Oh, please. If you know anything about me, it's that I love to spend money," She smiles. Stopping in front of our cars, I watch as she opens her trunk and grabs a box before placing it under her left arm. "Need help?"

"Thanks, but no thanks."

I laugh at her reply, both of us walk side by side as she takes a bite. "What'd you want to talk to me about?" Her speech is muffled, cookie crumbs falling onto the concrete as she covers her mouth quickly. "Tiffany." She pauses in her steps, causing me to walk ahead before noticed she'd fallen behind. "What?"

"You better not be breaking up with that girl. She loves you too much." Surprised by her reaction, I laugh. She begins walking again, now back to my speed as we reach the corner. Looking both ways, we notice no cars coming before we begin walking.

"Actually, it's quite the opposite."

CHAPTER SIXTY-FIVE: BLESSINGS

TIFFANY

"Alright," Analease says before standing up. I do the same as we reach over her desk and shake hands. "I'll email you tonight whether or not you made it." She hands me my purse back right before I walk over towards the door. "Tiffany," She calls before I turn around. "You've really impressed me. Don't expect bad news, at all." Did she basically just say I made it? No way. There's no way she's allowed to do that. But technically, she's not REALLY telling me. She's just telling me she's impressed. Right?

"Thanks," I smile in response before walking out and heading down the hall, passing a few of their older articles along the way.

Some are from 2019, 2015, and from 1990. I glance at each one, reading every single name that is on the front page. Each one impresses me, especially with the kind of wording they've used. These people have definitely gone somewhere. My phone buzzes in my pocket, and my ringtone blazers out not too long after. "Crap," I mumble, watching as other appointments for meetings stare at me, giving me looks of somewhat disgust. I silence it, walk out the doors, and head to the car before connecting my phone to the Bluetooth. Before driving off, I call Jayden hoping for an answer, but quickly dismissed by a decline.

JAYDEN

"You're planning to propose?" Emery shrieks. I caustically light punch her shoulder as employees turn to face us. My phone rings in my pocket, Tiffany's name on the screen as I decline it. "When?"

"Soon."

"And you want me to pick the ring?"

We walk down the aisle as she points out the Kate Spade purses. She picks up an orange one and looks in the mirror, doing occasional poses. "And Avery. I want you to call her when we go, okay?"

"Alright. when are we going?"

"Tomorrow. I need to head to her parents' house to get their blessing."

She continues to hold it as she goes to another one, but it's green with a floral pattern. "I literally cannot believe this is happening."

"You two know her jewelry taste more than me, and I figured you guys would pick the best one because, well," I pause, motioning towards her as she looks at the different bags within the section. "We know style, I know."

Three bags in her hand, we walk over to the cashier before she pulls out her card, and they immediately scan it before handing it back to her without breeze. "See you tomorrow, Emery?" How much could she shop for the cashier to know her name? Emery places her hand onto my shoulder as she speaks, "Yup, sure will. My best friends' boyfriend, here, is planning to propose to her."

"I bet she's a lucky woman," She responds before we walk away.

CHAPTER SIXTY-FIVE: BLESSINGS

* * *

The time reads 6:45 PM when I pull into the driveway.

I get out, briskly closing the door behind me as I shove my hands in my side pockets. The temperature dropped earlier today to around 60 degrees Fahrenheit, actually giving the feel to fall. I knock on the door after walking up the porch steps, greeted by the silence of nothing but light footsteps on the other side. It opens, and I'm face to face with Mr. Mohan.

"May I help you?"

"Hey, can I come in?"

I ask before putting my hands back into my pockets. He opens the glass screen before widening the main door, allowing me in.

"Just put your coat on the hook," He mumbles, and I watch as he walks into the kitchen. I place it onto the hook before sliding my shoes off and following behind him.

"Lyana."

"Hm?"

Mrs. M replies, looking over the couch as she notices me.

"Jayden! Oh my goodness, I had no idea you were down."

Standing up, she races over before giving me a hug, and I hug her back as I prepare myself of what to say.

"I need to talk to you guys."

Her smile fades, and I watch as she glances at her husband, both of them exchanging looks.

I breathe in before exhaling, my breath trembling.

"I'd like to marry Tiffany."

TIFFANY

A call request from Ever announces through my speakers, and I place the Chinese takeout box down before pressing accept. **"Hello?"**

"T!" She responds, her voice distant. **"Hey, what's up? You told Liam yet?"** I take a bite from the rice as the blinker goes off causing me to lightly multitask, one hand on the wheel and steering while the other feeds me. **"Yea."**

"How'd he react?"

"Not as bad as I thought. He actually recommended we head to a clinic together after our first class tomorrow. Telling our mom if it's positive."

I nod, glad she'd gotten it off of her chest.

"That's good. Hey, I picked up Chinese earlier, and I know Nadia and I aren't gonna be able to eat all this. Want some?"

"Yea, sure. I'll pick it up at 10?"

"Better hope it's not gone, it's still a possibility."

I hear her laugh on the other side of the phone before exasperatingly exhaling.

It's silent as I feel her emotions through the phone. Anger, Tiredness, Anxiety. Popping my knuckles against the wheel, I begin speaking, **"You're okay, Ev. I promise you're okay. Even if you are pregnant, I'm not leaving you alone. And I'm sure Liam won't."** I hear her shakily inhale.

"And I promise you, your parents are gonna be with you every step of the way."

Sixty-Six

CHAPTER SIXTY-SIX: IGNITION

JAYDEN

I watch as joy washes across Mrs. Mohans' face, tears aligning the rim of her eyelid.

"Oh my god."

I lick my lips, watching how my singular sentence impacts them both. Her dad stands there, rubbing her mothers' back as I notice his eyes turning red. "I give you my blessing. You're an honorable young man, and I'm proud to see her choose someone she loves to be around as much as you."

TIFFANY

Waking up, I realize I'd missed my first class, unfortunately.

And it's crazy because you'd think since you woke up so early in high school, that you could do it in college. But no, it's so freaking hard to even respond to your alarm. Starting to regret my decision of a 9 AM class.

I sit up, rubbing my face as I see Nadia's bed made up. She must've gotten up already. I grab my phone, which sits on the floor face down, probably from me knocking it over in my sleep. Lifting it, I see the screen has a notification from my Gmail, the subject line says 'The Californian'. Butterflies enter my stomach in excitement. Face ID opens it automatically as I press the notification, quickly loading into Gmail as a large paragraph loads onto the screen.

Tiffany Jessie Mohan,

I've been forced to type your full name for these emails, so just ignore those. But, hey! I'm pretty sure you got the hint by now, you know, since the email was sent. But anyway, I'm emailing to let you know, drum roll please, *insert drum roll here* , You made it into the Californian! Our very first official team meeting will be tonight, at 8 PM, which allows people to get at least half of their classes done. Anyway, can't wait to see you guys! Meeting will be in the newspaper room within Hearst Hall; which isn't that far from my office. See you soon! <3

XOXO,
  Analease

Oh my god, I actually made it into my first club!

I jump up and down in excitement before quickly noticing the curtains opened as I lean over the desk to shut them.

I pull my bonnet off before tossing it onto my bed, my curls slowly falling down my face as I head towards our dresser and I fish through for a pair of leggings and tank top. I grab hold of the things, sliding the leggings on after taking my shorts off, and swapping my shirts. I look in the mirror and put my hair into a middle puff, quickly applying some lip gloss on to finish the lazy morning look.

Sliding my feet into my slides, I head out the door.

CHAPTER SIXTY-SIX: IGNITION

Walking down the hall, I bump into Ryan, who seems like he was on the way to me. "What's up? Haven't seen you in a bit," He laughs. Shoving his hands into his pocket, he stands comfortably.

"Hey, yea. Been busy lately," I respond, noticing we'd met near the elevators. I press the button. "You sign up for The Californian?"

"Yea."

"You make it?"

I smile brightly before responding, glad I'd gotten out of my comfort zone.

"Yup. Someone told me there's also a campus news channel?"

The elevator doors open, and we both board on before I press the button leading to the lobby.

"Yea. There is. Auditions aren't until December, though. That's when the first few episodes air." I nod to confirm my attention before quickly grabbing my phone from my side pocket. Yup, you heard me right, my leggings have pockets. A message from Ever sits on my screen, along with an image of an ultrasound. I mumble under my breath before sending a response.

ME| let me plan the baby shower! :)

EVER| lol. no way. anyways, liam and i are heading to a ice cream place, wanna meet there?

Ryan clears his throat as the doors open. I send my reply to her question before turning my phone off and walking out. Ryan walks alongside me as we walk out the doors, quickly reminding me that Fall had recently begun. "Where you headed?" I check the time on my phone as it reads 11:02.

"Heading to get frozen yogurt with a friend."

"At eleven AM?"

"Yup," I respond.

Now clear of the path, I begin to speak to Ryan again, "How was your date?" We pause in our tracks, standing right in front of the gates that lead towards the parking lot. "It was cool. Nadia n' I headed to this comedy bar she'd found. Cool people." I nod lightly before shoving my hands into my pockets. "Ya'll dating yet?" I tease. He smiles before responding. "Nah. Might go to a few more." "Come on, she said y'all been tight since lord knows when," I playfully groan, punching his shoulder.

"Well, we have another movie date tonight," He trails, another smile growing across his face. "Lookachu!" I praise. I watch as he zips up his coat before standing with his hands tucked to the side. "Anyway, I should head out," I add, checking the time.

"See you around."

"See you around, freshman," He adds, the nickname coming back. I watch as he shoves his hands into his pockets before walking backwards, slowly erasing from my sight.

JAYDEN

A message from Tiffany sits on my screen as I look at my phone screen glow in the cupholder, my mind refraining my hands from grabbing it and responding quickly.

Emery sits in the passengers sit beside me, her nails tapping against the door as she watches me.

"Why not respond?"

"I may ruin the surprise," I say almost immediately as she chuckles lightly in response.

"I spill pretty much everything that's told to me. But look, I'm not telling her, it's surprising ain't it?"

"True."

We both laugh before the air becomes silent with nothing but the sound of the radio lightly playing in the background.

"Respond. Trust me, the mind can think of many different outcomes

CHAPTER SIXTY-SIX: IGNITION

when unwelcome."

We stop at a red light as I grab it, my eyes scanning the text as Tiff checks in.

TIFFANY| hey! how's memphis? could you check in on shi for me?

he was worried when i'd moved out.

Although he may not admit it, i know he misses me <3

"She's a very family oriented person," Emery says in a cheery tone, much like singing. "I can see that," I reply, my foot pressing the gas as the light turns green. I turn around the corner, quickly pulling into the Carriage Crossing parking lot.

Surrounded by other parked cars, we get out before getting on the sidewalk, finding ourselves coincidentally standing in front of H&M. Emery turns to me, her eyes saying it all as she doesn't even speak. "Go ahead, I'll wait here."

"Wait here?" She pauses, dramatically gasping.

"Oh, no, you're coming with."

Sixty-Seven

CHAPTER SIXTY-SEVEN: KEY ELEMENTS

JAYDEN

I watch as Emery pulls out a dark blue suit vest from the rack, quickly holding up against my chest as she contemplates how it looks.

"What're you doing? I have a suit back at home."

"Yea, but this is your proposal! Depending on where you're going to propose in the first place, you want it to be formal, and fitting." Moving it away from me, she hangs it onto her arm before going through the rack once again, picking up another vest and doing the same.

I stand impatiently, my hands resting inside my pocket as I wait for her to finish. "Okay, go try these on," Emery pauses, handing me the two pieces of clothing before walking to another section, where it seems the button up tops are.

"You should wear one of these vests with a white button up under."

"I'll look like a child."

CHAPTER SIXTY-SEVEN: KEY ELEMENTS

"Exactly. It's adorable. It makes you look like your overdressing, or trying to appeal her." She pauses.

"I could just wear a blazer."

"Sure," She sighs roughly before speed walking back to the previous rack, my feet leading me to follow directly behind her.

Placing the vests back, walks to the other side, and we're quickly greeted by blazers of all sorts. Black, Navy, Green, White, Red, Violet. "Pick a color."

"Grey?" I reply, unsure of what to say. She listens before briskly shifting through the clothes, her hands speedily sliding each hanger aside after her eyes scan the suits. Suddenly, she picks one up as I come face to face with a light Grey blazer, perfectly buttoned up within the center. "This?" I nod, and she hangs it onto her arm before walking towards the pants, almost immediately finding the matching pants.

We walk towards the register as she places the clothes onto the counter before grabbing her purse and reaching inside, quickly pulling out a wallet containing her card.

"Your total is $117.89."

I watch as Emery pulls out her wallet before handing them her card, and they quickly slide it into the card reader before handing it back. They place the clothes into a bag, hand it to her, and I watch as she hands it to me. "Thanks," I mutter before grabbing it and holding it in my hand, my fingers tightly wrapped along the plastic handles. We head to the door before walking out, meeting the chilly breeze.

* * *

After walking slowly along the sidewalk for a while, we finally find ourselves in front of the Macy's storefront. Quickly, we cross the street, walk in front of the doors, and head inside.

Although it's only mid September, Christmas music is playing overhead, seeming to sound like an off brand artist singing a song. Emery's heels click against the linoleum flooring as we walk down the aisle, her eyes grazing the purses we pass by as we walk. She pulls out her phone, opens Face time, and I watch as her finger hits Avery's contact, the screen quickly loading up to a reflection of her face. "Alright, so Avery and I are gonna pick a ring for her, because over the years we've known her longer than you, we've definitely watched her taste for jewelry change and revolve over the years."

The screen changes from Emery's face to be quickly full of Avery's. "Hey, Em! Where are you?" Avery's eye engulfs the screen before Emery moves the screen from her face and directs it to me.

Pulling my hand out of my pocket, I wave. **"Hey! Since when were you in town? Is T with you?"**

"No," Emery interrupts, her feet boarding the escalator before I follow behind her. "Jayden, here has something to tell you." Turning around, Emery hands me the phone before we step off the moving stairway, our ears quickly disturbed by the loud sounds of the crowds around us.

People pass by, cups and bags in hands, laughing and talking.

"I'm proposing to Tiffany."

TIFFANY

Emery and Liam walk beside me as we walk towards the building, the chilly breeze blows through my sweater as Liam opens the door, Ever and I standing aside awkwardly before walking inside.

Light lofi plays overhead, and a bell by the door rings as it shuts behind us. "We'll be right with you!" An employee behind the counter calls. Ever's hand rests on the glass display, quickly lifting it to find a hand print left behind as she chuckles lightly, very clearly annoying Liam.

"What are we gonna tell mom?"

CHAPTER SIXTY-SEVEN: KEY ELEMENTS

"Liam, could we not right now? I mean, we're getting frozen yogurt and my friend is literally right there. Let's not argue in front of her, at the least."

He inhales before exhaling roughly, his eyes scanning the flavors in front of us. I look around the small shop, glancing at the photos of families smiling and laughing, small spoons in their mouths.

I hear footsteps behind the display before a person speaking. "Hey! You guys ready?" "Yup," Ever quickly responds, Liam moving out the way as she whisks to the side, where it seems like her choices are. "Can you put multiple in one?"

"Yes, Ma'am."

"Alright. Get me Pistachio, Almond, Mint Chip, and Rocky Road. Put something between the Pistachio and Almond, they do not need to touch."

The worker laughs at her sentence, their hands speedily scooping the cold cream with the scoop before placing it into the cup. They placing a small barrier with multiple small spoons, just as asked.

The price rings up on the register, Ever's hands quickly reaching into her pocket and grabbing a wad of cash, separating the bills into the required piles. "$10.57," She mumbles before shoving the remaining bills back. The employee hands her the cup, their attention reverting towards me and Liam. "You two?"

"I'll have Rocky Road."

"And I'll get Vanilla, add caramel on top, please."

They nod in confirmation, and we watch as they do so.

My phone buzzes in my pocket, Jayden's response to my previous message sitting on my screen.

JAYDEN| Sorry, babe, I've been busy. Yea, I've checked in earlier, Shiloh's doing fine.

I smile, glad he's okay.

"Your total combined is $8.99."

"I can pay," Liam mutters, his hand reaching into his pocket.

"No, I got it, Liam. Go sit with Ever."
"Really, Tiff, I don't mind."
"Liam."

I pause, his face looking at mine.
"Go sit with Ever, please."

My ice cream cup within my hand, I sit at the third chair at the table, between both Liam and Ever. "I saw you," Ever mumbles, the spoon quickly going from her mouth back to the cup.
"What?"
"You got excited. Jayden text you?"
"Nosy Rosy. Yes, he did. And what do you mean, I get excited?"
Ever glancing at Liam as they both give each other that sibling look.

Liam speaks as he tries to hold back a laugh, "Really? You forreal asking us this?"
I nod.
Liam chuckles lightly before coughing, his face immediately regretting his laughter as he beats on his chest, very obviously had inhaled some ice cream.

"Your face glows with happiness whenever he texts you. Whether it's just to check in on you, ask you a question, or respond, your face can just tell a person who it's from."
Embarrassed, put the cup down before jokingly covering my face.
"You're kidding."
Liam laughs again, this time, without choking.

"No, you're literally in love with that man."

Sixty-Eight

CHAPTER SIXTY-EIGHT: THE RITUAL OF LOVE

JAYDEN

"**W**ait a second." Her voice pauses, eyes darting around what looks like her dorm as she tries to process. "**You?**"

I nod.

"Proposing to T?"

I nod, once again. Her eyes turn red as she covers her face before leaning forward into the camera, her head resting against something. I hear light sobbing before Emery says something.

"And he's honorable, too! Dude came down to Memphis and asked for her parents' blessing, came to me, and straight up asked if we could help pick the ring." On the other side of the screen, Avery lifts her head as she listens to Emery speak.

    She gasps dramatically before we begin speaking again Emery looks around as she tries to find a store for us to stop at first.

    "Jayden had this plan and everything. Said we could call you and pick the ring out that way. He has no input, whatsoever. <u>We</u> pick the ring."

    "No."

    "Yes!"

    They both begin laughing, talking and planning.

Emery finally stopped in front of a storefront, KAY Jewelers.

    "Okay, you ready, Jay?"

My mind scrolls through my future, *each and every* thought including Tiffany.

    "Yea."

TIFFANY

"I should get going, I'm literally ten minutes late."

    I say, grabbing my purse before tossing the plastic cup thing into the trashcan. Ev and Liam do the same following behind me. "Alright, well," Ever pauses, reaching into her pocket as she pulls out a black sheet. Looking closer, I notice it's an Ultrasound scan.

    "Ever, I'm so planning the shower."

My hands grasp around the sides, holding it as I look around the frame.

"You know you are," She chuckles before taking it from my grasp and putting it back in her pocket.

    "We're from down here, so we'll just drive to our parents house and let them know."

CHAPTER SIXTY-EIGHT: THE RITUAL OF LOVE

She breathes deeply before continuing her sentence. "We'll see their response soon."

I give her a tight hug before backing away, quickly heading back to my car.

"See you at tonight's meeting!"

JAYDEN

I watch as Emery picks up random rings, Avery putting in her own input on each ring as time goes by.

"I think T fits a size seven?"
"No, that's you. I'm pretty sure she's an eight."
"Check her latest post, Avery."

Silence cracks between the two of them, Avery's fingers clacking away at the keyboard. We watch as she looks at the screen, her head moving closer to the camera every other second.

"She's a size Seven."
"Told you!" Emery shrieks, startling me as they begin bickering.

A worker walks behind us, glancing at the phone with Avery before speaking. She has dirty brown hair, curls waving throughout the style looks as if the were from a curling iron. Her skin is pale, freckles seeming to cover every bit of her skin, as she nibbles on her bottom lip.

"Anything specific you're looking for?" Em places the phone against the glass as she responds, causing an echoing bump throughout the room. "Yea. Any recommended Bridal Lines?"

"Yes, actually! One of our most popular collections is The LEO. Many people have come in requesting one," She says, walking around the glass chambers as we follow behind her, quickly coming to a stop as she walks behind a barrier only for employees.

She grabs the key pinned onto her chest, her hands unlocking the door before reaching inside and grabbing the ring insert.

The diamonds sparkle as the light reflects off them, Emery freaking out about the look and feel almost immediately, "Oh my god, these are gorgeous!" Placing one onto her finger, it just barely fits; as it's the wrong size; as she shows Avery, who's continuing to sit on the other side of the phone.

"Gold doesn't fit her tone. I would say pick something either rose gold or silver," Avery mutters, gathering the attention of the employee in front of us.

"Ah, picking something for a significant other?"

Emery says something before I can get the chance.

"Yea. He's picking something for his girlfriend, she down in California. He flew all the way down here for her," She coos, giving puppy eyes before continuing to look through the foam casing, trying each ring on throughout the way.

Looking through the options, I pick a up ring as it catches my eye.

The shank is silver, the size thin as it holds a white diamond within the center, one small stone on each side. The inside has an engraving which reads 'Ideal Cut'.

"What'd you find?" Emery says, practically snatching it out of my hand as she glances at it, giving me a look as she hands it back. "What?" I say, confused as to why she'd glanced at me like that. "Thank god you came to me and Av. That looks more like a promise ring than an engagement. Can you show us this line?" Her finger points towards a case with much bolder, larger rings.

I put the ring back in the lining as the woman places the container back into the casing before locking it with the same key. She scoots over a bit just as she unlocks the other door, grabbing the container Em pointed to. "This line is 'Now & Forever'. One of our third most demanded collections for the past year."

CHAPTER SIXTY-EIGHT: THE RITUAL OF LOVE

The phone glitches as Avery begins speaking, the audio going in and out throughout her sentence.
"I.. Tiff.. It's g.."
"Av, we can't hear you!"

The audio clicks back in right as Emery screams that, everyone within the store looking at us.
"Look at that one, it's gorgeous. Tiff might like that."
"Which one?"
"Third one down in the fourth row to the left."

Emery points to that ring, the worker picking it up as she holds it, each of the many diamonds glistening. It has a split shank, an engraving near the diamond within the inside that states *Always and Forever*. "Yea, that's an option, definitely," I say, my eyes watching as the worker places it inside a black felt tray.

I look through the glass, a certain ring sparkling in my eye as I look closer at it, the diamonds glistening from the display lights.
"What line is that?" I point, both Emery and the worker turning around. Emery walks over, her jaw dropped as she looks at it, repeatedly jamming her finger against the glass as she shows Avery.
"Ah," The employee coos, grabbing the ring before handing it to Em.
"This is our Neil Lane line. One of our most requested."
"It's hella beautiful, I can say that," Emery says, moving her hand around as it rests on her finger. She holds her hand up to the phone camera, displaying the silver ring to Avery.
"That. That's the one. Tiffany will love it."
Emery looks up from her phone, placing it down onto the glass case as she takes the ring off before handing it back to the worker. "Women's seven."
They quickly nod before walking into the back, coming back in the front with the gloves from before off of her hands.

"It'll be ready in two weeks."

"I don't have two weeks," I mutter, my hope slowly fading. Hearing a phone hit the glass, it's quickly followed by the ruffling of cash before a plastic card against the counter and Emery's voice.

"15,600 extra. 15,600 for you to have it in an hour."

"Consider it Done."

Sixty-Nine

CHAPTER SIXTY-NINE: SERVICE WINNER

TIFFANY

"Alright, Tiffany and Cali, you two will work on the Sports column for this week. I'll send you any information you'll need to start, you guys find the rest."

I turn to my side, face to face with the girl I'd sat with on the plane here with mom. Standing up, she grabs her satchel before sitting on a beanbag beside me, immediately grabbing her laptop before typing away.

"Hey. Long time, no see, huh?" She faintly mutters, her eyes glued onto her screen. This isn't how I remember her. The last time I'd seen her, she was all bouncy and full of energy. Non stop chatter, constantly touching my shoulder to gather my attention. Now all of a sudden, she's drawn to her computer screen and not saying a word?

"Yea," I respond before awkwardly grabbing my a journal out of my bag. Mom bought me a new Macbook, but it hasn't delivered yet. And I know, I should be making my own purchases, but it's too expensive for me within my budget. Besides, while my dad insisted I learn to live in the real world, Mom stood up for me and offered to purchase any large priced items. Such as said Macbook.

The campus website loads slowly on her screen as she begins scrolling, quickly pressing a link to the sports page. "Our Volleyball team won a game against Saint Mary's yesterday," She mutters, her hand ushering me to write. My fingers click against the top of the pencil, the lead slowly sputtering out.

"Jeez, they suck. 3-0. Lydia gave the most kills, blocks, and aces. Won her number 1 in ranking."

My hand scribbles across the pages, struggling to keep up with what she's saying. Her nails clack against the finger pad, scrolling even more down the page as she clicks another link. Glancing at the screen, I watch as it loads to the game box.

My phone buzzes in my pocket, my mind ignoring it as I finish writing a sentence.

Placing the pencil down, I reach for my phone before it buzzes once again, two messages from Shi sitting on my phone screen.

SHILOH| T. Jayden's having dinner with mom and dad tonight.
SHILOH| Lord, come save me. They're bringing out the tux I wore to D'liya's wedding!

Lightly, I chuckle under my breathe as I put the clipboard onto the ground, my fingers quickly typing away at the screen.

ME| lol. he's just tryna get to know you guys.
more than just you hitting him up about playing COD or GTA or smth

Leaning over, I grab the clipboard again as I continue writing, glancing back and forth between my paper and the screen every so often. Cali quickly clears her throat as she loads the screen to another page. "I never

CHAPTER SIXTY-NINE: SERVICE WINNER

got to know you on the plane."

"Yea, because you babbled on and on about you returning from break."

"I get nervous on flights, okay?" She laughs before checking her watch. She shuts the laptop as she places it back into the bag and slings it across her shoulder. "I have to head out, but you have my number, right?" I stand up as well, unsure if I should shake her hand as if we were in a formal event. "Yea. You practically forced me," I lightly chuckle, unsure if it were a good joke. She doesn't laugh. "Right. Okay, well I hope we can talk at a good time. Text me whenever, we'll get stats, alright?" I watch as she walks towards the door, not even waiting for my response.

* * *

Nadia opens the door after I knock, her face confused as she looks at my hand to see nothing. "I left my card in here." Understanding, she nods as I walk in, shutting the door behind me. Tossing my bag onto the ground, I reach into the bookshelf as I grab *Blood Like Magic* before sitting onto my bed, quickly startled by Ryan as I look at Nadia's bed directly in front of me.

"Crap, Ry! You scared me."

"I thought you saw me."

"Well, I didn't," I mutter, bending over to untie my shoes. I kick my feet up onto the mattress, quickly diving my body underneath the wad of blankets before I remove my bookmark leading to my labeled page.

"When's your next class?" Nadia says, her voice readily followed by the creaking of her bed springs. Reaching for my pocket, I check the time as my home screen glows with a mirror selfie of me and Jayden. "An hour." My phone makes the click sound as I turn it off, the screen lightly dimming before it glows from a notification from Instagram.

Ryan and Nadia chat for a bit, their voices quickly followed by silence as

I turn around and immediately regret it, viewing as they make-out with one another. My face turns warm at this, quickly drowning any thoughts of the book.

And it's funny, because we all hear complaints of people saying roommates will quite literally engage their romance life in front of you and not care, all of us refusing to believe so. TV shows even bring this up, but constantly seeming to be made up and fictional. What. A. Lie. Pretty much any time Ryan's in here, the only "studying" they're doing is of one another. Different subjects each day.

"God, maybe you could've waited until I ditched," I groan, standing up as I slide my feet into the shoes I had on, unbothered to tie the laces at the moment. Nadia chuckles lightly before I get hit by a small pillow. Turning around, I give her a look and watch as she stands up, leaving Ryan resting against the headboard in with a face that just expresses confusion. The room is silent, Nadia's smile growing as she begins to speak.

"I'm in the mood for ice cups. You?"

JAYDEN

Running through the door, I shut it behind me before rushing upstairs, my hands quickly digging through the shelf in my closet.

The Hobbit. The Hobbit. The Hobbit.

It shouldn't be this hard to locate a simple book with the most noticeable cover. If I remember correctly, it's the deluxe, so it should be easy to locate compared to my other books shelved.

After what feels like ages of searching, I finally catch glimpse of it, very quickly snatching it off before taking it out of the slide cover and tossing it onto my desk. I'd bought it from the bookshop T and I worked at, so it's fairly used. Surprisingly, after the owner had it, they still managed to keep up with the cover box. "Uh," Emery stutters, her head moving around as she looks at the empty room, nothing but my posters from when I was 12

CHAPTER SIXTY-NINE: SERVICE WINNER

on the walls. "I actually forgot I had you with me," I chuckle awkwardly, sitting onto the bare mattress as I untie my shoes. "Right. So, why are we here?" "I had this idea," I respond, purposely hitting my hand against the door frame to signifying my quick exit.

I walk down the small hallway, quickly opening Mom's door before heading towards her desk, digging through the drawers to find a box cutter.

Walking through the doorway, I knock on the door before speaking to signify my return. "We Tiffany and I first met, you remember when we wrote in the journal?" She nods, and I sit in the rolling chair beside my desk. "Right.Well, I had a feeling it was gonna be more than just a short-term," I say, my words lingering on as I open the first page of the book, Tiffany and I's words trailing along the sideline of the page. I smile at this, thinking back at the moment and how excited I felt when someone wrote back.

"So I kept it." I hear her gasp at my sentence before the blade hits the center of the page. I slowly move my hand a bit, just enough room within the center for the ring. A bit more space for the cushion. "I swear, this is gonna be the best proposal in the world, Jayden. T's gonna love this," She says, the floor creaking underneath her footsteps as she walks to me. Bending over my shoulder, I feel her breath against my neck. "That's too cute." I smile, sending over a quick signal of my thanks. The paper now in a small stack within the page, I reach and grab it before pulling it out, doing the same thing once again.

"Yea, it's worth my time, you know? I remembered how we met, and after realizing I want to move forward, I thought to do something similar."

20 minutes into doing this same system, Emery sits on the ground as she waits, her phone in her hand, and random audios playing every other minute. Multiple small sheets of paper sit in stack beside me, the hole in the center deepened more than before. Just a few more pages and it'll be ready. I hear Emery laugh, then a buzz before she's silent. "What?" I ask, confused as to why she'd gone quiet all of a sudden.

"The ring. It's ready."

CHAPTER SEVENTY: REACH OVER

JAYDEN

The glass doors separate as Emery and I pace through, side by side. We slow down our speed as we reach the glass counter, the worker from earlier manning the register. "Hudsen," I state, the girl smiling before she walks into the back room, coming back with a black bag with white tissue paper sticking out in her hand.

"Thank You for shopping at KAY's. Hope we see you again soon," She blankly says, and we thank her before walking out, Emery snatching the bag from my hand as she looks inside.

Sitting on a nearby bench, we both make peace as I grab the box, immediately greeted by the very same ring from earlier, the right size and everything. Turning to face Emery, I watch as her eyes slowly turn red, her emotions probably spilling over.

"Thank you. Tell Avery I said thank you, too. I couldn't do any of this without you guys," I chuckle, my voice wavering as my eyes become glassy. Leaning in for a hug, she doesn't respond, but instead hugs me tighter before releasing. "Treat her right." A grateful smile aligns her cheeks as a tear falls from her left eye. We stand up together, her hands wiping her face as she grabs her purse and slings it across her shoulder.

"Because, god, I'll kill you if you don't."

TIFFANY

Checking my phone, I look at the time as I walk up the building steps, grateful for having left early.

Reaching for the handle, I open the heavy door before walking inside the cool building, my eyes adjusting to the dim lighting. Quickly heading towards the lecture hall, I open the door to find myself awkwardly greeted by a full class.

"Ms. Mohan," Professor Kade states, his glance maneuvering from the class to me. "You're late."

"One O'clock?" I say unsurely, speed walking towards my desk. "If you checked your assigned email," He pauses, grabbing a sheet of paper before whispering to a person in front of him to pass it on. "You would've seen my email about class times changing." He leans against his desk, arms crossed.

People snicker in the back row, annoying me. You'd think that since it's college, maybe people would mature.

The paper quickly gets me as I look at the blank sheet in front of me. Pop Quiz.

"And unfortunately, due to the fact you'd come in late, you will not have the glorious courtesy of having your notes. Please sit in the very back to work on it, then hand it to me at the end of my lecture." Grabbing my stuff from the ground, I slowly walk towards the back, where the chuckling people sit. Face-to-Face with a Sociology quiz I have no idea what to answer; due to the fact I haven't studied at all for it; I already know I'm about to bomb this.

JAYDEN

Walking through the parking lot, we make our way back to my spot as I grab my keys and unlock the doors, both of us sitting inside the cold car.

"You need a place to stay?" I turn the key into ignition as *24K Magic* by Bruno Mars begins playing on the current station, my hands quickly leading to turn it down. Before I can even respond, she continues offering. "I mean, I saw your room. Nothing is in there but large pieces of furniture, and literally your sheets are gone." I hum along with the song as I begin to think. "And I have a roommate, just to signify," She adds on, quickly pulling her phone out of her purse. "My parents said I had to, because apparently I'll end up thinking I own the world." I chuckle at this, the thought of her parents telling her she has a roommate cracks me up. "That's not funny. But," She exclaims, looking up from her phone as she continues speaking. "She's extremely sweet. I love her, she's just like me. Attitude, but sweet."

I scoff jokingly as I turn the corner, quickly leaving the Carriage Crossing area and heading towards the freeway. "Yea. Thanks for the offer, I really didn't want to stress my Mom out with my sudden appearance. I hope I'm not a burden to you, either," I respond, taking her up on the room. She laughs, her hand immediately grabbing the aux before she changes my car input. Chloe x Halle blares through the speakers as she sings along, knowing each and every line. She turns to me, hoping I know the upcoming lyric as it plays by, nothing but air singing along.

"Oh come on. You're telling me Tiffany hasn't played them before?" "Emery, no," I chuckle as I lean back, waiting for the red light to turn green. "Type in your address." Leaning forward, she types it in, blocking the street name with her left hand. "Reflex, my bad."

"No, you're good. I get it, people can be creeps. Believe me, I'm not one." She laughs muffledly before reaching for the volume knob and twisting it, turning it down.

"You know, I watched as she fell in love with you, Jay."

I pause, listening to both her and the GPS, telling me to turn right.

CHAPTER SEVENTY: REACH OVER

"Really?"

"Yea. I mean, first it was a look. A look I remember too often. From CJ, Justin, Malcolm," She pauses, quickly realizing she's talking too much before I assure her it's alright.

"But then it turned into something more. Her look turned more into a gaze. A gaze I watch my parents give one another as they dance in our corridor. A gaze I see my grandmother give to my grandfather." She pauses, taking a breath before saying the next sentence.

"A gaze I watch you give her."

TIFFANY

I'm only 3 questions away from the end as I hear Professor Kade announce the end of the class.

People shuffle to gather their things, the sounds of backpacks rubbing against someone echoes through the room.

"Does anyone have any questions? I expect one essay on the Youth Culture of today. Compare to previous times, including examples."

Quickly, I rush through the page, continuously reading as I struggle to circle the correct answers. Looking up, I watch as he slowly prances towards me, his hand out for the paper.

"You had an hour."

"Give me more time. I have three more questions left, I can have this done in five minutes, tops," I request, continuing to read the questions.

He inhales roughly before leaning against the chair in front of me. "I don't have a class for another fifteen. Have it done before then." Silently, I thank him as he walks off.

My phone vibrates against my leg as I quickly grab it, handing the flimsy paper to Professor K. "Your grade will be in tonight. Tiffany," He says, reverting my attention from my phone to him.

"Keep up with your email. Everything you need is on there." Annoyed I mumble a goodbye before heading out, the wooden doors shutting behind me.

Ever waits beside the couches within the main building lobby, quickly standing up as she notices me.

"I told my parents."

* * *

"Well, What'd they say?" I respond, both of us stopping in the middle of the doorway, people giving us looks as we speak.

"They're okay with it. Sure, they're surprised by my irresponsibility," She inhales deeply before continuing to speak. "But, they're in support of me."

A smile aligns her face as her eyes glow. Quickly, I lean in for a hug as she holds tightly, slowly breaking down on my shoulder.

"I know we've just met, but I swear I don't know what I'd do without you."

I chuckle lightly, rubbing her back in consolation as she lightly cries.

"Trust me, I needed you, too. I couldn't last a second on this campus without a friend like you."

Seventy-One

CHAPTER SEVENTY-ONE: 2 YOU

JAYDEN

Emery and I both walk into her kitchen, immediately greeted by the scent of multiple spices floating through the air.

"Hey, Em!" A voice calls, a girl quickly exiting a side room following it.

She has brown hair with dark blue highlights, dark caramel toned skin to top it off. Emery takes her purse off before setting it on the counter and sitting down on the bar stool. "Hey, India. This is my friend's boyfriend, Jayden. He came down to get a ring for her." She has dark brown eyes and an oval face shape, her hair a dark brown with blue highlights, much like characters in Sci-Fi movies.

She doesn't respond as she opens the oven, a faded cloud of smoke exiting as she uses an oven mitt to remove a glass tray. "Get that towel." Quickly, Emery listens as she grabs the nearby towel and places it against the counter, India swiftly putting the tray on the towel before taking the foil off.

Inside the dish are chicken breasts, very well seasoned. Reminds me of a restaurants' recipe, every part of the chicken covered with something.

"India's a good cook. Literally anything she makes, just know she put her foot all up in that stuff," Emery says, walking towards the cabinets as she grabs three plates. I stand up, immediately grabbing glass cups out the very same cabinet, closing it behind me right after. "No, you're the guest," India pauses before grabbing the glasses from my hand. "Sit. I'll pour us some drinks. Emery, get the salad out the fridge. You make dinner tomorrow, you know that right?"

"Yes, Indie, I do," Emery groans, the fridge shutting as I hear the glass bowl against the counter. "Learning to cook?"

"Always knew how, never felt like it. I mean, it makes sense. Why cook when you have a chef?" I scoff before leaning against the body of the chair, glancing between my phone and Emery. "But, hey, I don't live down there anymore. Can't depend on someone else," She adds, the end of her voice whining as if she were mocking someone. The time reads 8:57, 3 minutes until 9.

India comes back from the side room, probably the pantry. A wine bottle sits in her left hand as she pours some into the cups. "I literally bought glasses a week ago."

"And?"

"You put wine in the glasses, not in cups."

Emery snatches the bottle from her hands as she reaches over the fridge and opens a cabinet, one glass in her hand before pouring the wine in and handing it to me.

"Wine?"

"My family owns an orchard. Cheesy, yes. But hey, comes to use when it comes to the good stuff," India says, sitting down on the stool on my side.

The plated chicken sits in front of me, along with a serving of white rice and salad placed beside it. She hands me a fork, allowing me to quickly get a taste of the food. "This is good," I mumble, chewing the bite I have in my mouth. Shyly, India smiles before saying thanks. "So," Emery pauses, taking a sip from her wine glass. "What's your plan for the wedding?"

CHAPTER SEVENTY-ONE: 2 YOU

"I mean, I'm intending for T to plan it. She seems like she'd have one hell of a time with it, so why not?"

She nods lightly as she chews, her finger in front of her mouth, much like if she were a teacher.

"Good answer."

* * *

Placing the empty plate into the sink, I head over to the couch as I grab my phone and open messages, quickly sending Tiffany a text.

ME| Hey, babe. Heading back tomorrow morning. You available all day?

The I hear the floorboards creak before I turn around, Emery walking over with a wad of blankets in hand. "When are you leaving?"

"Tomorrow," I respond, clearing my throat as I walk to her and grab the wad from her. Walking back, I kick my shoes off and place them neatly beside the couch, tucking my feet under the blanket as I toss my phone to the other side.

"Can I come? I mean, sure, I don't have break until like, next month, but," She continues, "I wanna see this. Tiffany's proposal?" She walks closer to me before sitting on the armrest. "I have to see it." Tired, I nod. "Sure, I guess. But your classes gotta be covered for."

"Done. Just consider it done already," She replies, excitedly standing up. "Besides." I sit up, realizing she added another thing.

"Avery's already down there."

TIFFANY

Opening the door, the room is pitch black, and nothing but the sound of crickets chirping echoes throughout the room. Closing it behind me, I kick my shoes off and toss my bag to the ground, walking to my bed before falling face forward with no intention of changing clothes. My phone buzzes in my pocket, the glow quickly shining on my face as I grab it and unlock it, Jayden's message on the screen.

> JAYDEN| Hey, babe. Heading back tomorrow morning. You available all day?

Moving my hand from my chest, I quickly type a response.

> ME| hi. yea, im clear all day. saturday's one of my only days to rest lol.
> wanna hang when you get here?

I wait for the chat bubbles to load, and nothing but a 'Delivered' label sits underneath the message.
Quickly, it reverts from 'Delivered' to 'Read' as the bubbles pop up.

> JAYDEN| Alright :) Yea, I wanna hang out tomorrow. What's on your mind?

My eyes open and close, struggling to stay open.

> ME| anywhere off campus, lol. i've very quickly realized i spend all my time here.

The phone vibrates in my hand as he responds, causing me to quickly wake up.

> JAYDEN| Be ready at 10AM. Tomorrow is a day for just us.

CHAPTER SEVENTY-ONE: 2 YOU

* * *

I wake up to music on blast, someone singing along with the lyrics. Sitting up, I realize I hear two voices before its followed by laughter.

"Mornin' T."

My eyes adjusting to the bright lights, I see both Mariyah and Nadia in the room, standing in front of the mirror as they put makeup on. "Good Morning," I respond, stretching. Standing up, my feet hit the carpet as I walk towards my bag, grabbing the journal inside. "Take a break, Tiffany."

"I gotta get this done, first. I'm not doing it on my own, although I wish to," I respond, grabbing a pencil from the pen holder before sitting down on the white pouf in the middle of the room, between Nadia and I's beds. My phone buzzes within the blankets, causing me to get up and dig through the wad to resurface it.

Jayden's name rests on my home screen, the current time sitting above.

10:50 AM

JAYDEN| On my way, now. Plane just landed, so apologies for the late timing. Hope you're ready. Wear a causal outfit for now, we'll go back and forth between activities.

Activities? We're doing multiple things today? "Jayden?" Mariyah says, somehow knowing exactly who it was. "Yea. We're hanging out today."

"You guys are cute," She responds, closing the mascara bottle in her hand. She places it down onto the desk in front of her as she uses her fingers to be sure the lash is applied properly.

"Where you two going?" I ask, tossing my phone back on the bed as I walk towards my dresser, grabbing a pair of ripped jeans, bra, and underwear before heading to the compacted closet and grabbing a yellow sweater.

It started getting chilly around last month, definitely throwing us off guard. And I know, California usually has the chilliest temperature compared to Memphis, but I really had no idea when it would really drop.

I grab my hygiene basket off the shelf before scooping up my pair of matching Jordans and digging for my phone.

"Imma get ready. Text me as soon as Jay gets here?" "Alright. If we ain't here, don't get mad at me!" I shut the door behind me as she finishes her sentence, playfully rolling my eyes.

Walking down the hall, I head towards the showers, exhaling a breath I hadn't known I'd been holding when I see it practically empty.

The sweater I picked is like a dark mustard yellow, and the matching shoes are yellow AJ1s, a pair my Dad sent over not too long ago. Putting my shirt on, my phone vibrates against the wood bench, a message from Nadia on my screen.

NADIA| jayden's in the room now. we finna leave so get your behind up here

I chuckle at her text before opening the changing room door, my pajamas hanging on my left arm and my basket resting in the other.

Walking back down the hall, I catch them leaving just in time before walking in the room.

Jayden stands in the middle, a white rose in hand as he leans in for a hug and holding me tightly.

"How's Maddison doing??"

"Being there for a week calmed her down a bit."

I nod lightly as I look in the mirror, groaning at my curls as they matte together, quickly separated by my brushing. Quickly, I put my hair into a high bun with an elastic.

I feel Jayden's hands wrap around my waist as I grab some gel and apply some, quickly laying my edges. "Ready?" I say, my mouth muffled from a hairpin sitting in my mouth. Grabbing it, I hand it to Jay to place in the

CHAPTER SEVENTY-ONE: 2 YOU

back and hold the puff he place. He does so, very quickly helping me in the best way possible.

"I should be asking you that. Hell, yea, I'm ready."

I laugh at his response before grabbing a black chain bag and applying gloss.

"Let's get outta here, then."

Seventy-Two

CHAPTER SEVENTY-TWO: LOVE YOURZ

JAYDEN

The book with the the ring sits in the backseat in one of my suitcases. Yea, I haven't unpacked yet, nor even brought the bags inside, but hey, I want to get this day going.

Emery and Avery checked into a hotel right when we got here, and I told them every place we're headed to. Hopefully, we won't bump into each other. Crazy, but you'd be surprised with how much you can bump into a person when you don't want to.

I open the car door for Tiffany as she gets inside, closing the door behind her. I get to my side and hop in, quickly putting the car into ignition. Personally, it takes a moment for me to get used to another setup. For the past week, I've been driving my Mom's 2007 Honda; Which she refuses to let go of; and to suddenly switch to a newer model, it kinda throws me off.

"Where we headed first?"

CHAPTER SEVENTY-TWO: LOVE YOURZ

"Brunch. Found this french spot call *La Note* while I was riding around, it seems like a place you'd like."

I add a false french accent in the middle of the sentence as I repeat the name, Tiffany giving me a playful look. I continue facing forward as I drive out the campus, turning the corner into the busy road.

Lightheartedly, T lightly hits my shoulder, chuckling at my accent.

"What?"

"The accent doesn't sound right on you," She responds, her voice seeming to have the very same false sound.

Falsely, I gasp before placing a hand on my mouth in shock.

"Oh, really?" I respond, bringing the accent back again.

"I think I sound pretty french to me."

She chuckles before I hand her my phone, and without looking, she types in the password and opens Safari. Her fingers type in the restaurant name as the search engine loads to the results.

She presses the first link, quickly led to the website. I turn another corner, remembering where I'd drove earlier. "This looks good!" Tiffany says, showing me a picture of a waffle with powdered sugar on top. I stop at the red light as I grab the phone, looking more at the menu than I had before.

"I'm guessing that's what you're getting?"

"Hell, yea. This and an orange and lime juice virgin mimosa. Hopefully they'll take special requests." Grabbing my phone from my hand, she withdraws her arm before going onto my Spotify, quickly pressing the playlist I'd labeled 'Tiffany'.

"I haven't heard this playlist in a few months. Started missing our song, not gonna lie," She chuckles, shifting her body to sit in a comfortable position.

She's Mine by J.Cole plays almost immediately, Tiffany glances at me before looking back towards the window. "What?" I ask, a light chuckle in my voice, already knowing why.

"Nothing."

I sing along with the chorus as the slow-ish song plays through. Tiffany sighs before grabbing her phone and opening it, the screen slowly loading onto Instagram.

"So, you sign up for any clubs?"

"Me?"

I respond, my pointer finger towards me.

"Yes, you. Ryan told me a few weeks ago you were going to try to get into the campus Red Cross?"

Of course, he tells everyone everything.

"Yea, yea. I was thinking about it. I missed the meeting last week, so it doesn't matter, really."

"Jayden," She pauses, her voice becoming consoling.

"The moment we get back on campus, you're emailing that president."

"Why not now?"

I stop the car briskly at the red light, my eyes glued to the stoplight as the green arrow towards the left flashes.

"Because, I'm out with you."

* * *

Jazz plays overhead as we enter, and the chatter of people flows through the room.

The theme in the building is a style inspired straight from Paris, and just by glancing at Tiffany I can tell she's stoked.

A woman with pale skin and blonde hair waltzes towards us before speaking. "Bonjour et bienvenue sur La Note! How many in your party?"

"Just two."

I respond, watching as she grabs two menus from behind the podium at signaling for us to follow her towards an available table.

It's completely crowded in the place, but somehow, the host had managed

CHAPTER SEVENTY-TWO: LOVE YOURZ

to snag us a spot not too far, but far enough from the crowd.

"My name is Claire, and I'm the host. You're waitress, Charlie, is on her way. May I get you two started on drinks?" She quickly grabs a pen and notebook from her back pocket before getting in pose to write.

Tiffany immediately begins speaking, keeping her statement from the car.

"Do you guys take drink requests?"
"Yes, of course!"
"Great, I'll have a Orange and Lime virgin mimosa."

Her hands dash around the notepad as she looks at me, waiting for my response.

"Orange Juice with a dash of Apple Juice."
"Alright. I'll have this out with Charlie!"

We both watch as Claire dashes away, stopping in front of a brunette as before she turns around with her.

Tiffany turns her phone face down against the table, her 'Do Not Disturb' on, along with her notifications muted.

"So, how's this day planned?"
"Just simple, fun stuff, you know?"

She nods, crossing her arms as she leans against the table.

"I can't wait for November, Jay."
"You wanna ditch already?"

She laughs at my comment before continuing to speak, her arms uncrossing as she reaches across the table and plays with the salt shaker that sits in the middle.

"Nah. I just miss family, you know? And Shi, god, he shook me up when he actually showed concern for me. Like, he actually was genuinely nervous for me to leave."

I nod as I listen, signaling to Tiff that all my attention is on her.

"Yea, I get you."

The brunette from earlier walks over with our drinks in hand, quickly placing them onto the table before she grabs the notepad from her apron pocket. "Hey! My name is Charlie, as you may know, and I'm your waiter for today. Have you decided on your order?"

"Yes, actually," Tiffany replies, handing her both our menus. "I'll have the Creme Pancakes; Short Stack, please." Charlie speeds her hands across the page.

"The I'll also get the Fromage Omelet, no toast. Three strips of bacon."

"And for you?"

She turns towards me, my eyes still scanning the menu.

"Right, I think I'll just have a chefs' choice," I say, handing her the menu as she holds them in her left hand. "Alright. Your order will be out in just a few minutes." Flashing a smile, I watch as Charlie turns around and walks around the crowded room, quickly finding her way to the kitchen.

"God, I'm stuffed."

I grab my card from the black bill holder before standing, friskily grabbing my jacket off the back of the chair. "You ready?" I ask, watching as Tiffany stands up to stretch.

Her jacket lifts slightly before she grabs her purse. "Yea."

Reaching for my phone, I check the time to be sure I'm on schedule.

11:50 AM

Yup, on time. Walking towards the exit, I open the door as Tiffany exits, also holding it for a small family entering. "Thank You," the mother mumbles, and I nod as I mouth a *'No Problem'*.

Getting inside the car, I get the car started as Tiffany leaps towards the heater, immediately turning hers up to 86. I laugh at this, finding it funny of her immediate reflex.

"What?"

CHAPTER SEVENTY-TWO: LOVE YOURZ

"Nothing, just the way you perked up," I reply, looking at the side mirrors as I back up. Pulling away from the curb, I pull up Google Maps on my phone, quickly typing the next spot. Tiffany watches me, an immediate smile escaping her lips.

"Lookachu! Whole day planned, huh?"

Oh, yea.

"Yup. Missed you the past few weeks, so I figured a day should be enough time for us."

She nibbles on her bottom lip before she glances at the window, watching the cars speed by as we drive.

Since the next place isn't far from the restaurant, it was nothing but a quick drive, even shorter than expected due to the light traffic.

* * *

We pull along the curb, quickly getting out before I pay the fee on the parking meter.

"Rasputin Music," T reads, mesmerized by the aged records displayed within in the window. "It caught my eye while I was looking for places to go to with you." I reach for her hand before she quickly grasps it, my other opening the door as both of us walk inside.

Seventy-Three

CHAPTER SEVENTY-THREE: BEST PART

TIFFANY

The music played throughout is from a turntable connected to a preamp.

My Girlfriend is a Witch fuzzily plays as it turns off, the clerk changing the record to a different song. It sounds much like jazz, the trumpet playing with every end sentence.

"You looking for a particular thing?" The worker asks, watching as Jay and I glance through the casing beside the entrance. "Not really. Just browsing for right now," I respond, sending over a quick smile. "My name's Jared, let me know whenever y'all need help."

The clerk has curly red hair, freckles covering his entire face. His skin is pale, and he's wearing a black hoodie.

Jayden walks behind me before placing his hands onto my hips, kissing my forehead as I shuffle through the records. "You know, anything you

CHAPTER SEVENTY-THREE: BEST PART

have in mind, they may have. I don't mind anything, old or new."

"Jay," I groan, knocking his hands off my waist as I turn around. "I really don't wanna blow your money in one day. Records are expensive." He rolls his eyes jokingly, a light scoff slips from his mouth. Almost as if it didn't matter to him. "T, trust me, I don't mind."

"Jayden-" He places his right pointer finger against my lips, causing me to become silent. "I don't mind. Buy as much as you need. Again, used or new, it doesn't matter."

Unsurely, I agree, lightly hiding my excitement before I turn around and begin digging through the vinyls once again.

I ended up picking out ten records, grateful for Jayden's offer with my collection.

The ones I picked were Lemonade by Beyonce, One in a Million by Aaliyah, an Album by Donna Summer, and a few others that consisted of Jay-Z and J. Cole. Walking out, we're hit by the unexpected chill of the wind, the temperature unfortunately dropped within the past thirty minutes we'd been in there. My phone buzzes in my pocket before I grab it, messages from the group chat with Em and Av ringing it off the chain.

AVERY| yo yo yo imma come down to memphis next week.
EMERY| alri. but your classes?
AVERY| i asked for a break. lied and said it was a family emergency.
EMERY| it's not good to lie, avery.
AVERY| oh well, arrest me.

I laugh at the two of them as I put the plastic bag, containing the records, in the backseat, shutting the door behind me.

When I get in and sit in the car, it's already warming up as Jayden got in before me.

"Any other place?"

"Duh," He replies, a smile warming up his face as we pull off.

The Bookposal

"God, Jayden you really don't have to," I say as I step out, my shoes hitting the pavement. Jayden parks hella close to the sidewalk, and I just noticed this.

"Come on, this one isn't just for you. I like reading, too, you know," He says, reaching for my hand. I grab it, my heart leaping as his pinkie grazes my thumb. Someone from inside opens the door for us, the toasty environment immediately feeling welcome.

"Hello! Welcome to Mrs. Dalloway's. Anything you looking for in particular?" Jayden places his left elbow against the counter top, his fingers flicking the air as he thinks.

"Yea, actually. Where are your Fantasy novels?"

"Right in the back. The newest will be to the far right of the shelf, and the used and/or donated are to the left of it." Lifting his arm from the counter, our hands part as he heads towards to back.

Looking around, I notice as there aren't any particular signs to show each genre and category. And it's not like it's a big deal, it just takes a while to get around a place that does that. Mrs. Deliare did that when I first started working there, but over time she decided to add signs.

I could ask where the Romance novels are, but I feel like I could easily find it on my own, just walking around the place. I mean, how hard could it be?

JAYDEN

Looking through the shelf, I find myself searching for books I know I already have.

Only flaw? They're in Memphis.

My hands grasp the book Divergent, very quickly flipping through the pages as I realize I hadn't read this one. I feel a tap on my shoulder before I turn around, quickly greeted by Tiffany.

CHAPTER SEVENTY-THREE: BEST PART

"Hey, I thought you were looking for the Romance?"
"Right, actually, I have no idea where I'm going," She chuckles in response, her voice unsure. "I'll ask. Get me book real quick, pick absolutely anything. New or old, just pick something," I respond, walking backwards in the aisle before turning around and walking to the cashier. "May I help you?"
"Romance novels?"
"Yes! To your left, right beside the Contemporary."

"Thank you," I reply, the worker humming in response as I walk back to the Fantasy, where Tiffany is.
"What'd you pick out?" She turns around from the shelf, at least five books in hand.
"Okay, so I found Wings of Ebony, The Final Gambit, The Wicked King, and Blood Like Magic." Each book displays in her hand as she says the title, moving it to the other hand in progress of saying the others.

I grab Wings of Ebony, quickly reading the blurb within the jacket. "I'll definitely get this one," I say, my finger hitting the cover. "This sounds good." She smiles, glad I'd picked something she grabbed. Although she has other choices, she places them back on the shelf.
I tell her to follow me, leading her towards the Romance.
"Now, let me do the same with you. I'll pick a book."
"Jayden," She pauses, her voice wavering as she begins laughing. "You have no idea what books I like within Romance."
"Oh, really?" I reply, going through the books in front of me. Continuously grabbing each book that gathers my attention, I quickly become disappointed each time.
After about ten minutes of this process, I notice a book I remember seeing on GoodReads, the plot and cover grabbed Tiffany's attention almost immediately. Grabbing it I hand it to Tiff as I watch her eyes glow.
"By The Book? Oh my god, and it's on discount here! Brand New!" I watch as she beams with excitement, quickly feeling what she'd probably felt when I'd picked the book she chose.

"Your total is 10.96."

I hand them my card, watching as they scan it before handing it back and giving us our bags.

"Have a nice day!" The cashier calls, my mind scanning through my next stop. We walk through the doors, walk to the car, and get inside. The moment I get in, I turn the ignition on to get the heat flowing. Grabbing my phone, I check the time, quickly realizing we'd spent almost and hour in there. Turning my phone off, I hand it to Tiffany as she unlocks it all over again and opens the playlist, Jhene Aiko's voice flowing through the speakers. "Where to next?"

"You in the mood for painting?"

"Hell yea."

I turn the corner, the view of the campus slowly coming within my view.

"When we get to the dorms, change into something more lazy."

I pause, my eye on the streetlight as I wait for the light to turn green.

"I would hate for that sweater to become stained."

TIFFANY

See, Jayden sometimes scares me with the statements he makes.

We pull into the parking lot, quickly jogging towards the gates as we walk onto the campus, surprised by the amount of people scattering around in the cold.

Due to both of us having separate dorms, we have to part near the center, going in different directions. Walking inside my building, I feel my phone buzz in my pocket before reaching for it and seeing a message from Jayden.

JAYDEN| Don't forget your coat. You felt that chill, it's gettin' cold out here! :)

CHAPTER SEVENTY-THREE: BEST PART

Sliding my key card inside the scanner, I pull it out before opening the door, the room pitch black. Turning the light on, I waltz towards my small dresser, scrambling through clothes that I wouldn't mind getting stained.

After searching through for what feels like ages, my hands grab a hold of a tank top and dark gray sweats. Putting those on, I grab a pair of Nadia's beaten up converse, gratefully realizing we wear the same size. There is no way in hell that I'm wearing a single pair of my J's while painting. But the thought is quickly shut down as I think about how she could be sneaking a pair of my shoes.

Walking towards the door, I look at the mirror hooked to the back as I fix my puffball.

A few finishing touches such as lip liner, gloss on top, reapplication of mascara, and we're done.

My phone buzzes against my bed as I go over and check it, another message from Jayden on my screen.

JAYDEN| **In the union. Come down when you're ready.**

Seventy-Four

CHAPTER SEVENTY-FOUR: PERFECT

JAYDEN

We walk out the building, T and I laughing at the multitude of things that happened while we painted. A stripe of green paint rests on her right cheek from me putting it there, and three stripes of red paint rest on my left cheek from her doing the same to me.

The entire time we'd painted, it was just us dying from laughter at each others art. Her canvas sits in her left hand, multiple splatters of random designs on hers. A few attempts to paint something genuine, but very obvious signs of her just giving up.

"Really," I pause, pointing to a certain part of the painting. "Is that an alpaca?"

"Yea! You like it? I gave him a tassel collar," She laughs as she responds, almost tripping over her shoelaces.

Catching her balance, she begins laughing at herself once again, quickly calming down. Looking at the sky, I notice the sun has began to set, a smile

CHAPTER SEVENTY-FOUR: PERFECT

aligning my face as I think more into the night.

"Whatchu smilin' at?" Tiffany says, her shoulder colliding with mine.

"Nothing," I respond, lying straight under my breath.

"God, today was fun."
"It's not over."
"Oh, really?"

We reach the car, my arm grasping a hold of the handle as I open it for her. Tiffany doesn't get in immediately, instead standing against the car facing me, her eyes gazing between mine and my lips. Her tone lightens, more calm and smooth.

"What else do you have planned, then?"
"Oh, just dinner."

Letting go of the door, it stays open as I get closer to her, our hands wrapped around one another as my chest touches hers.

Our noses touch, her eyes closing as it initiates an immediate kiss between us.

Her lips were warm and soft, completely opposing against mine. Trailing my hands towards her face, she seems to almost do the same. Now on her face, my hands graze her face, causing her to chuckle lightly against my lips as I do the same.

My body becomes warm inside, now feeling nothing but assurance.

Releasing from each other, I notice that T can't help but smile after that, her face enlightened with joy. She gets inside, my hands immediately shutting the door behind her as she sits comfortably. I walk over to my side, open the door, and get inside, quickly pressing the key fob button as the car starts up, my seat adjusting to my preferred setting. The radio plays light jazz, slightly fitting the mood before I connect my phone to the Bluetooth. I open Spotify, this time pressing a different playlist; *Our Playlist*.

A different song plays, something slow as a pull off the curb and down the street, leading into the highway.

"Alright, we're gonna stop at our dorms again, changing into something nice. I bought you an outfit I'd like for you to try on, it's in the backseat in a white lace box." Turning around, she glances at it before her jaw drops. "I bought myself a matching suit. When I drop you off, I'll be ready in thirty minutes. Take as long as you want, but I have dinner reserved for 8."

She looks at the time displayed on the touchscreen on the dashboard.

6:15 PM

Slowly, I turn the curb before turning into the campus parking lot.

And yes, everything I'd picked is nothing but a small drive away from campus.

We get out, quickly jogging towards the gated entrance before she types in the code, allowing the gates to be opened. Walking along the sidewalk, I notice it's pretty empty aside from the few couples walking along the path, holding hands like we do.

We go to Tiffany's dorm building, walking inside as we get to the elevator and step on. She presses her floor level, the doors close before we get lifted, and we're on our way.

The doors opening, we both step off as we walk down the left hall, quickly getting to her door. The white box in my hand, I give it to her as she opens it, finding herself face-to-face with a light purple dress Emery had picked while we were in Memphis. "Oh my god, this is gorgeous," She mumbles, her hand reaching in as she feels the fabric.

A pearl necklace and Swarovski earrings also rest inside, both the next things that she grabs as she looks around. "Jayden, you really didn't have to." "Yes, I did. I love you, and I wanted this day to be all about you," I respond, watching as she puts the things back into it before leaning in for a hug. Holding her tightly, I rub her shoulder before she lets go and digs in her back pocket for her card, scanning it as the door unlocks.

"See you soon, babe. I won't take long, promise."

CHAPTER SEVENTY-FOUR: PERFECT

TIFFANY

I shut the door behind me, internally panicking inside as thoughts of the day replay in my mind; primarily the kiss; over and over again. Without looking, I notice Nadia sitting on her bed, writing something down in her journal before realizing I'm in the room. "Hey," She says without looking up. "Hi," I respond breathily, kicking off my shoes as I toss them to her bed. "That's where they were. I was finna wear those earlier today, you know," She mumbles, standing up as she grabs them and places them into the corner with her other shoes.

I roll my eyes before grabbing the box and opening it once again, mesmerized by the contents. "Nadia, I really need to get this dress on, and I'm not going in those stalls." "Okay?" She replies, sitting back onto her mattress. "Turn around?" I request, rotating my finger in a circle as a symbol for her to spin around. Annoyed, she sighs before grabbing her books and turning around on her bed, her back now facing me.

"Better?"

"Yes," I respond, giving her annoyance right on back.

The dress slips on perfectly, each movement I make blessed with the feeling of the cool fabric hitting my skin. I look at myself in the mirror, smiling at the sight as I look beautiful. "Alright, you're good." Nadia turns back around, her face still sucked into her textbook.

Walking back to my bed, I dig in the box once again before grabbing a hold of the pearl necklace and earrings. I put the necklace on first, the cool pearls slowly hitting my collarbone as I clip the two clamps together.

Next, I put on the earrings. They're drop earrings, with the ends almost touching my shoulders. Again, I look in the mirror, this time looking at the full outfit. I haven't put shoes on yet, so I glance at my feet as I realize I'm barefoot. "Hey, you have a pair of white heels I can borrow?" I ask Nadia, grabbing a bottle of lotion from my nightstand before putting the proper amount in my hand and rubbing it along my left leg. "Yea. They're strap around's though. You still want 'em?" Standing up, Nadia walks towards her pile of shoes and grabs a pair of heels by their straps. "Yea." She tosses them to me, one by one as I catch both, putting them on.

I hear a knock on the door before a muffled voice, my mind quickly recognizing it. "I look good?" "Hell, yea," Nadia responds, her hands grazing the dress fabric. Smiling, I walk towards the door as my heart leaps with excitement, feeling just as I did on our first date.

"God, you look," Jayden pauses. I hold my breath, hoping it was the look he was hoping for.

"Beautiful."

JAYDEN

Tiffany smiles shyly as I say this, her eyes glowing with compassion.

"Really, you look amazing," I add on, slowly walking into the room. Getting closer to her, she places her arms on my shoulders as I place my hands onto her waist, the both of us staring at each other in nothing but awe.

"Alright, get a room."
"Nadia, you're one to say," Tiffany pauses, slowly thinking of a thing to snap back with.

"What?"
"You and Ryan make out, while I'm in here, every other day."
Nadia smiles, rolling her eyes before grabbing her pencil and writing inside the journal that sits in front of her.

"Whatever. Enjoy your night," She mumbles, her focus now towards the work rather than us.

"Will do."

CHAPTER SEVENTY-FOUR: PERFECT

We walk along the sidewalk, holding hands as we talk.

"What's the place you got us reserved at?"

"Providence."

"Oh my god. I've seen so many good reviews of that place! Em and Av both recommended I go there at one point, whenever we can, really."

I smile, glad they'd both put in a good word.

Getting closer to the parking lot, we walk off the sidewalk, now walking along the street as she walks on my side, laying her head on my shoulder.

"Can you believe it's almost October?" She says.

"I know. You better expect those constant parties," I reply, laughing immediately after. She laughs, too before responding.

"Yea, yea. Imma have to get used to Nadia coming in at 3 in the morning again," She sighs. Now at the car, I open her door before she smiles at me and gets in, my hand shutting the door behind her.

I walk over to my side, my eyes catching glance of my bag still in the backseat, my mind spiraling through thoughts as I think of the ring sitting in the book. Shaking my head, I clear them out before getting inside and closing the door behind me.

My hand hits the button as my seat adjusts once again. Digging in my pocket, I place my phone into the cupholder before gathering a glance of the time.

"You ready?"

She nods, her hand in the middle of the console, requesting mine.

I accept her offer, placing my right hand there as she grabs it, our fingers intertwining. My left hand on the wheel, I begin backing up, careful not to ding any of the cars around us.

Let the night begin.

Seventy-Five

CHAPTER SEVENTY-FIVE: ENDLESS LOVE

TIFFANY

We've been driving for about, what a hour? My playlist has literally been the only thing keeping me sane.

And it's not like I have something against the both of us sitting in a car for an hour, I can definitely deal with that. It's just that Jayden's hyped this night up so much to the point where I physically cannot refrain myself from feeling bored. Usually in a long car ride, I fall asleep, but I, for one, don't wanna fall back asleep during dinner. And for two, don't wanna mess up my makeup. It's literally what took pretty much half the time I had to get ready.

We pull into the busy city, cars everywhere, lights illuminating the packed street, people walking along the sidewalks.

Pulling along the curb, Jayden stops the car before moving the gear stick to park.

CHAPTER SEVENTY-FIVE: ENDLESS LOVE

"Okay, we're a few minutes late, but I let them know ahead of time, so they still have our table." I nod, ignoring, but also listening to the things he says.

We both get out, the chilly breeze going through my coat and straight to my skin. Going around the car, Jayden gets to my side before we begin walking.

"How was Maddie?" I ask, stopping as he reaches to open the door. "She's good. A small relapse due to my absence. We plan to call every other day now, both for me to keep up and for her to see me." I nod, glad to hear her progress.

Walking inside, we're greeting by a dark skin woman, her hair in Bantu knots. She's wearing what looks like maroon shaded lipstick, which looks gorgeous on her.

"Hello! Do you have reservations?"

"Yes, actually. Hudsen?"

Her fingers speed across the keyboard as she types away, her head nodding as she seems to have reached the correct page. "Alright. Follow me." She grabs two menus before walking through the crowd of people, bringing us towards the back of the building, in front of a window.

The table Jayden reserved literally had an entire view of the city. Like, I could take a picture and it would be one of those photos you see on stock websites. "Okay, your waiter, Walter, will be with you in just a moment. Wanna get started on some drinks?" Jayden glances at me before giving her a response. I nod, already knowing what drink I want to order. He gives me a look, which I know all too well.

"We'll take one Holywood cocktail, and one Gin and Tonic."

"Alright, just let me see your ID, sir."

Digging in his pocket, Jayden quickly grabs his wallet before showing the woman his false ID. She looks at him before looking back at the card. To me, it looks very obvious that it's fake. I mean, that person (that looks like Jayden as is) has an entire goatee, while Jayden purely doesn't. But somehow, we always get drinks with it.

Looking at him once again, she doesn't say anything, but instead, winks. She tosses in a smile before speaking.

"Got it. Your drinks will be out in just a moment with Walter." Turning around, she walks back down the hall and into the crowded room, shutting the door to the private room behind her.

JAYDEN

A few minutes after the woman had walked away, the doors open again, this time a white man with a what I like to call "Soccer Boy" cut comes in, both of our glasses in his hand.

"Holywood Cocktail," He pauses, passing the drink to Tiffany as she waves her arms up, glad to have the glass in hand. "And Gin and Tonic." He places the glass against the table, quickly grabbing a small towel from his back pocket to wipe off the cup ring. "You guys decide yet?" Turning to my side, I notice Tiffany still looking at the menu. "Give us five," I mouth, and he nods before walking away.

"Anything catch your eye?"

She doesn't respond, continuing to read the page.

Suddenly, she snaps up as she points at something, quickly gathering my attention.

"Sashimi and Salmon."

"Sashimi?"

"Yes. Emery said it was bomb, and Avery just said it sucked. So, I wanna try it for myself."

"Alright," I respond, grabbing the folded menu in front of me.

"What're you getting?"

"I might get the salmon along with you, that's about it."

"Not in the mood for tasting something new?"

CHAPTER SEVENTY-FIVE: ENDLESS LOVE

I shake my head no.

"Nah, I'll just have some of your Sushimi," I laugh, purposely pronouncing it incorrectly.

She inhales roughly, sitting up as she begins to correct me. "Sashimi."

"Sushimi."

"Sah! Sashimi," Tiffany says, sounding it out as if I were a kid. Realizing I wasn't gonna let go of my pronunciation, she rolls her eyes before chuckling under her breath and taking a sip from her glass.

The waiter comes back over, a notepad in hand.

"We ready?" He says, a large grin on his face. "Yup," T responds, handing him both our menus. "Sashimi and two Salmons," She says, Walter writing each thing down.

"Alright, your order will be ready soon." He tucks his pen into his pocket, before turning around and exiting, also closing the private doors behind him.

"I don't like the way you say Salmon," I mumble, laughing at the sound of my own sentence.

"What? It's Sal, Sal-Mon!"

"Salmon."

"No, you're adding Sam. It has Sal in it, doesn't it?"

I agree with where she's coming from, both of us continuing to playfully banter about how each of us are wrong.

"I mean, my entire family pronounces it that exact way, all of them saying I'm saying it wrong."

"You are."

"But it has Sal!"

With the argument slowly coming to an end, we slowly break down in laughter, finding it hilarious on how we just had an entire feud about a words pronunciation.

A few minutes later, we both continue to talk, each topic starting from random sentences.

The doors open once again, Walter walking through, this time with a tray of food.

"Woo!" Tiffany cheers, unconsciously doing a dance she seems to do whenever she eats. "Sashimi and two Salmons," He mumbles, placing the three plates onto the table.

"Thank You!" Tiff cheers, excited to try the new item.

"You wanna taste first?" I ask, grabbing the fork from the rolled napkin.

"Yea," She responds, watching as I pick up a piece of meat from the plate and place it in her mouth.

Slowly, she chews it with a sour face, having no choice to flauntingly swallowing the bite. "Not good?" She shakes her head no as she grabs her glass and takes a sip, probably to wash the taste out her mouth. "Try it," She stutters, pointing towards it.

I take a piece before putting it in my mouth, despising the texture, but enjoying the taste. Swallowing the bite, I wash it down as well with my drink.

"Not the best texture, but I give it credit for that taste."
"No way."
"Yeah, I mean it's not favorable, but it's good," I respond before taking a piece of my salmon and chew it. With nothing but silence between us now that the food has arrived, Tiffany manages to bring our chatter back by one quick sentence:

"Whatchu wanna get for desert?"

***

I open the thing that holds the bill before grabbing the card, surprised by

CHAPTER SEVENTY-FIVE: ENDLESS LOVE

the low price of our dinner.

I worked my behind off the past few months. I knew the prices of dinner here was skyrocketed, so I went ahead and got the money ahead of time.

"One last place," I pause, sliding my coat on.

Tiffany laughs lightly as she does the same. Walking towards the door, we open it and walk into the dining room. It's not as crowded as it had been earlier, but it's still pretty packed.

Many couples sit at two-seated tables by the windows, multiple people taking photos of the view before continuing to eat.

Opening the doors, the cold breeze allows me to thank myself for putting my coat on ahead of time. "Where to, now, Jay?" I chuckle at this, thinking of what I already know what I'm about to do.

"You like stars?"

Seventy-Six

CHAPTER SEVENTY-SIX: ETERNAL SUNSHINE

TIFFANY

The only hint Jayden gave me for the next place is stars.
And I swear I'm not dumb. I know exactly where we're going, it's just that I wanna be sure, you know? I mean, we could be going to a field and looking at the stars for all I know. I look out the window as we drive, my memory instantly bringing me back to my childhood as I do so.

Kendrick Lamar plays on the speaker, Jayden rapping along with the lyrics. He pauses, holding an imaginary mic up to my mouth as I turn around. I don't continue that lyric, but instead bust out my own "mic" and begin singing the next verse.

We continue singing, going back and forth within the line as needed.
And just like that, we're here.

CHAPTER SEVENTY-SIX: ETERNAL SUNSHINE

Pulling into the parking lot, I glance out the window once again, amazed by the sightful view.

I open the door and get out, my shoes crunching on top of the asphalt. Jayden waits at the back of the car, his phone in his hand as he types something in, quickly shoving it into his pocket as I come by.

"Why are we here, Jay?"
"What? I can't see some stars with my girl?"

With a smile, I roll my eyes as he grabs my hand and we begin walking. My heels continue crunching against the ground, Jaydens' shoes doing the same until we step onto the sidewalk. Looking ahead, I notice it's a long walk, so I tuck my hands into his pocket to keep them warm.

Close to the center of the path, I look over the cliff. If the view down there was gorgeous, oh god, then this is out of my words. I can see every building, the main city in a distant cluster. Reaching the building, we walk up the steps before reaching the entrance. Jayden opens the door, allowing me to step inside before him as we enter.

Looking at the ceiling, it's not like a planetarium with stars, but like one of those light projectors from the 2000s. It's adorable, and the feeling is hella nostalgic. All across the walls, there are 3D models of the different planets plastered on the wall, many people crowded towards that pertained area. Aside from the stars, the ceiling has what seems to be a mural of some sort, nothing really clicking in my mind of observation.

Walking up to the front desk, Jayden begins talking to the receptionist, my eyes watching as she hands him a pamphlet. Now distanced from them, I find myself look at a NASA rover, my eyes scanning through the label that sits on the glass.

"What do you wanna check out first?" I hear Jayden say from behind me. "Believe it or not, I actually don't know," I laugh, looking around the room as people exit.

"What time do they close? You know it's 9:50, right?" "Yea," He responds, licking his lips as he goes through the pamphlet. "She said she'll let other workers know we're here." I feel my eyes widen as he finishes speaking, a slight laugh exiting his lips at this sight. "I let 'em know we're new and just wanna take a look." Raising my eyebrows, I give him a look I tend to give Emery and Avery.

"You don't gotta believe what I'm sayin' at all, we just have time in here," His attention begins to revert towards the same display, his head bobbing as he reads. I've quickly realized that Jayden tends to do that. Whenever he reads something, he nods his head as if there were music playing.

Looking around, I catch glance of another display, something that actually kinda looks like R2-D2 from Star Wars. Call me immature, but that's what I see. Walking over, my hands graze the cool glass as I view before I look down and read the plaque. Not paying attention, I feel a hand touch my shoulder as I turn around facing Jayden, him once again startling me.

With a chuckle in his voice, he says, "You really gotta start paying attention to your surroundings."
"I already do," I respond, holding his hand as he stands beside me.
"I just scared you."
"I was zoned in!" I laugh, playfully hitting his shoulder. "These exhibits hella boring. I got so many recommendations from people around campus."
"Maybe they were talking about the stars?" I say, both of us facing each other now as we speak. "Yea, I think that might've been what people were talking about," He mumbles, licking his lips. It becomes silent between us, with nothing but the intensity of our gaze wandering in the air. Breaking the ice, I snap back to reality and lightly tease him.
"Why're you carrying a book?"
"Why not?"
"Jay, that's like carrying a book to the movies."
"No it's not," He chuckles, clutching it close to his chest.
"Which one even is that?"

He turns it towards the cover before showing me, my mouth dropping almost immediately. "Bro," I mutter, holding my breath as I read the cover. He nods, a smile slowly creeping up his face. "Yup, rereading the book we'd met with."

CHAPTER SEVENTY-SIX: ETERNAL SUNSHINE

"You bought a new one and everything?"
"Yea, it was one of the books I brought with me from home."

I continue reading the plaque, this time, Jayden doesn't speak until I visibly finish.

"Wanna go check out the sky?"
"But it's cold," I groan, holding my shoulders tightly, already imagining the cool breeze against my body.
 "I'll hold you," He offers, his arms out as like a hug.
 Giving in, I reply, "Fine."
 Glad I'd given in, he pumps his fist in the air as if we were in a concert, his face scrunching up as well.
 "Oh, quit it."

JAYDEN

We walk through the doors to the balcony, my eyes amazed by the sight of the overhead city. It's crazy, because when you're walking around the place thinking it's so cool and amazing and huge, but when you see it in the bigger picture; It just confirms those thoughts.
 I sit down on the bench, continuing to hold the book in my left hand as Tiffany walks towards one of those railing telescopes, placing her face into the eye rest before looking through.
"It's amazing, Jay. I can't believe you don't wanna see this view."
 I scoff, quickly opening the book to the page.
 Inside rests the ring in the center of the page, held up by a white cushion. A multitude of words are highlighted throughout the page, each word describing T in some kind of way. The sides of the page has our notes, from the very beginning with our signatures signed away beside them.
 Walking towards her, I stand beside Tiffany.

Crouching onto my knee, I open the book to that page, now waiting for Tiffany to raise her head from the binoculars.

TIFFANY

"Man, I wish Em could see this. Like really, she would love-," I pause, lifting my face from the Eyepiece. Turning around, I look to the ground to find Jayden. Jayden crouched on his knee, a book in hand as it contains a ring. My eyes water, emotions filling my mind as I blink away the tears. Before I can even speak, Jayden opens his mouth instead.

"I know we've only been together a year. I know dang well it's still the beginning of the relationship. But I feel as I've known you forever. The way I can relate to the things you say, the way you talk, the points you make."

I hold my hand close to my mouth, my mind still trying to process everything.

"Tiffany, you're everything a person could dream of. You're compassionate, caring, gifted, talented, embracing, so much more I can't even describe with one word.

I'm gonna be real honest here, I can see us living life together. Moving in together, Working together, reading together."

This small joke gets a chuckle out of me, causing the tears to spill over.

"Just living together. So here I am, on one knee, with a ring."

Inhaling, I wait for him to say the next sentence before I respond.

"Will you marry me?"

CHAPTER SEVENTY-SIX: ETERNAL SUNSHINE

JAYDEN

There's silence from her for a moment, which causes me to become nervous.

Thoughts swirl around my mind within that one second, multiple things telling me I'd done this too early. That I should've waited. That it's not gonna last. That she's gonna say no.

But one thing she says cancels all of those out, each thing replaced with nothing but excitement for the future.

"Yes!"

About the Author

Zoe Harris is a high school student born in Memphis but moved to and still resides, in Mississippi when she was 10. The oldest of 3, she hangs out with her siblings and can often be caught playing Roblox with them. You will almost always see her playing Sims, Reading, Writing, or Crafting in her free time. The Bookposal is Her first novel.

As a young author, Zoe tends to write primarily around the topics of Contemporary Romance, and many of the books she reads seem to reflect this throughout her work. She writes as an escape from the world, which works pretty well. With many ideas in mind, Zoe plans to keep up to date with her readers and publish more books in the future.

She also owns a book blog, Black Girl Reads, where she reviews books with a few friends.